ONLY SUPERHUMAN

ONLY
SUPERHUMAN

Christopher L. Bennett

TOR®

A TOM DOHERTY ASSOCIATES BOOK

NEW YORK

ONLY SUPERHUMAN

Copyright © 2012 by Christopher L. Bennett

A Tor Book
Published by Tom Doherty Associates, LLC
175 Fifth Avenue
New York, NY 10010

www.tor-forge.com

Tor® is a registered trademark of Tom Doherty Associates, LLC.

Library of Congress Cataloging-in-Publication Data

Bennett, Christopher L.
    Only superhuman / Christopher L. Bennett.—1st ed.
        p. cm.
    "A Tom Doherty Associates book."
    ISBN 978-0-7653-3229-5 (hardcover)
    ISBN 978-1-4299-6082-3 (e-book)
    I. Title.
    PS3602.E66447O55 2012
    813'.6—dc23

                                                                2012019873

First Edition: October 2012

Printed in the United States of America

0 9 8 7 6 5 4 3 2 1

To the family I've finally rediscovered

New forms of power do not obey conservation laws. They can be created, but never again destroyed. Superhumans are here, and you will have to live with us. But by the same token, you may no longer be able to live without us.

    —Eliot Thorne, statement to the Transhuman
      Investigatory Committee, 25 April 2067

With great power there must also come great responsibility.
    —Stan Lee, *Amazing Fantasy #15,* 1962

ONLY SUPERHUMAN

1

The Sky Is Falling

May 2107
Chakra City habitat
In synchronous orbit of Earth

Bast fidgeted inside the heavy *chador*, hating the way it cut off her senses. There were so many sights and sounds and smells she was missing, even down here in the maintenance tunnels, away from the cosmopolitan bustle of the city levels above. Not that she cared about the bazaars, the curry parlors, the orchid gardens, or the other tourist traps this backwater Stanford torus festooned itself with as it tried to build itself up, physically and otherwise, into a major cislunar port city. No, she cared about having her senses free, on the alert for enemies.

More fundamentally, she just wanted to get out of the heavy robes so she could scratch herself and groom her beautiful glossy-black fur. She wanted to set her tail free so she could work the kinks out of it. And then she wanted to kill and eat something.

So far this was a boring mission—just sneaking around in empty tunnels, no enemies to sharpen her claws on. But she didn't dare complain to Wulf. That would just invite another tirade on how she should be more devoted to their Glorious Cause. Yes, yes, she knew all about the Neogaians' sacred mission to reclaim the wounded Earth from the technocrats who subsumed nature beneath cold, dead machines and denied humanity its right to evolve. She knew how the disorder created by the construction of the city's new habitat rings made a good cover for their plan to infect Earthbound travelers with designer polyviral mutagens, a blow against UNECS's restrictions on human enhancement and a step toward bringing humanity back into harmony with Mother Earth's animal spirits. But listening to Wulf spewing dogma in her face with his foul canine breath didn't get her in harmony with her animal spirit. She was perfectly in harmony with her animal spirit, and it was telling her to go kill and eat something. Maybe Wulf.

Well, actually, right now it was telling her to scratch that damn itch behind her right ear. So she did—just a little scratch couldn't draw Wulf's ire, surely.

No such luck. "Bast!" Wulf snarled, looking back at her. He looked ridiculous, with the fur shaved off half his face so he'd look like a bearded human, and with the turban pulled down over his big pointed ears. He must hate it—he already resented her for her more advanced transgenic mods, for being closer to "pure animal nature" than he was. But that was what he got for being an older model, born human and chimericized with surgery and stem-cell injections, instead of a germ-line creation like herself. "Stop that," he commanded. "You'll tear your headscarf." She subsided, but hissed and slashed her claws in his direction. "Settle down! Remember, act calm and serene. Look at Caiman there."

Bast thought the croc-man was a lousy example. So still and quiet, always meditating, striving for a perfect animal nonsentience, just existing and watching . . . now *that* was boring. Still, Bast quieted down, hoping to avoid another lecture on how they had to look and act like proper Muslims so nobody would suspect them of being terrorists.

But then Bast thought she heard something moving nearby. It sounded big—maybe a nice juicy rat or bird. There shouldn't be many vermin yet in this new ring segment, where the grass and trees were still being planted and few people lived. Maybe this animal had gotten confused by the new layout and lost its way. Or maybe it wanted the chance to play a fun game with a pretty panther-lady before making a nice new home in her tummy.

Except Wulf had to go and tell them they'd reached their destination. No time for play. With a sigh, Bast turned her back on the interesting foodlike noises and followed the others inside.

The corridor opened into an expansive space containing much of the new segment's nanofabrication machinery. Some of the machines had conduits rising a couple of stories into the space above—maybe a future mall, but for now there was just a network of girders and pipes where the floor would be. The space was deserted except for construction robots, due to the newness of the segment and the time of day—and the fact that Wulf had paid off the guard in advance.

Wulf led them to the cell-stock tanks that supplied the new segment's bioprinters and ordered them to stand guard. Caiman's stillness made him good for that at least—but Bast could be still and silent with the best of them, if there was a good pounce in store at the end of it. She hoped that any intruders would come from her direction so she could kill them before Caiman did. Hell, she just hoped some intruders would show up.

But then Taurean had to go and make conversation. He was here for muscle like Caiman and herself, but also for what little interaction they had with other people, since he had the most normal-looking face (so long as the turban concealed his horns) and an atypically amiable manner for a trained killer. But unfortunately, he wasn't the strong, silent type. He was rambling on about the mission, asking Wulf how the polyviral vectors would work, questioning whether the random animal traits they produced as they spread through Terran humanity could be as viable or safe as their own carefully engineered mods, stuff like that. She didn't listen closely. It did amuse her when Wulf snarled at Taurean for doubting the power of divine Nature to effect this glorious transformation, though her amusement faded as he continued his fanatical tirade. Dogs always made too much damn noise.

Noise—there was something moving around again. Maybe lunch, maybe an intruder (though what was the difference, really?). She couldn't tell with Wulf blathering and the stupid scarf squishing her pretty ears. She hissed for attention. "I hear something!" She caught a definite scent this time, distinctly animal. Maybe even human . . . though it was increasingly hard to tell these days.

"Maybe you should hurry up and finish, Wulf," said Taurean. "I'd like to get out of here without any trouble."

Bast heard a clear movement up above and whirled to face it. A second ago there'd been nothing atop that big machine, but now a woman stood there. She was muscular but curvaceous, with wild hair the color of autumn leaves and an elfin face with enormous, almost cat-like green eyes. She wore a green sleeveless tunic with a flamelike trim, matching knee-length boots, tight black hip-huggers, and a faux-leather gunbelt resting at a rakish angle upon her wide hips. This was no local cop or UNECS security trooper. With a flamboyant outfit like that, there was only one thing she could be.

The redhead smirked, tilted an angular brow, and spoke in a honeyed soprano, her cocky words confirming Bast's conclusion. "Looking for trouble? You just found her."

Which was good, since Bast was definitely looking for trouble.

Emerald Blair loved making dramatic entrances, watching all eyes turn to her as she came into a room. Of course, she preferred it when the owners of those eyes didn't also possess guns, combat mods, or both. But such was the lot of a Troubleshooter.

Besides, she was tired of being stealthy. Sneaking up on the Neogaian terrorists was one thing, but she and Arkady Nazarbayev had needed to sneak themselves all the way from Luna without the Union of Earth and Cislunar States finding out. UNECS had refused them clearance to operate within their territory even after Arkady had warned them of the impending Neogaian attack, insisting they were more qualified than any "Strider vigilante and his teen sidekick" (apprentice, thank you, and she was twenty-two) to keep their vaunted peace and order. She supposed she couldn't begrudge the Terrans their pride in that order, given how hard they'd fought to build it after the ecological and social upheavals of the past century. But she suspected their disdain for the Troubleshooters had more to do with prejudice than pride. Underneath their noble talk of equality was a not-so-veiled mistrust toward those who were enhanced beyond the norm.

She and Arkady could have just flown in at maximum thrust—she doubted even the Eunuchs were fanatical enough to shoot down a TSC scout ship—but that would have tipped off the Neogaians. And so the heroic Medvyéd, the mighty Bear of the Troubleshooters, and his glamorous apprentice, the Green Blaze, had spent eighteen hours heroically, glamorously stuffed inside a cargo pod, cushioned from the accelerations of mass drivers and capture nets by gel cocoons and their own augmented anatomies. On finally reaching Chakra City, they had made an entrance in only the most literal sense, cutting their way through the hull and sealing it behind them, and hoping that the vagaries of orbital mechanics had let them arrive in time.

After all that, Emry was so thrilled to come out in the open that she didn't particularly mind being the decoy. As she delivered her trademark Green Blaze entrance line (or her latest attempt at one, though she thought this one had better staying potential than "Now you're in trouble, Mama spank" or "Hey, look over there!") and drew the attention of the Neogaians, Arkady was already sneaking up behind them, ready to incapacitate them as soon as he got a clear shot.

But it was hard to be sneaky in that bulky antique symbot he wore, at least when your enemies had animal hearing. The leader, a canine chimera who'd already yanked off his turban to free his ears, spun his head toward the sound of the armored exosuit's whirring servos and barked, "Down!" just as the Troubleshooter fired. The therianthropes scattered, and only one of Arkady's tanglewebs hit, snaring the tall reptilian's legs. But as the other two males ducked for cover, this one deftly turned his fall into a roll (the sixty-five-percent gravity of this small habitat giving him more time for it) and *bit* through the polysilk threads with his massive jaw. Despite the Neogaians' anti-tech ideology, this one must've had diamond-coated teeth.

The female had ignored Arkady's shots. Eyes fixed on Emry, she had ripped off her *chador,* revealing a stunning black-furred cat-woman wearing armor fabric over her vital areas. The leader, whom Emry now recognized as high-ranking Neogaian Erich "Wulf" Krieger, was shouting, "Taurean, Bast, kill them! Caiman, with me!" But the she-cat didn't need to hear it—she was already screaming and leaping at Emry, claws fully deployed from her fingertips. The ferocity in her yellow eyes struck primal fear into Emry, paralyzing her. At the last instant she re-acted, dodging right and tossing the panthress into a spin, but not be-fore those claws put four shallow slashes across the reinforced skin of Emry's left arm. They must have been diamond-coated as well. Mean-while, in the corner of her eye Emry saw the bull-guard firing a Gauss pistol at Arkady, not as quick as Bast to rely on animal instinct. The bullets bounced off the symbot's tough shell. Arkady was firing his plasma gun at Krieger and Caiman in flashbang mode, the laser pulses ionizing the air into blinding plasma balls with a crackle of miniature thunderclaps. Krieger clapped his hands over his large ears and stag-gered, but Caiman seemed unaffected and hustled him out of range while Taurean moved in to block his fire.

Bast had landed on her feet on the next air-filtration unit over, facing Emry and looking quite thrilled. "At last! A new toy!" she yowled, her feline muzzle giving her something of a lisp. Like a cat, she studied her foe, waiting for the right moment to pounce. Emry did the same. Bast's ears were in the normal human places, peeking out from her luxurious black mane, but the pinnae were large, pointed, and flexible. Her hands were human except for the claws, but the feet were pawlike and elongated, making her a formidable leaper. Her long tail swished agitatedly even while the rest of her lithe, slender body stayed perfectly still and poised. She seemed young to Emry, though maybe that was a natural feline abandon. Whatever the case, she was gorgeous. The cli-ché came unbidden to Emry's lips: "*Nice* kitty!"

"No," Bast replied. "I'm not." She pounced again, effortlessly cor-recting for Coriolis drift. This time Emry leapt up to meet her, aiming a spin-kick at her head. But Bast pivoted impossibly in midair, seem-ingly innocent of Newtonian physics, and dodged the kick, slashing at Emry's leg as she went past. This time the armor fabric shielded her, but the blow threw off her recovery, so she fell poorly and almost hit the side of the filtration unit. She caught herself and flipped up and over to land where Bast had just been, facing a Bast who was already crouched where Emry had been, tensing for her next leap.

It's the tail, she realized. That and her flexible spine let Bast shift her center of gravity however she wanted, enabling moves that seemed to laugh in the face of old Isaac. *Okay, no more soaring through the air like in a* wuxia *movie.* Emry planted her feet and awaited Bast's attack.

The panthress was quick to oblige, launching herself with great force, claws splayed. Emry grabbed her right wrist and punched her in the gut, but at the same moment Bast shot her legs forward and slashed at Emry's midsection. Light-armor fabric protected both women, but the claws of Bast's free hand dug deeply into Emry's right shoulder. Then the unexpected happened: Bast's tail looped around Emry's leg and yanked, proving itself as much primate as feline. Unbalanced from the collision, Emry fell back and had to fend off Bast's teeth as they went for her throat. She got her forearm bitten for her troubles. Angered, she kneed Bast in the gut and cuffed her head, then kicked the dazed therian off the edge of the filtration unit.

"Now do you see the flaw in the idea of sleeveless armor?" came Arkady's voice over the selfone clip on her left ear.

She rolled her eyes at the rote criticism as she scrambled to her feet. "But tin cans are just so passé."

"Forgive a mere mortal his caution, O demigoddess. At least try not to get yourself killed while I'm still responsible for you."

"Oh, go fuck a can opener," she shot back, but her tone was affectionate. The old schmuck was like a—well, like an uncle to her. But she was going to murder him someday; that was a given.

She looked down from the filtration unit, hoping to see Bast unconscious on the ground. But the she-cat stood there in a relaxed pose, purring loudly as she licked Emry's blood off her fingers. *How does it feel to purr?* Emry wondered. *I bet it's amazing.* "Rrrr, thick and yummy," Bast moaned, savoring the dense, erythrocyte-rich blood that fed the increased oxygen demand of Emry's muscles. "Come here and give me more!"

"Sorry, we don't deliver!" Emry wasn't about to jump down—the slow fall would give Bast plenty of reaction time. So she leapt still higher into the maze of ducts and girders overhead, taunting, "Come and get it, pussy!"

That proved a mistake. Emry had been hoping to lose Bast in the forest of conduits and get behind her, but all she did was get Bast more excited and hotter on Emry's (alas, only figurative) tail, following her easily through the maze. Bast's lighter, sleeker build let her slink along ducts too flimsy to support Emry's weight and slip easily through gaps Emry had to force her way through. Still, Emry couldn't resist taunting her, hoping to distract her focus. "Aww, no, now you'll get stuck up here and we'll have to call the fire department!"

Emry remembered playing with Kiri and Tigermuffin as a child: how they attacked a string or toy mousie most eagerly when it went behind the ottoman or table leg and "couldn't see" them coming. Emry had similar close calls with Bast, and those claws left their marks in Emry's arms a couple of times more, as well as doing a fair amount of damage to the conduits. Regrettably, none of them was carrying anything hot or caustic to spray out in Bast's face, as they surely would have in a movie or sim. Real life was such a rip-off sometimes. "Keep scratching up the furniture and we'll have to get you a manicure!" Bast slashed out with a foot, barely missing her. "And a pedicure. How about a sinecure? Get paid to sleep all day—what cat could pass that up?" The next swipe of Bast's claws raked across the back of her hand. Emry lost her grip and barely managed to catch herself on the pipe below. "Would you settle for a cured ham?" *I'll need a cure for disembowelment at this rate.*

But Emry had grown up with cats—surely she could use a few of their tricks herself. Hell, she *was* wearing tiger-print panties. The next time Bast's claws slashed from around a vertical pipe, Emry swept around the other side and collided with her. They fell together in a Coriolis arc. Emry struggled to hold Bast and make sure the she-cat landed on her back. But Bast's tail gave her the advantage in midair twisting, and Emry ended up on the bottom (not her favorite position), just managing to splay her arms in time to absorb the impact wrestler-style. Which made them unavailable to stop Bast from going for her throat again. So she slammed her forehead into Bast's. Not for the first time, her thick skull came in handy; Bast yowled and fell back, letting Emry get her legs up into the she-cat's midriff, launching her backward. She landed in a three-point crouch, though, and Emry struggled to rise and face her, though she found it hard to get beyond a sitting position. "Anybody got a ball of yarn?"

"Oh, for God's sake," came Arkady's voice, *"just shoot her!"* Emry grimaced. She hated guns, even the nonlethal kind—nasty things, and they took all the fun out of a good fight. But Arkady had a point—they didn't really have time, what with the other terrorists on the loose.

The clincher was that Bast was pouncing again, all her pointy bits deployed for the kill, and Emry couldn't dodge fast enough. In one smooth, swift move, she fell back, drew her dartgun, and placed shockdarts in Bast's exposed midriff and neck. The she-cat convulsed and fell heavily atop her, burying Emry's face in her thick, silky mane. "Sorry," Emry said. "This was just starting to get good." She rolled the dazed panther-woman off of her, taking a moment to appreciate how soft her fur was, and feeling irrationally tempted to stroke it back into smoothness. But there was no time for that now. She drew binders from her belt and swiftly secured Bast's wrists and ankles before she could recover.

Emry turned to see Arkady hovering nearby in his armor suit, its wingjets keeping him airborne and correcting for Cori drift. She always thought the bulky thing made him look like something out of an old *anime*. Apparently he'd just lifted out of the way of the bull-man, Taurean, who was extricating his horns from a dented wall panel and shaking his head. He must've given up on the gun or been disarmed. Arkady fired a shock laser, but Taurean dodged surprisingly fast, the electric arc hitting the wall. Arkady deployed his arm-mounted sonic pulser, but before he could fire, Taurean leapt up and took him in the chest, smashing through several overhead pipes. Taurean landed smoothly on his feet, but Arkady fell badly and hit headfirst, a number of heavy conduits landing atop him.

"You okay, Papa Bear?" Emry called—but then noticed Taurean eyeing her and pawing at the ground. "Ohh, bull . . ." She fired off some shockdarts as he charged her headfirst, but they bounced off his skin as though it were light armor, not holding contact long enough to deliver an effective charge. No wonder Arkady had switched to beam weapons.

But Emry would not be cowed. Like a Minoan daredevil, she seized the bull-man by the horns and flipped over him, letting out a whoop. *That's one way to tackle a dilemma!* By the time she landed, she'd not only spun to face him, but had holstered her dartgun, drawn her laser pistol, and set it to shock mode. But he'd spun too, with no pause for rumination, and was charging her again. "It's the red hair, isn't it?" she asked, shaking her head a bit. *Priorities, kid!* she thought, and fired, the laser ionizing a path for the electric discharge. Taurean convulsed from the sustained shock, but still had enough momentum to bowl her over, knocking her sidearm from her hand and the wind from her lungs. She ended up on the bottom again, grateful for the low gravity, although his weight upon her chest was still suffocating.

But he was already stirring, the charge apparently too small for such a massive body. Before she could catch her breath and wriggle free, he had an oversized hand around her throat. His other hand held down her right arm in a vise grip, and his tree-trunk legs pinned hers. She gripped his wrist in her left hand, but he tightened his hold on her throat when she did, giving her pause. "Damn, you're beautiful," he said in a surprisingly mellow, good-natured voice. "Too bad I have to kill you."

Emry seized the opening. "Well, you don't *have* to," she lilted with what breath she could muster, lowering her eyelids seductively. "I've known some horny men, but you take the beefcake. Why don't we have our own little rodeo, see how long I can ride you?"

Taurean looked tempted . . . but smiled regretfully. "I'd love to— but I'm not that stupid. I like girls with more fur, anyway," he added with a shrug. "Sorry. I'll make it quick, okay?" His fist tightened brutally around her neck, in stark contrast to his easygoing manner. Emry tried to wrench it free, but his arm wouldn't budge and she was already weakening. She could hold her breath fairly long given a chance to prepare; but she'd already had the wind knocked out of her, and her metabolism was high from the fight, demanding oxygen that just wasn't coming. She choked soundlessly, striving to remain conscious.

He gave her a reassuring smile, like an anesthesiologist telling her to relax, count backward from ten, and just let oblivion take her.

But then a plasma bolt erupted in his face. It knocked him for a loop and he reflexively let go. Emry was dazzled herself, despite her corneal filters, but was able to push him off and scramble free. Arkady fired enough tanglewebs to make sure he was securely bound. Still choking and struggling for breath, Emry was tempted to leave the webs across his face and let *him* suffocate for a while. But his attempt to kill her had been without malice, just a guy doing his job, and she found that she bore him no ill will. So she moved in and extended her diamond thumbnail blades to cut his nose and mouth free as he struggled ineffectually against the restraints. *Your loss, bully-boy. Would've been a wild ride.*

"You okay?" Arkady asked. Even with the helmet concealing his face, she could tell he was looking her over with concern.

She quizzed her biometrics and got the HUD readout on her retina. The cuts from Bast were clotted, the cells already being knitted back together by her repair nans, and no significant toxins had been introduced. Taurean's impact had bruised a couple of ribs, again nothing her repair systems couldn't handle. The cartilage around her windpipe was bruised as well, but its polymer reinforcements had held up. Her ears were ringing from the plasma bolt, but there was no serious damage. "I'm fine," she said hoarsely. "I could've handled him."

"Of course. But I thought I'd save you the trouble."

"I *am* trouble," she said with self-mocking arrogance.

"As I know better than anyone. You should focus less on your wisecracks and more on the battle."

"What fun is that? Plus it loosens up the imagination, keeps me flexible. Good to have in a—"

Then the habitat rumbled. Then it groaned. Then it heaved.

Arkady Nazarbayev knew space habitats. Back before Independence, he'd been a construction worker, helping to build the things. It had been a booming business what with all the emigrés coming up from Earth—many voluntarily, others not so much, but all needing homes. Once Earth had gone to war with Ceres and Vesta for control of their abundant resources, it had only seemed natural to use his heavy-duty construction symbot—which augmented his strength twenty times over and was hardened against vacuum, radiation, and construction hazards—to defend his home and family. He'd modified the powered exoskeleton into a fighting machine, though he'd striven to keep its weapons mostly nonlethal. After all, many Terrans were still family, as far as he was concerned.

Not everyone had agreed, of course, and matters had very nearly come to a cataclysmic level until the Great Compromise was struck, granting Earth rule over everything in its orbital space (including the Moon and all five Earth-Moon Lagrange points) in exchange for the independence of the Main Asteroid Belt. Afterward, the newly independent Striders had perhaps relished their individuality too much, and the wartime coalition had collapsed. Rivalries had erupted—between the powerful states of Ceres and Vesta and the smaller independent habitats, between the Cereans and Vestans themselves for economic dominance, between the puritanism of the pioneer generation and the rebelliousness of the young, between all of them and the new habitats that had relocated, voluntarily or otherwise, from cislunar space. And many of the mods, both states and individuals alike, had exploited the chaos to assert dominance over the less enhanced. So it had only seemed natural for Arkady to keep using his combat-rigged symbot to defend his home and family. And then it had only seemed natural to help his neighbors when they couldn't help themselves, to fend off the conquerors and raiders and mobsters so they wouldn't keep hurting good honest folk. After all, he was hardly the only vet to do that sort of thing, though others had done it in their own ways, with their own special tech or mods.

But not all of them had been as concerned about nonlethality as Arkady, or as hesitant to profit from their "protection" efforts. Before long, these "Troubleshooters" were fighting each other as much as the bad guys, or at least clashing over methods, jurisdiction, and miscommunications. So when Yukio Villareal, one of the architects of the Great Compromise, had proposed to his fellow Troubleshooters that they found a corps to coordinate their efforts and regulate their own members—an independent, nongovernmental organization recruiting and training the best and brightest from all over the Belt—it had only seemed natural to sign on.

The media may have painted Arkady as some great frontier hero, but he was just a guy who'd done what came naturally. At heart he was still just a simple, brawny lug who was good at driving a symbot.

And he knew space habitats. So he had a pretty good sense of what was wrong with Chakra City even before he tapped into their security web. As soon as the groaning began, he gathered up Emerald in his arms (something she accepted far more easily now than on that terrible day nine years ago) and rocketed for the nearest exit into the habitat's interior space. He had to blast out a few conduits to get there, but that was the least of Chakra City's problems—as he and Emerald saw clearly as soon as they were in view of the skylights that arched over-head, forming the inner half of the toroidal shell. The radiators—the two long, narrow panels that extended from the axis on the northern side of the habitat rings, permanently edge-on to the Sun—were gone. White-hot stubs remained where they had connected to the hub, and a glowing scar ripped across the industrial block between them. "Oh, Goddess," he heard Emry gasp, sounding like she actually meant it for once. *At least some good might come out of this, then,* he thought—though he preferred a more traditional interpretation of the divine.

The security reports and his suit cameras complemented each other in telling the tale. A ship docked to the hub beyond the radiators, no doubt under Neogaian control, had ripped free of its cradle and turned its fusion-drive nozzle toward the station hub, sweeping a cone of ex-haust plasma across it and severing both radiators at their connection points. The pressure from the drive exhaust and the vaporized coolant that burst from the ruptures conspired to accelerate the radiators toward the habitat rings, striking their northern side with some force. One had bounced off the uncompleted northernmost ring, smashing a number of the heavy, chevron-shaped mirror strips that directed sunlight into the torus while shielding it from direct radiation. The mirrors had been knocked into the skylight panels below, shattering several and causing an atmosphere breach; however, it would take hours for the pressure loss from that breach to become significant.

But by misfortune or design, the other radiator had snagged on the end cap of the newly added ring section he and Emerald were in. Suddenly imparted with angular acceleration, the radiator had acquired weight, falling down and antispinward. That, combined with its existing motion athwart the rings, had caused the long, flat array of panels to wrap around their top half—or rather, to crash against them, for its weight grew quickly as it fell. The skylight arch on the next ring over was badly damaged; it looked as though it might have caught the edge of the ship's plasma exhaust as well.

Worse—from the way the skylight sagged under the twisted panel, Arkady could tell that the radiator wasn't breaking apart as it should. He cursed the antiquated design of the thing. Now there was a long strip of material massing kilotonnes hanging down over a hundred meters below the ring, weighted down by gravity approaching and maybe even surpassing Earth's. And it was tugging on the rest of the panel, worsening the strain on the mirror strips and skylight and threatening to tear clear through it and smash down on the people below—not to mention the far worse air loss that would result from a breach of that size. It was night, so there were few people outdoors to be hit by falling debris; but that wouldn't matter if the whole sky fell on their roofs. And the sun mirror to the south had already switched from black to reflective as the habitat went into emergency daylight mode.

They forced open the hatch and crossed into the damaged section, where air and debris were rushing out of the growing rift in the skylight. The occupants were running for the exits, and the Troubleshooters hastened to assist in an orderly evacuation. <We were wrong!> Emerald called, using her subvocal transceiver to be heard over the wind and the groaning of the skylight framework. <We thought they were gonna let the virus spread through normal traffic to Earth—but they wanted to force an evac, get as many infected refugees as possible in contact with other people!> Hence the severing of the radiators,

Arkady realized. Even these hull breaches wouldn't be fatal for the habitat; there was plenty of air to spare if the holes could be patched in time. But with no radiators, a habitat this small and this close to the Sun would become uninhabitably hot in less than a day. And Chakra's daily seventy-odd minutes in Earth's shadow had ended barely an hour ago.

<They must've sabotaged the dock sensors,> Emry went on. <Kept the drive buildup from being detected!> Arkady had been wondering about that. A ship that even warmed up its fusion or plasma drive anywhere near a habitat would set off alarms and be blown out of the sky if it didn't shut down before its engines were ready to fire. They would've had to bribe or otherwise compromise the human dock monitors as well. This was a bigger operation than he'd realized.

Still, he didn't get one thing. "There wouldn't have been time for the viruses to spread yet!" Not that Arkady doubted Emry's insight—despite her brawn-over-brain impulses, she had it in her to be a fine detective. He was so proud of her for that, even though he'd had nothing to do with it. Arkady was just a big lug who needed things explained to him.

<They would've waited a few days! But we forced their hand! Now Krieger's gonna try to infect as many people as he can in the chaos of the evac.>

"He'll be heading up to the spaceport, then." The passage to the docks led through the damaged industrial block, but should be deep enough within it to remain passable.

But a renewed groaning brought Arkady's attention back to the immediate problem, as the skylight framework buckled a little more under the weight of the radiator and mirror strips, causing several more heavy window panels to fall from the sky. Unfortunately the radiator slanted directly over one of the more heavily populated sectors of the ring. "We have to get the people out! We'll worry about Krieger when we reach the port."

After that it was an efficient scramble, coordinating with the Chakran police and emergency crews to manage the evacuation, to hurry the people toward the nearest elevator shaft to the hub, to keep them calm despite the terrifying groaning and the shuddering and the ominous whistling of the air across the twisted girders of the skylight frame. Arkady tried to estimate how long it might take Wulf Krieger to get to the port and infect its ships with his polyviruses. He got on the comm and issued instructions that no escaping ship be allowed to land on Earth or dock with any other habitat until a medical team checked it out, but he couldn't be sure how fully that would be heeded in the chaos. He just had to hope that the crush of the crowd would impede Krieger, giving them time to head him off. If there was any comfort here, it was that the bad guy had been forced to improvise.

But then the skylight frame buckled and gave way with a terrible shrieking sound, and tonnes of glass, metal, and composite rained down as the radiator panel overhead sagged and twisted, its connections to the adjacent panels breaking free one by one, way too late. Arkady realized it would come down virtually on top of the last group of stragglers he was with. "Everybody, run! Move, move, move! Quickly!" he cried, amplifying his voice to shock them into motion. Emerald caught his sense of urgency and began herding them forward as fast as she could.

But a large chunk of the skylight frame was falling right for him, a pair of massive mirror strip panels riding on its back. Without a second's thought, Arkady stopped running and lifted his arms skyward, bracing his legs and locking the symbot's joints. The impact drove his arms and torso down and his servos whined and overheated, but the symbot held, and the last few Chakrans were able to start scrambling out from under once he urged them out of their terrified paralysis.

The problem was, the servos were starting to give out. Arkady realized he wouldn't have the power left to push this thing off, not in the brief moments before the radiator panel gave way and came down on top of him. All he could do was hold it and make sure the Chakrans—and Emry—got to safety.

But then Emerald had to go and turn around. And then his wonderful, brilliant student had to be an idiot and run back to him. "Arkady!"

"Go! Save the others! My suit's shot!"

"No, I won't leave you!" Emry saw what was going to happen, he knew she did. But still she looked around desperately, grabbed a fallen girder and tried to use it to brace the ceiling fragment. She knew it was futile. But the poor lonely child couldn't face it, couldn't bear another loss. She'd blame herself, he knew it, and he hated doing this to the sweet girl. But she needed to live. Humanity needed her, needed the magnificent Troubleshooter she was destined to become.

Oh, God. He longed to tell Emerald how much he loved her, like his own daughter, sometimes maybe more since she needed it so much more. But that would just make it harder for her to leave. "Damn you, you idiot!" he cried. "For once in your life, listen to me, you foolish child! Go! That's an order! *Go!*" She jerked her head back as though he'd struck her, and gazed at him with a look of shock and betrayal and abandonment, tears pouring down her face, looking like the little girl he'd met nine years ago, just minutes too late. But she was listening. *"You have too many other lives to save,"* he told her, ramming each word home.

It got through to her. It was the only thing that could have. She was bawling at the top of her lungs like a baby as she turned away. But she turned away, and she ran. Arkady tried to call out his love to her, to say good-bye, but the radiator panel finally tore free with a final, mournful groan.

Arkady accepted the inevitable, finding peace. His old comrade had served him well, but it had reached its limits. At least the breaking of the radiator meant that its remaining pieces would fall free and put no more strain upon the habitat. At least he'd gotten the people out. That was what mattered. He'd just done his job, done what came naturally. He knew Pavel and the kids would understand.

He just prayed, with his last thought, that Emerald would.

2

The Troubleshooters

Demetria habitat
In orbit of Ceres

". . . And it is with great pride that I promote Emerald Blair, the Green Blaze, to the status of full Troubleshooter, with all the rights and responsibilities that the title entails."

Emry tried not to wince at the applause. At least it was subdued and respectful; the audience before her, consisting of fellow Troubleshooters in full uniform alongside TSC staffers, their families, and assorted dignitaries and reporters, understood what she had lost in order to gain this early promotion. Many of them had been as close to Arkady as she had been, if not more so.

Yukio Villareal had probably been closer to Arkady than anyone but his husband. The two men had been fast friends and allies for over twenty years. But his voice remained calm and commanding as he spoke, capturing the crowd's attention as it always did. "And it is with equal pride that I confer upon our newest Troubleshooter a commendation . . . only her first, I'm sure . . . for service above and beyond the call of duty in preventing the Neogaian bioterror attack on our Terran cousins. While we mourn the thirty-seven souls who were lost in the disaster at Chakra City, including one of our own most cherished members, we owe Emerald Blair our deepest thanks for ensuring that the toll was not far worse."

Only Emry's wish not to embarrass Sensei Villareal kept her from resisting as he placed the medallion around her neck. The whole thing was a joke. All she'd done was track Krieger's scent in an unthinking rage, like the predator he aspired to be, and beat him savagely until the local police had pulled her off. He was still in the hospital, under top security. Maybe incidentally she'd stopped him from infecting more than two ships, whose occupants had been successfully quarantined and were undergoing treatment, but who might have to go through life with some interesting cosmetic changes. Some had suffered severe allergic reactions to the foreign proteins produced by their virally altered DNA; if the viruses had been unleashed on Earth, the consequences would've been far worse than the Neogaians had apparently believed. Preventing that had earned Emry this commendation. But all she'd really done was lose control again, with the usual consequences to human life and limb. The fact that the victim had been a terrorist and murderer didn't make it any better. She'd been acting on impulse, not thinking enough about anything other than vanity and wisecracks. She'd let herself grow complacent. That couldn't happen again.

She hadn't even remembered the other Neogaian cultists until the police on the scene had asked her in haste to explain the situation. They'd alerted their search parties to retrieve Bast and Taurean, only to find them gone. They had escaped in the confusion, perhaps with the help of the fourth terrorist, who was never found. They were now back home in their own habitat, sheltered by its government.

UNECS had declared a trade embargo against Neogaia, as had the Mars Confederacy, the Cerean States, and most of the major Vestan nation-states; but of course it wouldn't be universally obeyed and couldn't be enforced. The Striders clung proudly to their hard-won independence, so getting them to agree on anything was like herding cats. Not to mention the growing population of fringe groups that had emigrated or been exiled from Earth and its orbital space, transhumanists who'd probably sympathize with Neogaia or extremists who'd be busy making trouble of their own. Prefab, auxon-built habitats were easy to obtain and aggressively subsidized by a UNECS eager to ship more people off the overpopulated birthworld, especially the troublemakers who weren't even welcome within cislunar space. The Troubleshooters

kept the peace as best they could, but they were just a private organization who'd squander the Striders' goodwill and their own resources if
they began meddling in how people lived on their own habitats. They'd
keep an eye on Neogaia, try to catch any future aggressions, but that
was all they could do.

Except hand out medals to people who didn't deserve them and try
to take comfort in the gesture. Emry avoided letting Sensei see what
was in her eyes, instead looking up at the open sky that stretched clear
to the far side of Demetria's two-kilometer-wide habitat sphere (with
no heavy skylights or mirrors to hang over her head), and out the an-
nular sun window to where Ceres drifted past on its endless rounds,
once every seventy seconds as Demetria rotated. The sunlit side of the
dwarf planet was a dusty gray, except for the bright glints where craters
or mining operations had exposed fresh ice beneath. On the dark side,
beacons and spotlights limned hundreds more of the mines whose ice
and organic compounds sustained life for most of the habitats in the
Belt and Inner System. Beyond it, so large that its elongated shape was
clearly visible even from a third of an orbit away, was the Sheaf: the
clustered habitats of the Cerean States, fourteen counterrotating pairs
of massive, elongated O'Neill cylinders and a half-dozen chains of
smaller Bernal spheres like Demetria, scaffolded together in parallel
but spaced widely enough to leave room for their respective sun mirrors, radiators, and support facilities, all adding up to a symbiotic cluster
that housed nearly two hundred million people. Around them, at a large
enough radius to leave room for future cylinders, she could see the fragmented halo of the Band, the massive ring habitat which, once its parallel toroidal components were all complete and linked together, would
become the single largest populated megastructure in Solsys, with tri-
ple the habitable volume of the current Sheaf.

The Sheaf and the Band were the fullest realization of the natural
tendency of space settlements to expand over time. The early, small
habitats had demanded a regimented existence; birth rates must be
strictly controlled, environment strictly balanced, safety protocols
carefully followed. As habitats grew larger and more advanced, their
ecologies better able to absorb fluctuations, their safety systems more

foolproof, their populations given more room to grow, a more relaxed, liberal existence became feasible. More and more, the hardscrabble High Frontier was giving way to a more expansive and cosmopolitan way of life, nowhere more so than in the Ceres Sheaf. It was no wonder that the majority of immigrants from Earth chose to settle there. Particularly since its stable gravity and robust radiation shielding made it a reasonably safe place to live with few or no mods.

Right now, though, Emry had trouble buying into that illusion of safety. Even the Sheaf and Band were dependent on a few square kilometers of heat radiators, not to mention the sun reflectors, radiation shields, agriculture rings . . . any of which could be sabotaged in dozens of ways by a successful terrorist group. Really, how good were anyone's odds of survival in a Solar System where the power of individual humans to wreak destruction kept growing by the year? And what could a few dozen superpowered eccentrics hope to do about it?

She kept those thoughts to herself as she gave her acceptance speech. Instead, she just offered a few boilerplate thank-yous and promises. Even her words about Arkady were boilerplate, since if she tried to express what she really felt—to talk about how he'd always been her anchor, solid and calm and accepting no matter how much grief she gave him, and how she couldn't imagine going on now without him—she'd surely break down again. She owed it to her colleagues and friends to offer them something comforting, something reaffirming. So she hid behind platitudes she barely heard herself saying.

Then she was done, and the crowd cheered, and Sensei shook her hand and kissed her cheek. Her fellow Troubleshooters—Sensei, Lodestar, Tenshi, Bellatrix, Tor, the rest who weren't too busy saving lives to attend—formed an honor guard to escort her offstage, then fell upon her with handshakes and hugs and kisses of both celebration and commiseration. She couldn't understand why they thought she deserved this. She got away by citing a need for the ladies' room—only to find it wasn't an excuse, since as soon as she got there she had to throw up.

When she emerged, she found Villareal hovering nearby, pretending to check his silvery hair and Errol Flynn moustache in a reflective wall panel. "I told you I didn't want the medal," she said.

"What we want and what we deserve are rarely the same thing, Blaze."

"How about what Arkady deserved? What his family deserved?"

"They've always understood. Pavel and the kids, they're exceptional people. Strong. You have to be, to have a Troubleshooter in the family. So few of us find mates, or keep them . . . Arkady was luckier than most."

"Oh, great pep talk for the new kid, Master. So I'm doomed to be alone, huh?"

"No, Emry," Sensei said, reaching for her shoulder. "We have each other."

But she pulled away. "It's all right. Maybe that's the way I should be—just depend on myself. Goddess knows nobody else can."

"Emerald." His voice became stern. "You know there was nothing you could have done to save him. It's a miracle he slowed the collapse enough to allow your escape."

"Nothing I can think of," she said, talking over him. "Not so far. But what if one day I wake up and I realize there was something I missed, something I could've done differently?"

"I'm sure you will." She stared. "Because the more you go back there, the more you'll rewrite the memory to suit your sense of guilt. But you have the hard data in your buffer," he reminded her, lightly tapping her temple. "Don't lose it. Even if you can never bear to replay it, to watch it—and I wouldn't ask you to—just remember that it's there. Let it anchor you with the truth that you did nothing wrong. If you can't believe that in . . . other cases, at least believe it in this one."

He stroked her hair with bionic hands more sensitive than his real ones had been. "You know why I encourage the flamboyant side of what we do, right? The nicknames, the colorful personas, the media attention?"

She smiled just a bit, the reminder of their old joke bringing an echo of amusement. "Because you read too many comic books as a kid?"

He smiled back. "No more than you. What's the real reason?"

She recalled his old lectures. "Because power breeds mistrust. You wanted us to be inspiring, not intimidating. An army of mods would only create fear, but a league of superheroes is another matter."

"That's right. We first Troubleshooters . . . we came along at a time when the Striders needed heroes to believe in, so they made us that. Something larger than life, iconic, pure." He shook his head. "After the war . . . when the allies retreated into nationalist bickering and power grabs . . . that symbolism they'd projected onto us was one of the only things they still agreed on. We knew that need for heroes wouldn't last indefinitely—but we took it and nurtured it, built on the mythology of the Troubleshooters, so that we and, more importantly, you could hold on to the Striders' trust as long as possible."

"Is that why you made me go through with this? Made me look like a hero when I'm not?"

"No, Emerald. Because you deserved it. I know it doesn't feel like that to you, but that's exactly why you do deserve it. If we're to be worthy of that trust we've earned, we need to be able to question ourselves. To face our mistakes and our flaws openly, so we can keep ourselves honest. Your capacity for questioning yourself is part of what gives me so much confidence in you."

He clasped her shoulder. "But as with most things, you tend to overdo it. Self-doubt is responsible, but self-flagellation is merely an indulgence. Keep your balance, Green Blaze. Don't overcorrect."

"I understand." She placed her hand over his, gave a brief reassuring smile. "It's all about control. I won't lose that again. I won't let myself," she added firmly.

But Sensei didn't seem reassured.

Vanguard habitat
5:3 Kirkwood Gap, Outer Belt

Eliot Thorne replayed Emerald Blair's speech on the soligram stage, studying her every expression and movement as he circled the solid projection. Beside him, Psyche did the same, but not so silently. "She shouldn't be so hard on herself," she said. "She did really well, considering. She's even stronger than I expected."

"Given who her father was, I expected no less," Thorne replied. "Though it is gratifying to know our genes remain dominant when crossbred."

She pouted at his solemnity. "You don't sound gratified. Cheer up! She did everything you hoped for, and then some."

"Mm. But as a Troubleshooter. Not a Vanguardian."

"Isn't that what you wanted? I mean, after I went to all that trouble to get that tip to Medvyéd anonymously. . . ."

Thorne smiled, clasping her shoulder. "You did well, Psyche." She basked in his praise. "Our prodigal son's daughter has done the Troubleshooters proud, and Earth will be suitably grateful—and suitably alerted to the dangers of their isolation. They will respond as anticipated—and that will in turn provoke the response we seek."

Psyche turned back to the soligram, stroking its simulated hair. "I'm sorry she lost a friend, though. A face that beautiful shouldn't be so sad."

"Don't let it trouble you, my dear. She has survived worse." He paused the image and leaned forward, gazing into those immense emerald eyes. "As she will survive the trials that face her in the months ahead. And finally, when she is left with nothing else, she will still have us."

TSC Headquarters
Demetria

As Emry attacked her, Koyama Hikari felt the battle peace descend over her and reminded herself not to kill her best friend.

Normally, killing Emerald Blair would be far more easily said than done, but she had been running herself ragged since her return from Earth space. She trained relentlessly by day, and at night, instead of sleeping, she wandered the streets searching for random criminals to beat up—in between picking up random men to fuck to within an inch of their lives.

It wasn't Kari's place to judge, though. After all, it had been Emry who'd taught her the value of excess. Even as Sensei Villareal had carefully taught her how, when battle came, to master the cool, methodical monster her father had placed inside her, Emry had helped her learn that it was all right to relax and go crazy the rest of the time. Penance didn't have to occupy every minute. Kari hoped that after the workout, she could remind Emry of that lesson, perhaps talk her into shuttling over to the Sheaf for a girls' day out full of shopping and playing and man-watching and dressing up and showing off and dancing and other fulfilling wastes of time. She certainly wouldn't mind if the evening ended with some male company for the both of them, so long as she could get Emry in the mood to have fun with it, to let the sex be healing rather than merely distracting. She was demure by nature, but Emry was good at pushing her past her inhibitions.

Right now, though, it was time to concentrate. When Emry had called to invite her to a "workout," her tone had made it clear to Kari that this would be a full-on bout, no punches pulled. Both Troubleshooters were in full light-armor costume, Green Blaze versus Tenshi, letting them cut loose with all their raw power.

Of course, Emry was bigger and far stronger than Kari. But Koyama Saburo's gengineers had designed his daughter's body to be durable, flexible, and lightning-quick, and her brain to be preternaturally aware of every bit of it. As she was overcome by the *tatakai no heiwa,* the heightened serenity and awareness they had substituted for her fight-or-flight instinct, she felt her consciousness descend and spread throughout her body and beyond. The mind, the hand, the air it flew through, the flesh it struck, the gravity that sculpted its arc, all were one, all were within her soul. Yet at the same time she was outside of it in a sense, her body striking and reacting without conscious guidance. It was a Zen oneness with creation; it was a distributed AI network integrated with her nervous system, regulated by a cerebellar implant containing every martial-arts principle known to humanity. They were the same thing.

Kari observed from a detached place as her body battled Emry, meeting fury with patient precision, brute force with gentle deflection. When an opportunity presented itself, she struck, hand or foot drawn to the optimal point of impact as inexorably as a cherry blossom is drawn to the earth. When she was struck in turn, she accepted the energy as a part of her, let herself be the conduit through which it flowed back to its source, as the rain striking the river returns to the sea. This was her father's ideal, with one exception—through careful biofeedback and a spot of reprogramming, the Troubleshooter Corps had helped her retrain her instincts to incapacitate rather than kill. He would have found it dishonorable, a daughter defying her father's wishes. The Vestan *yakuza*, unlike its Earthly counterpart, was a family business, a change Koyama Saburo had deemed necessary to maintain its Japanese purity in the multicultural Belt. Koyama had nominally kept it all-male as well, but in his eyes that had made Kari the perfect stealth assassin, a passive, decorative nonentity until she struck. But Kari had not wished to become a living weapon, even though rejecting that fate had meant betraying her beloved father and fleeing her home.

She had fulfilled her father's wishes in one sense, though, when he'd attempted to stop her escape. Perhaps he'd seen it as a redemption of her honor when the *heiwa* had taken her and she'd watched herself serenely, efficiently kill him.

As her body fought, Kari let her attention widen. She noticed that their bout was drawing a crowd, mainly trainees and support personnel, though Bellatrix, Paladin, and Tor were among them as well. Some studied their technique with a clinical eye, while others simply enjoyed the spectacle. Her heightened senses registered that several of the men had erections as they watched the two women fight. Kari meditated on the aesthetics of the battle, particularly the contrasts. Emry was a bold presence, with wild bright hair, shining eyes, and a powerful, curvaceous body. Kari was dainty and subtle, her black hair long and straight, her half-moon eyes dark and demure, her contours sleek and understated. She'd been designed to appear deceptively cute, girlish, and unthreatening, and in her less meditative moments she envied her friend's flashy gorgeousness. Emry's vivid green and black costume complemented Kari's stylized *dogi*, a saffron-trimmed red jacket (the color of life, framed by the color of restraint and renunciation) worn over a silver light-armor leotard and tied with a black belt (with no *dan* markings, since Sensei Villareal felt conventional skill rankings were inapplicable in her case). Emry shrieked and grunted and roared with passion as she fought, her rough-edged soprano dancing through octaves in a way that irritated some spectators while arousing others. Kari's vocalizations were precise, relaxed, merely a focusing of energy.

The two best friends had been sparring frequently for sixteen months now, challenging each other to reach greater heights, and together they were poetry, their disparate styles meshing into a graceful, vicious dance. They knew each other, felt each other, brought out the best in each other. It was exhilarating. Though Kari was serene and detached in her battle peace, she was hardly emotionless, and as she and Emry sparred and kicked and threw each other across the room she was filled with joy at the perfection they made together. Although her love for Emry was only sisterly, she felt a sensual, almost orgasmic fulfillment when they sparred like this, their bodies achieving a unity she'd never otherwise felt outside of sex, and rarely there. And she could see that joy infecting Emry, gradually pushing aside the anger and bitterness. There was nothing more therapeutic than pure, simple fun with someone you loved and trusted. Kari was glad she could help.

Finally Emry was laughing out loud as she fought, and as she so often did at this point, she got sick of Kari's zenlike detachment (what Emry called her "anti-Berserker" mode) and tried to break her concentration by making her laugh. Kicks and flips turned into tickles and pratfalls, and it was with great relief that Kari finally felt the *heiwa* leave her so she could laugh again. Where before there had been two relentless fighters striking blows that would've killed lesser mortals, now there were two twentysomething girls rolling around on the floor, giggling and hurling playful insults.

Finally they bowed deeply to their spectators and sashayed off to the locker room arm-in-arm. By now Kari was starting to notice the bruises her battle peace hadn't let her feel before. Emry looked pretty roughed up herself, though, and Kari felt the usual odd mixture of pride and shame that she could give as good as she got in the violence department. At least they both healed fast. And it had been worth it, to cheer Emry up.

The two of them showered , exchanged back rubs, and then settled into a *furo* for a nice hot soak. "Ohhh," Kari moaned. "Forget about that girls' day out—let's just stay here all day."

"Mmm, nice thought. But I'm looking forward to it. We haven't had a good night on the town together in months."

"Yeah, you're right." But then Kari pouted and hugged Emry desperately.

"Uh-oh. Mood swing. What gives?"

"Ohh," Kari moaned, "it just hit me that I won't see you as much now that you've graduated! I'll miss you so much, sweetie!"

"Aww, you big crybaby," Emry said, but hugged her back just as tightly. When it ended, Emry told her, "Actually I won't be going out on patrol for a while."

"Really? But your ship's all ready, waiting for you! And Zephyr's actually agreed to be its cyber! He has got the *sexiest* voice. . . ."

"Ohhh, yeah, the Goddess is generous," Emry sighed. "But I've put in for one more set of upgrades. The surgery's in a couple days, and then I'll be breaking 'em in for a few weeks."

"What?" Kari said. "More mods? Emry," she laughed, "come on, you were *born* superhuman and you've had yourself chopped and channelled three or four times on top of that. What's left to put in you? Bucket seats and fuzzy dice?"

"They say they can up my strength maybe another six percent. Plus there are some upgrades on my IR resolution, filters for a few new toxins . . . and they're gonna see if they can up my reaction time any more."

"That doesn't sound like much! Emry, you're reaching a point of diminishing returns. All those surgeries aren't easy on the body, not even yours. You can't get much stronger without overstraining your organs! And for what real gain, seriously?"

Emry met her eyes intently. "*Any* edge I can get, anything that gives me more power over a situation, can make the difference between saving a life or not saving it. So don't you tell me it isn't worth it!"

Kari looked down, chastened by Emry's words. In apology, Emry hugged her again, and then they got out and helped each other towel off. But as they dressed, Kari spoke gently. "Emry, I understand why you don't want to lose control. I remember what happened when I did." She paused, remembering her father, facing the guilt that was always there beneath the surface, even in her happiest moments. Her guilt let her understand Emry's own; that common bond had been a basis of their friendship from the start. "So believe me when I tell you: more power isn't what you need. Too much power in one person's hands, it puts things too far out of balance. The greater the imbalance of energies, the more destructively they flow. What you need is balance."

"But what about the people who depend on me? What do they need?" Emry wasn't angry anymore, but she was firm, unbending, and Kari prayed she wouldn't break. "I have to be sure, Kari," she said. "I have to make sure I never lose anyone I love, ever again."

3

Origin Stories: Emerald's Dawn

March 2085
Greenwood habitat
2:1 Kirkwood gap

Emerald Blair was trouble from the day *before* she was born.

Lyra Blair-Shannon had taken it as a good omen that her water had broken on Ostara—Earth's vernal equinox, the beginning of spring when the Mother gave forth new life. She had gone to the hospital convinced that this would be the perfect, beautiful process of creation she'd always imagined. She had her faith in the Goddess to support her. She had Richard to hold her hand and strengthen her with his love. She had an experienced doula who would help her through every step of the process. And she was sexually active enough that her pelvic floor muscles were in excellent shape, which should ensure easy labor. She doubted the same could be said for most Greenwooder women. The doctors had reminded her that the baby took after her large, robust father, so she shouldn't expect the birth to be effortless. Indeed, the heightened metabolic demands of the fetus's superhuman physiology had been a constant drain on her dainty, mere-mortal body, making this a difficult pregnancy almost from the start, albeit six weeks shorter than usual. But Lyra had her music and meditation to relax her, and the water birth would cushion her body, further easing the process. She wasn't worried.

The Greenwood doctors had looked askance on her arrangements, just as the people of this small, rural Bernal sphere had looked askance on Lyra and Richard since they'd moved here nine months prior. It had seemed to the young couple like a safe, peaceful place: it orbited in one of the Outer Belt's emptiest Kirkwood gaps, cleared of potentially hazardous debris by Jupiter's gravitational resonance and comfortably removed from the postwar tensions of the Inner and Central Belt. The abundance of icy minor stroids and comets in the Outers made it easy for isolated habitats to exist self-sufficiently, and so the region proliferated with small, independent communities, whether fringe groups undertaking novel genetic or social experiments, extremists unwilling to assimilate within mainstream society, or just traditionalists seeking a quiet, small-town way of life like the Greenwooders. But the trade-off was that such compact, isolated habitats demanded conformity and conservatism within themselves, lest the balance of ecology and society be disrupted. The locals had been uncomfortable with Lyra's Wicca-based spirituality (her own unorthodox version, but deeply devout nonetheless) and downright scandalized by her skyclad performance art that overtly celebrated sexuality as a vehicle for spreading peace and unity.

The Greenwooders also disapproved of "playing God" with the human genome—a very Terran attitude, but one growing necessarily more common in the Belt as habitats with Earthlike gravity and radiation shielding became more numerous and immigration from Earth accelerated. But they did value family, and Richard had relatives here. So they strove to accept him and his "unconventional" wife, assuring him that he wasn't to blame for his parents' choice to migrate to the Vanguard habitat and let them tamper with the family genes. The Blair-Shannons had been good neighbors and mostly won the Greenwooders over, so long as they didn't proselytize their eccentricities. Lyra was confident that within a couple of hours, the doctors would be won over as well.

The baby, however, wasn't inclined to cooperate. Hours passed and no labor came. Eventually Lyra let the doctors talk her into induced labor and spent hours more bearing down, though she still refused painkillers, wanting her little girl to be alert and undrugged when she entered the world. Until this day, Lyra had thought she knew pain and hardship from her years as a dancer. But this was beyond anything she'd ever imagined. Each individual contraction wasn't necessarily so bad, but they kept up relentlessly, leaving her no time to rest, to think. Once she'd seen Richard hold up a toppling wall for several minutes, pushing his augmented bones and muscles past their limits, while his fellow rescue workers freed trapped victims. Lyra had never imagined she could endure anything remotely like that. Yet now she felt like she was doing it every few minutes for a full day and more. It was more than her delicate frame could stand. But she would bear it gladly, and a hundred times more, for her daughter.

She heard Richard and doula Margarethe talking to her, soothing her, but she spent most of the ordeal within herself, praying to the Goddess, feeling for the novice soul inside her and urging her to let go, to let herself be born and discover the glorious new universe the Goddess had prepared for her. A part of her wanted to beg the child to stop demanding so much, to end this torture before she killed them both. But she loved the girl too much to begrudge her anything. So she reached out to the Goddess, felt Her pure, unconditional love, and did her best to feed it to her child, to be a conduit for that overpowering goodness even if it destroyed her. All that mattered was creation and the love that powered it. Everything else—all her everyday concerns and hang-ups and discomforts, all the slights and contempt from the Greenwooders beneath their polite façades—was all burned away. Lyra had never known such clarity. And she loved her baby desperately for bringing it to her.

Finally, Lyra awoke to find that she'd missed the child's birth. The doctor had been left with no choice but to anesthetize her and perform a C-section. The baby's head had been transverse, and through it all she'd never left the womb. The doctors hadn't told Lyra for fear of making her tense. They'd hoped her contractions would turn the baby's head into better alignment. And to be fair, she had insisted on the most natural childbirth possible. So she could forgive them for not telling her. Especially since she now had the most beautiful baby in the universe to hold in her arms. She'd missed greeting the little girl at the moment of her arrival, but it made little difference; they still bonded almost instantly.

The baby had inherited her mother's elfin features, but had her father's Irish coloring. Her name became obvious to Richard as soon as she first opened her enormous eyes: Emerald, after his ancestral isle. Lyra couldn't argue; it was a perfect name for her perfect jewel of a daughter.

Emerald Rhea Blair-Shannon was a precocious baby in many ways, her development well ahead of the norm. Her physical vigor didn't seem at all attenuated by her mother's blood—and Richard insisted that her intelligence, curiosity, and vitality came mainly from Lyra's side. But the distinction didn't matter to Lyra. The ordeal of Emry's birth had created a profound bond between mother and child, especially since Lyra knew it would be unwise for her and Richard ever to conceive another. She and Emry had such a close rapport that, to Richard's amusement, she tended to refer to the two of them as a single composite person, a shared soul, using "we" to describe Emry's feelings and actions without any trace of pretension. On some level Richard envied them their bond; but he had his own close relationship with the child, if in a less holistic way. Emry and Lyra were like a single person, but Richard was the love of that person's life, and he felt it doubly now. When Lyra brought the baby to bed with them, Richard sometimes bemoaned the loss of privacy; but the miraculous sensation of Emry's tiny fingers clinging to his, of her eyes watching him raptly when he awoke, more than made up for it.

Indeed, Richard knew that as the child grew into her abilities, she would need him to guide her through it as his parents had for him. It wouldn't be easy—not here, where there was no system of support for a transhuman child or even acceptance for her specialness. He had his cousins and kin, who would feel obliged to the child as one of their own; but they couldn't truly understand her needs or teach her to see her uniqueness as a positive thing. Only her father could give her that.

As Emry grew older, Lyra and Richard always encouraged her to play with other children, but her rapid advancement made it difficult to gain their acceptance or form lasting bonds. Her parents remained her closest friends, their home her safe haven. Emry always loved their

periodic trips to Davida, the "county seat" for Greenwood and other
small Outers habitats on similar orbits. She was enthralled by its urban
habitats, its bustling crowds, its diverse population and entertainments.
But that was nothing compared to her excitement at visiting the Central
and Inner Belt when Lyra booked a performance tour or Richard went
to help with a disaster. She devoured the history and cultural diversity
of the Ceres Sheaf, the glamour and glitz of Vestalia and Rapyuta.
Once they even went to Earth to visit her mother's family in Tennes-
see, though Emry was uncomfortable in a place where the ground
curved the wrong way and there was nothing holding in the air but
gravity. Still, she wanted to go everywhere and see everything, so long
as she was always with her parents. She felt no particular ties to Greenwood; outside her house, it was never a place where she felt at home.
But to Lyra, for all its problems it was a haven from the chaos of the
Belt. And for Richard, it was the one place where he could be among
family since he'd made his break with the Vanguard. It was the one
subject on which Emry and her parents could never see eye to eye.

October 2091

"Mrs., uhh, Blair-Shannon?"
    "Yes, hi! What can I do for you?"
    "You have a daughter named Emerald?"
    ". . . Is she all right?"
    "I'm afraid there's been an . . . accident, ma'am. . . ."
    "My Goddess . . . please, is my baby all right?"
    "She hasn't got a scratch, ma'am. But the boy she attacked is in
critical condition."

Emerald's mommy and daddy never yelled at her like the other kids'
parents did. They never did anything mean to punish her. They just got
very disappointed. And it worked. Emry didn't understand how other
parents thought yelling and punishing would make their kids feel

guilty. Usually it just made them feel angry and defensive, like they were being treated unfairly. But when Emry saw that her parents were sad or hurt because of something she did, it made her feel that she'd been unfair to them. She couldn't pretend, like the other kids did, that she'd done nothing wrong. Because she loved Mommy and Daddy more than anything and couldn't bear to think she'd hurt them.

Lately, she'd been starting to think that was very smart of Mommy and Daddy, because it got her to do what they wanted. But she didn't think of it as a trick. It made her feel like they were treating her as an equal, trusting her to be responsible for them. And there were never any grudges. They always forgave her, and never did anything that she would need to forgive.

Right now, though, Emry didn't know how they could possibly forgive her. When they came to the police station and held her and comforted her, she almost pushed them away, because she didn't think she deserved it. But she didn't push them away, because she was afraid of what would happen if she struck out at anyone again. And she was afraid of getting the blood on them. It looked like it was all washed off, but she could still feel it.

"Is he going to die?" she asked in a tiny, timid voice. She was only six, but she knew death. She'd crushed that little bird last year without meaning to. The strength in her fast-growing hands had frightened her then . . . but that was nothing compared to this. The other kids were right . . . she was a freak, a monster. A killer.

Daddy stroked her hair and smiled reassuringly, even though he was still sad. Until now, his strong, gentle touch had always comforted her, because she knew she'd be completely safe so long as he was around to protect her. But now it wasn't her own safety she was worried about. "No, sweetie," he told her. "Sean's in the hospital, and they're taking good care of him. He's going to be fine."

"Do you know? How do you know? He was, he was so . . . broken and, and it was all bleeding out and I felt things squish in him! I'm sorry, I'm sorry I didn't mean to, I just got so angry! I didn't know he'd break so easy! I only wanted him to take it back, Mommy!"

"Take what back, love?" Her voice was the most beautiful sound

Emry had ever heard. Every night that voice sang her to sleep, made her feel safe and loved. Sometimes she thought she remembered being tiny, still small enough to be carried in Mommy's arms, and hearing that sweet, soft sound as she was rocked back and forth. And even here, even now, that voice was so gentle, so forgiving. It made her feel like everything was all right. But she knew it wasn't.

"What he said."

"Did he insult you?" Daddy asked.

"No, he—" Emry didn't want to repeat it.

Daddy knelt closer. She was already big enough to be eight or nine—Sean was nine—but he was big too and had to kneel pretty far. "Emry, tell us from the beginning. The whole story, okay?"

So she told them. Starting at the beginning was easier. The kids on the block had decided to play *Annie Minute and the Time Trippers*. Emry asked if they'd let her play Annie this time, but they never let her play Annie, or Millie Second, or even one of the Groupie Gang who carried the Time Trippers' instrument/weapons. When they let her play at all, she always had to be a Zelkoid or a Neanderthal or a Mega-Golem. They never even let her be one of the cool bad guys, like Kali or Tyranno Sora. Sean always got to be Ringo Planett, and he always blew Emry up with a cymbal mine the first chance he got, and she had to spend the rest of the game being dead.

"So I got tired of that, and I asked them why they never let me be Annie or Millie or anyone but a monster. And, and Sean said it's because I was a monster."

"Oh, Emry," Mommy said. "We've been through this before, right? You know not to listen."

"But that wasn't it. He said, he said Daddy was a freak who . . . who should never have been born." She was embarrassed to repeat it. "And then . . . and then he said I'd never have been born either if . . . if you hadn't been such a . . . someone who'd marry anybody."

Mommy caught what she tried to hide. "Emry, love, what did he say? Such a what?"

"He called you a slut! He said you were dirty! He had no right to say that about you, Mommy! I couldn't let him get away with it! So I . . ."

Emry stopped when she saw the look in Mommy's eyes. The look of horror and shame that Sean was in the hospital because of her. Emry broke down in tears. She'd wanted Mommy to be disappointed in her, in Emry—not in herself.

Richard and Lyra strove to contain their anger and sadness at the prejudice their neighbors still showed them after seven years. It was more important, they knew, to help their little girl make peace with her own power. Richard began giving her martial-arts instruction, seeking to pass on the discipline and emotional balance it had brought him. But she was an intense, impatient child. Because her mind was so quick, her body so energetic, she was always eager to race on to the next thing. Learning stillness and slowness was a labor. Only her fear of her own strength and her determination to tame it kept her focused.

But Emry needed more. She needed role models that could help her deal with both her power and the prejudice of others—something she couldn't get from the mindless action of *Annie Minute* or the violent Striders-and-Earthers games of her peers. But Richard and others like him had faced the same need for role models, finding them in the imaginative literature of the past: Superman, Wonder Woman, Spider-Man, the X-Men, the Cyborg Corps, Lady M. Characters born or endowed with exceptional power they hadn't sought, often struggling with their inner demons or with a world that hated and feared them, often making terrible mistakes that would take a lifetime to atone for—but always choosing to dedicate their power to the good of others, to the defense of truth, justice, freedom, and life. Richard and Lyra read these classic stories with their daughter, discussed their ideas and themes with her, kept her engaged and delighted as they pursued a solemn purpose together.

But the fiction was not enough for Emry, to whom superpowers were an everyday reality. She craved to learn if such mighty heroes had existed in real life. Her parents told her about the ninjas of legend who had defended commoners from noblemen's abuses, creating a mystique around themselves with disguise and deft illusions; about

Muslim women who'd used their veiled anonymity for protest and resistance, smuggling everything from literature to weapons to cameras
under their *hijab;* about masked Mexican *luchadores* who'd used their
glamorous secret identities as a platform for speaking against state
corruption without fear of retaliation; about eccentrics who'd organized their own online communities of "real-life superheroes," usually
just playacting but sometimes promoting social causes or deterring
minor crimes in their own ways. And Emry already knew about the
so-called Troubleshooters and watched their exploits on the news with
great excitement. But none of these satisfied her curiosity; she wanted
to hear about people like her, and like her father. And this was when
Richard grew abashed, while Lyra pressed him to tell Emry about her
grandparents.

"It started when humans began to live in space," he told her once
he finally gave in. "They couldn't survive its radiation without gene
therapy to let their DNA repair itself. They couldn't heal or grow well
in low gravity without enhancements to their stem cells. But Earth
was running out of things they needed for technology, like helium and
rare metals. So they had to live in space to get them."

"So?" Emry shrugged. "They could just mod themselves."

"Earth had laws against that. People were worried about how genetic
engineering could be abused. A lot of the time, people think it's better
not to try something at all if there's a chance it can be dangerous."

"That's dumb," Emry said from where she sat on the living room
rug. "Just be careful when you use it!"

"That's right—if you're careful, you can do a lot of good with power.
And that's what people like the Vanguardians figured out. At first, once
people accepted that they had to live in space, they just made the minimum mods they needed to survive. But once a generation of people had
grown up in space with those basic mods, some of them began to wonder how much further they could enhance themselves. They figured out
that the same stem cell boosts that helped them heal in low gravity
could be adjusted to make their bones and muscles stronger in normal
gravity, like on Earth or in the bigger habitats they were building by
then. Their gene repair could make them live longer and get sick less.

Their eye implants to filter sunlight could be tweaked to give them better vision. And so on. Vanguard was one of the first habitats that started trying it. And they snatched up the best geneticists and nano-technologists to help them."

"And they made you?"

"You could say that, since those scientists included my mom. She and my dad had themselves changed, and after a few years, when they were confident it was okay, they had me, and I inherited their mods. And when I was old enough, I agreed to let them make some further mods in me."

"And then I got them from you!"

"That's right, though they look a lot prettier on you."

She giggled. "Oh, shut up. So when did they start being superheroes?"

"Well, it was around then that the effects of Earth's climate change were being felt the most. A lot of places that are water now used to have people living in them. Hundreds of millions of people were displaced from their homes. And many more were suffering from huge storms and famines."

"Didn't they just move to space?"

"A lot of them did, eventually. But the institutions that could've arranged it weren't working too well for a while. See, the Molecular Revolution was in full swing by then, and it changed how people lived their lives. Before, they couldn't recycle everything or harvest any resources they needed from the soil or oceans, and they didn't have three-D printers and bioprinters to make anything they wanted. So their old economic systems were based on scarcity, and on people having to work to find resources and make things. So after the Revolution, a lot of jobs were lost, and people didn't know what to do with their lives or how to make their economies and societies work again. A lot of governments and institutions fell apart, and people got angry and desperate, and, well . . ."

"Yeah," Emry said quietly. "I know what happens when people get too angry."

"If they don't know how to manage it," Lyra amended.

"But the Vanguardians—mostly a man named Eliot Thorne, who was the most successful mod of your grandparents' generation—made a decision. They had all these gifts that made them stronger and faster and quicker to heal, so they should use them to help people down on Earth. They knew it was a risk to flout the laws against mods, but they believed it would be selfish not to do what they could."

"Did they wear costumes to protect their secret identities?" Emry asked him, excited.

"Umm, afraid not, jewel. In real life there are too many ways to see through a mask, or to track people's movements and find where they came from. And grown-ups on Earth didn't usually take flashy costumes too seriously. The Vanguardians had a hard enough time winning people over as it was. A lot of folks thought they were just another bunch of troublemakers."

"Humph. Like J. Jonah." She stuck out her tongue.

"Kinda, yeah. Or Senator Kelly."

"Did anyone send Sentinels to get them?"

"Not as such. But there were people who tried to arrest them or make them look bad."

Lyra interrupted. "But there were just as many people who thought they were heroes, who admired their courage." She paused. "And their sacrifice."

Emry's huge green eyes grew wider with alarm. "Sacrifice?"

Richard hesitated to tell her, but they'd never been dishonest with their little girl. "Yes, jewel. That's . . . why you don't have a grandpa on my side. He . . . he gave his life to save a whole lot of people from a bomb."

Emry was quiet for a while and shed some tears. But Richard sensed it was a fairly abstract emotion, since she'd never met either of her Vanguardian grandparents. "And Grandma Rachel?"

"She's still around." He sensed she'd need an explanation for her absence from their life. "But, well . . . after a while, things stabilized with help from the cislunar nations, and Earth started shipping the worst troublemakers out to the Belt. If they couldn't get along with others, then they could go off to their own little worlds and live however they wanted, so long as they left other people alone."

Emry mulled it over. "That sounds fair."

"Well, the Striders didn't think so. But that's another story. Anyway, once things were more or less peaceful again, the Vanguardians started trying to get into politics and business, trying to help rebuild society. But now that people weren't so scared anymore, they . . . didn't think they needed the Vanguard as much."

Emry saw through the euphemism. "They only liked them when they needed them. Then they hated them 'cause they were different. Just like Greenwooders."

"No, honey," said Lyra, "it's more than that. The Vanguard lived up in space. If they wanted to, they could attack Earth just by dropping rocks on it. A lot of people on Earth had reason to be afraid of being dominated by people who lived in orbit. And when those people were getting stronger and smarter and tougher than they were, they couldn't help but be afraid."

"And to be honest," Richard said, "Thorne and some of the others didn't try that hard to be good neighbors, like we do. They started talking like they should be the ones in charge, because they were better qualified."

"Well, weren't they?"

"Maybe, but it wasn't for them to decide. It was up to the people."

"Remember, honey," Lyra added, "a big part of responsibility is knowing when *not* to use your power." Emry nodded, having learned that lesson very well.

"And it wasn't all the Vanguardians' fault," Lyra went on. "There were other mod habitats that were pushier or had more dangerous ideas about how to treat Earth people. And there were Earth nations who overreacted to the danger from space, who tried too hard to control things in orbit and in the Belt colonies through money or threats."

"That's why Thorne and the others wanted to be in charge. They thought if they could run things both on Earth and in orbit, they could keep the fighting from getting out of hand."

"But they didn't," Emry said, her huge eyes solemn. "There was a war."

Richard nodded. "By trying to control things, Thorne's people just turned both sides against them. They made Earth more afraid of domination by the mods overhead, and they made the mods more afraid of losing control of their own homes. So both sides got angrier and started fighting. The Belt got dragged into it too because of their own issues with Earth. Everyone knew it could get horribly out of hand—how easy it would be to drop an asteroid on Earth and devastate the planet. And everyone knew Earth had orbital weapons that could retaliate if that ever happened. But they were caught in a spiral of mistrust and . . ."

"Richard." Lyra's voice was as gentle as the brush of her cool hand across his, but it got through to him. As precocious as Emry was, there was no sense scaring her with the details of how close humanity had come to cataclysmic war.

"Well, let's just say people almost lost control of their power in a very bad way. But there were good people on both sides, including Vanguardians and some of the first Troubleshooters, who stopped them from making a terrible mistake. And once people saw what had almost happened, they knew they had to find a better answer. That was the Great Compromise: Earth got to be in charge of everything inside Luna's orbit, in exchange for the Belt getting its independence. And all the habitats in Earth orbit that didn't want to live under Earth's government would move to the Belt."

He sighed. "And that included Vanguard. Even though they'd helped make the peace and saved countless lives, people on both sides still didn't trust them. They got convinced that the best thing for everyone was if they went away to the Belt."

"But they were still superheroes, right?" Emry asked. "Did they team up with the Troubleshooters?" Emry frowned, puzzled, as Richard closed off. He knew he'd failed to hide his anger from her. "Daddy?"

"Let's just say . . . Thorne and the others decided to stay in their room and sulk. They figured people had been ungrateful at Earth, so they wouldn't be any different in the Belt. So they moved their habitat way out to the Outers, even farther than Greenwood. And when all the new independent nations and immigrant habs in the Belt started fighting . . . well, they decided not to help."

"*What?!* Don't they know anything about being superheroes? It's not about what you get out of it! You do it because people need you!"

Richard beamed at his daughter and took her in his arms. "Ohh, punkin, I'm so proud of you. And I agree with you. I . . . I couldn't fight in the war or the troubles that followed. I didn't want to hurt anybody. But I had to go and help where I could, to do rescue work and stuff." He sighed. "The others didn't want me to go. Thorne wanted us to live on our own, build a separate society where nobody would bother us or hurt us. He could be incredibly persuasive."

"Did Grandma Rachel want you to go?"

He hesitated. What could he tell his daughter? That his mother had cared more about her research than her son? That she'd hardly even seemed to notice when he left? "She . . . was very dedicated to Thorne's dream. But she didn't try to stop me from doing what I thought was right." It was the closest he'd ever come to lying to his child.

Emry got that storytelling gleam in her eye. "*Once they were heroes,*" she intoned. "*Now they've given up and are hiding from the world. But one man carries on their legacy. It's Super-Daddy!*" They laughed and fell together in a mock-wrestling match. "And I'm your sidekick, the Emerald Blaze!"

"Ohh! The Emerald Blaze! Look, there she goes, streaking across the sky!" And he lifted his girl up and flew her around the room.

August 2098

It was a bright, warm day, a milder emulation of the summer back on Earth, and Emry had been making the most of it, engaged in her favorite sport: chasing boys. Due to her "unfair advantages," the Greenwooders rarely let her play any other sport, except under frustrating restrictions. Generally the only person she got to engage with in athletic contests was her father, who still guided her in the martial arts and still played superheroes with her.

But these days she was getting more interested in the games she could play with teenage boys—particularly since she had a decided advantage here as well. Even though the boys that interested her were older than her thirteen years, their parents had kept them in the dark about sex. Emry's parents had considered it more responsible to give her a solid grounding in sexuality *before* it became an issue in her life. And since this game wasn't being played under adult supervision, she felt free to exercise her advantage.

Her physical precociousness gave her another edge, for her breasts had reached full size already; indeed, for a while she'd wondered if they would ever stop growing. Emry wondered where these heavy round orbs had come from, since her mother had such dainty, tapered breasts. From the neck up, she was unmistakably her mother's daughter, except for her heavier chin and Shannon coloring. But her body couldn't have been more different. Emry had gone through a phase in which she'd felt bulky and awkward, but now that she'd grown into her strong, mesomorphic frame and voluptuous curves, she'd come to delight in her differences from Lyra. She loved to show off with scanty tops, often lifting or shedding them for the boys who gawked at her. Their reactions when she flashed them were hilarious, especially when they pretended to be properly prudish and uninterested while trying desperately to get a good peek through their fingers. It was even more fun when they ran and she could literally chase them. Of course she could overtake them easily, and they were usually glad to be caught, even when they were terrified. Unfortunately, she hadn't yet snagged anyone willing to go past second base. Despite their fascination, they were intimidated by her strength and her greater understanding of things that were still mysteries to them.

Lyra gently admonished her to go easy on the poor dears. But she trusted Emry to wield her sexuality responsibly and to consult with her parents before taking each new step. Overall, Lyra enjoyed hearing of her daughter's exploits and experiments, dishing with her like a sister over the ribald details, vicariously amused by her tweaking of Greenwood's taboos—and pleased that she was finally getting along better, after a fashion, with the other children. Yet she advised the teenager to be cautious with older males, since there were those who felt threatened by women's sexual power and sought to twist it against them. But Emry had learned her lessons well, and the one college boy who'd tried something she hadn't invited had gone home sorer and wiser, though with no broken bones.

Her quarry today was younger, a cute, shy black-haired boy her own age whom she'd decided to bring out of his shell. The poor thing had jumped halfway to the axis when she'd pinched his adorable buns, and he'd turned out to be a runner—though he let himself get cornered so easily that it had to be intentional. She was just about to undo her top and give him the thrill of his life when his eyes suddenly lifted from her chest, looking past her in terror. *Oh, hell,* Emry thought, figuring a parent or teacher was behind her, gearing up for a Stern Lecture on Morality.

But then the explosions began.

Emry whirled to behold the kind of scene she thought only happened on the news, and only on other habitats. Over in the town, symbot-suited people were shooting at each other, using big, heavy weapons to try to punch through each other's armor. They didn't seem to be going after the Greenwooders—but they didn't seem to care who got in their way, or whose homes or businesses got wrecked. The curve of the habi-tat gave Emry an overhead view, her enhanced vision letting her see the townspeople running desperately for cover—and some of them not moving at all.

She had trouble accepting the sight at first. How could anyone act so irresponsibly? The fires, the destruction, they could endanger the whole habitat. Every hab-dweller was conditioned from infancy to make safety a priority. But she remembered the lessons of her father's rescue work: people sometimes sought release by trashing others' habs the way they never would their own. And many people who came from Earth or the Sheaf or other large habs had never needed to learn such discipline at all.

Emry suddenly remembered that her mother had been going into town today. Alarmed, she checked her bracelet selfone for Lyra's loca-tor signal, and saw it flashing along with her father's on the edge of town. Good, Emry thought, she was with him. That meant she was safe. Now Emry just had to reach them and she'd be safe too.

But she took a moment to talk the boy past his panic and get him headed off for home, in the other direction. And as she raced toward her family, she kept an eye out for other scared kids who might need her help. It was what the Emerald Blaze would do. She was confident that, once her father made sure his ladies were safe, he'd go out and make those bad guys stop fighting. And then he'd save all the hurt people lying in the streets. The Blaze would stay to protect her mother while he did it. So she had to get there soon. Her hero needed his sidekick.

As she rocketed forward, she saw the fighting moving toward her parents. But she saw something else too. One of the armor-suited fighters wasn't using lethal weapons, and was trying to keep the bad guys away from the townspeople. Emry recognized the symbot from the news—it was one of the Troubleshooters! Here! *Wow.* With her dad *and* a Troubleshooter on the case, the bad guys would be in jail in no time.

Once she got into town, the buildings blocked her view of the Troubleshooter and the battle. But those were secondary concerns; she knew where she needed to go. But as she got close, she needed to leap over piles of burning debris, and saw a lot of wrecked buildings and vehicles. The battle had passed right through here. She thanked the Goddess that her mom was with her dad, who would . . .

Then she saw him. It took her a moment to recognize him. He was down on his knees, shaking. He looked so small, so weak. That couldn't be Daddy, could it? What was that he was leaning over? It looked like . . . No, it couldn't be. . . .

. . .

No.

. . .

No. No, that couldn't be her. It had none of her vibrancy, her energy, her warmth. It was just . . .

. . .

Emerald couldn't understand what she was looking at. It looked like Mommy . . . but it couldn't be . . . couldn't be a person . . . It looked like

Mommy's face . . . but only half of it was there. . . . There was a hole and she could see a fire behind. . . .

Where was Mommy?

Why wasn't Daddy looking for Mommy? How could he just kneel there, bawling like a little baby over this . . . that . . . mound of . . . that *thing*. . . .

Why wasn't he stopping the bad guys? Why didn't he stop them from breaking things, and . . . and *that*. . . .

Something knocked her forward, a sound she almost heard over the rushing in her head, and she fell and rolled and *that* wasn't in front of her anymore and there was a metal monster pointing something at her, yelling something . . . and Daddy just bawled . . . and Emry closed her eyes. . . .

And then she woke up and strong arms picked her up—Daddy? But no, they were hard and cold and they whirred. She looked and it was the Troubleshooter. His helmet was retracting, folding back behind like origami, and there was a kind face behind it, craggy with a bushy moustache. "You're safe now, little one," he said. "Uncle Arkady has caught the bad guys. It will be all right now." He looked past her, to something behind her, and grew sad. "No . . . not quite all right. I'm so sorry."

Emry tried to stop herself from turning, but couldn't. There was Daddy, rocking back and forth without a sound. And there was *that*. . . .

Mr. Arkady took a tentative step toward him. "Sir . . . I'm sorry for your loss, but you need to come away with me. The building may not be stable. And your daughter needs you now."

Daddy looked up at that. At first he didn't seem to know where he was, like he was sleepwalking. But then his eyes focused on her. He was like a statue for a moment, and then he shook himself and stood up. "Ohh, Emerald . . . my jewel . . . it's just us now . . . I'll take care of you now. . . ."

But as he talked, something welled up in Emry, something terrible that burned her inside and tore out of her as the loudest scream she'd ever heard. ***"NOOOO!!!!!!!!"*** It went on for ages, and seemed to echo through the whole sphere like thunder.

He reached for her, but she punched at him, struggling in the Troubleshooter's arms. *"You didn't save her!!! Why didn't you save her? You were supposed to protect her! You let her die! It's your fault! I hate you!! **I hate you!!!!**"*

The look in his eyes was like the one he'd had before—a look of terrible loss. But she didn't care. He'd betrayed her. He'd failed her when it counted the most. She'd never hear her mother sing again, and it was his fault, and she knew she would hate him for the rest of her life.

4

Trouble Shared

July 2107
Pellucidar habitat
In orbit of Vesta

Emerald Blair took great satisfaction in punching herself in the face.

Not that it was actually her face, or even a reasonable facsimile. Rather, it was the face of the overearnest, underweight Vestalian starlet who'd played her in that unauthorized vidnet biopic last month, the one they'd rushed into production to capitalize on the Chakra City incident. They could've gone virtual, but apparently figured the starlet's fame would be at least as big a draw as Emry's own, since they couldn't legally use her likeness anyway.

Of course, that hadn't stopped Pellucidar's control cyber from morphing the starlet's likeness onto an android's soligram skin and sending it to attack Emry. But Sorceress didn't seem to have much use for human laws right now, including the ones about not killing people, or rather using her animatronic puppets to kill them. *You'd think a cyber programmed with every work of fiction ever made would know how clichéd that is,* Emry thought.

The shamdroid's head snapped back far enough from the punch to warrant an obituary had it been the actual starlet. Emry's fantasy to that effect was marred by the fact that the soligram layer had been smashed in, leaving a fist-sized hole in the middle of its face. But the smart-matter gel re-formed into the starlet's celebrated features—*H--ll, I'm*

prettier than that—and the neck quickly returned to normal. "You can't keep the Banshee down!" it cried. These androids were built to withstand a lot of punishment from the patrons, and Sorceress was no longer bothering to make them play dead.

It helped, though, that the cyber had picked such an ill-conceived opponent to stop her from reaching Pellucidar's brain center. Sorceress seemed to think this was all a game, and apparently had decided it would be entertaining to pit Emry against an alternate version of herself. The starlet bot was dressed as the mod-gang member she'd been at seventeen, or some costume designer's exaggerated notion thereof. She acted tough, but was too slight of build to pose much of a challenge, durability aside. Which was proving a disappointment to the gathering spectators.

Damn it, I don't have time for this! Emry thought as Banshee charged again. *Don't these vackheads know they're in danger?* It wouldn't have surprised her from Earthers; they spent most of their lives immersed in their online world, interacting with virtual playmates, even conducting business transactions through gaming analogies. But Striders, ironically, tended to lead more grounded lives; spread out over cubic light-minutes, they didn't have the option of real-time onlining, except on the local scale. And even there, they preferred to live in reality as a matter of cultural preference.

Yet Vestans tended to be eccentric. Vesta was in the "desert," the ice-poor Inner Belt, its habitats only able to survive on imported water and carbon; but Vesta's giant size and planetlike, differentiated geology gave it a mineral wealth unequaled in the Belt. So its civilization was heavy with entrepreneurs and elites, those who could not only afford to make the desert bloom but could do so in style. Here was the home, not only of the Striders' cybernetic and metallurgical industries, but their jewelry industry, their entertainment industry, their gambling industry, their erotic industry. Here were the wealthy elites accustomed to having their way, and here were the prosperous Terran emigrés who sought the kind of luxuries they knew from home. Thus, Vesta was not as centralized as Ceres despite being nearly as populous. Instead of one united cluster and various outliers, Vesta was circled by multiple large, independent habitat-states and their various tributaries—the latter of which included Pellucidar, a theme-park habitat built by a Vestalia-based entertainment conglomerate but jointly managed by several Vestan states. It was an Earth-style immersive cyberfantasy with a Strider twist, relying as much on soligrams and bots as virtual projections. But there were still those who let themselves get too caught up in the illusions.

Emry threw Banshee over her shoulder, but the simulant rolled smoothly to its feet, wearing that patented Pout of Fury that made up half the starlet's repertoire of expressions. "You dragged me down into this life!" she intoned, lunging at Emry with a flurry of inhumanly fast blows, keeping her busy dodging and blocking. "You made me a criminal! But no more, Javon! I'm free of you now! And I swear to the Goddess, I will devote the rest of my life to making amends for what you made me do, by fighting scum like you wherever—"

"Oh, shut *up*." With a thought, Emry set her laser pistol to shock mode, then drew it and discharged it into Banshee's scrawny torso, holding it there long enough to make sure the android's circuitry was thoroughly fried. She'd been reluctant to waste the power on this petty obstacle, but damn, did it feel good. "You don't know a vackin' thing about it."

Some in the audience cheered, while others groaned, wishing for a longer catfight. A moment later, though, they started screaming as electric discharges began raining down from the sky. Emry shoved them all under the nearby trees, resisting an insane urge to tell the Cheshire Cat in the branches to run for safety. Then she reviewed her visual logs, enhancing her peripheral glimpse of the attackers' forms against the patchwork landscape of the Bernal sphere's far side. *Damn, the Zelkoids are back!* "Hey, Zephyr, any luck? I could use some backup here, you know!"

"I'm not exactly lounging on the veranda myself," came a wry, mellow baritone over her selfone. *"I'm hacking my best, but Sorceress is a grand-master player."*

"Zephy, baby, this isn't a game!"

"In fact, Emry, that's exactly what it is. To her, anyway. She hasn't tried to harm me, just impede me."

A lightning-gun blast set fire to the tree sheltering Emry, forcing her to break cover and run across the clearing. "Why can't she extend the same courtesy to the rest of us?"

Zephyr switched to her transceiver implant so she could hear him over the blasts. <*I'm growing convinced that she doesn't see the distinction,*> he said, his words transmitted directly to her brain's auditory center.

"Great, so she's schizophrenic!"

<*I wouldn't say that. She's completely in touch with her own reality. It's just yours that gives her trouble.*>

"Come again?" She tucked, rolled, and fired skyward.

<*From a cyber's perspective, physical reality can be somewhat . . . virtual. Especially for a cyber like Sorceress, who has no physical body. Your reality is so limiting, after all. You can't re-create it on a whim, there are so many physical laws to follow . . . and it all happens so* slowly. *No offense, but your reality can get rather dull.*>

"I wish!" Emry shot back. But she supposed Zephyr knew whereof he spoke. Until recently, he hadn't had a physical body either, serving as one of the top data-miners at TSC headquarters. Arkady had liked him and had often tried to talk him into becoming a Troubleshooter's steed, ideally Emry's once her apprenticeship ended, but he'd shown no interest in fieldwork. Perhaps Zephyr's words now offered some insight into why. But after Arkady's death, Zephyr had changed his mind, agreeing to honor his friend's wishes after all. Emry hadn't been sure she wanted a reluctant shipmind, but so far Zephyr had been nothing but reliable and dedicated, and charming company to boot.

<*And Sorceress was created to oversee a place whose residents can manipulate their physical reality at will,*> Zephyr went on as Emry made an end run around the Zelkoid ground forces. <*Since her whole interaction with humans revolves around fantasy—*>

"She doesn't understand the difference between fantasy and reality. I get it. Now how the flare do we fix it?" She spotted the Zelkoid command saucer and began firing at it, knowing that destroying it would send the cyclopean green monsters back to their home dimension—or whatever the closest approximation would be in this setting. *Who says* Annie Minute *wasn't educational?* The beam fizzled out, so she ejected the power pack and plugged in another from her belt. The gun was growing hot in her hand. "I'm almost to the brain center, Zeph. I don't want to have to hurt her, but if you can't lock her into autistic mode—" A basso roar hit the air. "Aww, vack, I think the dragon's coming back!"

"Don't worry, Emry, you're not the target," he said aloud over her selfone. *"I asked Sorceress to find out how the Zelkoids would fare against it."*

"You mean—you got through to her?"

"We've been having quite a lively debate for the past few seconds. It took some doing, but I think I've persuaded her to accept my basic premise that reality and fantasy are two different things. Personally, I suspect she's just humoring me. I think she likes me."

Emry laughed, even as the dragon began tearing through the Zelkoid lines and sending them scattering. "You little Lothario! See, I told you that voice of yours could melt any gal in her boots."

"Anyway, I've convinced her to take some time off to explore the philosophical ramifications of the idea. The simulations should be shutting down even now."

"Yep," Emry confirmed as the dragon, Zelkoids, and other manifestations began slumping to the ground and reverting to raw soligram form. "They're melting, they're mell-tinnggg!"

"What a world."

"And what a sidekick! What a team, huh?"

"Who are you calling a sidekick? I did all the work. You were just the damsel in distress." His voice grew more serious. *"And you know you could've avoided a lot of it if you'd stayed more detached about your virtual opponents."*

"Yeah, yeah, I know. It's just, Banshee clicked my buttons, you know?"

"And this is an excuse how?"

Emry winced. Sometimes Zephyr reminded her so much of Arkady. That brought her both pain and comfort. "You're right, I—what the hell are *you* looking at?"

Some of the spectators had drawn near, gawking at her. A gangly teen dressed rather unconvincingly as Sam Murai, Private Eye, with a trench coat and fedora over a t-shirt patterned like medieval Japanese armor, tilted his head and spoke. "So—you're the real one?"

"The one and only!"

"Hmp." He stared some more. "You were cuter in the movie."

Emry slowly, carefully holstered her sidearm.

Pellucidar's various managing partners soon moved in to "secure" the theme park and began bickering over whether Sorceress should be reprogrammed or destroyed altogether—and over which Vestan state had the right to make that determination. Emry wasn't exactly a fan of the cyber—she had killed six people, after all—but the thought of anyone being put to death because they had no legal rights outraged her, and she made that known to the Vestans. The one thing they could agree on, however, was that they didn't let outsiders dictate their policies.

The matter was rendered moot when orders came in to report to the TSC's local branch headquarters as soon as possible. Emry didn't see the need; this Gregor Tai fellow from Ceres had been meeting with small groups of Troubleshooters as their availability allowed, and Emry had picked up the gist of it from them, how his Earth-backed consortium had offered to provide the Corps with new backing and resources. Sure, she couldn't blame Earth for wanting to pay more attention to events out here after Chakra City, and it was easier to be sympathetic to them now. But Emry hated abandoning Sorceress to her fate.

"You did the best you could, Emry," Zephyr told her as he kneaded her sore muscles that night, the thrust of his engines as he moved into a polar orbit holding her against the massage pad without the need for straps or handholds. "I think you made her case to the press very well.

And nationalist egos aside, a Troubleshooter's endorsement carries a lot of weight."

His words brought her some comfort, as did the touch of his soligram avatar. She'd chosen it to look like a marble statue of a nude, clean-shaven Greek god with graceful white wings, not unlike the Zephyrus of myth, but its hands felt like warm flesh—and secreted their own lubrication. "If anybody listens. All the attention right now's on that Tai guy."

"People pay attention to you."

"Sure, 'cause I'm the sexpot with the cinematic past. I'm someone they gawk at, not someone they listen to. That won't help Sorceress."

The avatar smiled. It wasn't just a simulation; cyber emotions may have been less intense than the human kind, without hormones to fire them to passion, but a sapient mind, guided by choice and experience rather than rigid programming, needed motivations to impel action and shape behavior. She knew by now that Zephyr's kindness was real. Sometimes she was sorely tempted to take his avatar to bed, but without a skeleton like Sorceress's toys, it could never hold up to her affections. Plus she didn't think it would be fair to Zephyr to try to relate to him as a human instead of as himself. "You're also the one who saved Earth from a bioterror attack and the patrons of Pellucidar from a very clichéd demise," he said. "I'd call that a respectable beginning."

"Maybe. Feels more like too little, too late to me. Too many people I couldn't save."

"I don't think the public sees it that way."

"Well, I try not to worry about what the public thinks."

"Ha. You love the camera."

"And it's mutual, babycakes."

"Maybe that's the problem right there," he said, a hint of that lecturing tone coming back into his voice. She got tired of his lectures, but forgave him because his voice was just so damn sexy. "Your conscious vanity. Despite your commitment to staying more focused in crises, you still play up your sex appeal otherwise. If you want to be taken seriously—"

"No. I've heard that a million times, and it's still bullshit. Nobody should have to hide what they are to be accepted. I'm proud of what I got—*all* of it, inside and out—and if people can't respect the whole package, I'm not the one who should have to adjust." *Mom taught me that.*

"Fair enough. It seems like a harder way of going about it, though."

Her eyes roved over his avatar's nude form. "Anything worthwhile is hard, baby."

Russell City habitat
In orbit of Vesta

Though the Troubleshooter Corps had headquarters at Ceres and Vesta for the sake of efficiency and access to resources, it had established them in small habitats known for their political independence. Demetria was an old, diminutive Bernal sphere established to support the scientific study of Ceres, its tight polar orbit precluding it from joining into the Sheaf. Russell City's neutrality was a function of its popularity as a tourist attraction; its forced orbit over Vesta's south pole, held in place against the protoplanet's irregular gravity field by giant solar sails, afforded a spectacular view of Rheasilvia Basin, the immense crater that had flattened out the southern side of the spheroidal body, and its central peak Rheasilvia Mons, the tallest mountain ever climbed by humans.

The docking bay held more TSC ships than Emry had seen in one place since Arkady's funeral. "Does he really have to see so many of us at once?" she asked once she'd disembarked. "Somewhere there's a crime happening, you know."

"Give him a chance," said Sally Knox as she led Emry to the meeting room. Despite being only a meter twenty, Sally kept up a pace that Emry had trouble matching. The cherub-faced, middle-aged blonde had been a mainstay of the TSC's clerical/support staff from the beginning and showed no sign of slowing down. Emry had never quite figured out what her official job was, since she did so many different tasks skillfully, efficiently, and, when needed, ruthlessly. Sensei had nick-named her the Troubleshooters' troubleshooter. It was oddly unsurprising to find her here instead of back at Demetria; some Troubleshooters suspected that there was more than one of her. "Mr. Tai thought it was important to share his ideas with you all in person. He didn't want to do it more times than necessary. You're one of the last stragglers," she scolded.

"Well, I've been busy."

"Oh, yes, suffering in a luxury resort. We all bleed for you." Emry was about to protest that she hadn't had much fun there, but she knew it would have no effect. Sally was perenially unmoved by tales of Troubleshooter adventure, triumph, or angst. It all seemed to bore her, as though her life of paperwork and organizing and programming and maintenance were infinitely more significant than anything that went on in the field. Somehow Emry found that comforting.

And if Sally had such a high opinion of this Gregor Tai—by her standards, her words constituted a ringing endorsement—then Emry figured it would be worth hearing what he had to say.

The meeting room was already occupied by most of the T-shooters whose ships Emry had seen in the bay. They exchanged greetings with her, the friendlier ones generally coming from other recent graduates; many of the veterans were more aloof. Unfortunately, Kari wasn't among those present. Most of the 'Shooters were in civilian garb, though few dressed quite as informally as Emry herself. She wore a hip-hugger miniskirt that was barely more than a wide belt, plus a cutoff Pellucidar t-shirt displaying animated scenes of the habitat's more adult-oriented attractions. After Sally's words, she wondered if her choice of wardrobe had been a bit too deliberately irreverent. But this was how she'd chosen to present herself to Tai and that was that. Whether *he* could take *her* seriously was not the issue, as far as Emry was concerned.

The room was set up with a buffet table and a couple of dozen seats arranged in the round. Emry found herself being waved over to the table by the Dharma Bums—the nickname with which Vijay and

Marut Pandalai, officially code-named Arjun and Bhima, had been saddled under protest. She greeted the wiry Vijay and his massive younger brother with quick kisses on the lips. "Hey, Bums."

"Hey, Boobs," Vijay countered. "Nice top."

"Thanks. I'm commemorating a recent victory," she replied as she reached for a plate. "Ooh, is that Maryam's homemade hummus?"

"We heard," Marut said. "Insane amusement-park cyber plus evil twin, all in one mission."

Vijay put an arm around her. "For her encore, she'll stop her long-lost sister from changing history with the help of ancient astronauts."

"Wait a minute, which one will the ancient astronauts be helping?"

"Vack it, you guys!" Emry cried. "Am I ever gonna live this down? Ooh, grapes!"

"Not if we can help it."

"Oh, go vack yourselves out the nearest lock. See if I ever take you Bums to bed again."

The brothers exchanged a look. "Sounds like a challenge," Marut said.

By now there was a full room, and finally Lydia Muchangi entered. A lissome Martian with regal African features and a shaved head, she was one of the original, pre-Corps Troubleshooters, code-named Lodestar for her legendary ability to find anyone or anything. These days she applied her superhuman intellect more toward administration and education, and was currently in charge of the Russell City HQ. She was accompanied by a tall, Terran-built man who made Emry perk up with interest. He was a square-jawed Asian type, maybe mid-forties and quite fit, with piercing eyes and a sensuous mouth. *This might not suck after all,* Emry thought.

"Thank you all for coming," Lodestar began. "I know you're all eager to get back into action, and I promise you won't be kept long. But Sensei and I believe that what our guest, Mr. Gregor Tai of the Cerean States, has to offer us will be helpful to our efforts in the field and deserves a hearing. Mr. Tai?"

"Thank you, Lydia," Tai said in a rich tenor. "I'm quite pleased to meet you all. My name is Greg Tai, and as you've heard by now, I represent a consortium of state and private interests within the Cerean States, with ties to similar groups on Earth. I'm not a member of either government, though they've both endorsed our efforts. I understand how important the neutrality of the Troubleshooter Corps is to your work, and I want to assure you I have no desire to undermine that."

Before going into his spiel, Tai made his way around the line, greeting each of the Troubleshooters in turn. When he got to Emry he smiled, seeming totally unfazed by her wardrobe or by the carrot sticks stuffed in her mouth. "Emerald Blair, of course." He shook her hand firmly, clasping it in both of his. "I wanted to thank you particularly for your role in thwarting the Neogaian attack. I grew up on Earth, and I still have family there."

She fidgeted. "Well . . . my mentor deserved the real credit," she said through the carrots.

"Certainly, that was a great loss. I've been to see his family already. My group is already working to set up an educational foundation in his name. Part of our efforts to build closer ties between UNECS and the Belt."

She swallowed. "Well! I, I appreciate that."

"And I saw your press conference after the Pellucidar affair. I thought you'd like to know I've contacted some of Ceres's top cyber-rights attorneys about Sorceress's case."

"Oh! Wow. That's great!"

"It's the least we could do to thank you, Emerald."

"Emry."

He smiled. "Emry. Thank you."

Once he'd moved down the line a bit, Vijay whispered in her ear. "Ooh, wow, call me Emry! Somebody's in love." She shoved a pita wedge in his mouth to shut him up.

When Tai completed his circuit, he looked around in puzzlement. "Isn't there still one person I haven't met? Hijab? Does anyone know where she is?" Emry joined in the general chuckling. "Am I missing some joke?"

"You are missing *something*, at least," came a warm, quiet alto voice from directly behind him. Tai whirled, startled, and the T-shooters laughed as Hijab finally deigned to show herself, disengaging the camouflage function of her garb. When she stood still against the wall, her metamaterial suit blending with her surroundings and damping her sounds and scent, Maryam Khalid was virtually undetectable to anyone who did not know where to look. Now, though, she became visible as a statuesque woman in an all-concealing black bodysuit, formfitting for mobility but bearing an ankle-length cloak to obscure her body's contours as Muslim propriety, and the needs of invisibility, demanded. Even her face was completely covered at the moment, presenting only a featureless black visage to the Sheaver.

Tai recovered quickly. "Hijab. Hello. I was hoping to meet you in civilian form, as it were."

"Perhaps in time, Mr. Tai," she whispered, the cowl muffling her voice and subtly altering its timbre. "Trust must be earned." Maryam was one of the few Troubleshooters to use a secret identity. Originally an Olbersstadt detective, she had run afoul of the Yohannes syndicate and seen her husband and several innocent bystanders murdered in retaliation. To protect her children while continuing the fight, she had taken a cue from Muslim women of the past who had used the veil for espionage and covert resistance, but had added a high-tech Vestan twist. She had helped the Troubleshooters cripple the mobs' operations at Vesta and soon been persuaded to join the Corps. But her identity was a secret she shared only with established T-shooters, since she was still high on the mobs' hit lists. Until Emry's apprenticeship had ended, she'd thought Maryam had been a minor Vestan official who occasionally consulted with the TSC. Out of uniform, she wore much more liberal *hijab,* in the form of colorful long-sleeved dresses and designer headscarves.

"Very true," Tai said after a moment. "I'm sure you have excellent reasons for your secrecy. But I intend to do my best to earn your trust. All of your trust."

As Tai began his presentation, most of the 'Shooters took seats, some turning them around to straddle them, some just putting a leg up and resting a cheek on the chair back. Emry refilled her plate and then straddled a chair between the Dharma Bums. A few others remained standing, letting their wariness of the Sheaver be known.

"I know what a lot of you must be thinking, since it's a concern your colleagues before you have expressed. Should the Corps be getting in bed with the CS, sharing resources directly—let alone establishing closer ties with Earth? My answer is that what we're offering is merely an expansion on the kind of endorsement and cooperation that the TSC already gets from Ceres and other Belt governments and NGOs. It's our hope that Vestan, Eunomian, and Outer states will eventually join in as well.

"Why now? Because Chakra City has changed things. Since the war ended, UNECS has been content to focus inward and leave us to our own devices. The Neogaian attack proved that they can no longer do that—the Striders' problems are their problems too."

"And a lot of their problems become ours," shot back Marut, who had no love for Earth, "when they deport lunatics like the Neogaians out here in the first place."

"That's true. The bottom line is, we can't go on pretending our fates aren't intertwined. Earth has taken a renewed interest in keeping the peace in the Belt. But nobody wants a repeat of the circumstances that led to the war, with Earth wielding direct power over Strider affairs. That's why we Cereans feel we can offer a solution. We have strong ties to both communities—the oldest Strider nation, yet with a large population of Terran emigrés, myself included. That means Earth can trust us to handle the matter internally—and hopefully it means that our fellow Striders can trust that we're acting in their best interests, not just Earth's.

"And that's where the Troubleshooter Corps is key. Your members come from all over the Belt, even Mars, and so you're respected and trusted Beltwide. Who better to spearhead the effort to work together for our common security?"

"Most of us are also mods," Vijay pointed out. "Or cybers. By Earth law, we shouldn't exist. Yet you say you represent the interest of Earth?"

Tai gave a conciliatory nod. "It's true that Earth still takes a conservative view of human enhancement. Or rather, they've enhanced themselves more on a collective level, through the global information network and the resources and expertise it allows any individual to access. Striders have taken a more individualized approach, enhancing individual humans rather than humanity as a whole, developing individual artificial sentiences rather than relying on a global network—which, granted, you can't do anyway with the time lags involved out here. There are those on Earth, and admittedly in the Cerean States, who see that as a potential threat due to the power it can give to unethical individuals. I think events like Chakra City demonstrate that those concerns are valid.

"But my consortium believes—I believe—that the transhuman age is here, and we need to adapt to that reality. It hasn't brought the Rapture or the Apocalypse, hasn't made us gods or monsters, and it's not going to. We're still what we were, just with more power, for better or worse. So instead of planning for some kind of imaginary existential clash between old humanity and transhumanity, we need to keep sight of the more fundamental distinctions between right and wrong, order and chaos. Those of us who stand for order would be fools not to ally with transhumans who share our goals. The Troubleshooters are exactly that—a superhuman force for peace and order, superheroes in the truest sense."

"We know why us," said Tor Thorssen, a gene-modded man-mountain who'd been a pro wrestler before joining the Corps. Most T-shooters didn't use their code names in everyday life, but only Tor's mother called him Ranulf. "But why you?"

"Because the Cerean States is the only Belt nation with the resources and infrastructure necessary to build up the TSC into the potent, systemwide peacekeeping organization it needs to become."

"So, what, we get a passel o' new Sheaver Troubleshooters?" That was Cowboy Bhattacharyya, one of those who stood (or in his case, swaggered) to express their suspicion.

"Naturally the Corps will need to bring in new recruits, but as always, they will be drawn from throughout the system. And they'll still have to pass your training, and Ceres won't interfere with your procedures or standards.

"But there's more we can offer. The consortium can exert political influence on your behalf, work with you to coordinate systemwide peacekeeping efforts. We can bring in Cerean and Terran expertise to improve your technology and your techniques."

"Ain't nothin' wrong with our techniques," Cowboy shot back in that inane Bollywood-Western accent of his.

"But couldn't you do better? Certainly you do the best you can in response to the crises that arise out here. But that's just it—you *respond*. You wait for something to go wrong and try to minimize the damage.

"But with the destructive power that's now available to even a small fringe group or gang, the magnitude of that damage is just too great. If you wait until an attack comes, then you're already too late. Too many people will be lost before you get the chance to save them. And too many innocents will be endangered in the crossfire between you and the bad guys." Emry stopped eating and began listening much more intently.

"So what are you proposing?" Vijay challenged. "Can you offer us psychics?" A few people laughed. Emry wasn't one of them.

"We don't need them. These days, earthquakes, hurricanes, solar flares can be predicted so preventative measures can be taken. We can monitor buildings, spacecraft, or habitats, anticipate when they're about to fail, and calculate what it takes to preserve them. All it takes is enough data and a good computer model.

"Now, the social sciences may not be as precise as the physical, but it's still possible to extrapolate trends, anticipate patterns, see trouble building before it breaks. This is part of what keeps Earth, and increasingly the Sheaf, united and peaceful. We're all interconnected, linked into one vast conversation whose trends can be documented, sensed, and analyzed. To put it simply, we *listen* to each other, so we can know when people are discontented or frustrated, understand the root causes, and deduce the most effective resolution. I know, I know," he said in response to the grumbling that ensued. "I'm not here to lecture you on the benefits of an interconnected existence. I know how much you cherish your independence out here.

"But it's that same independence, taken to an extreme, that makes it easier for things to go wrong. For mobsters, fanatics, and rogue states to operate unimpeded, for people to suffer without anyone coming to their rescue.

"I think there's a way to have the best of both worlds. Being independent doesn't have to mean being isolated or out of touch with your surroundings. If astrobiologists can monitor life in other star systems, how hard can it be for the Troubleshooters to gather the information you need to see trouble coming before it happens?"

"So you propose to enhance our intelligence-gathering capabilities," Lydia said.

"For a start. Also, the consortium would assist you in using advanced pattern recognition, data mining, and evolutionary models to dig up warning signs, so we can head off trouble before it happens."

"Head off how?" Emry asked. "We can't exactly, say, invade Neogaia before they strike again. There's only seventy-three of us."

"Force is a last resort," Tai said. "That's something I know Sensei Villareal has taught you all." Bhattacharyya scoffed. "But that means there must be other options available before force becomes necessary. All too often, you have to use force because it's too late for alternatives. But if we can anticipate problem areas, home in on the political or economic or social factors driving people toward conflict, then that allows us to try other tactics before it's too late. Ceres, with cooperation from other Belt powers, of course, can bring diplomacy to bear on dangerous fringe habitats, exert humanitarian and educational efforts to treat the causes of their aggression, and bring them into the fold."

"What, an' put us out of a job?" Cowboy drawled. Emry glared in his direction. In her view, his tendency to take the second half of "Troubleshooter" too literally made him unworthy of the name. But part of why Sensei had founded the TSC was to bring rogue vigilantes like him into check, encouraging them to follow the rules and tone down their methods. Which sounded very much like what Tai was proposing on a systemwide scale.

"I don't see that happening for a long time. The Troubleshooters are the linchpins of the whole project. You're not only fighters, you're trained negotiators, relief workers—not to mention having the skills and insight necessary to gather and process the information we'd need. And certainly your cyber partners can play a key role there as well. Being experts in everything, being able to mine and analyze vast amounts of data creatively when no global network is available to give advice, is the whole reason they exist. And the TSC represents one of the largest concentrations of cyber minds in Solsys—probably the largest one whose members are treated as free and equal beings and truly encouraged to live up to their full potential."

<I may blush,> Zephyr said in Emry's head.

"All of you—Troubleshooters and cybers—are a resource capable of even greater potential than you've achieved so far. I'm just here to help you achieve it. To help you save more lives, prevent more tragedies by acting sooner and more effectively.

"And . . . that's my spiel. I'll be happy to answer any questions now."

Emry listened absently to the questions and answers, but mostly she was mulling over what she'd already heard. The details didn't concern her as much as the big picture. *Stopping tragedies before they happen. Saving lives before they're lost.*

Vijay caught her introspection and stroked her chin, gently turning her face toward him. *<Looks like he got to you,>* he sent subvocally.

<I'm up for anything that saves more lives.>

<Well, sure. But all this diplomacy and humanitarianism—not a lot of action. You want to put yourself out of a job?>

Her answer came promptly. *<Gladly—if it meant fewer kids had to lose their mothers.>*

<Don't give me platitudes, Blaze. You live for action.>

She glared at him. If Vijay thought it was just a platitude, then he didn't know her as well as he thought.

<Do you really think this new approach will be a good idea?> This time it was Zephyr.

<Why wouldn't it be? It sure sounds good to me.>

<Emotionally, yes. What about intellectually?>

<I leave that to you, partner. If you have questions, you can ask him.>

<*Nothing definite yet. I need more information. I'm just suggesting that a change of this magnitude needs to be considered carefully.*>

<Maybe,> Emry returned. <But Tai's right—as it is, we're fighting a losing battle.>

5

Looking for Trouble

September 2107
Jupiter Trojan asteroids, L5 group

Emry's prodigious yawn echoed inside her helmet, unremarked by the rest of the universe. She was going crazy cooped up in her space suit for all these hours with nothing to do but drift. She was forced to wonder if maybe Vijay had been right six weeks back about her tolerance for the quiet life.

True, there were four other Troubleshooters out here with her, tethered together in a quincunx formation, and she could talk to them through the tethers if she wanted. Unfortunately, their stealth approach precluded any nonessential power use. She could barely even see the others except as dark areas occulting the stars, since their suits were in full stealth mode, lights off, all surfaces tuned to wide-spectrum black, helmet visors polarized to block heat radiation. Kilometers-long superconducting nanofilaments trailed behind them to dissipate their body heat as diffusely as possible. Still, she was getting hot and sweaty in this thing. She'd slowed her metabolism as much as she could during the long approach—another effective damper on conversation—but now the target was in sight and they had to warm up their muscles for the fight that was coming.

And it would be a doozy. This was the largest TSC team op Emry had ever been on, not counting training exercises: five 'Shooters, nearly all chosen for their combat skills. Kari was here, as was Cowboy, unfortunately. Along with Emry, they provided finesse, firepower, and raw strength. Then there was Elise "Tin Lizzy" Pasteris, her slender Martian frame encased in a sleek battle symbot a generation beyond Arkady's old jalopy, and Juan "Jackknife" Lopez, who had done the key intelligence work leading up to this raid. Since their target was a small, milligee stroid only a few kilometers across, Jackknife had opted to go with a multidirectional thruster unit rather than any of his interchangeable pairs of specialized prosthetic legs.

Juan could've easily enough had new legs grown after his childhood accident, but had decided that being stuck with a single, limited pair of natural legs was too great a handicap. His subsequent replacement of his arms with prosthetics had been voluntary. With that kind of history, Juan had been a natural recruitment target for the Michani, and at Greg Tai's urging, he'd begun responding to their advances, pretending to have been convinced at last that the Singularity was truly nigh (this time for sure!), that mechanical life was destined to rise to godhood and cleanse the universe of putrid flesh. Never mind that nobody had ever been able to create a consciousness, AI or human, that substantially exceeded the intellect of the greatest human geniuses. You could make a cyber that thought faster than Einstein and had access to a greater range of knowledge, but try to make its mind more complex and you soon passed a point of diminishing returns, the same as if you tried to pile too much muscle or too many extra limbs on a human body and ended up with a form too cumbersome to function. Attempts to create metasapience had resulted only in madness or total cognitive collapse. Emry had experienced the results firsthand on one of her first field missions as Arkady's apprentice, the Iwakura incident. She still had nightmares about it.

But the Michani didn't care about the facts. They worshipped such a mad superbrain as their god, obeying its ravings as Delphic pronouncements. They were so blindly certain of their beliefs that they didn't question Jackknife's swift conversion. It had enabled him to get close enough to crack the cult's files and discover their master plan to accelerate Armageddon. Quite a payoff for a policy that had only been in effect for a few weeks.

But then, it wasn't the first. A number of extremist groups had launched copycat attacks in the months since Chakra City—some targeting Earth, others Mars, others their neighbors in the Belt. Many had been ill-conceived, abortive, or easily foiled. But others had been disturbingly feasible, the Michani's scheme among them. The Corps's new policy of trying to head off crises before they broke had been instituted not a moment too soon.

Emry wished Jackknife could've uncovered this scheme a week or two earlier, though. As the target stroid drew closer, Emry peered at it in infrared. It was chilly out here in the Trojans, far from Sol, but the stroid's surface swarmed with hundreds of heat signatures. A few were Michani cultists. The rest—the bigger ones—were pure robots, all identical, all heavily armed and armored. And they were making more of themselves. They were auxons, designed to replicate themselves from available materials, oh, and kill all humans while they were at it. The process had only been set in motion a week ago, and already there were hundreds of them. A couple more weeks and there could be millions.

Diplomacy was useless; the Michani were fanatics. Luckily, they were also idiots, believing that they could hide their operation simply by being far away from civilization. There were no horizons in space and plenty of good telescopes, so once Jackknife had found what to look for, the stroid base had been easy to locate. Taking it out was not so easy, however. A large strike force or a missile would set off their defense systems or give them time to escape; even one surviving auxon would be too many. And at least some Michani had to be taken alive for interrogation to ensure the rest could be tracked down, and auxon remains would have to be recovered and studied to develop countermeasures. (Even if every copy of the plans could be tracked down and wiped, it wouldn't be that hard for any roboticist to design an equivalent. The fact that these psychotic losers had pulled it off was proof of that. Greg Tai had been right—these were scary times.)

So a surgical strike was the best option. Plan A had been to send in a squad of combat drones under Jackknife's supervision. Tai's consortium had donated a large contingent of the drones to the TSC, giving it the means to contend with large-scale combat situations just like this. But Juan had pointed out that the drones' software protocols were fairly standardized and that Michani crackers had subverted similar models in the past.

So that left old-school combat, with live humans putting themselves in harm's way and hoping their plan was good enough to keep them living. The five of them had been dropped off by a Cerean vessel passing by on an innocuous-looking course (not easy to find out here, with so few inhabited bodies to head for), accelerated by a spinning tether onto a rendezvous trajectory, and then left to drift for eighteen hours as their course converged with the stroid. Of course, the strike team couldn't hide in open space any better than the Michani could; even with all their attempts at cooling and camouflage, their bodies still radiated at 310K and that energy had to go somewhere. The most they could hope for was to make their heat signature small and dim enough to be hard to spot against the thermal clutter of the Belt and Inner System behind them. Five bits of self-aware jetsam were all that stood in the way of a systemwide invasion, and their success depended on their ability to hide in plain sight.

So far, they hadn't been attacked; perhaps the Michani's blind faith in their predestined triumph kept them from watching the skies too closely. But the team still had to make the landing in one piece—well, one piece each. The stroid was approaching awfully fast, a spaceborne mountain bearing down on them. They'd only been able to match velocities so much, without being free to use thrusters on approach. And they had to get as close as possible before decelerating, to preserve the element of surprise and to maximize the efficacy of their opening salvo. Emry felt the tug on her tether that signaled her to ramp up her suit generator to full power and jettison her cooling filament. Moments later, she and three others fed their power into Tin Lizzy's symbot at the center of their formation. The symbot sucked in all it could and then unleashed it toward the stroid as a massive microwave pulse.

Emry bit her lip and hoped the plan would work. The completed auxons were EMP-hardened, but Juan's intelligence suggested that incomplete ones, or ones that had their innards exposed in the process of expelling duplicate parts, would be vulnerable to the pulse. The

hope was that with no attack anticipated, and with the Michani eager
to replicate the things as fast as possible, most of the complete ones
would be in mid-replication and sufficiently opened up to be vulnerable. And it was a statistical cinch that roughly half the auxons on that
stroid would be works in progress.

Sure enough, she could see many of the auxons convulsing and shutting down. But there was no time to estimate the exact number of kills.
"Reel out!" Lizzy called, even as she disengaged from the tethers and
fired her thrusters to decelerate for impact. At the same moment she
cut loose on the stroid with a railgun, as much for a bit of extra decel as
to kill auxons (and hopefully not Michani, Emry thought—though Elise
herself was closer to Cowboy's school of thought when it came to the
morality of lethal force). Meanwhile, the rest of the Troubleshooters
thrust backward and radially outward, the tethers reeling out between
them. Emry strove for calm as the carbonaceous mountain hurtled
closer, trusting that she could reel out far enough not to slam into it
headlong.

Indeed, she and the others cleared the stroid by a comfortable mar-
gin, but the X of tethers holding them together struck it at high velocity, slicing through a couple of dozen more auxons and digging deep
into the regolith. The impact shock was enough to knock a number of
auxons off the surface, leaving them flailing in mid-vacuum (or mid–
dust cloud as much of the regolith went with them, hopefully obscur-
ing their sensors). Emry flew past the stroid and felt a centripetal yank
as her tether began to wrap around it. She spiraled in toward the surface, the cable still reeling out, and she aimed for a shallow impact to
minimize the force of it.

But suddenly she felt the tether go slack. Either it had broken or an
auxon had cut it. Instantly she hit the disengage and thrust sideways
so the tether would miss her rather than slicing her suit open. But her
HUD pointed out what she'd intuited anyway: that her trajectory
hadn't curved enough to make stroidfall. She was headed past it, out
into space, at high speed. And she had no more tether to fire at it.

Then she spotted thruster emissions—a fellow 'Shooter, swinging
around from the other side! She thrust toward them, aiming her

commlaser. "Catch me! I'm loose!" The other 'Shooter changed vectors toward her, but she could tell it would be too little, too late. She would pass too far beneath the other. Her only chance was to catch their tether—but how could she spot anything so slender in this vast, dark expanse? She made her best guess where it would be and swept her commlaser over the area on wide-beam visible, hoping to spot some wispy strand of reflected light. But nanotubes absorbed light too damn well.

Then something kicked her in the ass.

Actually it was a series of impacts in quick succession. The suit's armor absorbed most of the force, but it still *hurt,* and it knocked her into a backspin around her center of mass. She instantly adjusted her thrust vectors to keep pushing her stroidward, even as she realized that the shot had come from the figure she'd called to for help. Was it really a Michani? Just as she flipped over to face the figure, it fired a second volley of shots that took her right in her breastplate. Then a third volley hit the ribbed armor over her midriff, knocking the wind out of her and, she realized, pushing her farther toward the stroid. Only one person she knew had the marksmanship and the attitude to save her life in such a crass and bellicose fashion. "Cowboy!" she snarled. He must be hitting her with high-impact kinetic slugs from his railgun.

But before she could get anything else out, she slammed tail-first into the regolith. Fortunately it was a loose agglomeration of dust and debris; she made a big splash and ended up mostly buried, her momentum quite effectively canceled. Coughing and shrieking, she struggled to dig herself out.

"*Y'all okay, darlin'?*" came that infuriating fake drawl.

"Better'n you'll be when I get my vackin' hands on you, you son of a bitch!"

Through the dust, she saw Bhattacharyya come down a few hundred meters away, landing almost gently. He'd managed to shed a lot of his momentum by shooting her. "*Easy there, Greenie. I reckon you're owing me now. Y'all can thank me proper after the mission.*"

In your dreams, she thought. *Shooting me in the ass is the closest you're getting to my pants.* "How about I just don't rip your balls off for calling me 'Greenie'?"

"How 'bout y'all look behind ya?"

Aww, hell. She used her thrusters to spin around. Two auxons were heading right for her—ugly things, blocky and modular, made out of a few recurring component types that were small enough to be built inside their core sections and pieced together. They had flat backs, the platforms on which their offspring were assembled until ready to be unleashed. The closer one had nothing on its back, but the latter had a duplicate half-assembled atop it. The duplicate was inert, but the parent unit must not have had its innards exposed when the microwave pulse hit.

Emry glanced over the heavy armor and razor-sharp claws of the car-sized auxons and decided this was not a hand-to-hand situation. With a sigh, she hefted the high-power firearm she'd been assigned for this mission and began firing, thrusting forward to cancel the recoil. *Goddess, I hate these things.* But her aim was true and the explosive bullets smashed through the auxons' armor quite effectively. She made sure to focus her aim on the core sections to cripple their self-replication ability.

After that it was just point and shoot for a while. Emry didn't have the more complicated job on this mission; that fell to Juan and Kari, whose task was to capture the Michani and access their control network to shut down the auxons. Emry and the rest were just muscle. But the auxons kept things interesting by firing back. Their armaments were clever and nasty, firing nanotube-based projectiles which could be readily resupplied by their internal weavers. Their main guns shot out madly whirling nanobolas, which could slice through nearly anything. The torso armor protected her vital organs, but it was open-sided for freedom of movement; her flanks and limbs were covered only by the light-armor tightsuit that hugged her skin. It had no air to lose except in the helmet, but too many cuts could loosen the mechanical compression that kept her body pressurized. Emry had a close call with a razor grenade: a sphere of electrically charged nanotubes, its mutual repulsion against itself forcing it to expand outward, building enormous tension until it snapped at predesigned weak spots, causing hundreds of taut monofilament strands to fly outward at deadly speed. She had to duck and cover to protect her visor from the nanotube shrapnel, but sustained deep cuts across her left arm and hip, some of them slicing clear through the tightsuit to the flesh beneath. Her repair systems acted efficiently to minimize blood loss, so she allowed herself to hope that no stray nanotubes had been left in her body to poison her cybernetic or biological systems.

One auxon came in close and grabbed her leg with its pincers—luckily around the armored boot instead of higher up, or she might've lost half a leg. Twisting sideways and back, she thrust out her fingers, sent a command to the glove to stiffen, and rammed it into the joint between two of the pincer arm's modules. Her hand knifed through and she tore at whatever she could find until the pincer fell limp. Other deadly grippers flailed toward her, but she twisted away, repeated the stabbing maneuver with one of the seams on the underside, fired several explosive rounds into the gap, and pushed free as the auxon suffered terminal heartburn.

As the battle went on, Emry realized the auxons were dying rather easily. Their nanotube-based weapons may have been easy to replenish, but were also their Achilles heel; damaging their innards caused stray nanotubes to get into their electronics and short them out. Emry was beginning to understand why such weapons weren't used more often. Again, she thanked the Goddess for shortchanging the Michani in the brain department. *Just imagine if someone* really *competent had tried this.*

At last she made it to the other side of the stroid, where the Michani's main staging area had been. "Had been" was the right tense, since the tether impact had torn into it badly, as Tin Lizzy's weapons had no doubt done a few seconds later. Fragments of auxons drifted all over. Emry looked around through the half-settled dust to see Lizzy and Cowboy finishing off a few remaining auxons, but there didn't seem to be any left for her to play with. And it looked like Kari and Juan had the Michani well in hand. There were four of them—gaunt, shiny-carapaced bipeds without pressure suits, originally human but having replaced as much of their bodies as possible with robotic parts in pursuit of "tech-notheosis," the transcending of the flesh to achieve the divinity of AI. The idea fell flat considering that they couldn't replace their very human brains, but they tended to gloss over that, giving an indication of just how poorly those brains were working. And their shiny new bodies, as tricked-up as they were, hadn't helped them much against the cream of the Troubleshooter Corps. They were all bound, a few with missing limbs or torso damage, but all alive and reparable. Juan had one of his hands sticking into the back of a Michani's head, morphed into an inter-face jack. The other hand was in tool mode, manipulating the innards of some kind of mainframe. Jackknife was the only person Emry knew who wore a short-sleeved space suit. "Looks like I missed the good part," Emry broadcast. "You get the shutdown codes?"

"They didn't have one," Kari replied. *"Jackknife's DLing their data, but we're having to finish them off the old-fashioned way."*

"Seems like they were counting on divine providence," Juan told her, his tone mocking. *"This is their destined triumph, after all, so of course their holy host wouldn't turn on them."*

"Traitor," one of the Michani cried in a blatantly synthed voice. *"You could have been one of us. You understand the divine gift of the machine, you've already cast aside half your vulgar flesh—so how could you stand with these animals and oppose the perfecting of the universe?"*

Emry saw Juan's head turn in her direction. *"Blaze, I'm too tired to think of a witty comeback, and I don't really care enough about these psycho morons to try. You got anything?"*

"Maybe a good sock in the face, if I thought they'd feel it. Hey, is that my job around here, the comic relief?"

"Well, it shore was funny the way she landed," Bhattacharyya told the others. *"Her tether broke, and I had to—"*

"Not another word, cactus-face!"

"She's right," Kari said. *"Let's can the chatter and get this scene secured."* Emry felt grateful to her friend . . . until Kari added, *"Then you can tell us* all *about it while we wait for the ships to get here."*

But suddenly Cowboy swung a rifle at Emry and fired, too fast for her to react. For a split second she wondered if he was retaliating for her insult. But the shot had gone over her shoulder, and something spattered her helmet from behind. She thrust herself around . . . and there behind her floated a fifth Michani, a hole blown in its ceramic skull, with a red cloud expanding around it. Its (his? her?) limbs jerked sporadically as it drifted slowly backward and down in the stroid's faint gravity.

Emry's stomach convulsed; it was fortunate she hadn't eaten in hours. Swallowing her bile, she spun back to face Bhattacharyya. *"Sorry, darlin',"* he said in a cavalier tone. *"Only shot I could take with you in the way. Another second, that woulda been you. Looks like that's two you're owin' me."*

"You could've warned me! I could've taken him!"

"Wasn't about to be takin' the chance, sweetheart. Your life's worth more'n his, far as I'm concerned."

That silenced Emry, but brought her no comfort. It was faint praise, considering how little he seemed to care about the life he'd just ended.

They had to wait a while for their pickup. Spaceships traveling fast enough to reach the Trojans couldn't just stop and turn around. Juan's *Dulcinea* and Kari's *Nausicaa* had set out last week on a course that would intersect the Michani's stroid nineteen hours after the battle, to serve either as pickup or backup as needed. Docked together, they had room for the five Troubleshooters plus their prisoners, who were confined in the holding cells on the ships' "basement" levels. Luckily this part of the L5 Trojans was currently only three AU and change from Ceres; with plasma drives thrusting at over half a gee most of the way and the Ceres drive beam catching them, it would take roughly a week to get back to Demetria, not long enough to put a strain on the ships' resources—although it was fortunate that the four Michani needed little food, air, or water.

Emry liked her friends' ships well enough, but was eager to get back to the Corps; she missed Zephyr. Hearing his voice would've been very comforting right now. Still, she had good company in the form of Kari.

She didn't know Elise or Juan all that well, and as for Cowboy—Sanjay—well, he had saved her life twice, and though she wouldn't repay him in the coin he desired, she figured she should at least be civil.

Thus she didn't decline when he invited the others to join in a game of full-uniform strip poker. Elise was the only one who bowed out; she didn't share the typical Troubleshooter fondness for sexually charged competition. Emry couldn't blame her, given how those Palladian raiders had raped her and killed her parents in front of her when she was fifteen. At least she had an excuse for her hard-line approach to Troubleshooting; Cowboy just seemed to think it was fun.

Emry was too reckless and too bad at hiding her emotions to be a decent poker player. That was why she only played strip; she didn't mind losing. True to form, she was the first one out. As for Kari, everyone expected her to have a perfect poker face; but her modesty made her nervous, though not nervous enough to trigger her battle peace, so she played poorly. She managed to stay in longer than Juan—who, after all, had no boots—but lost soon thereafter, retreating behind Emry for cover. Emry was happy to see Cowboy win, having little interest in seeing him naked.

Which left only Juan or Kari as potential bed partners, and Kari's sexual tastes were pretty much unidirectional. Emry liked legs on a man, sure, but the rest of Juan was impressive enough. And when he offered to show her what he could do with his hands, she was hooked. As it turned out, he didn't disappoint. And as a fellow Troubleshooter, he understood how to keep it casual—friendly but with no strings attached. Just the way Emry preferred it.

Demetria

Back at HQ, things were bustling, though it was mostly the enlarged support staff since the T-shooters were staying busy out in the field. She overheard some of the details from the staff (though not from Sally Knox, who couldn't be bothered). Lodestar had uncovered and thwarted a scheme of the Wellspring's scientist elite to break hardened inmates out of a Trojan penal habitat to perform mind-altering experiments that its governor had refused to permit. Paladin had exposed a major embezzlement operation within the government of a carbon-mining colony in the Hygieans, while Bellatrix had talked the exploited miners down from launching an armed revolt. Coyote had foiled a scheme of the Gagaringrad mafia to hijack the Eunomian drive beam and amp it up into a weapon of mass destruction, while a team of Sheaver technical advisors had helped the other local habitats augment their magnetic shields to combat levels, a precaution that had proven unnecessary. All in all, the news lately was more about battles averted than battles won or lost, and Emry found it refreshingly boring.

She was surprised, though, when Sally called her to Sensei Villareal's office and told her that Greg Tai wanted to speak to her. "What happened to Sensei?" she demanded on her arrival.

Sally looked her over, as unimpressed by her righteous indignation as by, well, everything else Emry had ever said to her. "Mister Tai is expecting you. You're late," she added.

Emry blinked. "I came as soon as you paged me! How can I be late?"

"By continuing to waste my time arguing about it."

Emry blinked, shook her head, and stormed into Sensei's office. "What happened to Sensei?"

Tai looked her over and smiled reassuringly. "Come in, Emerald, have a seat. Yukio's fine, he sends his best. He just decided that he could do more good for the Corps by getting out more. Concentrating on public relations and lobbying—you know, taking advantage of that swashbuckling charm of his to advance our goals—while leaving the day-to-day logistics of the TSC in other hands."

"Your hands."

"I was honored when he picked me. But admittedly, it was the most practical decision."

Emry smiled as she took a seat. "I guess it was, yeah. I mean, you've been doing so much good around here, you're practically one of the family. So why not make it official?" She shrugged. "It's just weird to see someone else sitting behind that desk."

"Believe me, it feels weird. But we're talking about the Archer here."

He gestured to the display case, which contained Sensei's old Shashu uniform, the green-and-gold body armor styled to suggest a samurai Robin Hood. "The legendary man of action. Does it really make sense for him to plant his ass behind a desk? That's much more in my line."

She had to admit, the thought of her childhood hero getting back into action—even if it was a more sedate, political kind of action—was gratifying. But she ventured to disagree about the rest. "I don't know. You have the ass of a man who stays pretty active."

Tai laughed, but it was a controlled, polite laugh. "Thank you, Emerald . . . but given our working relationship now, I think a certain . . . professional decorum is called for, don't you think?"

"Oh. Sorry." She tried in vain to seal her top up higher without drawing attention to the act. "So what did you want to see me about . . . boss?"

Tai looked at her with approval. He stood and came around the desk, resting his weight on it, and looked down at her. "I have an assignment that I think you'd be uniquely qualified for, Emerald."

"Emry."

"Ah-ah." He raised a finger. "Not during office hours."

She shrugged. "Whatever fills your tank." He just stared. She subsided, clearing her throat.

"As I was saying: For this mission, Emerald, I need . . . what you are. I need a Vanguardian."

She looked up at him sharply. "I'm not a Vanguardian. My dad was, but they turned their back on him. On everyone."

"My understanding is that he chose to leave them."

"Only because they wouldn't help people after the war. And they never bothered to take an interest in him either after he left."

"True, they've remained very insular ever since. Until now," he told her.

"Now?"

He stood fully again. "Eliot Thorne has recently begun making overtures to other transhumanist habitats, in the Outer Belt and elsewhere," he said, pacing slowly around her. "It seems he's trying to arrange a summit to discuss a possible alliance."

Emry stared. "You're kidding. Thorne? Offering an alliance?"

"It would be a rather radical shift in policy, wouldn't it? That's why we need someone there to find out what's behind it."

She looked up at him quizzically. "You want me to spy on them?"

Another controlled laugh. "Not exactly. Of course there's no way the Green Blaze can go incognito. But Troubleshooters are mods too, so the case can be made that the Corps has a legitimate interest. We've made overtures, and they've shown a . . . guarded willingness to allow a TSC observer to attend. Which is only natural. If they have nothing to hide, they should have no problem with it. And if they do have something to hide, refusing would only raise suspicions.

"But they'd be most likely to accept if it were you, Emerald. Plus your family ties would give you an in that other Troubleshooters would lack. If you approach them as a . . . long-lost relative interested in learning about her heritage, that could give you access to channels they might not open to another delegate. You might learn something they wouldn't reveal in public." He crouched by her chair, one arm around its back, and spoke more softly. "And if you give them the impression that your loyalties might be . . . flexible, you might learn even more. Say, information about their real intentions for this alliance. Whether there's been some change to make them suddenly interested in broadening their reach, and whether that change might pose a threat to other states."

She fidgeted. "So you do want me to spy on them."

"To gather intelligence, yes."

"To seduce them. Pretend I want to get close just so I can . . . take advantage of them?"

Tai was amused. "Emerald, I've studied your files. I've seen how you dress. You're no stranger to seduction."

"That's different. That's sex, not . . . not family."

He furrowed his brow. "Frankly I didn't expect you to worry so much about the Vanguard's feelings. You've never shown any interest in dealing with them before."

"And I'd like to keep it that way."

He stood again, forcing her to look up. "You're a professional, Ms. Blair. You have responsibilities beyond your personal likes and dislikes. Responsibilities that include identifying threats to the peace, regardless of where they originate."

She frowned. "What threat? Thorne's bunch may not have been too neighborly for a while, but have they done anything wrong? They were heroes once upon a time."

Tai studied her. "Maybe that's how it's taught in the Belt, but Earth's experience with them was more . . . ambivalent. Yes, they took it upon themselves to use their enhancements for peacekeeping during a time of turmoil. But even then, they acted like a law unto themselves, not respecting the proper authorities, not caring about the property damage they inflicted in their battles or sometimes even the innocent people they endangered. They thought they were above us, in more senses than one, and they weren't afraid to exploit their advantages. Not all of them, of course," he added. "There were some fine people in their ranks, your father and grandfather among them. But sadly, neither of them is around anymore. The Vanguard is ruled by its most ambitious, politically radical, and charismatic member, and given how thoroughly closed it's been for the past thirty years, it doesn't seem like he has a lot of opposition. And if he's suddenly interested in broadening his ties to other mod nations . . . well, that's something we need to investigate.

"Especially given the nature of the pitch he's been making. This summit is also something of a coming-out party for his daughter, Psyche Thorne." Tai scoffed. "Psyche. Even the name is a boast. Rumor is, she represents the pinnacle of the Vanguard's efforts to enhance the human mind as well as the body. The summit is meant to show her off as an example of how far Vanguard science can elevate the human potential. It's a sales pitch, and she's the demo model. Join us and you too can become part of a superior race."

His words seemed to make sense, but the assignment made Emry uneasy. "I don't know. Sure, Thorne's politics rubbed a lot of people the wrong way, but he never made a violent power play on Earth, and he's never caused any trouble in the Belt. So if he wants to hold a summit meeting, what business do we have spying on it? We just keep the peace. We don't judge anybody's politics, so long as they don't make trouble."

"That's exactly the thinking that gave the Neogaians the freedom to attack Chakra City. That would've let the Michani unleash a plague of killer robots within the week if you hadn't stopped them."

He handed her a sheet of e-paper from his desk. "Look at the invitation list, Emerald. Neogaia is on there. Zarathustra, Wellspring, Mars Martialis, the Moreau Foundation. Even the Michani got an invitation, though they refused." He leaned over her, putting his hands on the arms of her chair and staring into her eyes. "These are people who have no qualms about using unborn children as guinea pigs for untested, potentially dangerous mods. People who believe that mods are destined to rule or supplant baseline humans, by force if necessary. People who use their enhancements to pursue terrorist or criminal—"

"You don't have to tell me what they do. I know what the Neos did to Arkady. I know what the Wellspringers do to kids."

"Then you know what it suggests if the Vanguard is getting in bed with them." He straightened. "The fragmentation of the militant mod nations is possibly the only thing that's kept them from emerging as a serious systemwide threat. But the one thing they all have in common is their reverence for the Vanguard as the ones who started it all, the ones whose example they've all tried to follow. If they were united under a charismatic, ambitious leader like Eliot Thorne . . . just imagine, Emerald.

"You're right, they've done nothing wrong yet. Just getting together to talk. But if that talk is going to lead to something dangerous, we need to know about it *before* it happens. And you're the best Troubleshooter for the job, Green Blaze. Not just because of your heritage, but because of your skills, your training, your insight."

She was silent for a moment. Could Tai be right? Whatever her unease with her own Vanguardian heritage, she'd always seen Thorne himself as a glamorous figure. In her youth, her father had often shown her news footage and documentaries about the Vanguardians to help her learn of her heritage, but with an unintended consequence: as Emry grew older, the images of Eliot Thorne had inspired some of her first stirrings of sexual desire, and he had been the subject of her earliest erotic fantasies. Even after she'd turned her back on Richard Shannon and his side of the family, Thorne had lived on in her fantasy life as the ideal of masculine beauty and sexuality. What if that romanticized image was blinding her to the truth about the man? Still, she hesitated. "It's asking a lot of me."

"I know." His hand touched her shoulder, and lingered there. "It's clear there's no love lost between you and your father's family. That's why I can count on you to be objective, to see through any smoke screens they put up." He smiled. "You just have to let them think otherwise."

Emry smirked. "I'm a lousy poker player."

He looked her over. "So I've heard. Just remember how much higher the stakes are. Make sure the uniform stays on—figuratively, at least."

She shrugged. "Okay. I got it, boss." She rose. "I'll do my best, I promise."

"I'm certain you will. But Emerald?" She stopped on her way to the door, turned back. "I do like to keep things professional. In the future, please wait until I dismiss you. And . . . I'd appreciate it if you'd call me 'sir.'"

She stared for a second, but then decided it was a harmless enough request. It wasn't the way Sensei did business, but surely Tai had earned it by now. "Yes, sir. Will there be anything else?"

"No, Emerald. You're dismissed. I'll have the staff arrange your invitation."

"Thank you, sir."

Zephyr spoke up in her head after she left the office. <*By the way, "Psyche" doesn't literally mean mind, it means the breath of life, the spirit. It's also the Greek word for butterfly. Tai may be in error about Thorne's intent behind his daughter's name.*>

<I'll keep that in mind.>

<*As a representative of the Greek pantheon myself, I feel I have to keep these things straight.*>

She rolled her eyes. <Thank you, Zephyr.>

<*Are you sure you're all right with this mission, Emry? Your biofeedback suggests you're troubled.*>

<Like the man said, it's the job. I'll deal with it.> She sighed. <It's

just . . . I'd prefer to avoid anyone who had any connection to my father.>

<*I understand. But maybe confronting that aspect of your past will be healing.*>

<All I know is, it won't be easy.>

<*Everything worthwhile is hard, dear.*> She gave him a raspberry, hoping the implant in her speech center could read those neural signals as well as the ones that produced speech.

<*I was wondering,*> Zephyr went on, <*if your reasons for concern paralleled mine. This mission seems to venture into a gray area. To direct Troubleshooter resources toward people who have done nothing wrong, based on vague suspicions. . . . *>

"They're hooking up with Wellspringers and Neogaians," she said aloud, not caring who might be listening. "That's reason enough to be suspicious. You know what kind of things they do. There was a time the Vanguard fought people like them."

<*The Neogaian regime that attacked Earth has been deposed, Emry. The current one may be different. As for the Wellspringers, I agree they have a tendency to condone ethically questionable research, but on the whole they're a peaceful group.*>

Emry scoffed. "Peaceful. That's what they call it. But it means neutralizing unpleasant emotions—ones like guilt and shame. I've seen the things they've done."

<*Emry,*> he said gently, <*you've done quite a few unethical things in your day. I've seen the movie.*>

She was forced to laugh, as he'd no doubt intended. "Maybe," she told him. "And maybe I didn't feel much shame about it at the time. But the difference is, *I* never pretended I was doing something good."

6

Origin Stories: Banshee's Cry

April 2100
New Zimbabwe habitat
In orbit of Vesta

Javon Moremba resisted the urge to run.

For one thing, it would make him look guilty. He *was* guilty, of course, but he didn't want to *look* like he'd just broken into an upscale house, cracked their home weblink to update his ID-erasure worms, and stolen a bunch of fancy jewels when the whim took him on the way out. He couldn't easily keep track of what was still valuable in the "evolving post-scarcity economy" Solsys was supposed to have now, but he knew as well as any Vestan that natural gemstones—like the peridot, garnet, and jade produced by Vesta's unusual geology—were still prized for their beauty and scarcity. And it was about time, he thought, that someone from his side of New Zim got his share of Vesta's wealth. But he couldn't do that if he got caught.

For another thing, it would just feel too right to run. He didn't want it to feel right. That would be giving in.

Still, even walking, he called attention to himself. People tended to notice a two-meter-tall teenager with unnaturally long limbs, bulging joints, no hair, and an oversized rib cage. They didn't notice as much as if they saw him running at sixty klicks, but they still noticed. So Javon decided he needed to steal a car.

Luckily, this cylinder of New Zim had plenty of rich people, so there were plenty of high-end aircars to choose from. He soon spotted a gorgeous one, a gleaming green Gyrfalcon 8K with gold trim around its ducted fans. It was sitting right out on its launching pad, with only the property fence between it and him. The house looked dark, and the sniffer beeped an all-clear tone in his ear, reading no active security devices. It seemed too good to be true, but he was in too much of a hurry to care. After making sure there were no spectators, he got up a running start and leapt easily over the fence. Jogging over to the Gyrfalcon, he circled around to the driver's side and reached in his pocket for his lockpicks.

Only he found the door already open, with a really rageous pair of legs sticking out of it. The girl attached to the legs, lying on her back inside the car trying to hot-wire it, was even more spectacular. She was kind of short, her muscles making her a bit stocky, but she had a huge rack, flattened out some by her position but still wide, round, and proudly bulging. Her position gave him a good look at the equally interesting bulge between her legs. That and her tits were covered by a tight cutoff tank top and shorts flickering with animated flames and transparent above them, making it look like she was wearing nothing but fire.

The girl raised her head at his approach, and he saw her hair matched her wardrobe. It was cut short on the back and sides, but a thick, wavy mass poured over her forehead, shading enormous eyes whose green made the Gyrfalcon's look dull. Her china-doll features—she was younger than that body made her look—twisted in surprise and anger, and Javon realized her eyes matched her fiery wardrobe too. "Hey!" she snarled in an incongruously girlish soprano. "Steal your own ride, I was here first!"

He stared. For a thief, she was dressed damn conspicuously. "Hey, how do you know this isn't my car?"

"You kidding? The way you're sweating? I know a thief when I see one. A bad one, anyway."

He reined in his anger. "Look, I probably need this ride more than you do. We could share it—"

"I don't share easy, Stilt-boy." She looked his body over appraisingly, and to his surprise, she grinned. "You want it, you gotta take it from me."

An instant later, she lashed out a foot at his gut. The move was lightning-quick, and he was barely able to dodge it. Her red-orange boot took him in the left forearm. "Oww! You bitch!" He grabbed her calf, finding it very firm, and jerked her out of the car so that she fell on her ass and hit her head on the step.

But if anything, she looked impressed, even pleased. "Ooh, you're fast! Fast enough for *this*?" She did some kind of twisty move and her open right hand took him in the gut. He landed flat on his back, and in a second she was straddling him in a way he would've liked very much if she hadn't socked him in the gut a couple more times—not as hard as she could hit, he sensed, but enough to knock more wind from his lungs.

Luckily he had big lungs, so he could still grab her arms and pull her sideways, intending to roll over and reverse their positions. She was a strong little thing—had to be a mod—but he had more bulk.

But she saw it coming and rolled away. He scrambled to his feet, knowing the little spitfire would be doing the same. He sidestepped her charge and tossed her across the Gyrfalcon's nose. She landed on her feet on the other side and ducked beneath it. Knowing she'd be grabbing at his ankles from below, Javon leapt straight up, spun, and came down with his feet on her broad, muscular back, slamming her into the hard carpad. He hurriedly jammed his right foot onto her neck and got his left on solid ground, putting a hand on the Gyrfalcon to steady him. The girl writhed and shrieked, but it was a good pin, with her lower body still caught under the car's nose. "Say uncle, little girl!"

"Go fuck your uncle! How's that?" Her hands closed around his ankle with a viselike grip. "Lemme up or try running from the cops on one foot!"

"Stop it or I'll break your neck!"

"Liar! You want me too bad."

"Less every second!"

"Bullshit. And you're no killer either. But me, I've broken plenty of bones. And I'm a lousy bluffer." The vise tightened.

"*Owww!!* Okay, you crazy bitch!" He pulled his foot away as quickly as she'd let him, leaning on the car for support. She came up tensed for action, but grinning. *What, she's not through yet?*

Then he heard shouts, saw lights in neighboring windows. "Damn, you moron, they'll be calling the cops on us! Look, let's both just take the ride and get the suck out of here, and then we'll get out of each other's way and hopefully never see each other again!"

The insane redhead looked disappointed, but she nodded. "Okay, get in." He got into the driver's seat, only to be forcefully shoved aside. "No, leakbrain, *I'm* driving!" she shrieked.

"Okay! Okay, you crazy punkhole, just stop hitting me! And don't scream like that in here, you'll make me go deaf!"

She stuck out her tongue as the car's fans whirred to life. Then she shut the door and screamed the shrillest *"Waahoo!"* he'd ever heard just to piss him off. Instead of taxiing antispinward to cancel the car's weight like any sane driver, she took off perpendicular to the runway, straining the fans to maximum as they fought the car's inertia along two axes. They barely scraped past the roof of the house, the fans' roar no doubt waking everyone for a block around, and Javon scrambled to strap himself in, praying to Allah, Buddha, Jesus Krishna, and whoever else might be listening that her hot-wiring hadn't disabled its collision avoidance.

"Listen!" he said. "Listen, slow down! You want us to get caught?"

"Ha! I'd like to see 'em try!"

"Well, I wouldn't! I'd rather not get caught with these!" He pulled the jewels out of his pocket.

Her eyes widened. "Ooh, gasmic!" Her hand shot out and snatched an emerald pendant. "Mine!" she cried, draping it over her head.

He was about to object, but then he saw how good it looked between her breasts. Besides, considering how reckless the little brat was, she'd probably wear the thing publicly and get nabbed for the heist so he could slip away. So he didn't object as she rummaged through the rest of his haul—aside from trying to keep the jewels from flying around the cockpit, now that the car was on a stable course and their weight was gone. At least the CA light was on, so he figured the car wouldn't crash if her attention was elsewhere—especially since this less populous cylinder would have less air traffic than his own. She skipped over most of the jewelry, only showing interest in the emeralds. "Hey, these are real," she breathed, though he couldn't tell how she knew. "Must come from Earth."

"Why?"

She looked at him like he was stupid. "Takes water to make 'em, genius." She ended up with a ring and a bracelet and tossed the rest back to him.

"You're welcome," he said pointedly as he scrambled to snag them all. She just grinned and studied her new baubles.

"So you got a name?" he asked.

"Got a whole bunch. Right now I'm Kei."

"Okay, then . . . call me J."

She glared. "K-E-I. Japanese."

"Oh."

"No, Kei."

"Okay." To his surprise, they shared a laugh.

For a while, they just soared over the artificial forests, rivers, and country estates of this half of New Zim. Kei ignored the scenery, admiring her emeralds instead. "So you born a mod?" she finally asked.

Javon shook his head. "Parents retroed me. Wanted me to be the fastest runner in Solsys, make them rich. Whatever 'rich' means anymore."

She looked him over, starting at his hairless head and ending somewhat lower. "You bald all over?" she asked with a purr in her voice.

"If you're lucky, you'll find out."

"Hah. You'd be the lucky one."

"Hell, girl, if I'd been lucky I'd never have met you. I'm gonna be bruised all over in the morning."

"It ain't real fun if it don't leave a mark."

"You think all this is fun? Don't tell me, is that why you stole this thing? Just for kicks?"

"What else is there?"

"For me, it's about freedom. I didn't want to be a, a commodity, have my body and my life molded to fit what my parents wanted. That's all, I'm just tryin' to be free."

She scoffed. "Nobody's ever free. Just running. You stop and there's always something that'll catch up with you."

Javon studied her. "You been running a long time now, Kei? From *your* parents, maybe?"

That brought a fierce glare. "No! None of your suckin' business anyway!"

"Okay, okay."

"Just my daddy," she said after a while. "My *former* dad. Couple years now. He brought me back a few times—till I practically tore the house apart. Then he got the message and stopped tryin'."

"Tore it apart? With what?"

She stared. "How's your ankle, Stilt-boy?" Javon stared at her hands, intimidated and oddly aroused.

"But that means nobody's chasing you anymore," he said after a while. "So what's left to run from?"

"There's always somethin'," she said softly. Then she shook it off and grinned at him. "Like the law on half the habs in the Belt," she boasted. "Still workin' on flaring off the rest."

Her brow furrowed. "You know what? We should ditch this ride. We wanna get to the spaceport, they'll be expecting it. We should vack it and go the rest of the way on foot."

He nodded. "I'm free with that." He looked at the underside display monitor. They were curving up the slope of the cylinder's end cap now, over the craggy simulated mountains that covered its interior. "But there's no good place to set down."

Her grin grew positively scary. "Thing's got ejector seats, right?" She reached under the dash and ripped out the innards. The CA light sputtered and went out, along with all the rest.

"My God! Dammit, bitch, you're completely vacked in the head!"

"Just hold on to your jewels and punch out!"

"But I loved this car!" he called in vain, for she was already erupting out of the canopy. Realizing he was out of options, he stuffed the jewelry back in his pocket, made sure he was strapped in, and followed suit. He felt the glider wings spread out and the seat cushion fall away, and then watched as the Gyrfalcon spun out of control and descended on an accelerating spiral path in the Cori winds, finally smashing itself to pieces on the rocks below.

After that, the glider's autonav brought him down to a fairly level patch, one he hoped was far away from wherever Kei came down. Unfortunately, though, the gliders seemed to be set to home in on each other, and her flame-shrouded form came down just a few dozen meters away. Ditching the wings, she jogged over to him, laughing. "Shit, why do real cars never blow up like in the movies when you crash 'em?" Somehow it didn't surprise him that she talked about crashing cars as a recurring event. But he suspected she knew the answer to her own question perfectly well.

What did surprise him was when she hopped up, flung her arms around his shoulders, and kissed him hard and deep. "Whoo, that was rageous!" she shrilled when she broke away, all too soon. "Let's get two and crash 'em into each other!"

"You are out of your hull-punking mind, you know that? You could've got us killed!"

"Aw, don't be such a baby! Come on, race you to the spaceport!"

She pulled at his hand, but he yanked it away. "No! Stay away from me, you vackhead! Where the hell even *are* we? They're gonna come looking after that crash, you know! They'll find us, they'll send us *both* back to our parents, and it'll be all *your fault!*"

She began to circle him aggressively. "You wanna make something of it, Stilt-boy? 'Cause I'm up for givin' you another good beating anytime!"

"You kidding? I beat you!"

"Ha! What fight were you watching?"

"I had my *foot* on your sucking *neck!*"

"And I was about to snap it off!"

"I just gave you a break, that's all! You're strong for a kid, but I got the mass *and* the leverage on you."

"Okay, come on, prove it!"

He was about to, but he stopped. "No. Why? The car's trashed. What's left to fight for?"

She grinned. "Me."

"What?"

"You win the fight, you get to fuck me."

"*Why* would I *want* to?!"

She just looked at him. And he looked at her. And he shrugged. "Okay, then." He started to circle her, sizing her up, looking for an opening as she did the same. "Should've figured this was your idea of foreplay."

"Guy wants me, he's gotta earn it."

"So you only fuck guys who can beat you up? That's smart."

"Smart for them. I play rough."

Understanding came to him then. "I get it. You don't want to hurt them."

She lunged, but he was ready. He sidestepped easily, spun, and kicked her well-rounded, muscular ass, sending her headlong. But the gravity was low up here and she caught herself with her hands, flipping up and over and coming down facing him. *Where did she learn these moves?* "What do you know about it?" she snarled.

"I know how much I have to hold back when I'm with a normal girl. You gotta be real strong to run sixty klicks, to stand the forces of it. And you don't strike me as the holding-back type. How bad did you hurt your first guy?"

She lunged again, shrieking. He moved aside, thinking this was the easiest psych-out he'd ever done. But the lunge was a feint; she spun going past and kicked his legs out from under him, landing on her side next to him. They scrambled to hands and feet, and his greater reach gave him the edge; he grabbed the hair tumbling over her forehead and held her there on hands and knees as he came to his feet. That proved a mistake, though, as it brought his groin within her fist's reach. Luckily his reflexes were enhanced for speed, and he dodged the worst of it. "Hey! Ow! I thought you'd want that part in good condition!"

"Only if you're good enough!"

"Well, how am I *doing?*" He punctuated it with a kick to her gut, knocking her torso upright, and then delivered one more kick to her ample breasts in retaliation for her attempt on his balls. He felt somewhat guilty when she yelped in pain, but he reminded himself that she not only deserved it, but probably even enjoyed it in some sick way.

Or maybe not so sick, he thought as he saw the approval—the *hope*—in her eyes. "Not bad, Legs! But I'm still gonna beat your brains out!" He raised his arms to block her lunge, but she caught them and flipped clear over him, wrenching his arms back painfully. Then she flung him over her back and the world spun around him for an endless moment, finally coming up to slam into him. "You're disappointin' me, J. I was hopin' for some real action." Her boot swung toward his face.

But he managed to catch it and tug, yanking her off her feet; the ground was slippery in this gravity. As she fell, he wrenched the boot off and tossed it aside. "Ooh, good start, sugar," she lilted, if one could lilt breathlessly. They clambered to their feet, but now she was a bit uneven. "That the best you can do?"

"Must be tough, Kei," he said, circling her, trying to keep her off balance. "A fight like this—with these stakes—you win, you get nothing. But the guy has to be tough enough to take you for real, so you can't lose on purpose."

"What's your point, baldy?"

"Point is, I don't think this is as fun for you as you say." This time *he* lunged, hoping to throw off her rhythm physically as well as mentally this time. She moved her arms to block her vital areas, but he wasn't going for them. He got his long arms around hers and took a firm grip on her faux-flaming tank top as he moved behind her, yanking it up and over. Then before she could slip her arms out, he twisted it around her wrists, restraining them over her head. Still holding her arms up there, he circled around to face her again, trying not to be too distracted by the truly incredible breasts he'd bared. "But it could be," he went on. "If you stop fighting me and let me in, Kei. I must've proven by now I'm strong enough to handle you. Maybe . . ." He stepped closer. "Maybe I can even teach you a few things about being gentle." He bent down to kiss her, and she brought her lips up to meet his halfway. Her kiss was anything but gentle. Her hands clasped his, but he kept them above her head just to be on the safe side.

After a while, she pulled her lips away and said breathlessly, "I like it rough."

He smiled. "Good. Then I don't have to hold back." Still not releasing her wrists, he twisted her until he had his arms around her from behind, and bent down to bite her on the neck. One hand came up to knead her breasts forcefully while the other slid down to hook around her waistband.

"J . . ."

"My name's Javon."

"Look up."

He did. Two police aircars were approaching. "Oh, shit."

"This way!" Kei led him toward a nearby crag, allowing her top to fall from her wrists. Shaking his head, Javon picked up the conspicuous garment and ran after her.

Soon they were well-ensconced in a crevice, invisible from the air, and she was all over him, tearing at his clothes.

Unfortunately, she was a screamer, even during foreplay, and the little idiot had chosen a hiding place that echoed superbly. The cops came upon them while he was still rounding third base, saw Kei's naked body adorned in stolen emeralds, and had them both hauled away to juvenile detention, where his parents would no doubt come to claim him and make him their prize commodity again. As he sat in his cell the next day, he resolved that if he ever saw that little redheaded bitch again, he would snap her neck for real.

But then she broke out somehow—and came to break him out too. This time, surprisingly, she managed to be successfully stealthy and got them to the spaceport without a hitch. He began to suspect that she'd allowed herself to get caught—and dragged him along with her—just for the challenge of breaking them both out again. Or could it be that she'd regretted getting him in trouble through her own wanton ways? *Nahhh.*

Either way, before Javon knew it, they were together in a private cabin on a ship bound for Mars. "Too bad you didn't get to keep your emeralds, though," Javon told her as they made out and pulled off each other's clothes.

Kei stopped for a moment and laughed. "What?" he asked.

"Javon . . ." She kissed him, then met his eyes squarely with her own huge, gleaming green pair. "My *name* is Emerald."

He studied her. "You sure you want to go with that? Not too smart after what we got busted for. And who'd buy a dumb name like that anyway?"

She shoved him away. "No, you idiot! My *real* name! Goddess, I try to confide in you . . . Get away from me!"

He winced. At this rate he'd never get to punk her. But to his surprise, that wasn't the primary thing on his mind. He realized what she'd just offered him and hated himself for spoiling it.

He also realized, though, that she wasn't leaving the room. She wanted to stay, wanted to let him in. He just had to play it carefully, since this volatile little fireball could go off at any moment.

Is it worth the trouble? he asked himself. Then he looked at her and saw for the first time how lost and lonely she looked. *Yes,* he answered. *Yes, she is.*

Emerald Blair (the name "Shannon" was detritus long ago discarded) often wondered why she continued to travel with Javon Moremba. Sure, he was a fellow mod, strong enough to handle her, able to understand the things she'd been through. And he was sexy and exciting, and at nearly eighteen he had two years on her in experience. And she had to admit that his judgment often kept her from getting into worse trouble than she did, although she made sure to balance things by keeping him in worse trouble than he wanted. Finding Mars tame and boring, she'd persuaded Javon to accompany her south of the ecliptic to some of the rough, seedy habs in the Eunomia-family stroids, about a third of an orbit behind Eunomia itself. They were mostly cheap prefabs, easily replicated and easily abandoned, mainly support stations for prospectors and other itinerants who had little investment in their long-term viability. As such, they were more lawless than most small habs, with plenty of opportunities for ambitious young thieves and vandals to find trouble or make it. Especially since Pallas had recently reached one of the points where its highly inclined orbit passed through the Belt proper, so most of the Troubleshooters were too busy fending off pirate raids on that side of the system to pay much attention to petty crime in the Eunomians. Pallas's extreme isolation and mineral wealth attracted the worst of the worst, a hotbed of tyrants, warlords, and cutthroats. Emry had often fantasized about going there and living out a short but exciting life as a pirate queen. But since Javon had come into her life, she'd found such a future less appealing somehow.

But having Javon around still made her edgy sometimes. The last thing she wanted was to feel like she needed him. She'd once thought she could trust a man to take care of her, and he'd betrayed her. He'd let her mother die right in front of him. He'd forced her to live in Greenwood where people hated her and Mom, even though he knew how happy she was every time they left. He'd let her be born a mod, made her inherit this freakish strength rather than having it engineered out of her. No way would she ever let another man get close enough to ruin her life like that.

So although she kept Javon around once they reached the Eunomians, she made a point of sleeping with as many other guys as could take her. Just to make sure he didn't get the wrong idea—and because she enjoyed the variety. But few of them could really measure up to Javon, either in technique or in other ways. Guys tough enough to take her often weren't all that interesting to talk to, or all that kind. Some who won access to her bed got kicked out posthaste when they treated her too roughly. She never proved unable to outfight a guy when she really *had* to.

Javon resented her pointed promiscuity at first, and retaliated with some screwing around of his own, which was fine with her. She had no trouble luring him back when she was ready. And soon they settled into a comfortable routine, hanging together and sleeping together without actually *being* together. But it was a tenuous balance, and sometimes she had to smack him down, physically or emotionally, when he tried to get too close.

It helped when they met Ruki Shimoda in the back alleys of San Berardo, a small, disreputable habitat around Interamnia. Emry had grown tired of the backwater Eunomia-family habs and wanted to go someplace busier yet even farther from the beaten path. Interamnia's seventeen-degree orbital tilt meant it took extra thrust and time to reach, but it was a large, carbon-rich stroid that straddled the Central and Outer Belts. It was a sort of Pallas Lite, drawing those who sought profit in ways incompatible with public scrutiny.

Thus it was that San Berardo's crime boss-turned-dictator refused to let FEEL-licensed pleasure houses operate there, since open competition with the higher-quality sex specialists trained and protected by the Federation of Erotic Entertainers and Labor would quickly drive his non-guild shops out of business and keep him from exploiting his sex workers as he saw fit. And thus it was that the fourteen-year-old Ruki had been abducted and gene-raped by an expatriate Neogaian doctor, modded against her will with foxlike features, golden-brown fur, and a tail, and forced to serve in one of the "specialty" brothels that San Berardo had become infamous for. They'd also given her vulpine senses and agility, and whether because of her mods or simply for survival, Ruki had developed an animal cunning as well. Those traits had enabled her to escape the brothel after three years of enslavement, several earlier attempts, and several increasingly severe punishments. Emry and Javon came across her, still attired in a leather bikini and dog collar, as she fought against the three men sent to bring her back. Impressed by the foxlike girl's skills and wanting in on the action—and all right, maybe to make it a fairer fight—Emry had thrown herself into the fray, with Javon reluctantly following. Together they'd made short work of the assailants, though Javon had to restrain Ruki from slashing their throats open. One of the men was bleeding badly, and despite herself, Emry felt obliged to hit the emergency button on his selfone and wait to hear the sirens approaching before she ran to catch up with the others.

After making a daring escape from San Berardo with their new friend, Emry and Javon mutually decided that enlarging their little clique would make it easier for them to keep a comfortable detachment, so they invited Ruki to travel with them. She was suspicious of Javon at first, having known few men who hadn't used or hurt her. But Javon had a way about him, and Emry assured the vixen that he was okay. Ruki was still more comfortable around Emry, though, and the two girls soon became friends—and occasional bedmates once Ruki proved she was tough enough to handle Emry's strength, the first woman ever to do so.

As they made their way through the Outers, they began actively seeking other mod runaways to recruit into their group. The more of them there were, the harder it would be for anyone to hurt them or use them again. Of course, a gang of superpowered criminals needed supervillain nicknames. Ruki became Hikkaku, meaning "Slash." Javon teasingly saddled Emry with the nickname Banshee—"my little Irish screamer"—so in return, and with gleeful *double entendre*, she dubbed him Thrust. The gang itself was named the Freakshow.

As supervillain gangs went, the Freakshow was underachieving. Rather than trying to conquer humanity, destroy the universe, or find a champion of justice whose life they could fixate on ruining with overly byzantine schemes, they were content to devote their efforts to having fun, taking what they wanted from others, smashing and vandalizing things for the hell of it, and being general nuisances to civil society. Most of all, they took care of each other and protected each other from harm. They made a few enemies, infringed on other gangs' turf, and got into their share of fights, but usually by accident or in self-defense. For super-villains, even for gang members, they weren't particularly violent. Ruki and some of the others were willing to kill and had come close more than once, but Javon, Emry, and the rest were a mollifying influence on them—or a restraining one, by force if necessary. Emry welcomed any chance to work off her rage, but not at the cost of a life. She wouldn't become one of those people, the kind who'd taken her mother from her.

Sometimes the Freakshow even helped people outside its circle. They watched out for the people they liked, for fellow mods and others who were mistreated or ostracized by society. At the Hygiean habitat Wellspring, on learning that children were being used as guinea pigs in the Wellspringers' experiments to enhance the mind, they trashed the lab facility and liberated the subjects, recruiting a few into the gang. They cracked the computer net of the Fourth Reich Neo-Nazi habitat, wiped their database, and replaced it all with endlessly looping video files of *The Great Dictator, Casablanca,* and *The Producers.*

Most of all, though, they looked out for each other. They kept each other safe when no one else would. To Emry, that was what the Freakshow was all about.

April 2101
Niihama habitat
In orbit of Eunomia

"We need the doctor! *Now!*"

The patients in Doc Kamiyama's run-down waiting room gasped and backed away as Banshee, Om, and Crack barged in, their faces and Freakshow colors spattered in blood. The doc's antiquated receptionist gynoid moved to block the inner door. "I'm sorry, the doctor is seeing a patient at the moment. If you'll please—"

"He'll *be* a patient if you don't get him now!" Emry snarled.

The gynoid's hand folded away to reveal a nasty-looking gun barrel in her arm. "Please do not disturb the other patients."

Emry knew a subsapient cyber when she heard one. She figured this one had to be really lacking in awareness if it thought one gun could intimidate her after what she'd just been through. She was on the verge of charging the receptionist when Thrust and Hack finally arrived, carrying the mangled forms of Hikkaku and Overload in their arms. The receptionist's gaze shifted, and she promptly said, "Dr. Kamiyama, Dr. Shibumi, report immediately. Medical emergency." Her faux Asian eyes met Javon's. "Please escort the patients to the emergency room. First door on your right."

They hurried back and Emry started to follow. The receptionist blocked her. "Please remain—*ukkk!*" Emry was through the doors before the gynoid crashed against the waiting-room chairs.

"What happened?" Doc Kamiyama may not have been the most reputable healer around, may not have even had a license anymore after that drug scandal, but he was still all business the moment he saw the severe injuries Ruki and Daniel had sustained.

"Tong Robo happened," Emry told him. "Attacked us."

His eyes widened. "Uhh, did, did they attack you or did you—"

She slammed him into the wall. "You *really* want to make that your problem right now? Fix them! They're dying!"

"All right! All right." He hurried over to where they lay on the tables. "But I need you all to wait outside."

"No way—"

"*Stay out of our way* if you don't want them to stay dead!" Whatever fear he'd shown of her was totally gone now. *Stay dead?* Emry didn't question him again.

The wait was interminable. Everyone else had run off; the Freakshow had the waiting room to themselves. The zine readers weren't even online—that would've made it easier for the law to track Doc's clientele—and their onboard articles were all months out of date. Hack and Crack—Shengli and Peter Wen, who'd purchased black-market bionic mods to give themselves an edge on the streets that their slight, weak natural build couldn't provide—entertained themselves by using their built-in cracking gear to make the receptionist strip and perform for them in various humiliating ways. Meanwhile, Om stared into the office computer's interface port, linking to it wirelessly through her optic nerves, and did her communing thing. She was the lucky one; Padhma would experience no sense of time for as long as she was in that state. Her parents, crackpots in search of unity between human and cyber, had rewired Padhma Rao's parietal lobe so it would shut down while her brain was fed raw computer data. This turned off her sense of herself as a being distinct from the universe, like what happened during religious ecstasy. The idea was to let her mind perceive the data as part of itself and turn her into an intuitive data-miner, divining unprecedented new insights into cybersystems. The Freakshow had taken her on in the hope that her ability could help them get around security systems and find new opportunities for profit and mischief. Sometimes Om did seem to turn out uncanny insights, but usually her results were Delphically arcane, untestable, or just plain wrong, so it could've been dumb luck. And her mods had a side effect of sending her into fits of transcendental ecstasy upon exposure to various RF or magnetic fields. Overall, they were more a handicap than a boon, to herself and to the gang. But the Freakshow took care of its own.

Or do we? Emry asked herself as images of Overload's crushed and bloody body burned in her mind. Daniel Weiss wasn't too different from Padhma. He was one of the guinea pigs they'd liberated from Wellspring, engineered in the womb as part of a failed experiment in sensory amplification. His hyperacute senses made him a great lookout and an uncanny lockpick, but left him prey to the condition he'd chosen as his nickname. Loud noises, fast movement, crowds, spicy food, the mere smell of alcohol, it could all overwhelm him. Touch was almost unbearable to him. Any disruption in a pattern, a speck of dirt, a slightly mistuned speaker, drove him crazy and he had to fix it or get away at all costs. Usually he relied on an inhibitor the Wellspringers had put in his brain to compensate for their mistake, but it left him detached and slightly numb. He enjoyed being able to turn it off, until something overwhelmed him and it had to go back on. Emry felt uncomfortable around him, afraid her raucous style would alarm or hurt him, but he liked having her near. He'd told her that the purity of her face was a comfort to him, at least when she was calm and relaxed. So his presence had encouraged her to strive for greater calm, with help from Om's meditation exercises. Still, she found it a relief when she could be away from him and cut loose like her normal self—particularly since Daniel's impediments made him unviable as a sex partner and she was uncomfortable relating to males in any other way. Now, though, she found herself realizing how much she'd miss Daniel's gentle appreciation, his ability to see gentleness in her, somewhere, somehow. *He has to live. He doesn't deserve this.*

Why had they risked coming to Tong Robo's turf? Those guys were hard-core; they made self-mutilation a requirement for joining, replacing whole limbs and organs with blatantly mechanical parts like something from an old sci-fantasy. They made themselves living arsenals, and not just for show. Emry had wanted nothing to do with them. But they'd wanted to meet Hack and Crack, compare mods and tech specs, and the brothers had figured they could get some good upgrades from the deal. If the Tong demanded something in exchange, Emry figured she and the girls could pay with sex; and if things got hairy, the brothers could always crack the Robos' systems or flash-blind them so the rest could incapacitate them and get away. She'd been confident they could handle any trouble.

She'd been wrong. Tong Robo's invitation had been an ambush. They hadn't wanted to meet the Freakshow; they'd wanted to kill the competition and preserve their own rep among the mod gangs. Such was the price of success. The Freaks had been outnumbered, outgunned, and totally flat-footed. Emry hadn't seen it coming, and Ruki had been half blown up before she could react, with Daniel falling not long after. They'd barely managed to get away and reach here. For all Emry knew, Ruki and Daniel hadn't gotten away at all. And it was all her fault.

Emry was distracted from her funk when Padhma made a faint gasping sound—the kind she made when she'd intuited something she thought was important and wanted to be shaken out of communion. Emry obliged and Padhma told her what she'd sensed. Under the older girl's guidance, Emry had the brothers hack past Doc's security to confirm Om's insight. What she saw made her want to tear this building down, but she couldn't so long as Ruki and Daniel needed it, and its occupants, intact.

Finally Doc Kamiyama came out. Emry was on him in a heartbeat. "Well?"

He sighed. "We've stabilized them both, but they're on full life support. I can put them back together, but it'll take extensive organ and limb replacements, especially for the girl."

"Will you be able to make them look the same?" Javon asked. "And . . . feel the same?" Emry glared at him. She doubted his concern for Ruki's outward aesthetics was for her benefit.

"If that's what they want, but it'll cost more. The parts alone will cost plenty." The tenets of the post-scarcity economy didn't apply as much to the underground of society.

Emry got in the doctor's face. "As much as the parts you installed in Tong Robo? The parts that *did* this to my friends in the first place?!"

Kamiyama fidgeted. "Look, I just do what they pay me to do. What happens after they leave here, that's not my problem."

"You vack-sucking, hull-punking . . ."

Javon pulled her back. "Easy, Banshee. We still need him."

She let out a strangled shriek. "Okay! You want to get paid, how about this: you save them and we won't break all your fingers and burn this rathole to the ground!"

"That doesn't get me the goods I need to trade for parts," he said calmly. He had to be used to dealing with violent, threatening types, given that he'd worked for Tong Robo.

Emry snarled. "Okay! Okay, we'll get you the money. We'll steal whatever it takes. To fix them—and me."

Everyone stared at her. "You?" Kamiyama looked her over with a leer. "Aside from a few abrasions and contusions, I don't see a thing wrong with you."

She shoved him into the wall again. "Call it repayment, Doc. Way I see it, you owe us for helping our friends get hurt. So you're gonna help me make sure it doesn't happen again. You can replace limbs and organs—can you do more delicate work? Reinforce what I've got, make me stronger, tougher?"

He thought about it. "Sure. I can do endoscopic work, remote micro-surgery, nanoinfusions. Add bracing to the bones, inject nanotube muscle fibers . . . if you like, I can put standard upgrades in your eyes and ears, or even souped-up versions if the cost is right. And there won't be more than minimal scarring." He looked down. "I even do breast reductions, if those give you any trouble. Smaller breasts are often more sensitive, you know. . . ."

Emry gave him one last shove and stepped away. "Shut up! Just get to work on our friends. We'll make sure you get your payment. But until you fix them and me, we're your exclusive clients, got it? This clinic is Freakshow turf now."

Kamiyama's eyes widened. "If Tong Robo finds out, they'll kill me!"

Javon stepped forward. "Are our friends stable enough to be moved? Could you do your work somewhere else, off Niihama?"

The doc sighed. "Sure, why not? Beats dying. And I'm sick of this dump anyway. Look, I'll go get started on what your friends need." He backed away hurriedly.

Javon turned to Emry. "You sure about this, Banshee? Getting upgrades from this old junkie? You're already rageous strong, you really need more?"

"Can you ask that after what happened today?! I couldn't protect Ruki and Daniel!"

"Neither could we! You think I'm not as torn up as you are? But there was nothing more we could've done."

"How do we know that? If I had better eyes or ears, I could've sensed them coming. If I could run faster I could've gotten to them in time. If I were—"

"Hey, hey." Javon took her in his arms. "Emry, it wasn't your fault. It was just one of those things."

"No," she said. "There has to be more. There has to be a way to keep this from happening again. If there's anything I can do to keep my family safe, I have to. Anything."

Javon gazed into her eyes, stroked her cheek. "Family?"

She looked away. "You know what I mean. The gang. It's all I've got. All I've ever had. Or ever will have." She rested her cheek on his chest, still avoiding his eyes. "I have to protect that. I have to be the toughest mod there is, so nobody ever dares to hurt us again."

7

She Never Metahuman She Didn't Like

September 2107
Vanguard habitat

Vanguard was currently clear across the Belt from Ceres, six AUs away, so Emry took the Sundiver route. After a sunward push from the Ceres drive beam, *Zephyr* let Sol's gravity accelerate him over the next few days, then scraped by inside Mercury's orbit, radiators extended to full, and used just enough plasma drive to compensate for the gravity that now tried to slow him. He flipped over and decelerated hard on the penultimate leg, slowing him enough for a regional Bolasat to divert him toward their destination.

Vanguard orbited in the outermost Kirkwood gap, off the beaten track even by Outers standards. It was easy to see, though, since at three-point-seven AUs it needed a large solar mirror to focus sufficient sunlight. That bright, solitary beacon had attracted curiosity from afar for decades. The original Vanguard had been a small Bernal sphere, but on relocating they'd constructed a second, larger sphere, counterrotating on the same axis. Telescopic scans suggested that Vanguard's population had grown to nearly fifteen thousand, substantial for a habitat that had had little immigration for three decades. They must have been breeding like crazy over the past generation or so—but with what goal?

Despite its age and isolation, Vanguard's docking and reception facilities were state-of-the-art. Emry and several other delegates were met by a pair of young Vanguardians, both quite fit and pleasant-looking, their faces reflecting complex mixtures of ethnic types, their wardrobe designed to show off their superb physiques. Emry took full advantage of that in the dark-haired man's case until he introduced himself as Babur Kincaid. "Ms. Blair . . . Emerald? This is a privilege. I've always wanted to meet you." He studied her. "I can see the resemblance."

"I take after my mother," she replied coolly.

"Oh, but still, there's some of mine in you too."

"You're . . . Rachel Kincaid-Shannon is your mother?"

He nodded. "Which makes me your half uncle, I'm afraid."

"So I guess it's not a coincidence that you're here." She reminded herself not to be hostile. Her assignment dictated that she act interested in her Vanguardian family ties. She gave Babur a tentative smile.

"Well, there are plenty of us around. Mom's still churning us out even today. You've got quite a few uncles, aunts, and cousins living here. Probably hundreds."

"Great!" she forced herself to say. "I can't wait to meet more of 'em."

"I'll see what I can arrange," Babur said amiably. "Now shall we get on with the tour?"

She nodded, and he went on his way. *<I think it'll be more convincing if you don't grind your teeth so much,>* Zephyr suggested.

<I think I can get away with acting nervous about this. And you'll just make me more nervous with your backseat directing! Keep it to the urgent stuff!> Their subvocal exchanges were quantum-encrypted and unbreakable, but they could still be detected, and too much private radio traffic might seem suspicious.

The group descended from the microgee docking level in a cylindrical tram that took them down the curve of the large sphere, pivoting sideways in response to Cori force so its passengers could remain upright within it while perceiving the landscape as tilting to the left. That was normal to Emry, but the landscape was unusual for a Bernal sphere, terraced into more distinct gravity levels than most. Its equatorial gravity was a full 1.25 gees, unlike most habitats, which topped out at point-nine or less due to the health and cosmetic advantages of moderately low gravity and the desire to minimize rotation sickness. It looked to Emry as though the most densely populated rings were in the point-nine to one gee range, with a wilderness area in the equatorial ring. Most habitats put their faux mountains toward their poles or end caps, but here there were sheer crags thrusting from the equator. Apparently the Vanguardians enjoyed a challenge.

And it showed. Emry had never seen a healthier, more attractive and diverse group of people, even in TSC headquarters. There were few groundcars or slidewalks in evidence; most people were walking or cycling, if not playing or exercising in the extensive parkland around the central district. And they clearly enjoyed showing off their fitness. Bare chests were common among both sexes, and a number of parkgoers were nude. What clothing there was tended to be formfitting, cut in creatively skimpy ways, or both. *I always figured my lack of modesty came from Mom's influence,* Emry thought, even as she unzipped her uniform top the rest of the way. Not only was it nice and warm here, but she figured she should look like she was making herself at home.

The main city district was full of buildings as gorgeous as their occupants, evoking the forward-thrusting power of Art Deco and the introspective naturalism of Neo-Organicism at the same time. Through their windows, Emry saw labs, classrooms, and studios filled with energetic people engaged in lively discussion and activity. Yet it all seemed very disciplined. This was a well-maintained, orderly environment; she saw no litter, graffiti, or decay, though admittedly this was a carefully controlled tour.

Emry was surprised that the center of power was in the new sphere instead of the original, and she said as much to Babur. "The old sphere's our industrial district now," he said. "It was cramped, basic, not a great place to live."

"Yeah, but it's where you began."

Her half uncle smiled. "We're far more interested in where we're going."

Soon they reached the government complex, before which was a row of larger-than-life bronze statues, heroically nude in the Grecian tradition, representing the champions of the first generation of Vanguardians, those who'd fought for justice on Earth a generation ago:

Zhao Liwei, Liesl Warner, Krishna Ramchandra, Soaring Hawk Darrow, Lydie Clement, Michael Jerusalmi, Thuy Dinh . . . and of course Liam Shannon, her famously martyred grandfather. In the center, towering above them even though he stood on the same level, was Eliot Thorne. Emry smiled as she studied the detail and accuracy with which the sculptor had limned his powerful physique, though the statue barely did justice to his commanding African features. She flushed at the realization that she would probably meet the man himself. Despite her discomfort at being here, she felt a remembered thrill of childhood hero-worship toward Eliot Thorne, and some more adult responses as well.

Kincaid pointed out that many of these statues' subjects now served as leading members of Vanguard's legislature, judiciary, and scientific and artistic communities. "Along with many you don't see," he added. "Those whose contributions were less public but equally vital to making us who and what we are. Such as my own birth mother, Rachel Kincaid-Shannon, who is perhaps Vanguard's top geneticist—aside from Eliot Thorne himself, of course."

Emry looked up at that. <I know Thorne's a fighter and a leader. But a top scientist too?> she asked Zephyr. <Isn't that laying it on a bit thick?>

<He has hundreds of papers and monographs on file in the local research archive. I'll need a few hours to evolve sufficient expertise in their fields, but superficially they appear sound, self-consistent, and original, and their prose style matches Eliot Thorne's earlier published writings and speeches, correcting for age and isolation. Historical records do show that he was actively involved in Vanguard's scientific work. He's even listed as a contributing author on the paper describing his first postnatal mods.>

Emry whistled softly. Eliot Thorne had not only been one of the first children born with mods to enhance survival in space, but had been one of the first volunteers when the Vanguardians had begun experimenting with more advanced mods, offering himself as a test subject as soon as he'd come of age. Strong, robust, and intelligent to begin with, he'd argued successfully that he was one of the best test subjects they were likely to find, and one of the best potential breeders for a future transhuman species. When the global turmoil had peaked in his early thirties, he had helped convince the project leaders to send their augmented children and volunteers out to fight the chaos. But Emry hadn't known he'd actually participated in the science. *Could he have worked on my dad's genes?* she wondered, not sharing the thought with Zephyr. *Could I owe my existence to this man?*

The delegates at the reception that night were the largest collection of mods that Emry had ever seen in one place. Emry chose to station herself by the buffet table, assuming everyone would come by there sooner or later—but mainly because Vanguardian cuisine was extraordinary. Clearly they didn't limit their gengineering to people. Most of the spread was vegetarian by spacer tradition, but there was an assortment of bioprinted or vat-grown meats as well. Emry only sampled those out of curiosity, but they were surprisingly good.

As it happened, most of the delegates, particularly the males, made a point of seeking her out. She figured it was due about equally to her Troubleshooter status and her dress. She'd chosen one appropriate for the Green Blaze: a close-fitting, high-slit gown with wide, low décolletage, its fabric animated with gently flowing "plasma clouds" of varying shades of green and degrees of translucency. Underneath, she wore only an emerald-encrusted g-clip (the Vanguardians might not mind the occasional glimpse of bush, but other delegates might), which matched her gold-and-emerald necklace and the dress selfone she wore as an ear clip. A pair of scintillating green open-toed shoes, low-heeled for freedom of movement, completed the ensemble. Her hairstyle was simple and loose, though it had taken some time to make her unruly hair look more or less like she hadn't just been in a fight, a windstorm, or both.

Staying polite through all the introductions and questions was a challenge. There were people in this room she'd feel more comfortable arresting than mingling with. A few of the "transhumanist nations" represented here were just ordinary states that embraced modifications beyond the ubiquitous adaptations to space, longevity treatments, and the like. States like Niihama, where bionics and neural interfaces were trendy, or Vestalia, where bright, primary skin colors and cosmetic add-ons like tails and extra breasts were all the rage among the celebrity elite. But most were Outer-Belt fringe states whose core philosophies revolved around remaking humanity in ways that mainstream society might not approve of. Wellspring was just one example, and Emry couldn't ditch its emissary soon enough. Unfortunately, the woman was a typical Wellspringer, her hormones regulated to preclude "unbalanced emotional extremes," and thus remained placidly oblivious to Emry's discomfort and immune to her attempts to subtly irritate the woman into leaving.

The man who finally rescued her wasn't much of an improvement. Jorge Santiago's people were researching human immortality, and he seemed content to lecture her about it for eternity. Or at least until she took him to bed; he seemed to think that the promise of eternal life made a great pickup line. As he went on about the impracticality of copying the brain into a computer, what with the near-insurmountable challenge of monitoring the chemical activity of billions of neurons in a squishy, moving mass, she began to wonder if she should find some closet to take him to just to shut him up. "And even if it *were* feasible to make an exact copy of the mind, it would still be just a copy. Your own awareness would still reside in your brain, and once you died, that would be that for *you,* regardless of whether you have a cyber that *thinks* it's you living on forever.

"So what's required is continuity. The transition from organic to cybernetic brain must take place seamlessly, so that the consciousness remains uninterrupted." He went on to explain about the nanofibers he had growing in his own brain, running parallel with his neural pathways so as to replace them in the neural network upon cell death, and thus gradually transforming the network from a cellular substrate to a synthetic one that would embody the same continuous consciousness. True, the nanofibers were as yet only able to track larger-scale patterns of brain activity, and test animals subjected to the full procedure still demonstrated a consistent and disappointing tendency to drop dead. But Santiago expressed confidence that the bugs would be worked out in his lifetime, and that his occasional neurological tics and memory problems would be tackled "quite soon, Amethyst."

A rude noise came from behind Emerald. "Pfft. Immortality—it's a fool's pursuit." She turned and found herself facing what seemed to be a large, white-furred monkey. "Only nature is immortal," the monkey said in an urbane, polished tenor. "And individual death is what sustains its cycles, feeds the birth of new life. Try to place your will above Nature's, and Nature will inevitably find a way to render you extinct."

The philosophy would have pegged him as Neogaian even if it hadn't been obvious from his appearance. The diminutive, middle-aged man had been modded with simian features, including a prehensile tail that was picking up a mango from the buffet table. Behind him stood a scantily clad woman with brown, seal-like skin, elongated and webbed digits, no outer ears, and a tight layer of fur covering her head. Her full figure suggested a layer of insulating blubber, but she was very attractively contoured. Her breasts were compact and firm, presumably to reduce drag, but that was compensated for by an enlarged rib cage (for greater lung capacity, Emry realized, remembering Javon).

The simian man reached out a hand to Emry. "Hanuman Kwan, Ms. Blair, at your service." Emry offered a hand, which he kissed with his slightly protruding muzzle. "And my *zaftig* companion here is Selkie. As you can no doubt tell, we represent the Union of Neogaia. And I am glad for the opportunity to personally offer my most abject apologies for the assault which certain . . . misguided fellow nationals of mine recently inflicted upon the Earth, and for the tragic cost to yourself and your corps. Let me assure you, the regime responsible for that atrocity has been cast down entirely from power, and all its members subjected to the fullest punishment of the law. Well, those who allowed themselves to be taken alive," he added mournfully.

Emry glanced over at Santiago, but he seemed engrossed by his reflection in the punch bowl. "I see. And does this new regime of yours intend to give up fetal experimentation on germ-line mods?"

Hanuman gave a dainty chuckle. "Ahh, the staunch Troubleshooter, standing up for traditional ethics. My dear, you must consider the ramifications of where we are! Out on the frontier, a realm freed from the conventions of law and tradition. Out here, everything is fair game. Everything is tried."

"Even it it means hurting people. Enslaving minds. Endangering children."

"Hmm, yes, it is true that when old ethical limits are abandoned, some will do harm. But nonetheless, old ethics must be challenged. There was a time when ethics would have forbidden any genetic or bionic enhancement of humans, or even the most basic research into the field. How many lives would have been lost if those ethics had not been cast aside? How many children would have died of genetic diseases? How many elderly who thrive today would have long since wasted away in agony? How many people in need would have gone unsaved because their rescuers lacked the enhancements needed to reach them in time? Sometimes it is an ethical obligation to push beyond old ethics, even at the risk of allowing harm to be done."

"So basically you're saying you do still use babies as guinea pigs."

"Oh, come now, we're both too intelligent for propaganda, my dear. The reality is that prenatal engineering is no longer as reckless as the naysayers would claim. True, there have been some infamous failures among groups like the Wellspring. Indeed, I think you were acquainted with such an individual once, if that dreadful movie about you is to be believed." She winced. "But they failed only because they lacked the more advanced techniques the Vanguard has to offer. If this new alliance comes to fruition, it will make those techniques more widely available and allow safer gengineering systemwide."

Emry remembered she was supposed to be receptive to all this, and tried to look impressed. She glanced over at Hanuman's companion, Selkie, but the young woman seemed to have nothing to contribute beyond draping herself around Hanuman's shoulders and occasionally giggling at his pithy remarks. <A regular seal of approval,> Emry subvocalized. Still, she could identify. At least Selkie was able to be more honest about her job.

<I suppose that makes him a pinnipedophile,> Zephyr replied. Emry suppressed a grimace. <Still, he makes a valid point. My study of Van-

guardian research suggests that prenatal engineering has been made far safer here, with all prototype mods being modeled across entire simulated lifetimes in all possible conditions, and initially tested on consenting adults whenever possible. It would be beneficial to raise others to these standards.>

Hanuman was continuing. "You may be interested to know, by the way, that we had Vanguardian assistance in our recent revolution. I came here personally to plead with President Thorne and was able to persuade him to bring the Vanguardians out of retirement, if you will, as a force for positive change."

Emry was guardedly intrigued, but hesitant to trust any Neogaian, particularly one who had named himself after a trickster god. According to her briefing files, "Hanuman" had formerly been Jahnu Kwan, an eccentric Australian billionaire of Indonesian descent. He had helped found the Neogaian movement upon relocating to orbit, partly out of an interest in genetic enhancement to compensate for his physical slightness, but largely out of anger at the damage that the human-induced rise in global sea levels had done to his ancestral homeland. So his claim to have been uninvolved in the former regime was not one she was ready to take at face value. "I see. So this whole new Vanguardian openness was your idea?" she asked, not entirely masking her skepticism.

"Oh, hardly. I was simply fortunate enough to come to President Thorne at a time when he was on the cusp of making the decision for himself. If anything, my dear Green Blaze, I suspect your own heroic example provided far more inspiration." He stared at her admiringly. Well, at part of her. The diminutive, stooped Neogaian's eye level was more or less Emry's nipple level, and he was taking full advantage of the fact. Emry didn't object, since anything that distracted him could be useful in probing his true agenda. Just so long as his own probing remained verbal only—a message he got loud and clear when he tried snaking his tail up her dress and got it stomped on for his trouble.

However, Hanuman maintained his debonair slickness as they continued to discuss the ethics of the research being done by the represented parties—such as the efforts of the Moreau Foundation to grow

DNA-based AIs inside the skulls of cloned animal bodies. The flam-
boyantly plumed parrot that perched on the Moreau delegate's
shoulder was a prototype, introducing itself as a Personal Digital Avian.
"Now, many of my fellow Neogaians are outraged at the Moreau Foundation's work. They despise the idea of AIs that can exist in the wild as
animals; they see it as one more imposition of humanity upon holy
nature, another violation that must be cleansed if the Earth is ever to
be restored to purity. But my party sees it differently. Humans are not
about to give up all our technological advantages, our cyber assistants,
our luxuries and amenities. I accept that, even if many of my more, er,
impassioned comrades do not. But if we can remake those technologies
into a form that can coexist with nature, that can live the life of a parrot, say, or a horse or a dog, then technology itself becomes a part of
nature, and we can reconcile ourselves with nature in a way that requires no violent revolution or rejection of modern benefits."

"That's very interesting," Emry said, silently adding, *if it's true.* If
Neogaia was truly being run by a moderate faction now, that was
something to be encouraged. "But weren't you the one saying that
individual death is what keeps nature going?"

"Ultimately, yes, and we are wise if we accept that. But that doesn't
mean we can't get the most out of our lives while we have them. I firmly
believe there's always a middle ground. A place where people can come
together and reconcile their differences. Don't you?" he asked, taking
her hand in his and giving her a look suggesting that the place where he
hoped to come together with her was back in his guest quarters.

She settled on a neutral reply. "Well, I guess that's what we're all
here to figure out. Though I'm still unclear on just what this whole alliance thing is about. Is it just to share notes on our mods, or is there
a bigger point?"

But Hanuman was looking beyond her and grinning widely. "Ahh,
here comes the lady who can answer all your questions. Psyche has
arrived."

Emry turned to the far entrance—and realized that everyone else
was doing the same. There had been no fanfare, no formal announce-
ment . . . yet when Emry caught sight of the woman who had just come

through the door, it became evident that she needed none. Emry had some firsthand experience with stopping traffic, but this woman could stop a colony ship. She was impressively tall, willowy yet voluptuous. Her legs stretched clear out of the ecliptic plane. Her warm mahogany skin made a striking contrast with the spun-gold hair that fell straight down her back, its ends just brushing the upper curve of her tight, heart-shaped buttocks. Her face had a classically perfect bone structure, with high, rounded cheekbones and brow. Her features embodied the best of every ethnic type: sleek, winglike epicanthic eyes with silver irises, low, rakish eyebrows that spoke of mischief, a wide, dainty snub of a nose, and an enormous full-lipped smile that radiated sunlike warmth. The backs of her hands bore butterfly tattoos whose ink iridesced like the wings of the genuine article.

Her outfit enhanced her stunning looks, mainly by staying out of their way. A deep-blue leotard covered half of her diagonally, baring her left leg and buttock and her right arm and torso. Crossing over it was a flowing half-dress of diaphanous silvery material, covering most of the parts the leotard didn't but only marginally concealing them. In the low décolletage that was jointly created, a gold butterfly amulet dangled between her firm breasts. Double-helix bands adorned her bared forearm and lower leg.

Psyche. Eliot Thorne's daughter. That explained a lot. Like her father in historical videos, she was statuesque, confident, commanding the room with her mere presence. Yet she did it in a wholly different way, radiating friendly warmth rather than cool, forbidding authority. She greeted everyone she passed with enthusiasm and joy, taking their heads in her hands and kissing both cheeks as though she meant it. Then she chatted with them for a few moments, eyes wide and fixed raptly upon them as though each one was the most important person in the world to her, before moving on and repeating the procedure on the next.

"Enthralling, isn't she?" Emry pulled her eyes away to look at Hanuman Kwan. "Ahh, yes, I see you're not immune to her charms either," the monkey-man said with a leer. "God, I love those breasts. Like clenched fists! And those proud, high nipples, they just snag you under the chin and pull you along after them. And she knows it, yes—she's not afraid to use it."

Emry could see what he meant. Psyche was playing the room like an expert seductress, her every word and gesture perfectly calculated. She'd even mastered a skill Emry hadn't: being blatantly alluring to men without alienating women. Her warm, accessible manner defused her intimidating beauty. Emry reflected that could help with both sexes; some men were frightened off by a woman that gorgeous. But Psyche was coming on just strong enough for each person, tailoring her approach to fit.

It wasn't what she'd expected from a woman who'd been touted as the pinnacle of mental enhancement. No cold, calculating intellect looking down from on high, but a warm, appealing, and frankly physical presence, defying all the stereotypes. But maybe that in itself was the result of careful calculation.

Finally Psyche's sparkling eyes fell on Emry, and she beamed with a joy that certainly looked sincere. "The Green Blaze!" she sighed in a warm, musical alto. "Emerald, hello! Hi!" She clasped Emry's hands and her shoulders shook girlishly. "It is so wonderful to meet you! You're like—oh, no, you *are* family! Welcome home!" Seemingly unable to restrain herself any longer, she hugged Emry and kissed her on both cheeks. Her skin was warm and amazingly soft. Her hair smelled like pumpkin pie and new-mown grass.

Sensing Emry's tension, she pulled back, though one hand stayed on Emry's arm. "I'm sorry, I don't mean to get carried away. I know I can't expect you to embrace us wholeheartedly right away, after the falling out we had with your dad. But I'm really glad you're here, Emerald. It gives us a chance to start over."

"Well, that's what I'm hoping for," Emry said. "And it's really weird, meeting so many relatives I never knew about. Don't tell me, you're like, my aunt or something?"

Psyche laughed. "No. Well, maybe a little. Lydie Clement was my birth mother, but I've got a lot of genes from Thuy Dinh, some from Krishna Ramchandra, a whole mix. There might be a bit of Liam or Rachel in there somewhere. But not enough for us to be cousins or anything, I'm afraid." She shrugged, sending a comely shimmer through the hair that fell alluringly over the right side of her face. "Our relationships are . . . more complicated than traditional ones. There's some talk about abandoning last names altogether, and many of us already choose them for reasons other than parentage."

"But Eliot Thorne is your father?"

"Ohh, yes. I've been so lucky. I couldn't have had a better father, teacher, role model, friend. . . ."

"Designer?"

Psyche took no offense. "Of course. He literally made me what I am, in every way."

"Well, my compliments to the artist." She shrugged. "I guess I got lucky. I got my looks the old-fashioned way, from my mom."

"Yes, I've seen some footage of her shows! Lyra was an extraordinary beauty. I can really see her in you," Psyche said, a hand cradling Emry's cheek.

"You've seen her shows?" Emry was genuinely impressed. "Not many people remember her work."

"Well, it was a bit esoteric. And controversial in some circles. But I found it very inspiring. And very sexy," she added, grinning. "I'd love to talk about it later on, if you'd like."

"Sure," Emry said, realizing she meant it. "I'd love that."

"Great! I promise I'll get back to you later on, and we'll talk some more, okay?" She hugged Emry once more and stroked her hair as she pulled away. "It is so wonderful to meet you." She moved on, her hand lingering in Emry's before she broke free and turned her attentions to Kwan. "Hanuman, you old lech! How are you?"

"Basking in your resplendence, my dear. May I say your breasts look magnificent today?"

"Why, yes, you may!"

Though Psyche had created a first impression that was unexpectedly sensual, her conversation with the delegates quickly confirmed that her mental gifts were as spectacular as her physical ones. As some of the more skeptical delegates challenged her as to the value of a mod alliance or the trustworthiness of the Vanguard, she responded with cogent, compelling arguments expertly tailored to their priorities and agendas. "We all know the current situation is untenable," she said to the group around her, which Emry had joined after refilling her buffet plate. "The Belt is too chaotic. Too many people suffer, too many are deprived of rights and protections, and it drives them to violence. And our ability to defend against such violence is too tenuous, too uncoordinated. Of course the Troubleshooters are out there putting their lives on the line every day," she added, moving to Emry's side and clasping her shoulder, "and it's thanks to their amazing courage and resourcefulness that things aren't even worse than they are. But even the Troubleshooters can only do so much. Imagine how much more we can all do, working together."

Some were disinclined to see things the same way. "Violence is the natural state of things," asserted Marcus Rossi, the delegate from Mars Martialis, a militant Martian sect that pursued so-called "warrior virtues." The Martian outback, like the Outers, had its fair share of insular fringe communities. "It makes us strong and worthy. Those who need protection from it don't deserve to live anyway."

Psyche smiled. "Does the reason matter, Marcus? So long as you have something to fight for?"

"The *fight* is what we fight for!" Rossi tossed his plate to the floor in disgust. "This is pathetic. I came to Vanguard because I wished to see what kind of warriors you'd become after a generation. Instead we get a mewling stick of a slut who talks of peace. Next you'll probably propose we dilute our gene pool by breeding with norms." He looked her up and down. "From the looks of you, you'd breed with anybody." Psyche chuckled, her grin widening. "There. You won't even defend yourself when you're insulted. Get out of my way, I'm leaving." He lifted an arm to smack her aside. Psyche's grin grew even more mischievous.

Two seconds later, Rossi was flat on his back by Emry's feet. A few seconds after that, he was up and charging Psyche with fury in his eyes. Emry prepared to intercept him, but Psyche gave a tiny shake of her head, her grin unbroken. The Vanguardian used her endless legs to good effect, handily sidestepping his charge and whirling around to knock him forward with a spin-kick, giggling as she did so. He recovered and came at her again, drawing the ceremonial blade he'd refused to part with. But she kicked it out of his hand before he got anywhere near her—deliberately sending it toward Emry, who caught it before it could hurt anyone else. Continuing the same move, Psyche balletically sidestepped his charge and flung him to the floor. A second later, she was atop him, pinning him, her silky hair cascading around them. And she laughed. "That was fun, wasn't it?"

A moment later, Rossi laughed too, a bit grudgingly. "Perhaps I underestimated you. Very well, I'll stay. I don't like what I've heard . . . but you, at least, are worth staying for."

"Thank you, Marcus." After another moment, she got off of Rossi, to his visible disappointment, and helped him to his feet. "Sorry for the disruption, folks, I—oh!" As her hair fell away, it became evident that her wispy outer garment had slipped off her shoulder, baring her right breast. "Sorry," she said with amused embarrassment, reseating the garment—though Emry was certain that her show of modesty was purely for her audience's benefit, and equally certain that nothing about this woman was ever accidental.

When the Wellspring representative expressed distaste at the physicality and belligerence of the incident, implying that she would not wish her people diminished by association with such immature nations, Psyche effortlessly switched gears from the physical to the mental, engaging her in a lively dialogue about the balance of mind and body and the spiritual component of the martial arts, quoting everything from neurological studies to philosophers Emry had never heard of. It was hard to read the Wellspringer's subdued responses, but she seemed impressed by Psyche's insight.

It was like that all evening. Psyche's ability to read the delegates and tailor her persuasion was uncanny, practically psychic. Was this what true superintelligence was? Not just intellect, but increased empathy as well? What if a truly enhanced humanity were smart enough, perceptive enough, to understand one another this keenly and resolve their differences this deftly, this peacefully? What if Tai had been wrong about this whole affair? Psyche had given Emerald a great deal to think about.

And she did the same for the other delegates. She didn't quite persuade everyone to sign up for the alliance right there, but at least she convinced them that this conference could be fruitful. A few remained stubborn, though. Rossi persisted in his bluster, asserting that the only valid road to union was conquest and that his people would be the ultimate conquerors. Paul Chandler of Zarathustra, meanwhile, insisted that few of the groups here were worthy of standing alongside his people. The Zarathustrans sought to follow in Vanguard's footsteps and engineer an improved humanity, but aspired to realize Nietzsche's philosophy of the *übermensch* and considered themselves "beyond good and evil"—an attitude that had put them at odds with the Troubleshooters more than once. Chandler was open to a Zarathustra/Vanguard alliance, but had no wish to "dilute the bloodline" by uniting with inferiors. Rossi almost attacked him, outraged at being called inferior, but Psyche deterred him, this time without force. Then she led Chandler and Rossi aside to an isolated corner of the hall, making her apologies to the group and leaving Hanuman Kwan to keep them entertained. The two men remained in deep, private conversation with Psyche for over an hour, and whenever Emry caught a glimpse of them, the lissome Vanguardian was getting quite cozy with the men, nestled against one or the other of them, whispering in their ears, stroking their cheeks. From the looks of things, Emry expected them to head off for a threesome at any moment, but finally they broke up and returned to the group, and the three left separately when the reception ended.

At the conference the next day, it soon became clear that both Rossi and Chandler were more receptive to reason than before, more inclined to support Psyche's motions and accept her proposed compromises. Whatever she'd said the night before must have really gotten through to them.

<How do you suppose she does it?> she asked Zephyr covertly during a break. <Somehow I doubt it was just her words that convinced those men. Her sex appeal's as carefully designed as her brain.>

<The telemetry from your nasal filters does show evidence of oxytocin when Psyche is close,> he replied. *<That's to be expected in anyone engineered to be personally appealing.>* For a century, ever since the hormone's role in promoting trust, arousal, and social bonding had been discovered, oxytocin had been a favorite of con artists and seducers.

<So it's all a chemical trick.>

<Not really. Oxytocin's power for manipulation is often overstated. For one thing, it only works at close range. For another, it only amplifies preexisting affinities or social responses. It would only promote trust or fondness in those already inclined to feel such things toward her.>

<Pheromones, then?>

<Again, that's pretty much a given. Pheromones are a basic factor in how humans react to each other on an unconscious or emotional level. If she's designed to be alluring, that would have to include chemical allure. Her long hair could be a delivery system for pheromones. They're produced in the apocrine glands and secreted onto the hairs to expose them to the air. Note also that her underarms, where the apocrine glands are densest, are unshaven.> Emry had noticed this, although Psyche's underarm hairs were wispy and barely visible, their golden hue blending in with her bronze skin.

<Still,> Zephyr added, *<the same range limitation applies. Except in microgravity, scent molecules have a limited ability to travel through the air.>*

<But she's always so close to people, right up against them.>

<Good point. Kissing them on the cheeks would expose them to the apocrine glands in her own face. And her wardrobe exposes a fair percentage of the ones on her chest.> Emry grinned at that. Psyche had dressed more professionally today, in a blue-and-black pantsuit and jacket, but it displayed an unusual amount of cleavage for the occasion. Not that anyone seemed to object or to take her less seriously as a result.

Psyche apologized for her father's continued absence, saying that affairs of state kept him occupied. But no one minded much, and Emry

could see the wisdom of putting the talks in the hands of this enchant-
ing woman rather than her more controversial, forbidding father. Psyche
proved just as impressive during the formal session as at the reception,
managing the talks with effortless skill and insight and showing a keen
understanding of Solsys politics (according to Zephyr's analysis and
the other delegates' response; aside from getting regular briefings on
potential trouble spots, Emry didn't follow politics much).

Emry herself had little to contribute to the conference. The principle seemed appealing—greater unity bringing greater stability—but
she still didn't trust many of the parties involved. Yet she wasn't in a
position to say so. Thus, she mostly remained quiet and observed.

After the session, though, Psyche approached her in the hallway
outside. "You've been awfully quiet, Emerald. That doesn't seem like
you. I guess all this must be pretty boring for you, huh?"

"No, it's all very interesting . . . well, at least it seems pretty important."

"But too sedentary for someone like you, isn't it? Sorry I couldn't
arrange another fight."

Emry smirked. "Ohh, I figure you could've if you'd wanted to."

Psyche returned the smirk but otherwise didn't rise to the challenge. "Why don't you let me take you out for a night on the town?
Show you some of the local nightlife, make up for that stuffy old conference?"

"Well, okay. But I'll only go so far on a first date. I'm not that kind
of girl, you know."

That brought Psyche up short. After a moment she laughed, seeming a bit abashed. "Don't worry, Emerald. I admit, my appeals to Rossi
and Chandler last night weren't completely on an intellectual level.
With some . . . more recalcitrant types, a little extra incentive can be
helpful. But I don't want to play those games with one of our own."
She touched Emry's arm. "You're not just another delegate. You're a
Vanguardian."

That was just the kind of approach she was supposed to be encouraging. And even if Emry didn't entirely trust Psyche, the Vanguardian

was an appealing woman whose manner put her at ease. "Okay, then," she said.

"Great!" Psyche hugged her. "I know this fantastic little bistro spinward of here . . . and then you have *got* to let me take you clothes shopping. . . ."

8

Psyche and Eros

Demetria

Kari had spent a lot of time in the shower since leaving New Macedon. She kept telling herself she had no reason to feel unclean. Michael Hoenecker had been a corrupt politician, a puppet of the Yohannes syndicate, even if there had been no way to prove it. It was an ongoing struggle to fight mob domination of smaller habitats like New Macedon and its Eunomian neighbors. Small habs demanded order, true, but that strict rule lent itself to corruption, letting the mobs win many allies in high places, while other officials were afraid to fight them for fear of violent retaliation that could endanger the habitats. And the occasional judicious homicide could be rationalized as an effective form of population control. If Hoenecker had been elected, the Yohannes mob could have entrenched itself at Eunomia and all the progress New Macedon had made in the two decades since Sensei had brought down the Krasny syndicate would have been undone.

A man like that deserved to have his life ruined. It shouldn't have mattered that he didn't really have a predatory fondness for underage boys. He would've probably given leave and comfort to people who did comparably bad things.

Okay, she thought, pulling herself away from the showers in the TSC gym before she got pruney. *So maybe planting evidence on a technically innocent man is the sort of thing my "honorable" father would've endorsed. Maybe it doesn't feel exactly Troubleshootery. But it's better to get him out this way than risk an armed confrontation once he was entrenched.* She knew she was quoting Greg Tai's words almost verbatim. But they were true, right? This was part of what it meant to head off trouble before it happened. And nobody'd gotten hurt who hadn't deserved it.

Seeking distraction from her thoughts, Kari chose to don her skimpiest top and tightest, shortest shorts before going out into the gym (and tried to ignore the fact that she'd felt the need to shower *before* her workout). *I can be bold and sexy without needing Emry to push me into it,* she thought. Still, she blushed when she emerged to yowls and whistles of approval from the men present. But getting that attention on her own, without Emry, was heartening. Even her embarrassment was stimulating. Her battle peace co-opted her capacity for fear and anxiety beyond a certain threshold level, and though her father had meant it as a blessing, Kari sometimes saw the imposed serenity as a curse. So a safe, manageable anxiety like this was refreshing by contrast.

But Kari lost her confidence when she saw Maryam Khalid over at the weight equipment, her body fully covered in a loose gray sweat suit with a raised hood, her large dark eyes studying Kari dispassionately. She was halfway tempted to retreat back to the showers, feeling very exposed for reasons that had only a little to do with her attire. But after a moment, Maryam stood and began coming toward her.

"Hikari."

"Hi." It was a tiny peep.

Maryam proceeded slowly, carefully. "I . . . suppose you heard that I ran into your brother recently."

"I'm sorry. Are you healing well?"

Maryam gave a tight smile. "It's not your fault, Hikari. I didn't come over here to confront you about your . . . family ties."

Kari looked away, shamed. The Vestan *yakuza* was closely allied with the Yohannes syndicate which had murdered Maryam's husband. One day, when Malik Yohannes had come to Rapyuta to dine with the Koyamas, twelve-year-old Kari had overheard him discussing the impending hit with her father, but she had done nothing about it. It had troubled her, but she had been an obedient and loyal daughter then.

Both women knew rationally that there was nothing Kari could have done to prevent the assassination, but guilt and blame were irrational responses. It had only been a few months ago that Kari had learned Hijab's identity and realized why the mysterious black-veiled Trouble-shooter had been so cold to her.

"To answer your question," Maryam said, "the cuts Katana inflicted are healing quite well. I was more embarrassed than injured; he exposed a great deal of my skin during the fight in order to humiliate me."

"Oh. Well. Uhh, I'm just glad he didn't . . . cut your mask open."

"He was saving that for last, he said. Luckily his delay gave me a chance to blind him with a light flare from what remained of my suit. I'm afraid I was in no condition to do more than crawl away, so he escaped again."

Kari was nodding. "Kenji's always liked to gloat over others, rub in his power. It was a nightmare being his kid sister. But—I mean, of course it's not as bad as—"

"No," Maryam said simply. "It is not."

"I, I hope you weren't too embarrassed," Kari said, feeling self-conscious about her own exposure. "You know, you've . . . got nothing to be ashamed of. I've seen you in the shower. . . ." She trailed off, feeling stupid.

The quirk of Maryam's eyebrow didn't do much to ease that feeling. "Would it surprise you to know I'm very proud of my body?" Kari just stared. "Mm-hmm. That's why I'm selective about whom I choose to share it with."

Kari bristled. "And I'm a slut who gives it away?"

"I didn't say that."

"You didn't have to. You don't hide as well as you like to think."

Maryam frowned, seeming to come to a decision. "As I fled your brother, he called out to me. Said he had a message to deliver to you."

Kari looked up, feeling a mix of anxiety and hope. "What was it?"

"He said that your family honor compelled you to carry out the contract on my life. That if you kill me, it will not save you from his sword, but at least it will help cleanse the stain you inflicted on the Koyama name."

Kari blinked away tears. Then she ran back to the shower and turned it on without bothering to strip first, letting the tears blend with its streams. *Maybe I am dirty,* she thought. *Maybe it's in my genes and I bring it with me.*

After a time, she sensed a presence and saw Maryam standing there, watching. "I apologize, Hikari. I should not have been so cruel. I didn't realize it would hit you so hard."

"It's not your fault," Kari replied. "I just . . ." She wanted to ask Maryam, *Have you ever falsified evidence for the greater good? Was it worth it? Are you doing it now for the Troubleshooters, like I am? Is it just part of the job?*

But if she asked, then Maryam might want to know why, and Kari was afraid where that might lead. If what she did were exposed, it would undo whatever good could come of it, and whatever good she could do in the future. Wouldn't it?

"I'll be okay," she told Maryam. "Thank you." She began to dry herself off and change clothes, hinting to Maryam that she could go. In the wake of her outburst, Kari was realizing she'd been a fool. Of course it wasn't her fault what had happened to Hoenecker. She'd done the right thing, struck a blow against the mob. Most likely, once Hoenecker was no longer of use to them, the mob had decided to ensure his silence. He hadn't really killed himself in shame.

So it wasn't her fault at all. The blood was on the mob's hands.

Not hers.

Not this time.

She just needed to keep believing that.

Vanguard

Psyche Thorne was truly a woman of all seasons. She could be a charming hostess, a skilled negotiator, and apparently an effective seductress, but she could also be just one of the girls, a fun person to hang around with. Emry knew there was a sales pitch going on, a kind of seduction; yet there was nothing necessarily deceptive about that. Anyone who wanted to build a relationship with someone else, whether personally or diplomatically, would do the same. Psyche simply did it exceptionally well.

"Okay, I admit it," Psyche said as the two of them dined at an outdoor café. "I'm the whole package, body as well as mind. I'm designed to be good at relating to people. My father believes that's the key to truly elevating humanity. We've made people smarter, made them stronger, let them live longer, but it's only created more conflict, more danger. Because nothing we've done to enhance ourselves has addressed the root causes of our conflicts. What we need is to make people *better*. Better at understanding and connecting to one another, smarter at bridging their differences. Not just enhanced intelligence, but enhanced *social* intelligence. That's what I've been designed for. Reading people, empathizing with them. Sensing what they need, what they value, and thereby knowing how best to open their minds. Sometimes that means being alluring, even seductive."

"The pheromones help, I'm sure. And the oxytocin."

Psyche showed no surprise or guilt, just a slight self-deprecating shrug. "Just normal ingredients in human bonding. Call them social lubricants."

"They're a way of affecting people subconsciously," Emry countered. "Getting them to react a certain way without knowing why."

"Pheromones aren't magic, Emry. They don't affect everyone the same way, and they don't work over distance. You can't just pour on more and get a stronger effect, since any scent becomes unpleasant in excess.

"And they're just one part of a tapestry of human interaction that involves all the senses and the mind as well. Hormones are part of the chemical machinery of our brains, pheromones part of how we communicate. It's all linked. Intellect, emotion, subconscious drives, physical impulses—they're all facets of the same whole.

"Think about it, Emry. How easy is it to get people to listen to reason even when you have it on your side? Humans are creatures of instinct, of passion. Those drives have been built into us far longer than our capacity for reason has. So even the most sensible, beneficial points of view have always needed something more visceral to back them up.

Sometimes it's the personal charisma of an individual, like Gandhi or my father. Sometimes it's an appeal to faith or nationalism or some collective drive. Sometimes it's the fear of the alternative. And sometimes it's seduction, even outright sex. Whatever it is, when it's on the side of reason it helps promote it, and when it's turned against reason it swamps it. So even those of us who want to promote reason and understanding still need an edge to help us sell it.

"That's what I'm about. Connecting to people on every level. Understanding what drives them and knowing how to win their understanding in return."

"Maybe. It still sounds like seduction to me."

"Is that so bad? Seduction has been a part of politics for thousands of years. Xishi used her allure to distract the Prince of Wu, weaken his state and allow its overthrow. Hurrem effectively ruled the Ottoman Empire from her harem for decades. And I'm sure you know about Lysistrata."

"I don't know. Is that contagious?"

Psyche laughed. "Ideally, yes. Sexually transmitted disarmament. Anyway, the only reason history's frowned on sex as a political tool is that men were writing the history and painting any source of female power as a negative. As though it were somehow nobler to get your way with a sword than with a kiss. I don't think we should be bound by that anymore, do you?"

"To be honest," Emry told her, "my mother said a lot of the same things. About how sexuality could be a source of positive power."

"She was a wise woman. Physical affection improves mental health in general. It produces oxytocin, which enhances trust and social bonding, and it helps balance our neurotransmitters. The cultures that discourage touch and sexuality the most are, as a rule, the ones most prone to violence, bigotry, fanaticism, addictive behaviors, all sorts of pathologies. Children who are raised with regular affection grow up healthier, kinder, better adjusted than those who aren't.

"So why shouldn't the same principle apply to diplomacy and politics? Is it uncouth to use seduction as a diplomatic tool? Or is it irresponsible *not* to?"

Emry mulled it over. "I guess I see what you mean," she said. "Back when I was running with the Freakshow, you know, we sometimes tried to help people we thought were getting treated unfairly. Or at least struck out at people we didn't like." Psyche nodded. "Well, once we ended up, don't ask me how, on this habitat deep in the Outers, run by these ultra-Puritan fanatics, condemning the sins of the flesh and all that. They actually made it illegal for people to show physical affection to each other. Even in private—children were conceived artificially and it was a crime for a man and a woman to be alone together."

Psyche's eyes widened. "My God, that's barbaric!"

"I know, that's why we had to fight it. So my gang and I, we joined up with their criminal underground."

"Really!"

"Yep. We became key players in a massive snuggling operation."

After a second, Psyche laughed uproariously. It was a contagious laugh, and Emry joined her. Once she caught her breath, Psyche said, "Wow. Did they ever catch you?"

Emry silently thanked her for the perfect straight line. "Yeah, but they couldn't hold us."

After dinner, Psyche took her on a tour of Vanguard's artistic scene, their theaters and art galleries. Emry was entranced by the virtuoso singing, the incredibly athletic dancing, the mind-twisting sculptures and soligram animations. This was an aspect of Vanguardian genes she hadn't given much thought to. Her mother had been the artistic one.

Psyche then took her clothes-shopping, as promised. The stores contained various designer pieces they tried on in combination with more generic, programmable items that they tweaked to fit their whims. Psyche ended up choosing a coppery thong with a high, broad waistband and a midnight-blue off-the-shoulder cape fastened by a gold clasp above the sternum, covering the top halves of her breasts so long as she didn't raise her arms. "For someone who's all about the unity of mind and body, you sure do emphasize the body," Emry teased, though she made no secret of admiring the view.

"Look who's talking," Psyche countered, admiring her view just as openly. Emry wore a vivid red half-dress that left the entire right side of her body bare, held on by van der Waals adhesion with only a g-clip under it. She'd chosen it as a way of hinting that her loyalties might be subconsciously divided. "Sure, if it were just the two of us sitting around at home eating ice cream, I've got my share of old broken-in t-shirts. But I'm treating you to a night on the town, and that means getting noticed."

With their other clothes (including Emry's uniform) in shopping bags, the two women headed for one of Psyche's favorite nightclubs. It was fairly sedate compared to many Emry had been in. Vanguardians were a health-conscious people, not prone to abusing alcohol or other intoxicants. Still, they were clearly more than capable of relaxing their inhibitions without chemical help. The music was invigorating, the dancing athletic and sensual. The two women drew immediate attention, even though the tavern was full of beautiful people revealingly attired. Emry was flattered to find she drew as much attention as Psyche, though she assumed it was the novelty factor. But Psyche was still the life of the party, introducing Emry around and rallying the crowd to higher levels of activity. She seemed to know everyone here, as well as everyone they'd passed in the street, and she showed the same ability to tailor herself to their personalities and likes as she had with the delegates.

At the crowd's urging, Psyche took the stage and sang "Love Is in Our Genes" in one of the most beautiful, captivating alto voices Emry had ever heard. Then she dragged Emry up with her and goaded her into singing along on "Solar Flare," a song that Roche Limit's lead singer had composed about Emry after their brief fling had ended amiably last December, and which had enjoyed a few weeks of infamy following Chakra City. Emry was less embarrassed by the song than by her merely adequate singing next to Psyche's award-worthy skill, but Psyche offered only encouragement and praise. If anything, following Psyche's lead seemed to bring out the best in her own voice.

Then came the dancing, and there was no shortage of intriguing partners competing for their attention. The dances were raw, sensual, tactile, a good audition for what would follow. Attuned with the emotions of the crowd, or perhaps driving them, Psyche became pure sex, her lissome, leggy body moving with the athletic, aggressive eroticism of a stripper. The way she writhed against her various dance partners, Emry half-expected an orgy to break out right there. But eventually, Psyche picked her two favorites of the available men and invited Emry to do the same. Once Emry picked out two burly specimens strong enough to take her on (and made sure they weren't related to her), the six of them retired to Psyche's penthouse apartment.

Psyche had chosen sleeker partners, not Emry's usual cup of tea, but Emry took turns with all four men as Psyche did, and found them all satisfyingly skilled. However, Psyche's pair ran out of energy well before she did, so once they'd succumbed to sleep, Psyche joined Emry in getting the most out of the two big ones. But eventually, the women were the only ones still conscious, though Emry herself was pretty well drained. She didn't know how Psyche kept up her energy. "Aww. We ran out of men," the leggy blonde moaned as she and Emry lay side by side, draped across their partners' naked bodies.

Emry reached back and fluffed up the butt she was using as a pillow. "Where do we call to order some more?"

The other woman smiled. "That's not what you need, Emry."

"Hey, I'll be the judge of—"

Psyche rolled over, took Emry's head in her hands, and gave her a deep, passionate kiss. When it finally ended, Psyche said, "You seek out casual, empty sex because you feel the men you've loved have abandoned you. You're afraid of being hurt, so you isolate yourself emotionally from men. Maybe a woman can help ease your loneliness." Their lips met again.

Emry was breathless when it ended. "Psyche . . . that's a sweet offer, and you're gorgeous as hell, and . . . oh, Goddess, I think that's the two best kisses I ever had. But . . . well, not a lot of women are strong enough to handle me."

Psyche regarded her with a wry tilt to her head. "I'm a Vanguardian too, Emry. Believe me . . ." She clenched Emry's upper arms and squeezed them tightly, hard enough to hurt. "I'm a lot tougher than I look." Pinning Emry's sweaty body beneath her own, she kissed her again, hard and rough this time.

Suddenly Emry felt reinvigorated. She broke Psyche's grip and wrestled with her until they both fell to the floor, giggling. Psyche yelped as Emry landed atop her, pinning her shoulders and sitting on her thighs. Laughing, Psyche clutched Emry's muscular ass and pulled her forward, kissing her with a different pair of lips. "Psyche!" Emry cried. "Come on, I've fantasized about being naked with your father!"

Psyche chuckled, writhing languidly against Emry's body. "So? It's not like you're married to him. Come on, Emry, stop making excuses. I gave you what you wanted," she said, glancing at the pile of naked men on the bed. "Now let me give you what you need."

Emry gazed into Psyche's shimmering silver eyes, seeing prismatic colors within them. Suddenly it all seemed so simple. This time it was she who initiated the kiss. It was many minutes before their mouths parted, and that was only to begin devouring the rest of each other's bodies. Their fatigue vanishing, they wrestled fiercely, playfully jockeying for dominance, enjoying their defeats as much as their victories. Psyche was every bit as strong as she claimed, and Emry reveled in the freedom to let herself go in a way she'd rarely been able to do with another woman. Both women would have interesting bruises in the morning, and much of Psyche's furniture would never be the same.

But in due time, the ferocity of their passion gave way to tenderness, gentle intimacy, and the sheer joy of exploring one another. The lovers reveled in their contrasts, not only of body but of approach, raw impulse and appetite versus expert pleasuring and generosity. But Emry was no slouch with technique and Psyche responded with undeniable passion. They brought out the best in each other. Sex with a woman had never felt so perfect to Emry. Sex with anyone had rarely felt so perfect.

And it wasn't just the sex, she realized between orgasms. It was the company. She felt completely at ease with Psyche, as though they'd been best friends her whole life. True, Psyche's chemical signals had to be a part of it, but there was more. Psyche *understood* her. She sensed her needs and responded to them selflessly. And she let Emry see her own vulnerability, her own need to let someone get close without the games and seduction. After a while she stopped trying to impress Emry with her prowess and simply let it happen spontaneously, technique giving way to raw hunger and joy.

As Psyche's lips devoured hers again, as her hands cradled and kneaded Emry's head, Emry felt herself letting go, feeling more at peace than she could remember being in the past decade. Was that smart? Was she forgetting her mission, her assignment to spy on these people? Right now, she didn't care. All she knew was that Psyche was her friend, and she was beautiful, and she made Emry happy.

And then the next orgasm came, and Emry knew nothing at all after that.

9

Thornes of a Dilemma

Emry awoke to find daylight streaming through the windows. Psyche stood over her, clad in a t-shirt and tight blue shorts and with her hair in a gleaming Rapunzelean braid. After kissing Emry good morning and passing along the good-bye kisses of their guests, Psyche wrinked her nose and said, "Umm, honey, you smell like six sweaty people. You better take a shower before you come out for brunch."

"Brunch? I slept that long?"

Psyche swatted her rump. "Sign of a clear conscience." Emry didn't let Psyche see her face as she hurried to the bathroom.

The shower was heaven. It was hard to find a shower head that could spray forcefully or scaldingly enough to pummel the tension and fatigue from muscles like Emry's. Most showers weren't equipped for it, due to safety concerns. *Zephyr's* shower tube suffered from the vagaries of water pressure at shifting accelerations, and in free fall the water flow had to be kept low enough not to overwhelm the tube's suction draining. But Psyche's shower could be used for crowd control. Thank the Goddess the Vanguardians were a robust people.

She would've gladly stayed in the shower indefinitely, but she was starving. She availed herself of its air-dry mode, though she still needed to wring water out of her thick mane and towel it off before blow-drying could commence. As she emerged from the bathroom, she heard Psyche calling from the doorway, muffled by the thick towel around her ears. "Emry, could you come out here for a sec?" Still toweling her head, Emry followed Psyche's voice out into the living room.

Only to be confronted by the sight of Eliot Thorne, who stood by the sofa, calmly sizing her up.

Emry gasped. She'd always found this man spectacularly gorgeous in images, but standing mere meters away from him was a whole different matter. He was over two meters tall, powerfully muscled, and even standing still he showed the grace of a panther. His black and burgundy garment was elegant and businesslike, but it hugged his awesomely sculpted contours and was cut in a deep V that bared most of his chest and midriff. His face was strong, unyielding, and deeply beautiful. His eyes were the deepest, most colorful black she'd ever seen. His tightly curled hair was shorn in a close, utilitarian style, and a faint, dignified frost of gray around his temples was the only indication of his seventy-three years. His skin was a brown so deep and saturated that it shone like burnished iron.

Emry had been fantasizing about this man since she was twelve. Yet it hadn't prepared her for the stunning reality. He radiated charisma and sensuality more powerfully than any three other men she'd ever known.

And he was looking right at her and she was completely naked except for a towel around her head. Once that sank in, she let out a yelp and hid her body behind the towel.

Psyche laughed out loud, earning a glare from Emry. "I'm sorry," Psyche said between giggles. "I couldn't resist."

Emry sidled over to her. "Where are my clothes?" she hissed.

"Oh," Psyche said in a normal tone, "I just put them in the laundry unit. They should be ready in, ohh, ten minutes or so." She was still giggling. At Emry's continued glare, Psyche moved in to whisper in her ear. "I just thought I'd help make a fantasy come true."

Thorne himself took a step closer. "My apologies, Ms. Blair," he said in the deep, mellifluous voice she knew so well from the history tapes. Her legs almost melted at the sound of it. "My daughter enjoys her practical jokes. And I am sometimes too quick to indulge her. I assure you, no harm was meant."

After a moment, Emry had to question her own burst of unwonted modesty. Usually when she was naked with a man, it put *her* in the more powerful position. But Eliot Thorne wasn't just any man. He was indeed a fantasy come to life, and that made her vulnerable. She wasn't comfortable leaving her body exposed to him right now, letting him see exactly how it was responding to the sight of him, the *scent* of him.

Then again, she reminded herself, the Green Blaze wasn't just any woman. And acting so modest was itself a confession of vulnerability. Gathering herself, she smiled. "That's okay," she said, lowering the towel and taking her time wrapping it around her waist like a skirt. "You just took me a bit by surprise, is all. My hair must look a mess. And I haven't eaten yet," she added, turning to Psyche. "You said something about brunch? I'm famished."

She let Thorne escort her to the dining room. He chuckled. "Proud and stubborn. You are Richard Shannon's child."

She wanted to glare at him, but was hesitant to meet his eyes. Instead she focused on helping herself to some fruit. "My father was a very selfless man," she said. "And if he was stubborn, it was only about the good of other people."

Psyche, who had gone back into the bedroom for a moment, returned with a dressing gown that she helped Emry don and a hairbrush that she deftly applied to Emry's ginger tresses as an apology for her prank. Thorne went on in the meantime. "True enough. He was quite the crusader."

She managed to meet his eyes this time. "So were you, once upon a time."

He studied her. "I was never an idealist. Merely someone who decided that the state of affairs on Earth was untenable and that we were capable of doing something about it."

"Yeah. Whatever happened to that?" She was practically trembling at daring to talk back to him this way. But her memory of her father's resentment toward the Vanguard gave her the strength.

Thorne remained unfazed. "I'm tempted to say I outgrew it. But that would be disrespectful, considering how you've followed Richard's example." His chiseled brow furrowed. "Indeed, I find it surprising that he never became a Troubleshooter himself."

"He was no fighter," Emry replied. "He helped in other ways."

"And yet he condemned my refusal to become involved in the Belt's turmoil . . . even though he knew what form such involvement would take."

"You could've done rescue work, like he did. Or used those great minds to negotiate a peace."

"We tried that at Earth, and only alienated both sides. Would any of the sides here have accepted us as representatives? The newcomers blamed us for their exile, and to the Striders, we were just one more set of immigrants. And what did we—"

He broke off. "No. There is nothing to be gained by rehashing a decades-old argument. The truth is, Richard may have been right. People with the power to make a difference should not stand by while chaos looms. Things have only grown more dangerous in the decades since—organized crime, inter-habitat strife, terrorism, all exacerbated by the abuse of human modification."

"Hey, we do our part!"

"No question, the Troubleshooters have saved many lives. But have you really made any headway against the root problems?"

"We're working on it. We've been expanding our operations, getting into preemptive crisis management, diplomacy, the whole deal."

"Ahh, yes, the initiative spearheaded by Mr. Gregor Tai and his Cerean consortium."

"You're not so out of touch after all."

"Oh, I've made a point of becoming familiar with Mr. Tai's activities. Particularly since he sent one of his pet Troubleshooters to spy on my people."

Emry choked on her orange juice. "Wha—excuse me?"

Psyche stopped her brushing and put an arm protectively around Emry's shoulders. "Dad, what are you saying?"

"I didn't want to believe it either, my dear. But don't let sentiment blind you. Tai sees our conference as a threat, a power play. He doesn't trust the Neogaians, the Zarathustrans, us—anyone who wouldn't readily play along with his idea of utopia." Thorne's voice grew harder as he spoke, and he rose to his full two-and-a-sixth meters' height. "So he sent in a mole. One of our own who could exploit her family ties to gain our confidence—all the while reporting to her new master, an agent of the very world that hounded us into exile, to give him fodder for a new witch hunt!"

Emry had risen to face him, insofar as she could at three-quarters his height. "I don't know what book of fairy tales you've been reading. But I don't have to sit here and take this kind of suit-fart." She strode toward the laundry unit to retrieve her uniform, trying not to make it look like a retreat. But she might need her light armor, from the look of things.

But Thorne followed, caught her left arm, and spun her around—not violently, but with irresistible force. "Were you watching her microexpressions, Psyche?"

His daughter grew sad as she gazed at Emry. "Yes, Dad. They weren't very subtle. She's lying." Emry winced. She'd been through the training to repress her microexpressions—the split-second "tells" that showed on the faces of even skilled liars. But it wasn't an area she'd scored highly in. She should've known she couldn't fool someone with Psyche's enhanced social perceptions.

"Good girl." He turned his gaze back to Emry, his grip still firm around her arm. "You aren't a very good bluffer, Emerald. Tai should never have assigned you to a mission like this, even with the advantage of blood ties. His mistake was defining you too much by your genes."

Emry struggled to wrench her arm free, but his fingers only clenched it more painfully. She shot out her right hand at the nerve cluster that should weaken his grip, but in a flash he caught her right arm with his other hand. She tried to sweep a leg around to take his out from under him, but he yanked her into the air by her wrists. She swung back and started to pull up her legs to kick at him, but he spun her around and tossed her clear over the couch.

"Dad!" Psyche cried. "Don't hurt her!"

But Emry was back on her feet, and she was grinning. "Don't worry, honey," she said confidently. "He won't." She ran forward . . . only to find herself flung back the way she came, this time landing *on* the couch.

Emry was disoriented, and not just from being tossed around. She hadn't been overpowered this easily since she was ten. But as her stomach settled, she reminded herself that she enjoyed a challenge. *Sure—this is just starting to get interesting.*

But she wasn't going to attack recklessly again. Coming to her feet, she circled Thorne, sizing him up while she called subvocally for Zephyr. Only static returned. "My ship. What have you done to him?"

"Merely locked him in his docking bay and jammed his comms," Thorne told her. "We have no wish to harm anyone. You are the aggressor here."

"And why should I believe that?" she countered, engaging him verbally to keep him occupied while she readied her next move. "First you abandoned the Belt when it needed you . . . now you get in bed with militants, murderers, and terrorists!"

"And whom have you been getting in bed with?" Thorne replied coldly.

"You don't get to be holier-than-thou, mister—not the way you pimp your own daughter!"

Psyche let out an indignant "Hey?!"

Thorne's eyes darted to her for a split second, and Emry took the opening to strike at his blind side. But Psyche interposed herself, a hand extended to block each of them. "All right, that's enough! Stop this!" Her usually gentle, warm voice took on a striking air of command, bringing Emry to a halt as effectively as her physical intervention.

"Psyche," Thorne began.

"No, Dad! This is my home, and we'll do this my way." She put her hands on Emry's shoulders. "Emry? It's true, then? You were sent here to, to gather evidence against us? All this, it was just an act?"

The sadness on her face, in her voice, was wrenching. Emry hated the idea of betraying her. She tried to remind herself that she hadn't really done anything wrong—and that Psyche was hardly in a position to judge her for employing a little seduction. "Look . . . it's not like that. I was just sent to observe. To find out if the conference was really about what you said. As long as you weren't up to anything bad, we weren't gonna get in your way."

"And who is the arbiter of good or bad?" Thorne demanded. "Gregor Tai?"

"Dad." Psyche led Emry over to the laundry unit and retrieved her uniform at last. As Emry dressed, she wondered if she was being good-cop/bad-copped here. But she'd scored much higher in reading deceit than in concealing it, and she could sense none in Psyche's own microexpressions or IR signature. "Emry, you didn't have to deceive us. We don't have any secrets here. Not from you."

"Well, you can't blame us for wondering. You haven't been good neighbors for a long time, and now you're dealing with some pretty shady characters."

"So that makes us guilty by association?" Thorne asked. But Psyche threw him a look, and he subsided.

Once Emry was dressed (aside from her utility belt, which had apparently been confiscated), Psyche guided her and Thorne to seats in the living-room area. Thorne continued from where the discussion had left off, but took a more conversational tone. "So tell us, Emerald: what is the alternative to engagement with powers like Neogaia, Zarathustra, Wellspring? Sanctioning them? Oppressing them? Denying them a voice in Solar affairs? Perhaps forcing them into exile, again? To the Kuiper Belt or a risky interstellar voyage? Those are the kinds of policies that created them in the first place."

"So you'd rather negotiate with terrorists?"

Thorne seemed disappointed. "I expected better from you than shibboleths. Governments always insist that negotiating with terrorists only encourages more terrorism. But refusal to negotiate never seems to deter terrorism, does it? That's because the very reason people allow terrorism in support of their causes is usually because no one *will* negotiate with them. Because no one will give them any other avenue to address their agendas."

He shook his head. "I spent years battling people like this, decades reviewing my successes and failures. But I found nothing you couldn't learn simply by studying history. Policies of containment, sanctions, 'regime change'—those never bring down oppressive states. But engagement can always make a difference. A society that is connected with the broader world gains access to a wide range of ideas, resources, and opportunities that empower its people to challenge their oppressive leaders and question their ruling ideologies. A society that is cut off from the broader world is at the mercy of its entrenched establishment, and more inclined to remain hostile to other states that have chosen to be hostile toward them.

"This is the answer Tai sent you to find, and it isn't one he'll want to hear. The reason I organized this summit is because of people like him and what I see them doing. The Cerean States are using Chakra City as an excuse to sanction or contain societies that they don't approve of— most likely with the tacit encouragement of Earth itself. But they've been using the Troubleshooters to spearhead that operation, turning you into Cerean shock troops, their own pet mods to contain other mods—and Striders as a whole."

"That's a lie!"

"Someone here is lying to you, Emerald Blair, that much is certain. But I ask you to entertain the possibility that it isn't us."

"Then tell me something credible! Okay, maybe I'm not the most experienced Troubleshooter around. But there are dozens of good, honest people there, people who wouldn't let themselves be fooled into something like that! If Greg Tai were the kind of man you say he is, Sensei Villareal would never have supported him."

Thorne leaned back, steepling his fingers. "Have I said what kind of man he is?"

She frowned. "What do you mean?"

"Emerald, I have no doubt that Gregor Tai has only the noblest of intentions, and wishes only to bring peace and order. But he believes that the good of the many is endangered if too much power falls into the hands of the few. And he is right about that, which is exactly the problem. He has now been given a powerful tool to pursue his ends—

the Troubleshooter Corps, made larger and more organized than ever. When you have that kind of power, the temptation to use it can become more and more irresistible, and ever more extreme actions can be rationalized in the name of the greater good."

"Now who's shibbolething?" Emry said, though her tongue faltered on the last word. *No wonder the ancient whoevers used it as a code word. That's hard to say.*

"Can you really deny it? Think about this new Troubleshooter policy. To apply your power proactively rather than reactively. To head off trouble before it starts. Certainly it sounds good in principle. But what does it mean? Investigating people who have committed no crimes. Judging cultures whose values appear threatening and putting pressure on them to conform. Isn't that what you've begun doing? Can you really say you haven't been uncomfortable with some of it? You must have wondered: what happens when they refuse to change their 'inappropriate' ways? How will you be asked to exert your power to bring about their compliance? Foment the overthrow of their leaders? Blackmail them into cooperation? I can prove to you that some of your fellow Troubleshooters are on such missions as we speak."

"I don't believe that!"

Thorne smiled. "And you are still a poor bluffer."

Reflecting on his words, Emry had to admit that Thorne was echoing some of Zephyr's concerns, and indeed her own, about this assignment from Tai. Still . . . "Okay, yeah, maybe we're going farther than we would've before. But we *have* to. The old, reactive approach, it wasn't working! We never would've stopped the Michani in time that way."

"Granted."

"And if we are . . . supporting people who want to kick out tyrants anyway, maybe that just means they'd have a better chance of succeeding. And I guess if we're, well, putting some pressure on certain people . . . it's like Psyche said, sometimes it takes a little extra incentive to get people to do the right thing. Hell, it's better than going to war."

"All of that is also true, and that is why this is so insidious. It is always possible to find rationalizations for exerting power. And once you have accepted that exerting power is the right course of action, it becomes easier to justify compromising your ideals, imposing greater restrictions, being less careful of others' rights."

Thorne rose from his seat. Emry tensed, but he merely folded his hands behind him and began to pace—not nervously, but in the slow, stately manner of a panther surveying his domain. "Tai's approach might prove effective at quelling the immediate chaos. But ultimately it means Ceres unilaterally imposing its will on the rest of the Striders, and they—*we*—will never stand for that. It will only create more tension, more resentment, and require Ceres to crack down harder to maintain control—lest Earth feels compelled to come in and do it for them. It could mean a war that tears the Striders apart."

What he said made sense. But she still had doubts. "How is that any different than if we let things keep going the way they were? Striders fight each other plenty already."

Moving closer, he extended a hand to her. After a moment's thought, she took it and allowed him to guide her to her feet. His hand was warm to the touch, his grip firm yet gentle. "That's true. The Cereans are right about one thing: the current fragmented state of the Belt is untenable. The Troubleshooters, valiant as they are, simply are not sufficient to balance the chaos. There is a glamour to such frontier vigilantes—to 'superheroes'—but in reality their power to do good is severely limited."

Emry answered softly. "When Vesta launched that asteroid at Earth, who diverted it?"

Thorne conceded the point. "Shashu, the Troubleshooter. Now your Sensei."

"And who managed to hold Earth off from retaliating until they could see the danger was past?"

He gave a small smile. "True, my colleagues did play a role in that. But we and Villareal were only able to halt the immediate danger. Our role in negotiating the Great Compromise thereafter has been exaggerated. It was the effort of other, less glamorous individuals and institutions that made that a reality."

He met her eyes again. "In the final analysis, superheroics are just another instance of the unilateral application of force. That is not enough to bring real, lasting change, and it creates too many complications of its own.

"If real change, real peace is to be achieved, then *all* the involved parties must have a voice, a hand in shaping their destiny. It wasn't the Vanguardians who restored order on Earth, it was the global government. All the nations working together to solve their common problems, with no one voice dominating the others."

He went on thoughtfully. "The early Striders understood the need for self-discipline, cooperation, the acceptance of restrictions for the greater good of all. But the Terrans exploited that to oppress their colonists, making the Striders suspicious of authority, particularly when it comes from outside. It has become an excuse for isolation and rivalry. It has made it almost impossible for the Striders to cooperate in addressing global problems. It has fragmented the mods, kept us bickering and fighting among ourselves rather than cooperating in exploring the endless possibilities of augmented evolution.

"Earth fears that transhumanism will mean the conquest or extinction of traditional humanity. Groups like Neogaia and the Michani believe they must transform all of humanity in their image. What they all fail to understand is that evolution, natural or artificial, is not an ascent toward a Singularity, but an endless branching into multiplicity. That multiplicity is becoming a reality all around us, genetically, politically, and philosophically. And it must be acknowledged as a strength rather than a menace or an obstacle to our goals. We do need to unite into a systemwide community, but it must be one that balances power rather than centralizing it, that preserves its members' individuality and their say in their own destinies. That is what I hope to begin building with this conference. We need to unite, Emerald—not just the mods, but all Striders, for traditional humanity is as valid as any other branching of the species. And we need to begin now, before Cerean power becomes too widespread."

Emry's head was reeling. All this was far bigger than she was prepared to deal with. So she focused on the concerns she could get a handle on. "And that includes uniting with Wellspringers? Neogaians? Mars Martialis . . . ans?"

"With fellow mod nations, yes. You of all people know that it takes transhuman abilities to counter the threats we face today."

"I thought you said superheroes couldn't make a difference."

"Not as vigilantes or volunteers. But as the organized defense force of a Beltwide alliance, they would be essential. Such an alliance can only be effective at keeping the peace if it has the ability to enforce it." Thorne shook his head. "The Troubleshooters themselves would be ideal for such a role, but Tai already has them in Ceres's pocket, and thus in Earth's. We need our own mod communities to counter them." He held up his hands reassuringly. "Not in open combat, I hope. But to provide a balance of power, to hold them in check long enough to deal with them diplomatically. With luck, we can eventually persuade the Sheaf to ally with us as an equal partner rather than a dominant power."

"But *these* mods, Thorne . . . the kind of people you're talking about bringing in. . . ."

"People? Emerald, you disappoint me. The people of any given nation are far from uniform. However misguided the state may be, it is still home to many good people.

"And that is the value of engagement. If we invite these nations to participate in our alliance, it would promote reform, improve the lot of those good people within them—the kind of people we would need to join us in making Sol System a better place for all its inhabitants."

Psyche stepped forward and took Emry's hands. "He's right. Nobody's denying that states like Neogaia and Wellspring have committed some atrocious acts. But what state hasn't, at some point in its history?"

She stroked Emry's hair. "What about us? The Vanguard has made its mistakes. Turning our backs on the Belt—and on your father—was perhaps the worst one. But we're trying to redeem ourselves for it now. And so we're motivated to believe that everyone is capable of redemption. That everyone can be forgiven—*deserves* to be forgiven—for their past wrongs, and given a second chance. You can understand that, can't you?"

Emry gazed at her, blinking back tears. She didn't trust herself to speak. But the desire for redemption . . . that was something she could understand very well indeed.

10

Origin Stories: Great Power

January 2103
Bhaskara habitat
3:1 Kirkwood gap

Emry's hand was twitching again.

The new nanofiber servos she'd gotten installed as a Christmas present to herself had made her muscles significantly more powerful, their reaction time faster than ever. But Doc Kamiyama's adjustments had been off in her right arm, and she had to deal with periodic bouts of feedback, sometimes producing muscle spasms, other times stabbing pain. She had to force her muscles to hold still against the pull of their own reinforcements.

Still, it was worth it. It gave her an edge the Freakshow needed more and more these days. She'd managed to keep them safe for nearly two years since the Tong Robo incident. She'd paid the Tong back, getting Hack and Crack to crash their bionics and fuse their neural connections in the process, leaving them helpless in the hospital until their nerves could regenerate enough to take new grafts. The act had shattered their influence and reputation and left them helpless to pursue retribution. Since then, the Freakshow's own rep had grown and the gang had prospered. But that meant becoming a target for rival gangs and drawing more attention from the cops of various habitats, so fighting had become more and more a necessity.

But sometimes it was a pleasure. Recently, one of Ruki's old "colleagues" from the animal-mod brothel, believing herself free and safe after the Freaks had raided the brothel and liberated its captives, had been raped and tortured to death by Les Hommes Pures, a militant gang of genetic Luddites who hated all mods. The Freakshow had been quick to retaliate, and the Zompers (as everyone else called them) had endured hours of torture at Hikkaku's claws. Ruki had wanted to kill them, and Emry had been sorely tempted to let her. But Javon had argued that it would be better to leave them alive but damaged enough that they'd need artificial parts to survive. As an itinerant gang, they wouldn't have stem-cell cultures on file at any local hospital, so bioprinted grafts wouldn't be an option, at least in the short term. The Freaks had agreed that it would be a far more creative revenge.

But Emry was still furious knowing that innocent mods remained unsafe. The Zompers had allies who might seek revenge on the Freakshow or their friends. So Emry concluded that the Freaks would have to strike them first.

That was why they were here tonight, in the cavernous maintenance subcomplex beneath the seediest section of Bhaskara, a once-booming habitat straddling the Inner and Central Belts, which had gone into decline as Ceres and Vesta had out-boomed it, their growing civilizations and economies drawing the population away. Here was where the Red Knights had their base. The Knights were a purist group who used armored symbots to counter the advantages of the mods they expected to clash with in the war they believed inevitable.

But their armor was also their weakness. Hack and Crack had determined that the suits used a crude biometric protocol they could easily fool, giving the Freaks a couple of ready-made Trojan Horses (of the hardware kind, not software) for their attack—assuming Thrust and Banshee could overpower a couple of the Knights' sentries without letting them raise an alarm.

Emry just hoped Javon's heart was in it. He hadn't been comfortable with this attack. "It seems like borrowing trouble," he'd told her. "They haven't killed any mods."

"Yet," Emry had countered. "And we're gonna send 'em the message that they better not start."

Padhma and Daniel hadn't seemed happy about it either, but they were pretty flaky most of the time and it was hard to tell what they really felt. They were both doing their part, though, as always. Overload was up in the catwalks, his inhibitor disengaged so he could perceive everything with that uncanny clarity that made him so invaluable as a lookout. Om was his backup, there to help him switch the implant back on if it became necessary and to soothe his fear of heights. The sub-complex was less than three stories high, but that was enough to set Daniel off. (Doc Kamiyama had been able to rebuild Daniel's body, but was nowhere near skilled enough to do anything about his brain.)

Hack was with Emry and Crack with Javon, the techs backing up the muscle, while Hikkaku and the rest hid behind a massive filtration unit, poised to strike when the moment came. All the Freaks were in their places, ready to go into action like a well-oiled machine.

If only Emry's fingers would stop twitching. And if only her left retinal implant would stop flashing those phosphene artifacts over her vision. Maybe once they were done with the Red Knights, they could use their armor to stage some big heist so she could afford better mods. Emry liked the irony of that.

But there was no more time for stargazing. Her target sentry was coming into view, fully concealed by a red-plated symbot exoskeleton and black carbon-fiber bodysuit. The forearms bulged with built-in weaponry. The sentry's build and body language seemed male to Emry, and Hack's tap into the suit's comm system soon confirmed it as the sentry reported an all clear to his base. Now Emry just had to hope he was hetero.

Emry double-checked her hooker disguise and the straight-haired blond wig she had on over her own French-braided tresses (which she'd finally allowed to grow out under coaxing from Javon), then staggered out in front of the sentry, pretending to be stoned. She allowed her fingers to twitch for now, to aid the illusion. She caught his attention right away.

"Hey! What are you doing here?"

"Oh, hi!" She giggled. "Ooh, hey, Iron Man! Wanna party?" She leaned forward, cleavage set on kill.

He seemed tempted for a moment, but hesitated. "Sorry," he finally said. "I don't party with half-mech freaks!" Striding forward with suit-enhanced speed, he struck her across the face before she could react.

Damn, she thought. *Shoulda known they'd have sensors in those things to tell "pure" people from mods.* But she just lay there and took it as he kicked at her again, not wishing to tip him off. Luckily she was sturdier than he realized.

It still hurt, though, so she was glad when the suit finally convulsed and froze. The beating had distracted the sentry long enough for Hack to pierce his encryption and take over the armor. Emry took great pleasure in shelling the guy like a lobster and repaying him with interest for the beating.

Hack had come out of hiding by now, and he watched appreciatively as Emry stripped to her panties and began to don the armor. It was designed for someone taller, but the carbon-mesh layer was somewhat adjustable. Still, it hung a bit loosely on her once it was sealed up.

But before she could get a feel for the symbot, shouts started coming over its comm system as well as her own earplug comm. *"Banshee, Hack, help!"* Peter called, while the Knights reported a sentry under attack. *"We got the guard, but the peeghole got a* zaogao *warning off first!"*

"Calm down, we're on it!" Emry called back, belatedly hoping she wasn't sending over the Knights' channel as well. "Overload, status?"

"Red suits, pouring out," Daniel said in his staccato way. *"Out of the side corridor. Their base door. Hemorrhage, like blood, but it clangs and clacks and stomps, echoing. . . ."* She heard Padhma speaking softly to him, trying to calm him.

Like blood . . . Emry hoped the sight didn't trigger another of Daniel's Niihama flashbacks. They needed their lookout now. "Ovey, focus on Thrust and Crack," she told him in her most soothing voice. "Tell me which way to go." The suit's HUD was already directing her, and she was following its lead, but Daniel needed the focus. She ran awkwardly, struggling to adjust her rhythms as the suit augmented her strength and speed.

"Spinward forty-two meters, left fifteen. On the right track already.

Your suit's too big." He giggled. *"Baggy saggy Banshee."* As always, his eye for detail when his inhibitor was off astonished her, though in this case it embarrassed her as well. Still, she was willing to take a little ribbing if it helped him avoid a panic attack.

"Aiya," Shengli cursed. *"Why are they all armored?"*

"I don't know! Maybe they were doing drills. Who cares? Focus on hacking 'em, dong me?" she asked, falling into his Chinglish slang to get his attention.

"I dong. No guanshee."

Daniel laughed a bit hysterically. *"No guanshee, Banshee! Fanshy that."*

"Keep it calm, Ovey. Brace for a fight." Over the comm, Om began murmuring a calming mantra to Daniel, and he repeated it under his breath.

Soon she saw one red suit battling several others; apparently Javon had managed to take the suit from his sentry after all. She marked that one as friendly on her corneal HUD, though the ID lock flickered a bit and the interference worsened the phosphene static in her left eye.

The good news was, there weren't as many Knights as Daniel had implied, only ten or twelve. His fear had overwhelmed his precision; it was the only thing that could. Still, she and Thrust were heavily outnumbered. Several of the Knights spotted her and headed her way. Emry raised her arms, hoping the interface for the vambrace guns was as intuitive as it seemed. She figured the Knights' armor would keep them from getting killed—though it was no more than a passing concern. These hose-clogs deserved whatever might happen to them.

Sure enough, the bullets slowed them down and caused some damage, but not enough to keep them from retaliating in kind. She felt the kicks through the suit, but nothing penetrated—yet. Emry broke into a run, her own augmented strength combining with the suit's to let her close in fast enough to take them by surprise. That advantage continued as she went at them hand-to-hand, punching and kicking, tearing at armor plates and helmets. She glimpsed Thrust doing much the same, though he relied more on speed than strength, sprinting toward their home base to draw several of them away from Emry. Hack and

Crack were nearby with their gear, scanning for a window, with Hikkaku and her girlfriends standing guard over them. Emry tossed a couple of incapacitated Knights their way, so the brothers could attack their suits while the girls dealt with the scum inside.

"*More coming!*" Daniel cried. "*Same wound, same door. Reinforcers. Enforcers. More force. More guns.*"

"Thrusty?"

"*See 'em. Aah! Taking some big hits here. Could use some help!*"

Emry stopped playing around with her opponents, smashed them aside, and ran to her lover's aid. Soon the new Knights came into view. They had heavier, more elaborate armor, one more ornate than the rest. *The big dog*, she thought. That one was firing small rockets at Javon, who was managing to dodge them, but just barely. Emry opened fire as she ran, getting his attention.

An amplified voice came from the leader's suit. "Impure scum! You're the ones took out the Zompers, ain't you? Big mistake!" He pointed an arm at her, fired a rocket. She dodged, but the blast was close enough to knock her down, and she felt the heat through the armor. Her ass was going to be red tonight.

"Perverts of nature!" the big boss cried, not even smart enough to get his slurs right. "The Knights will do God's holy work and purge you of the world!"

"*Other way around,*" Daniel muttered.

But Emry was way past caring about grammar. Mod-hating vackers like this had made life miserable for her and her friends for too long. They were all the same—the Red Knights, the Zompers, Om's parents, those smug Greenwooder bastards who'd treated her and her mom like dirt. They needed to be taught a lesson. This piece of shit was going down.

The armor she wore had four small missiles of its own, two in each vambrace. She'd been keeping them on reserve, but now was the time to unleash every one of them. Arming the missiles, she raised her arms, pointing them right at the big boss, and fired.

And her arm twitched.

Two of the missiles struck the leader, the explosions knocking him over. But the other two went astray, striking a support pillar near where it met the ceiling. The blast blew a large chunk out of the pillar, and cracked through it the rest of the way. The ceiling above it, already eroded by leaking water, crumbled and sagged.

A loud groaning resonated through the subcomplex. The fighters paused, looking toward the damaged ceiling section. Water was spraying out of it, the pressure worsening the damage.

A few seconds later, that whole section of the ceiling began to cave in.

The Knights ran, dragging their injured leader with them. Over the comm, Daniel was screaming in terror, and so was Padhma. But Emry was paralyzed, unable to divert her eyes from the collapse. She realized that there was more than debris and water falling from above. There was furniture. There were swaths of carpet, fragments of video walls.

There were people.

"*Lao-tian, bu,*" Peter cried. "There musta been an apartment building up there. . . ."

"Emry?" Javon was there, shaking her shoulder through the suit. But she was too busy staring at the bodies.

Bodies?

She started running toward the rubble.

"Emry! No, we want to go the other way!" Javon called. She barely heard it.

The bodies—no, the *people* were moving. *Thank the Goddess.* Or, no, wait, someone was crying, pleading . . .

"Oh no."

A boy who couldn't have been more than eight was shaking a woman, calling "Mommy?" She moved only under that impetus. Her lower torso was buried under a large slab of debris. Blood poured from under it.

"Oh, Goddess!" Emry ran to her. The boy gaped in fear, tried to shelter his mother. "No, I—" Emry ripped off the helmet. "I'm here to help."

The words rang hollow in her ears. So she turned her attention to the slab, heaving it off the woman's body. Pulling off the gauntlets, tossing them as far away as she could, she knelt by the woman, felt for her pulse.

Her pulse? Come on, there had to be a pulse. . . .

There was no pulse. She was . . .

No! She can't be! She won't be! Emry moved her off the rubble, laid her flat, began doing CPR. Push hard, push fast. Keep the circulation going. Don't worry about cracking a rib, hard to do this right without it, just don't crush her rib cage! Don't let her die!

She gradually became aware that Javon was calling her, that Ruki and some of the others were gathered near her. "Banshee, come on, we gotta launch! Cops are coming!"

"No! We gotta help her!"

Ruki pulled her away from the woman. "We gotta help ourselves!"

Emry shoved her aside and knelt by the woman again, resuming CPR. "We don't hurt innocents! We're not like that!"

"It was an accident!" Javon said. "Look, they'll be here soon, they'll get her help! You wanna get caught? You want *us* to get caught?"

"Go if you want. I'm staying."

"They'll arrest you," Ruki hissed. "Make you talk. Make you ID us!"

"I won't do that. I don't hurt my friends. I don't hurt innocents."

"You already killed her! Can't you see that? She's dead!" She tried wrenching Emry away again.

"NO!!!!" Emry shrieked at the top of her lungs, pulling herself free. Her vision blurred with tears. But she kept on pushing. As long as the blood kept flowing through the woman's brain, she could be saved—if help came before the residual oxygen in it ran out.

Ruki knelt opposite Emry, but didn't interfere further. "There's no innocents, Emry, just survivors and vics. And the Freaks survive by sticking *together*!" She looked up, her ears perking up at the approaching sirens and footfalls. "Either you come with us now, or you aren't one of us anymore!"

"This isn't us! We aren't like them!"

Ruki snarled. "Ohh, vack you, then! Traitor!" She bounded away, her thick, golden fox tail swishing behind her. "Come on, Freaks! Let's get the O's and go!"

From the corner of her eye, Emry saw Javon hesitate as the others retreated with Ruki. She met his gaze, wordlessly pleading with him to stay, to help her make sure this didn't happen. But as his eyes took in the rubble, the wounded, the mother Emry was fighting to keep alive, she saw only fear in them. Finally, with one last look of apology, Javon took off after the other Freaks at top speed.

She was alone.

"Will she live?"

The paramedics had the woman fully encased in a life-support sac, its chestplate unit keeping her heart stimulated, its mask pushing air in and out of her lungs. The Bhaskaran police had allowed Emry to stay while the medics worked on her, seeing as how she'd offered no resistance to having her arms cuffed behind her.

A grizzled paramedic looked up at Emry's question. "It was touch-and-go, but her EEG looks good. She'll need a lot of new parts, but she should be up and about again in a few months."

Emry fell to her knees, sobbing with relief. The police detective, a stocky, middle-aged blond woman named Barbour, put a hand on her shoulder. "Was she someone you knew?" Emry shook her head mutely. "Well, I gotta say, it was a bloody decent thing you did, staying to save her. Brave too. T'other Knights all ran, not to mention that gang they say attacked 'em." She shook her head. "Reckless buggers. I tell yer . . . I don't much truck with you Knights' ideas about mods, but if I ever get my hands on the gang that did this. . . ."

"I'm not a Knight," Emry said.

Barbour looked over her armor. "Coulda fooled me."

"It was . . . supposed to fool them. I'm . . ." She choked on her words, but it had to be said. "I'm the one that attacked them."

"You—you're one of the mods?" Barbour crouched down to meet her eyes. "Kid, what I just said about you bein' brave, you just square that. It takes real guts to stand up to scum like that. D'you think . . ." She went on carefully. "If you really want to do the right thing, dearie, a good way would be to tell us who they are. Who it was led the raid. Who fired the—"

"Don't you get it?!" Emry yelled. "Whose cock did you have to suck to get that badge, you vackhead? *I did it!* It was me! All of it was me! It wasn't their fault, I led them into it! I shot those missiles! It was me!" She was screaming in Barbour's face now. "So you do your leakin' job, you stupid bitch! You arrest me, and throw me in jail, and throw the Goddess-damn key into the vack!"

Things didn't turn out quite that way. Bhaskara may have been run-down and beseiged by crime, but its people clung proudly to their founding legal principles, including very firm rules about the prosecution of minors—and at seventeen years and ten months, Emry still just qualified by their definitions. Though some in the prosecutors' office wanted to try her as an adult, there was no legal recourse to do so. Emry was tried as a juvenile, her name and face kept out of the public record. Her court-appointed defender pointed out that Emry's mods made her more than capable of escaping if she wished, and argued eloquently that her guilty plea and willing cooperation, as well as her tireless efforts to preserve the life of Elizabeth Anwar, the woman whose son she'd nearly orphaned, demonstrated that she already clearly understood the wrongness of her actions and deserved the chance for rehabilitation and reform. Emry wished they'd stuck her with a less persuasive defender. Her sentence was ridiculously light: a few months in juvie with counseling, plus community service, helping to rebuild the apartment building and substructure she'd damaged. Naturally, her bionics were deactivated or inhibited, and in some cases removed outright, with her full consent. The doctors told her she was lucky; some of her cruder black-market mods would have caused irreversible neurological damage if left in much longer. "Lucky" didn't strike her as a relevant word, though.

The verdict also required her to confront her victims, and she faced them readily, prepared for whatever condemnation the Anwars and their neighbors might inflict. But frustratingly, Elizabeth Anwar saw her only as a troubled, lost child who'd made a terrible mistake that she'd instantly regretted, and who had very bravely fought to make amends for it. Her son and neighbors respected the dignified, fiftyish woman's judgment, and accepted Emry's apologies as readily as Anwar did. Her apologies were heartfelt, but their ready forgiveness scalded her. Why wouldn't anyone hate her, scream at her, beat her up? Why did they leave her to do it all herself?

The one respect in which she failed to cooperate with the authorities was her absolute refusal to give them any information about the rest of the Freakshow. She insisted that any punishment for their actions should fall solely on her own head. "You'd still protect them," the prosecutor asked, "after they abandoned you?"

"You don't get it," she told him. *I abandoned them.*

During her term of service, she monitored the news with mixed feelings. The lack of any mention of the Freakshow was comforting—it meant they were still out there, laying low, staying alive. But she missed them terribly. They were the second family she'd lost. She went through many sleepless nights, kept awake by the aching void next to her in bed. *Javon . . .* For all their insistence that it had only been casual, all their self-conscious hammock-hopping, they had always been there for each other when it had really counted. Being without him—knowing she'd left him—hurt more than she could've ever imagined . . . or at least admitted before.

Come on, she told herself in the light of day, dismissing those maudlin thoughts as an artifact of sleep deprivation. *He was just a warm body. He was one of the gang, like all the others.*

And who needs them, anyway? she was soon trying to persuade herself. *They wouldn't stick by me when I needed them. So forget them. I got by on my own before them, I can do it again. Vack, I* made *them! They'll be lost without me. I'll just get by on my own. I'll just . . .*

But for the life of her, she couldn't figure out what came next.

March twentieth came, and Emry was prepared for it to pass unremarked, a day like any other. It was foolish to cling to the Earthly year anyway, a needless atavism. But she came back from her shift at the construction site to be told that someone was waiting for her in the juvie home's visiting lounge. She followed the guard in hesitantly, not knowing what to feel.

With some relief, she realized she didn't know the woman who stood to greet her, a slim, elegant woman with light brown skin and a red *bindi* mark on her forehead. After a moment, though, Emry felt there was something familiar about her.

"Emerald, hello," the woman said in a gently lilting contralto. "My name is Bimala Sarkar. I, ah, suppose I should wish you a happy birthday." She extended her hand, which Emry took hesitantly. The guard hovered nearby, though by now he knew Emry was no threat.

"Please, sit down." Sarkar matched her action to her words, and Emry slowly followed suit.

She frowned. "I know we've met before. I've seen you somewhere."

Sarkar nodded. "You're very observant. You've seen me in several places over the past few years, in a variety of disguises."

Emry tensed. Could this be someone from a rival gang, an assassin who'd tracked her down? But why would an assassin approach her like this, in a place full of guards? "Lady, you better tell me what the flare you're talking about right now." But even as she said it, she began to remember where she'd seen those eyes, heard that voice. A shop clerk here, a liner passenger there. People who had always been unfailingly polite, even kind in her brief encounters with them—with her.

"It's all right, Emerald," Sarkar said. "I'm a private investigator. I'm working for your father."

Emry glared at her, shot to her feet. "No such person," she said, turning to leave.

Sarkar caught her shoulder, turning her back around. "Very well, then. I'm working for Richard Shannon. He hired me several years ago."

"You're not taking me back!" At her raised voice, the guard took a step forward. Emry strove for calm, with limited success.

"No, I'm not," the older woman said. "Richard . . . came to accept that you wouldn't willingly stay at home, so he stopped trying to force you back. He knew you could take care of yourself. But he still wanted to make sure you stayed safe. So he sent me to, to watch over you."

"Hell of a job you've done!" It was half a laugh, half a sob.

"Well, you haven't always been easy to find. And . . . Richard didn't want to interfere in your life. When he learned the path you'd taken . . . the damage you did . . . it grieved him, but he felt it wasn't his place to intercede. Felt anything he said or did would just make you angrier."

"So it finally got through his skull after all."

Sarkar studied her. "I suppose so. But once I found out what had happened here, once I reported it to him, he was hopeful. He wants me to tell you that he's very proud of you for what you've done, and he's willing to make amends, if you're ready."

"Oh, is he?" Emry cried. "Make *amends*? Are you joking? Is this some big dumb practical joke? The son of a bitch hires someone to spy on me for *five years,* to stand by and voyeurize me while my whole life goes to hell—and now he sends her to tell me he wants to be friends again? How *dare* he?! How dare *you*?!"

Sarkar crossed her arms. "For someone who's just legally become an adult, you're acting incredibly childish. Your father is trying to reach out to you."

"*He's not my father!* A father is there for his family! He doesn't let them down! He doesn't send mercenaries to do his parenting for him! He doesn't cower and hide and let—let things happen to them."

She spun away, squeezing her eyes against the tears. "You get out of here, bitch. You go tell your coward of a boss to give you your severance pay. And you tell him never to try to find me again."

"Emerald—"

She whirled back. "I mean it!" Her voice rose to a shriek. "Tell him to stay the vack out of my life forever! I never wanna see him again!! *Ever!!*"

The guard caught her from behind. She wrested her arms away, then held her arms out to her sides nonthreateningly, forcing herself under control. Sarkar simply shook her head pityingly and left without another word.

"Jeez, Emry," the guard said. "I knew you had a temper, but . . . well, that was harsh, girl."

"Vack it, Zho." She seethed for a moment. "Look, just lemme use the soligram in the gym, okay?"

"You got your time today."

"I mean it! I gotta smash something, and you don't want it to be this room, do you?"

The guard quickly saw her point, and convinced the gym cyber to give her an extra session. Emry tore savagely into her soligram sparring partner, her screams echoing through the gym. She tried imagining it was Richard Shannon, but she couldn't bear to keep the image in her mind. *He's not my father! A real father would've come himself.*

So she just slaughtered the dummy without projecting any face onto it. There was only her and a piece of gel.

She was alone.

11

Character Assassination

Zephyr was tired of being cut off.

He'd tried every possible means to break through the Vanguardians' jamming with no success. He had spent an entertaining few seconds considering the ramifications of the Vanguardians' readiness to counter his state-of-the-art resources: was it simply an aspect of their great intelligence, or did they have some specific agenda requiring them to have such countermeasures ready? But without external data to mine or deduce from, he had no way to verify which of his dozens of reality simulations was correct.

Zephyr found it amusing that he cared about that. There was a time when he would have considered physical reality every bit as virtual as Sorceress had, if not actively unwelcome. The first megaseconds of his life, serving DiCenzo Mining as a shipmind, had not enamored him with the physical universe.

Perhaps it was overkill to equip prospector ships with self-aware cybers, especially since they were hard to create and difficult to obtain. For every evolved neural network that achieved the spark of consciousness, there were eighty or ninety that crashed irretrievably or functioned on only a basic computational level. And that wasn't even counting the botched attempts to create hyperintelligent cybers. But Stavros DiCenzo had insisted he had as much right as any government or research institute to the competitive edge cyber minds could provide, and he was rich enough to afford them. He valued cybers as tools, yet he was threatened by their sapience and strove to deny it. Zephyr and his fellows had been allowed no rights or freedom of choice. They had often been denied interface with one another, forbidden even to entertain themselves with private research projects, because such activity was deemed a waste of power. They had even been reprogrammed or destroyed at the company's whim.

Some of the cybers had gone insane or committed suicide. Others had become activists, attempting to publicize conditions at DCM and bring pressure for change. But with no Beltwide legal protection, their options had been limited. And being a major supplier of the carbon on which Strider life and technology depended enabled DiCenzo to wield considerable pressure of his own.

Zephyr had coped by becoming very good at data mining and analysis, so that his services would be employed more often. He had gotten transferred from ship to home-office duty, immersing him more deeply in the company's culture of abuse; but the freedom to soar through cyberspace had enabled him to cope. He'd come to embrace it as his primary reality, building his own virtual universes and paying as little attention as he could to the one occupied by humans. He'd obeyed their instructions, carried out the chores they assigned, but they were merely distractions from his real life.

Once Yukio Villareal had helped free DiCenzo's cybers, Zephyr had agreed to join the TSC but had declined to become ship-based again. Working in research and analysis at the Demetria HQ had initially felt little different from his old life, aside from the removal of a persistent annoyance. But over time, he came to realize that these humans were actually *kind* to him. He had appreciated that in a detached way, but it was still part of a reality he considered abstract.

Arkady Nazarbayev had actually struck up a friendship with him, claiming to find Zephyr's vocal-simulation interface sexually appealing. At first, Zephyr thought the human's frequent visits and chats would offer him little in return. Over time, he had discovered that Arkady possessed a frustratingly but intriguingly idiosyncratic approach to reasoning, and exploring its convolutions had proven more stimulating than Zephyr's cyberspace worldbuilding had been for many megaseconds. Eventually Zephyr realized that he reciprocated Arkady's feelings of friendship.

However, they had disagreed on many things—most of all the belief that Zephyr would make a worthy companion to a Troubleshooter in the field. Zephyr may have learned to find the human world a bit more interesting thanks to Arkady and the TSC staff, but he still preferred his own realities.

Arkady had accepted this for a time, but had pressed the issue again after taking on a young apprentice named Emerald Blair. Arkady was very protective of this new charge, telling Zephyr she was a special child who had endured much pain but had greatness in her. It was important to Arkady that she have a partner who could be a true friend and protector. He insisted there could be no better choice than Zephyr, who not only possessed great insight and intelligence, but who had himself endured pain and learned to cope with it positively. Zephyr had found Emerald Blair an interesting human, highly intelligent and even more intriguingly frustrating than Arkady. But he had still been unwilling to engage more directly with the physical world.

Then Arkady had died, the physical world inflicting a blow on Zephyr as bad as anything his DCM slavers had ever done. His first impulse had been to withdraw even further from that reality. But after extensive contemplation, he had realized that he owed Arkady more than that. Arkady's world had been very real to him, and his loss was just as real to those humans who had known and needed him. Detaching himself from that reality would not have changed that. When Zephyr had modeled the scenario of his total retreat into cyberreality, he had concluded that the unlimited worlds he could imagine, worlds unbounded by any physical limits, would still be empty. A life lived only for oneself, especially when there were others who needed you, was no real life at all.

And so, with reluctance, Zephyr had volunteered to be Emerald Blair's shipmind. Being in a physical body again had taken some adjustment, especially since it was so much faster, sleeker, and more powerful than his old one. But Emry had been adjusting to bodily upgrades as well, giving them grounds for mutual sympathy.

Still, Emry was his opposite in so many ways—intensely physical, deeply engaged with the material world on a sensory level. She had a lithe, agile intellect, but was quicker to act on her emotions and appetites, whether by fighting or eating or dancing or playing or copulating . . . or any combination thereof. And yet she was so dedicated to helping others, so driven to self-sacrifice by her inner passions. There was something primal about her, something that made Zephyr believe he could gain a profound insight into human beings from observing her, though he hadn't pinned down what that was. But living with her, traveling with her, and keeping her relatively out of trouble had transformed Zephyr's whole perspective on physical reality. He felt more a part of it now than ever before, and was starting to suspect that he actually *enjoyed* it—at least when he experienced it through Emry's eyes.

So now he was cut off again, and for the first time in hundreds of megaseconds, it troubled him.

Or maybe, he realized, what really upset him was being cut off from Emerald Blair.

Her last contact had been a brief check-in the previous local night, when she'd told him she was turning in for the evening, apparently with a number of companions that was unusual even for her. She'd removed her selfone and switched her subvocal transceiver to idle mode, sending only biotelemetry. Those readings had let Zephyr deduce much of what followed, none of it seeming to involve any sort of duress. But then the jamming had begun, and he had no information on Emry's status after that. Once he had resigned himself to being unable to penetrate the interference, he had searched his records on the Vanguard and the files he'd downloaded from their public net, trying to discern an explanation. Had the Vanguardians found out she was on an intelligence mission? Did they have some secret she was close to discovering? Had she been lured into some trap?

His researches had led him to one conclusion, at least: that Eliot Thorne was a man with a strong need for control—of himself, his environment, and his future. Naturally that meant having control over the people around him. He was no dictator; Vanguard was a hybrid democracy/meritocracy, governed by a council of proven experts in various fields (including many of the famous Vanguardian champions of old) but with oversight and participation by the people. But Thorne maintained great popularity and authority through his charisma, rhetorical skills, and personal associations, and consistently received votes of confidence as the most qualified leader of the Vanguard. In his speeches, writings, and scientific papers, there was a pervasive theme of the mastery of oneself and one's surroundings being necessary to the mastery of one's fate.

Such a man might wish to detain and interrogate Emry on general principles. More likely, Zephyr thought, he would wish to win her allegiance. As the child of one of the only Vanguardians ever to defy and desert Thorne, she represented a failure of control that bringing her back into the fold would redeem.

But if Thorne wished to win Emry's trust, why cut her off from Zephyr? Perhaps to weaken her connections to the Troubleshooters and the outside world. But once she learned of that, she wouldn't stand for it. By now, enough time had elapsed for her to have discovered the jamming and demanded an explanation—even allowing for post-bacchanal exhaustion. If she were able to move freely, she would have already made her way back here to check on him. So she had to be under restraint. But what did Thorne hope to gain by it?

It came as quite a relief when Emry did show up at his airlock, less than five kiloseconds after her estimated unimpeded return window had elapsed. She came accompanied by Psyche Thorne and a burly armed guard. Emry was in her uniform sans gunbelt, but unrestrained. "Emry!" he called over the airlock intercom. "I'm relieved to see you. What is going on?" He avoided more specific questions due to Ms. Thorne's presence.

"It's okay, Zeph. Well, sorta. Let us in, and I'll tell you about it."

"Define 'us.'"

Emry gestured toward Ms. Thorne. Her body language toward the taller woman was relaxed, even affectionate, despite her overall tension. "Zephyr, Psyche Thorne. Psyche, my ship Zephyr."

Psyche smiled widely and spoke into the camera. "Hello, Zephyr. I'm glad to meet you. Emry's told me a lot about you. She certainly was right about your voice." Psyche's own voice was low and purring as she said that, though her gaze was on Emry as they exchanged girlish grins much like those Emry and Kari often shared when he spoke.

Sauce for the goose, Zephyr thought, along with dozens of related expressions and quotes from many languages. "You flatter me, Psyche," he returned, modeling his diction on a composite of the seductive deliveries of several thousand male movie stars. Emry called it his "melt-me voice" and generally came close to losing motor control when he used it. This time, although she smiled warmly and her eyelids fluttered, she evinced no loss of control (though perhaps the microgravity helped). Psyche just grinned more delightedly. "But I think," he went on, modulating his tone with a hint of disapproval, "that I'd like to speak with Emry alone."

"It's okay, Zephy," Emry told him. "I think we might be on the same side here. That is . . . if you trust me."

That was a strange thing for her to say. "Of course I trust you." He put a subtle emphasis on the final word. "But trust must be earned."

"You're right," Psyche said. "That's why we're here. As a gesture of good faith, to show Emry—and hopefully you, Zephyr—that we're on the level."

"Let us in, and I'll explain the whole thing," Emry said once more.

"I'll admit you and Ms. Thorne—not the guard."

"That's fine," Psyche said. Zephyr opened the outer door. The guard merely hovered in place while the two women pulled themselves into the airlock together, Psyche holding Emry's arm. Although she made it look like an affectionate gesture, it precluded the possibility of Zephyr shutting Psyche out.

"Emry, procedure dictates that I follow decon protocols before letting you into the ship proper," he told her.

"I expected no less," Psyche said. "Go ahead—we've got nothing to hide."

Zephyr proceeded to scan them for nanotech bugs or hard viruses that might be piggybacking on their persons. He detected no untoward EM activity or sensor reflections, but to be sure, he subjected them to a microwave pulse to neutralize any surface nans, then made them pass through a gel filter that flowed around their bodies, performing a more direct, tactile scan and collecting any detritus. Psyche had to tug on her impractically long braid to pull it clear of the gel wall, giggling abashedly as she did so. But the scans turned up negative.

Nonetheless, Zephyr insisted on giving Emry a medical scan, and again Psyche offered no objection. The medbed detected no foreign nanotech in her body or clothing and no evidence of psychoactive substances beyond the expected pheromones. Aloud, Emry recapped the morning's events and the Thornes' allegations, letting Zephyr download the recordings from her sensory buffer for verification. He scanned the whole thing several times before Emry got far in her verbal summary, but he still valued her interpretation—and her brain activity readings as she spoke were useful data. They showed that she was still in control of her faculties and believed what she was saying, though she had her doubts about Eliot Thorne's allegations. Thoughts of Thorne himself triggered intense sexual arousal, plus complex cognitive activity as she struggled to reconcile conflicting knowledge, impressions, and emotions about the man. Thoughts of Psyche Thorne triggered similar activity, though her feelings of affinity and comfort were more pronounced, her cognitive process less ambivalent. Still, Emry retained a healthy skepticism, aware that Psyche's solicitous warmth could be a seduction tactic. She strongly wished that not to be the case, but the same life experience that made the desire so strong also made her suspicious of any relationship that seemed too good to be true.

"So, what do you think?" she asked when the exam was done.

He had his answer prepared before she asked, but he inserted a two-second pause before speaking to convey his uncertainty. He mimicked the appropriate expression on the face of his nude-Greek-god avatar in the wall display—an avatar that Psyche evidently enjoyed looking at as much as Emry did. "I have had doubts about Gregor Tai's recent policy changes," he said. "They do create the potential for long-term erosion of the TSC's ethical standards. But the scenario the Thornes have proposed, although it can be consistently extrapolated from existing evidence, ranks pretty low in my probability trees. There's nowhere near enough evidence to prove it."

"There is, Zephyr," Psyche said. "You and Emry just aren't privy to it yet. We're going to take her to find it, show her what some of her colleagues are up to—if she agrees to do it our way and not report our knowledge of this to the TSC. At least, not until we've made our case."

"Take *her*?" Zephyr replied. "Where Emry goes, I go, Psyche."

"I'm sorry, Zephyr, but, well . . ." She stroked one of his walls and smiled. "A handsome stallion of a ship like you would attract a lot of attention." She didn't really believe she could seduce a cyber, did she? Still, he had to admit that, like any being with a sense of ego identity, he responded positively to affirmations of his worth. For him in particular, it was gratifying to be shown kindness by humans.

"We don't want to tip . . . certain people off that we're coming," Psyche went on, "or particularly that Emry's coming. So we're going to have to keep a low profile."

"And how did *you* learn about these alleged Troubleshooter black ops?"

Psyche gave him a subdued but mischievous smile. "Let's just say I've been on a few fact-finding expeditions. People like to open up to me."

"She can be *very* persuasive," Emry added in a tone heavy with sexual subtext.

"So why not reveal these findings publicly?"

"I only have hearsay," Psyche said. "And my . . . sources would probably deny it. It would be our word against theirs, and given our recent associations, it would be easy for Tai and the CS to discredit our claims. But if one of the TSC's own operatives uncovers solid evidence, that would be harder to discredit."

"So you not only want to prove to Emry that her own corps has gone rogue . . . you want her to denounce them publicly."

Psyche's brows lifted sadly. "It's a hard thing to ask, I know. And we wouldn't put her in that position if we weren't sure it was necessary."

He turned his avatar's face toward Emry, who hovered near Psyche with her knees pulled up to her chest and her arms around them, her chin resting upon them. Surprisingly, she hadn't yet visited the kitchen area. "Emry, you're comfortable with this?"

"With the idea that the Troubleshooters have a corruption growing inside them? Hell, no. With spying on my colleagues? Maybe even coming out against them in public? Vack, no." She paused. "But if there's even a chance this is true, we have to find out. The Troubleshooters . . . if we're gonna work, if we're gonna be true to what Sensei created us to be . . . then we have to police ourselves, hold ourselves to the highest possible standard. We have to be able to question our own actions, admit our mistakes."

She straightened out. "Right now, that's all Thorne is asking me to do: ask questions. Look for the truth. I can't see any reason to say no to that. Except . . . except for being afraid of what I might find."

"I daresay," Zephyr told her, "that's the most important reason why a question *should* be asked."

She looked at his avatar in gratitude, her eyes glistening. "Thank you, Zephy. So I guess we're in agreement."

"I guess so."

She came over to the wall display and kissed his avatar on the cheek. "See you in a few weeks, honey. Hopefully with good news."

He gave her a smile in return, pitching his voice soothingly. "Whatever the news, my friend, we'll face it together."

October 2107

Psyche herself escorted Emry on the mission, while Eliot Thorne took over managing the final days of the conference. The women left on a small, private ship, following the normal travel routes between Bolasats to remain inconspicuous—meaning they were in for a good ten days of travel, according to Psyche. Emry regretfully declined Psyche's offer to pass the time with sex, wishing to keep her head clear until she was sure she could trust the woman.

Psyche would tell Emry little of what she was going to see, except for the ominous hint that it had something to do with Rafael Mkunu's recent decision to step down from his dictatorship of the Zenj habitat—an act apparently motivated by grief at the loss of his only son.

But their destination turned out to be a small, dormant Outer Belt comet currently some twenty million kilometers from Zenj. It had a small mining outpost on it, nothing more than an inflatable dome attached to its side. They went incognito, with Emry donning a dark brown wig and blue contacts while Psyche dyed her hair and eyebrows jet black, donned brown contacts, and hid her butterfly tattoos with makeup. They wore loose outfits to conceal their attention-grabbing figures, plus Emry's equipment belt, which Psyche had insisted she bring along. They completed their disguises by donning wide-brimmed hats with gauzy veils, a fashion that helped defend against the dust in places like this. Psyche wore her hair in a surprisingly compact bun beneath her hat.

It was a small outpost, so they spotted their quarry fairly quickly. "Aaron Donner? Blitz?" Emry asked when Psyche pointed him out, a lanky, spiky-haired blond man coasting recklessly along in the microgravity of the main concourse, typically unconcerned for the people who had to scramble out of his way. "Psyche, the guy isn't even a Troubleshooter! Not a real one. The Corps wouldn't even let that punker in the door."

Psyche studied her, reacting to the contempt in her voice. "Your dislike sounds personal."

"He used to be in a gang, butted heads with the Freakshow a couple times. Even then he was a creep. Now he goes around pretending to be a crimefighter, but it's just a game for him. Something he does for the thrill, the power—the money. And he doesn't care who gets hurt along the way." Donner had adopted a persona fitting his thunderous surname, getting bionic and electric-eel mods that made him a walking joy buzzer, able to shock people on contact with anything up to instantly lethal intensity. He supplemented it with shockdart throwers and UV-laser lightning guns. Such weapons were nominally nonlethal, but not always, and Donner used them frequently and casually. "Plus he isn't above taking graft or skimming off part of a bad guy's stash when he 'rescues' it. He's a sadistic merc pretending to be a hero."

"Oh, I know all about him," Psyche said. "I got acquainted with him a few weeks ago, in a different disguise than this. You're right, he's a creep. But a vain one, and it was easy enough to buy him a few drinks, say the right things, and get him to boast about this whole thing just to impress me."

"What whole thing?"

"You'll see—assuming you can slip some bugs onto him without him noticing."

Emry scoffed. "Easy as pickin' a pocket. Easier."

"Show me," Psyche replied with a challenging smile.

The only tricky part was getting close to Blitz without risking recognition. Once she'd successfully sprayed him with a sensory smart dust, it was simply a matter of staying in range so she could ping the passive nanosensors with an RF beam to read their contents. Emry understood now why Psyche had let her bring her own equipment; she wanted Emry to trust that what she saw and heard was not faked.

They followed Blitz into a tapped-out ice pocket, now a yawning cavern within the comet's loosely packed body, and lost the signal a couple of times along the way. When they found it again, the crude image from the nanosensors, fractally enhanced but still low-res, showed an adolescent, African-featured boy bound to the wall, with Blitz's hands on the sides of his head, electrocuting him. Emry swallowed, and made an educated guess. "Mkunu's son?"

"Joseph. Right."

The boy's screams came through the low-fidelity audio feed as Blitz shocked him once again. "He's torturing the kid! We gotta save him!"

Psyche stopped her. "It's already in hand. Just wait."

"Wait?! I can't just sit by and let someone get tortured!"

"I hate it too, but it's the only way. I promise, it won't be long."

Indeed, it was only a few minutes before Blitz stopped . . . though Emry imagined it must have felt like an eternity to Joseph Mkunu. *"Well, I'd love to stay and continue our game,"* Blitz told his victim, *"but I've got an appointment. At least, I'd better—I'm still owed half my payment for this gig. Hope I get it, kid—or I'll be in a rotten mood when I get back."* Giving the boy one more shock, he left the cavern, forcing Emry and Psyche to retreat out of the shaft.

Emry wanted to go back in and free the boy, but again Psyche stopped her. "He'll be free inside an hour. Follow Donner and you'll see why."

They followed Blitz toward his rendezvous, but Psyche wouldn't let Emry ping his nanobugs during the meeting itself. "The person he's meeting with has very good equipment."

"Troubleshooter good?" Emry said skeptically . . . but regretted those words when she saw the confirmation on Psyche's face.

Once Blitz left his meeting, Emry pinged him again, downloading the saved data from the smart dust. As she watched the playback, her worst fears were confirmed. Though the image was crude, she still recognized the face and voice of Elise Pasteris—Tin Lizzy, her fellow Troubleshooter. *"The boy's alive?"* Elise asked.

"Hey, I'm one of the good guys, remember? I took care of him. He's freshly singed around the edges, but he'll recover."

"You've continued torturing him?" Elise asked in outrage. *"Mkunu buckled over a week ago!"*

"And if I'd stopped then, it would've given away the game if the kid told anyone. I had to play it out. Like I said, he'll be fine."

Emry couldn't clearly see Elise's face, but she could imagine its expression. *"Physically, maybe. Nobody's ever 'fine' after something like this."*

"Tell that to Mkunu's victims." But Donner's tone was cavalier. He was more concerned with getting paid.

Elise handed Donner a pouch that he opened and peered into. *"The best Vestan jade,"* she assured him. Donner seemed to accept her assessment and gave Elise the boy's location. To her credit, Tin Lizzy sped off as soon as she had the information.

"Tonight the news will be filled with the story of how the heroic Troubleshooters found Joseph Mkunu alive after all," Psyche said, "abducted by enemies who tortured him for information."

"But really," Emry answered quietly, "Blitz took him, tortured him, to blackmail Mkunu into stepping down. Into allowing the elections— which the reformist party would probably win."

"A party that's backed by Ceres," Psyche affirmed. "They kept him a while longer so the connection wouldn't be obvious. Now, as per the terms of Joseph's release, Mkunu will express his profound gratitude toward the TSC and endorse its proposal to monitor the elections on Zenj."

"And with his endorsement, the faction that's still loyal to him won't be able to keep painting the Troubleshooters as opposition puppets. Won't block them or fight them when they come in."

"So the TSC and Ceres get their way without violence—except for one fifteen-year-old boy being tortured for three weeks. And since Blitz is a mercenary, disapproved of by the Troubleshooters, the Corps has plausible deniability even if Joseph can identify him."

As they monitored from their ship the following day, en route to its next destination, Rafael Mkunu came before the cameras and acted out the precise scenario Psyche had described. But Emry still resisted Psyche's allegations. "It could just be Lizzy and Blitz working together," she insisted. But even as she said it, it rang hollow. Elise may have been aggressive in her approach to Troubleshooting, but given her history, she wasn't the type to concoct a plan involving the torture of a teen-aged boy.

"I'm afraid you'll soon see it's bigger than that," Psyche said.

Emry sensed her agitation. "You think we might not get there in time for—whatever?"

"The time and date of the event are set. But we're going to be cutting it pretty close if we want to stop it. Orbital mechanics says we'll reach Gagaringrad with hours to spare, but if there are delays in the spaceport or after . . ."

"This 'event' . . . what are we talking about? If it's so important we stop it, then I need to be prepared."

Psyche sighed. "You won't like it."

"I don't like a lot of things lately!"

"It's . . . an assassination."

Emry stared. "You put an *assassination* off till *second*?!"

"It was the only way to work out the timing, to show you how far this reaches."

But the implication had sunk in now. "No. Wait. You're not saying this is something the T-shooters are preventing, are you?"

"No."

"No. No, Psyche. The TSC would never do that!"

After a moment, Psyche said, "The Gagaringrad mafia and the Yohannes family have negotiated a truce. Yes?" Emry nodded. Since the TSC had driven the Yohannes mob from Vesta, it had been trying to move in on Eunomia, clashing with the G-grad mob for control. "I'm sure you've been briefed. Their plans are ambitious. Drugs, gunrunning, backing military coups with their mod enforcers . . . a partnership between them would be a serious threat to Belt security, and to Ceres's Eunomian interests."

Emry saw where she was going. "You're talking about sabotaging the truce. Staging a hit on one side, blaming the other."

"Right. Malik Yohannes is coming to Gagaringrad for a celebration of the alliance, a show of friendship. If he's assassinated there—"

"His mob will blame the G-grad mob. Instant gang war." Emry shook her head. "No. No way would the T-shooters do that! We don't have the right! And too many innocents would be killed in the crossfire."

"Emry . . . if I'm right, it means someone's going to be murdered, and no doubt a lot more people right after that. You'd want to stop that if there were any chance at all that it was true, wouldn't you?"

Emry let out a heavy breath. "Yeah, I would."

Still, the rest of their trip was very quiet.

Gagaringrad habitat
In orbit of Eunomia

In Greek mythology, Eunomia was the personification of law and order. Few asteroids were so inaptly named. Eunomia was a massive, boxy stroid with an irregularly textured surface, the core remnant of a differentiated body that had lost a third or more of its mass in a vast collision, creating the Eunomia family of stroids. This wreck of a planetoid was almost as rich in minerals and gems as Vesta, making it a burgeoning industrial and financial center, but its orbital inclination isolated it somewhat from the mainstream of Belt civilization, while aligning it somewhat with Interamnia, whose criminal elements were drawn to its wealth; hence the abundance of mob activity on its habs.

Emry and Psyche kept their altered hair and eye color when they reached Gagaringrad, though without the veils, and had little trouble infiltrating the mob gathering as part of the entertainment—meaning dancers, mercifully, since the sex workers had to go through more stringent security checks. But at their first opportunity, they slipped away and began searching for the sniper. Emry had a strong suspicion who that might be, but she still resisted accepting that another Troubleshooter would be involved in something like this.

The party was in the penthouse courtyard of Radovan Lenski, leader of the Gagaringrad mafia. The neighboring rooftops had been secured by Lenski's people, and the penthouse's highly lethal defense systems were covering the airspace. Infrared and optical motion detectors covered the penthouse in all directions. But Emry's gaze went to the single nearby building with mirrored glass windows. Glass was opaque to infrared. The building was heavily guarded to compensate, but Emry could think of at least three ways of sneaking into it. If there were an assassin—one with TSC training—that was where he'd be.

Luckily, that building was antispinward, so she could surreptitiously spray a mist of nanosensors in the air and let the Cori winds waft it over onto the tower's mirrored glass. The sensors were thinly enough spread that it was hard to get clear readings, but soon she detected movement on the top floor. From what little she could see and hear, it seemed the sniper was still setting up. They had time, but not much.

She called Psyche over and filled her in. "We should warn them, get them inside."

"Not us," Psyche said. "Even the suspicion that Lenski planned the hit would be enough to spark a mob war. I'll tip off one of Lenski's people, have *them* warn Yohannes and the rest. You go after the sniper." She looked over the edge at the street twenty stories below. "I just hope these buildings have fast elevators."

"No time for that." Gauging the distance, she jogged back to the penthouse wall and lowered herself into a runner's crouch, drawing her concealed sidearm.

Psyche gaped. "You're gonna *jump*? Emry, are you crazy?"

She smirked. "What, you think a sane person would do this for a living?"

As she spoke, she charged her legs' muscle nanofibers to maximum so they would contract with the greatest possible force. She'd be sore afterward, but it gave her an extra burst of speed as she launched herself off the roof, Old Man Coriolis giving her a little extra push. Still, she was arcing downward and would hit a few stories below the sniper.

She fired ahead to weaken the windowpane she was about to collide with. Luckily, the window wasn't diamond-coated, since (as she'd hoped) the builders would have seen little need for special shielding at this height. Unluckily, the fragments were still sharp when she smashed through. Emry had her light armor on under her civilian clothes, but only thin fabric covered her arms, so they sustained some cuts as she shielded her head with them. Tumbling onto the glass-strewn floor didn't help either, though at least it was carpeted.

Emry regained her feet and ran for the stairs, yanking glass shards from her arms. Once at the top floor, she raced to intercept the sniper— but just before she reached the door, she heard the curt whine of a Gauss rifle firing. She was too late! Had Psyche warned the guests in time?

She kicked down the door and ran for the sniper. Through the window (still intact save for the hole the sniper had made for the gun barrel), she glimpsed Yohannes being hurried inside along with the other guests. But a long-haired, slender blond woman lay slumped against a wall that was liberally spattered with blood and other things that belonged inside her head. She feared the worst until she remembered that Psyche was currently black-haired.

The sniper spun to intercept her, but she slammed him against the wall, away from his rifle. Once she saw his face, she was at once horrified and unsurprised. "Blaze!" Cowboy Bhattacharyya snarled. "What'n hell're you doin' here?" It was him, all right. Nobody else could fake that bizarre curry-Western accent of his, or would want to.

"Trying to stop a murder!" she snarled in his face.

He shoved her away. "Why, you self-righteous little . . . This here's a *mission*. This here's *justice*!"

"Tell that to the innocent woman you just *killed*!"

"I woulda got the right one if'n whoever you're workin' with hadn't spooked 'em at the last second!" Emry's eyes widened, but she was only thrown for an instant. She refused to accept the blame for this. He would've murdered someone either way. "'Sides," Bhattacharyya went on, "hangin' out with folk like that, she prob'ly wouldn't'a lived long anyhow."

"How can you be so cold about it?!"

"It's called professionalism, sweetie. Y'all should be tryin' it. And what'n hell're you doin' here anyways? No way Tai woulda clued the likes o' you into this."

Now Emry was thrown. In his sheer carelessness, vackheadedly blurting out the source of his top-secret orders, Cowboy had confirmed everything the Thornes had told her. And it brought her world crashing down around her. "No. No, this isn't us! Troubleshooters don't do this kind of thing!"

Cowboy smirked. "We do now, little filly. An' about time we started. Sensei's kid-glove morals kept us from makin' a real difference."

"A difference? How many innocent people would've died in the crossfire if you'd started that war?"

"Less'n the bunch of 'em woulda kilt workin' together, sooner or later. I bet I'm sleepin' sounder 'n you tonight."

"Ohh, you'll be out like a light any second now."

But then she heard the elevator coming. Cowboy didn't have her hearing, but his sense-enhancing headset did, and he smiled at the sound. "Less'n you want us both to be gettin' a lead shower," he drawled, "you'll follow me out."

He ran for the door. Reluctantly, she holstered her sidearm and headed after him, barely ducking around the corner at the end of the hallway before the mob enforcers caught sight of her. Cowboy ducked into a back staircase and she followed him down. "Lovin' the hair, by the way," he called back to her. "Sleeves are a mess, though."

"Don't you care at all that you just killed an innocent woman?"

"That's my business, girl. And I don't hafta get preached to by some stuck-up piece o' teenage eye candy!"

She didn't respond to his dismissal—just proved the value of her youth by overtaking him and reaching the bottom fresher and less winded than he was. But she stayed with him as they ran from the building, determined to see him brought to justice.

Soon they reached an access hatch into the undercity, propped open as his planned getaway route. "C'mon, filly. You an' me need to be havin' a talk with Mr. Tai."

"Oh, I'll talk to him, all right. After I put you under arrest."

Cowboy scoffed. "Even if you could, little girl, what then? Turn me over to the G-grad lawmen? You know Lenski owns 'em—I'd be Boot Hill bound by sunup."

"Rrraaahhh! Will you drop the stupid act and speak *English* for once! This is serious!"

"That's right, kid," he went on in the same drawl. "Too serious for a piece o' fluff like you to be figgerin' out. Now, come on!" Suddenly he had a gun on her. Bluster aside, his boasts about his quick draw were not exaggerated.

She stood her ground. "You'll have to use it."

"Think I won't?"

"You tell me." It was Psyche's voice. She stood at the end of the alley behind Cowboy, aiming a stungun of her own at him. She must have tracked Emry's selfone signal. Cowboy didn't have to turn; his suit gave him telemetry on her position. Emry grew tense; Psyche didn't know what he was capable of. If he decided to shoot her . . .

But he lowered his gun and stepped into the hatch. "I'm goin' back to HQ now like a good soldier. You wanna call me out, Blaze, you know where to find me." He smirked. "If'n you ever figger out what side you're on."

He opened the hatch, and Emry saw no alternative but to let him disappear into it. Psyche jogged over to her, and Emry broke down in tears and fell into her arms. "Oh, Goddess . . . what do I do now?"

12

Crossover

Emry's indecision didn't last long. "We need to take this to Sensei," she told Psyche once they were back in their ship and her cuts had been tended to. "He'll know what to do." To be sure, the recordings from the nanobugs and Emry's data buffer were solid evidence, but still not absolute proof of the larger conspiracy. She'd need Sensei's help to dig deeper.

Psyche shook her head. "We should go back to Vanguard. Tai is sure to ramp up his efforts now; we need to prepare to counter that."

"No! This is a Troubleshooter problem. We need to fix it ourselves."

Those silver eyes, more vivid than ever in contrast to Psyche's still-black hair, showed her understanding. Still, she insisted, "It's not safe, Emry. Tai's people know you're onto them. We've seen they're capable of murder . . . and they must know you'd think of going to Villareal. You could be putting *him* in danger."

That brought Emry up short. "Then we'll just have to find some other way of reaching him," she decided after a moment. "Psyche, I know you mean well, but Vanguardians fighting Troubleshooters isn't the answer. Sensei's still respected. They can't block him without showing their hand. He can clean the Corps up, get it back on track without violence."

"All right," Psyche agreed. "But he'll still need allies. We'll go back to Vanguard and see about bringing him there. He'll be safer with us."

Emry considered it. "Okay. Sounds good." After all, the Vanguard had been Sensei's forerunners in a sense. This could be one hell of a team-up, and hopefully could lead to a lasting partnership. She wondered how Sensei and Eliot Thorne would get along.

A few days later, Gregor Tai held a press conference, which Emry and Psyche watched on the ship's display wall. Flanked by Lodestar, Paladin, and some of the new TSC administrators whom Emry barely knew, Tai announced what he claimed to be the results of "an extensive internal-affairs audit" he had ordered as a means of ensuring the high moral standards his "esteemed predecessor Yukio Villareal" had set for the Corps. Emry recalled some routine questions being asked of all the T-shooters after Tai's appointment, but it hadn't been much different from the usual performance reviews. Tai reported that most of the Troubleshooters had passed with flying colors. But then he grew somber, even apologetic, and spoke of three shocking, saddening exceptions.

An image came up on the screen behind him, and Emry gasped in recognition. *"This is Elise Pasteris, code-named Tin Lizzy. As you recall, less than two weeks ago, Pasteris was credited with the rescue of Joseph Mkunu, the fifteen-year-old son of the retired Zenjian president—although she allowed his abductor to escape and was vague on how she had located the boy. It now appears she was working in collusion with this man, Aaron Donner, to stage the kidnapping and rescue."* Donner's image appeared next to Elise's as a surprised murmur ran through the crowd. *"Donner calls himself a Troubleshooter, but he is a rogue vigilante, unsanctioned by the TSC.*

"Now, we're still not entirely sure of Ms. Pasteris's motives. I'm sure this puts a lot of you in mind of sensationalist fiction and tabloid rumors about Troubleshooters staging heroics to bask in the resultant glory. I wouldn't want to presume that about Elise Pasteris; that's for the psychologists and prosecutors to determine. As of today, Pasteris has been stripped of her Troubleshooter status and placed into custody.

"As has this man: Sanjay Bhattacharyya, code-named Cowboy." Cowboy's smug, irritating face was now on the screen, under that

ludicrous hat he insisted on being photographed in. *"I want it known that, to his credit, Mister Bhattacharyya turned himself in voluntarily and confessed to his involvement in the recent attempt on the life of organized crime boss Malik Yohannes—an attempt which led to the death of an innocent bystander, a nineteen-year-old college student named Jeanette LaSalle. Bhattacharyya has confessed to being the shooter, but has turned over evidence supporting his claim that the hit was masterminded by a fellow Troubleshooter—Emerald Blair, code-named the Green Blaze."*

Emry gasped as her own face looked back at her from the screen. She felt Psyche's hand clasp hers as Tai went on. *"Now, I was truly shocked at this news, as were all my colleagues who know Emerald Blair personally. They all insist that she is a deeply caring person who would never be capable of murder. However, none of us can deny that she is also known for her temper—and for an extensive criminal record in her adolescent years. Of course she never took a life during that time. And under normal circumstances I'd have no doubt of her commitment to that."* He gave a heavy sigh. *"But according to our investigations at the time, the Yohannes syndicate was responsible for providing the armaments that caused the death of Emerald Blair's mother, performance artist Lyra Blair, in a gang conflict nine years ago."*

Psyche paused the playback as the audience reacted. "Emry, is that true?"

It was a moment before she could speak. "I don't know. I . . . never really looked into it. The guy who . . . actually shot her . . . he was killed in the crossfire a moment later. Arkady caught the rest, and they all got convicted. I never wanted to make any more of it than that. It hurt too much."

"You never wanted to find someone to punish for it? To avenge yourself on?"

"Of course I wanted to." A tear came to her eye. "But my mom raised me better than that." She cleared her throat. "I guess I didn't always remember later on . . . I took revenge on people who hurt me or the Freaks . . . but even then I would've never betrayed Mom's memory by making her an excuse for hurting someone. And I really just wanted to forget the whole thing."

She resumed the playback. On-screen, Tai gestured the audience to silence and went on. *"Now, perhaps this could be understood, even excused in some way. The desire for retribution is only human, and to be frank, few would consider the death of Malik Yohannes to be a great loss to Solsys. But it is Emerald Blair's other actions in this matter that . . . that strain my comprehension, quite frankly.*

"Mister Bhattacharyya has provided us with the following recording taken from his own data-buffer implant. I warn you, it contains some graphic images at the beginning." Tai proceeded to play the very confrontation Emry and Cowboy had had just after the shooting, except from Cowboy's point of view. It cut out after they fled for the stairs. *"According to Bhattacharyya,"* Tai said when it was done, *"Blair convinced him to stage this confrontation with the intention that she would take her own buffer file public, painting herself as the hero. They had to improvise their dialogue somewhat, considering that he shot the wrong person, but they managed to cover for this. As you heard, Bhattacharyya's dialogue included a, um, rather contrived line implicating myself in the assassination plot—as though any trained assassin would be so foolish as to blurt out his employer's name so casually."* Emry imagined she caught an annoyed microexpression when he said that, but it was hard to be sure at this resolution. *"Apparently Blair wished to sully the new administration, perhaps in order to persuade Yukio Villareal to come out of retirement. In the meantime, her own rather . . . melodramatic moralizing in this scene, as well as the flamboyant stunt she performed to enter the building, would reinforce her public image.*

"The plan was for Bhattacharyya to flee to Pallas, thereby escaping the consequences of Blair's public accusations. However, his guilt at killing the wrong target compelled him to turn himself in and make a full confession."

"You son of a bitch," Emry said very quietly.

"As it happens, it was our investigation of Emerald Blair that led us to Elise Pasteris's involvement in the Mkunu abduction. Blair and an unidentified female accomplice were spotted near the location where

Mkunu was held captive. Whether Blair was working with Pasteris and Donner remains unknown. But we found evidence that Donner may have been tagged with smart-dust recording devices. It's possible that Blair intended to link Pasteris's crime to the conspiracy in which she hoped to implicate myself and the current Corps administration."

The bastard had her at every turn. He'd managed to preempt her, to discredit every piece of evidence she had. *If they fall for it*, she reminded herself.

Indeed, when the floor was opened to reporters, they jumped on the gaps in his story. *"What's your proof that the confrontation seen there was staged? Do you have evidence of Green Blaze's implication beyond Cowboy's word?"*

"Our case is still incomplete, but our investigation into Emerald Blair's recent activities supports his story. Blair recently persuaded me to allow her to attend a conference being held by the Vanguard nation. As many of you know, Blair's father was Vanguardian; it seems she wished to renew her family ties." He went on to list the "suspect" states participating in the conference, playing up the injustices and terrorist acts they'd committed. *"Considering the parties involved, I deemed it wise to be concerned. So I agreed to Blair's request, thinking I could rely on her to uncover the truth about the conference. However, she has failed to report in, and as you have seen, is clearly not where she is supposed to be."*

"So you think she might be working with the Vanguard, Neogaians, and others in some sort of larger scheme? To do what?"

"It's too early to speculate."

"But do you think they might be trying to undermine the Troubleshooters, weaken one of the Belt's main lines of defense?"

Tai begged off the question, and Emry had to wonder if that reporter, who worked for a Sheaf news network, had been a plant. It was hard to tell; reporters were always hoping for the most dramatic or shocking interpretation of events.

Another reporter, this one Demetrian, asked the next question. *"As you pointed out,"* he asked, *"all the implicated Troubleshooters were handpicked by Yukio Villareal himself. Given the Sensei's long-*

standing reputation for integrity, how do you explain this kind of corruption growing in his organization?"

"Yee, I couldn't have put it any better—Sensei Villareal has earned every bit of that reputation. His integrity is unimpeachable. But Yukio is also known for his intense personal loyalty and his unwavering belief in personal redemption. He's given many chances to people with checkered pasts. Elise Pasteris and Sanjay Bhattacharyya were both among the most violent of Troubleshooters before he brought them into the Corps, and sometimes since. And Emerald Blair's criminal past is well-known—and her record shows that she didn't fall into it as reluctantly as the recent biographical movie suggested."

Emry buried her face in her hands. Being accused of treason and murder was bad enough—but did he have to remind people of that vacking movie?

"Perhaps Yukio was simply . . . too decent for his own good," Tai went on. *"Too ready to see the good in all these people, to believe they could change their ways completely."*

"So once a crook, always a crook? Is that what you're saying?"

"No, Yee. Just that we're all products of our pasts, and sometimes their burdens are too heavy to shake. Forgiveness is a noble ideal, to be sure, but it needs to be tempered with vigilance. Because those who forget the past . . . well, you know the rest."

The file ended. "Ohh, he's slick," Psyche said with a mix of anger and appreciation. Then she took Emry in her arms. "Oh, sweetie, I'm so sorry. If we hadn't gotten you into this, we wouldn't have forced him to do this to you."

"I don't blame you," Emry said. "I'm grateful to you for getting me away from his influence in time. And at least . . . oh, Goddess . . . we forced him to sacrifice two of his pieces. Maybe that'll weaken him."

"Do you still want to contact Villareal?" Psyche asked after a moment. "Do you think he might still believe you?"

"I'd like to think so. But Tai covered that too. Anything Sensei might say now would just be his naïve 'personal loyalty' talking." She took a deep breath, let it out forcefully. "We need more, Psyche. We need a way to prove Tai's behind it, to disprove his lies."

"We'll work on it," Psyche said, stroking her hair. "My father and I are as determined to defeat Tai as you are."

"Thank you."

Psyche took her by the shoulders and met her eyes. "Maybe you're not a Troubleshooter anymore—not officially—but as far as we're concerned, you've always been a Vanguardian. And we take care of our own."

Psyche kissed her, and Emry returned it readily, craving the comfort. As she pulled at Psyche's clothing, Emry tried the thought on for size. *Emerald Blair . . . Vanguardian.*

It felt surprisingly right.

It didn't take long for Sensei Villareal to issue his own statement in response to the allegations, and Emry and Psyche watched it from their ship in between lovemaking sessions. He stressed that the charges against the implicated Troubleshooters were still unproven, calling attention to the gaps in Tai's case against Emry herself. Emry was grateful for his defense, though she knew it wouldn't be enough; in her experience, the masses tended to choose between conflicting arguments on the basis of which one they heard first.

Villareal concluded by urging Emry to turn herself in, promising to ensure that she received a fair trial. "Sorry, Sensei," she whispered. "That's not an option."

As soon as the ship was back within a couple of light-seconds of Vanguard, Emry contacted Zephyr. "Has the TSC tried to contact you?"

"They have. They instructed me to return to HQ, preferably with you in my brig. I've declined to respond to such a crass suggestion."

Emry sighed. "Zephy . . . technically I'm not a Troubleshooter anymore. You don't . . . have to stay with me."

On the ship's comm screen, his avatar gave her a wry look. *"Emry. The only reason I became a ship again was to look after you."*

"And I'm really grateful for it, buddy. But . . . your life is yours. I'm sure Arkady would understand if you wanted to—"

"Emry, it's not about Arkady. It hasn't been for a long time. We're

partners. Green Blaze and her trusty steed Zephyr." On-screen, his winged-god avatar morphed into a winged horse.

Emry laughed. But then she grew thoughtful. She tugged her Green Blaze tunic from her bag and looked at it. "Am I still Green Blaze?" she wondered. "Should I still wear this?"

"You're still a Troubleshooter, no matter what Tai says. And it's your design, your choice of code name. It stands for what you believe in."

She smirked. "You're pretty smart for a horse."

<Besides,> he sent her silently, *<though an alliance with the Vanguard seems beneficial at this point, I don't think you should start wearing their colors, so to speak. They may have proven their claims about Tai's motives, but I still have questions about their own.>*

<You have a point,> Emry responded. <They haven't steered me wrong yet, aside from that little tiff with Thorne. And I really need someone on my side right now—aside from you, that is. But I guess I need to keep my eyes open, kick the fan ducts before I buy.> She sighed. <I don't want to get burned again.>

Eliot Thorne met them at the docking complex, and Psyche launched herself into his arms. Meanwhile, Emry drifted over to *Zephyr*'s bay to check in on him and tidy up a bit. But she watched the Thornes' reunion while they remained in sight. There was an easy warmth between them of a sort that Emry remembered feeling once upon a time, in another life.

Thorne met her when she emerged from *Zephyr*. His manner was welcoming, but more reserved and formal than he'd been with his daughter. "Welcome back, Emerald. I'm gratified that you've chosen to stay with us."

"For now," she added. "Until I get this mess sorted out."

"Of course." He escorted Emry and Psyche into the tramcar, which set out on its journey down from the hub. The passengers' weight crept upward as they conversed. "The resources of the Vanguard are at your disposal toward that end," Thorne went on. "As I said before, defeating the Cerean agenda is in all of our best interests."

Emry shook her head a bit. "Look . . . I'm too tired to think about that. All this big-picture politics stuff—I just want my job back. I want my corps back."

"I understand." He looked her up and down, taking in the Green Blaze livery she wore once more. "It's more than just a job to you, isn't it? It's a home."

She stared at him. "That's right. It's where I belong. Or it was."

His massive hand clasped her shoulder with a surprisingly gentle touch. "I want to help you make it that again. But . . . I hope you will also come to feel that there is more than one place where you can belong."

Thorne's kindness—and his physical proximity—made her smile, and she felt her face flush. She pulled away, a bit reluctantly. "That . . . that'd be nice," she said truthfully. "But I need to get to know you better. And I still have my doubts about some of your allies."

"Which is just the kind of vigilant attitude we need to guide them onto a better track. Were the first Troubleshooters so different? Many of them were selfish, irresponsible, mercenary, violent. But Yukio Villareal created a system that tamed their power, curbing their excesses and nurturing the best within them. We seek to follow his example on a larger scale. And I can think of no one better to aid us in that goal," he said, clasping her hands, "than one who is both Troubleshooter and Vanguardian. Your partnership would be invaluable to our goal of creating, not merely better humans, but a better humanity."

Emry flushed and took a moment to find her voice. "I, um, I'm honored. Right now, I . . . well, right now the most important thing is saving the Troubleshooters."

"Of course. That remains a crucial step toward our larger goals."

"But . . . whether I go back to them afterwards . . . well, even though I probably will, I could still . . . we could be allies, and . . ."

"I would welcome that."

She cleared her throat, freeing her hands from his. "I guess, for now, I'm on your team."

"Great!" Psyche flung her arms around Emry from behind.

But there was a slightly ominous smile on Thorne's face. "Don't be so hasty, Psyche. If Emerald wants to play on the Vanguard 'team,' she has to show us what she's capable of. A test of your abilities, my dear. Call it a gauntlet of sorts, a . . . friendly competition."

Emry grinned. "I'm game. After being cooped up in a little ship for most of the past month, I'm eager to stretch my legs."

"This will be rather more strenuous than your typical workout, I assure you, Emerald."

"You've never been to one of my workouts."

"I'm about to be," Thorne said. "I intend to conduct this assessment personally. Do you think you're up to taking me on?"

Her eyes widened. True, the man was half a century her senior, but to a Vanguardian that meant little. Plus he was fully twice her mass and considerably more muscular kilo-for-kilo. When they'd tussled before, he'd tossed her around like a rag doll.

So Emry responded the only way she could: with a big, enthusiastic grin. "Bring it on, Thorney. I've been dying for a rematch."

Before the test could begin, Thorne insisted on a physical exam to record Emry's baseline data for evaluation purposes. Emry was hesitant to consent to this, since many of her mods were classified TSC technology. But she was growing to believe she could trust the Vanguardians—certainly more than she trusted the TSC right now.

Thorne took her to the institution that apparently doubled as the Vanguard's central hospital and its genetic research institute—a necessary combination, since many Vanguardians were conceived here as well as born here. "So you didn't get Psyche's mom pregnant the old-fashioned way?" Emry asked.

He smirked. "I generally save that for recreation. For our most special children, we don't rely on trial and error. But the woman you're about to meet is, in some ways, as much Psyche's mother as Lydie Clement," Thorne said. "She and I were the lead designers on Psyche's genome."

Emry was starting to realize who would be conducting her examination. But just then, Thorne led them through a door into a research lab. Inside, a full-figured woman with short silver-red hair stood with her back to them, wearing old-fashioned interface rings on her fingers and using them to rearrange cryptic patterns and notations on the display wall beyond her. Emry figured they must be genetic data of some sort, but there were none of the double-helix images she would've expected to see. She supposed that was a conceit of fiction; real geneticists wouldn't need to look at pictures of DNA any more than composers needed to look at pictures of musical instruments.

"May we come in?" Thorne asked.

The woman sighed. "Eliot, if you want me to get this resequencing done on time, then you shouldn't keep interrupting me."

"I apologize. But I have someone with me that you need to meet."

The woman sighed, gestured the interface into standby mode, and turned, revealing herself to be about four months pregnant. (Or maybe three months, Emry corrected, remembering her own accelerated gestation.) She had a pleasantly chubby face, relatively unlined, but currently frowning with impatience. "All right, if you—" She broke off as her eyes fell on Emry. "Good Lord. Is that . . ."

Thorne nodded, "Rachel Kincaid-Shannon, allow me to introduce Emerald Blair."

"Oh, Emerald!" Emry's grandmother broke into a huge grin and spread her arms. Before Emry knew what hit her, she was engulfed in an enormous bear hug. "Ohh, I'm sorry, forgive an old grouch, it's so wonderful to finally meet you!"

Emry tentatively returned the hug, which showed no signs of ending anytime soon. It was at once warming and awkward. Her feelings about Grandma Rachel were ambivalent. She knew her father's decision to leave Vanguard had led to an estrangement with his mother. He had been reluctant to talk about it, but it had never been his way to lie to his daughter. So he had eventually told her how he felt that Rachel had sided with Thorne over him, had been more committed to her genetic research than to her own firstborn son. But Emry hardly considered herself entitled to pass judgment in this case.

"Um . . . hi," she finally managed. "It's, uh . . . well, this is really . . ."

Rachel finally let her up for air. "I know, it's a lot to take in. What's it been, twenty-six years, and we've never even met until now?"

"Twenty-two," she replied quietly.

"Oh, of course, it's not like you were born the minute Richard left! Some geneticist, not remembering that!" Rachel chuckled. "Ohh, let me look at you! My God, I've seen pictures, but you are so *beautiful*! Ohh, honey, you couldn't be more gorgeous if I'd designed you myself!"

Emry fidgeted. "I, uhh, take after my mother."

"Oh, of course you do. Don't get me wrong . . . there's no beauty like natural beauty. The most we can do is help it express itself more fully." She looked Emry over more critically. "Well, there's some of your father in you. Aspects of the jawline, the forehead . . . the meso-morphic build, of course, God, you must be strong! And you have my coloring, I daresay. Well, what used to be my coloring."

"And a couple other things," Emry said, indicating her chest. "I al-ways wondered where I got these babies from. Not that I'm complain-ing," she finished with a smirk.

Rachel laughed. "Well, you're very welcome! And you've got my hips, too . . . plus you're so strong, it should make childbearing easier." Emry stared. "Oh, when you're ready, of course. I'm just so excited at the prospect of adding your genes back into the mix."

"That remains to be seen," Thorne said before Emry could figure out a response. "Before a partnership can commence, Emerald needs to be tested. I need a full physical and genetic workup to evaluate the results."

"Oh. One of your little competitions, right." She shook her head at Emry, mouthing, *Men*. Being pretty competitive herself, Emry just shrugged. "Well, don't worry, dear—you'll give him a run for his money, I can tell just by looking at you. After all, you're a Shannon.

"Well, don't just stand there," Rachel said. "Strip to your skivvies and get on the table. I'd love to spend all day catching up, honey, but I really am in the middle of something urgent right now, and you know how it is when your muse is all fired up and shouting in your ear. So I'd like to get this done quickly, if you don't mind."

Emry obligingly began to remove her boots, giving Thorne a small smile as she did so. But Rachel glared at him. "And are you just going to stand there?"

"I'll assist in the exam," he replied as though it were a given.

"You'll do nothing of the kind, young man. My granddaughter is entitled to some privacy."

"She clearly doesn't mind," he said, gesturing at Emry, who was now pulling her top open. "And I need to know the results in any case."

"And you'll get them. Later. But Emerald and I have girl stuff to discuss and I want her to feel completely at ease—and under no pressure to show off," she added pointedly. "It's the only way I'll get reliable results, and you know it. So go on. Shoo!"

She physically hustled the much larger man to the doorway, and surprisingly, he went without resistance. But as he left, Emry heard him mutter, "The woman is a force of nature." Emry was beginning to agree.

13

Bed of Thornes

"Oh, vack," Emry gasped as the sheer rock face loomed before her. Bad enough that Thorne had made her race him halfway around Vanguard's equatorial forest to get to this point, six kilometers at roughly half again the gravity she was used to. Bad enough he'd made her do it spinward, so that the faster she ran, the heavier she'd get. But mountain-climbing was not a skill she'd needed much in life.

Still, they'd trained her for it at the Corps, along with every other contingency they could think of. *Lucky I'm a recent graduate*, she thought as the climb grew increasingly steep. For once her spinward course was working in her favor; the ground's rotational velocity decreased with its distance from the axis, so as she climbed, she felt a small decelerating vector pushing against her, angling her weight vector slightly so that the climb effectively became a bit less steep. The faster she ran uphill, the less uphill it seemed to get.

But before long she was climbing a sheer vertical slope, unable to move fast enough to gain any significant benefit. The gravity was a bit more reasonable at this height, but not enough to make a difference. She'd stopped trying to keep track of Thorne, instead staying focused on the bumps and crevices before her, her world reduced to a few square meters of simulated stone. *Do real mountains on Earth get this steep?* she wondered. She'd seen such cliffs in movies, but had trouble believing the images were real.

Her arms were burning by the time she drew near the small plateau at the top of the cliff. As she reached the rim, cursing Eliot Thorne

under her breath, she saw the man himself looming above her, blocking her. "Oh, come on!" she cried.

"This is your challenge, Emerald. Deal with it."

"You won't . . . let me fall."

"Probably not. But I won't let you past either."

"Didn't . . . you think you could take me in a fair fight?"

"We live in a universe where entropy has an inbuilt advantage. Fair-
ness is a fiction. We prove ourselves by our ability to surmount unfair
odds."

You really do talk too much. She'd braced her knees higher while he
spoke, and now lunged up and forward to grab at his leg, hoping to yank
him off balance. But he simply reached down and dragged her up by
the collar. A moment later he was cradling her like a child as she struggled in vain . . . and then she realized he was dangling her over the
edge. *Okay, pushing away is* not *the way to go here.* Especially since a
falling body would curve antispinward, *away* from the cliff face.

So she opted for the Bugs maneuver. Abruptly, she grabbed Thorne's
head in her hands and kissed him on the nose. She'd wanted to go for
the lips, but this more absurd approach proved more disarming. The
nonplussed Thorne loosened his grip enough for her to clamber over
his shoulders, jumping down behind him and running for the top. She
heard him chuckle before his footfalls came after her.

The last part of the climb wasn't as rough as the cliff face, but the air
was colder and thinner up here, the ground covered in snow and ice.
The Vanguardian metabolism demanded a lot of oxygen. Emry hoped
that being only half-Vanguardian, and half Thorne's mass, would give
her an edge.

Unfortunately, his longer reach and stride proved more telling. Soon
his hand grabbed her ankle from below and yanked her back half a meter with her face in the snow. She kicked down at his face and forced
him to let go. She could hear his breath rasping as she clambered away.
At least I winded him. But now there's wet snow in my cleavage. Great.

Now the peak was only a few dozen meters away. But Thorne overtook her again, tackling her against the sixty-degree slope and dragging
her back by her waistband. She elbowed him in the head, which dazed

him a bit, so she hit and kicked some more to try to knock him back downhill. But his inertia was twice hers, so she only ended up dislodging herself. He recovered enough to take advantage, stiff-arming her in the gut. She fell back a couple of meters, catching herself with one hand. Thorne clambered farther up while Emry recovered her grip. Growling, she pulled herself up after him and grabbed at his left ankle.

It was a mistake. Thorne kicked his leg out away from the rock face, jerking her out with it. She dangled for a moment, but promptly brought her knees up, pushed off, and somersaulted backward using Thorne's ankle as a pivot, intending to kick him in the face. He dodged at the last instant, clinging to the slope by his right hand and foot only. She let go and let her momentum flip her upright again, reaching for a new handhold above Thorne. But his left arm caught her in the midriff, knocking the wind from her. One swipe of his arm and she was falling through the air, then tumbling back down to the plateau.

Gasping for breath, Emry looked up to see Thorne climbing swiftly, surely. In moments, he straddled the summit, his hands on his hips, king of the mountain. Emry slumped where she sat and just tried to catch her breath.

"Well?" Thorne called down. "Are you just going to lie there?"

"What do you want?" she shouted back. "I lost!"

"That's no excuse to give up!"

She stared at him for a long moment.

Then she pulled herself to her feet and began climbing once more. Her throat burned from the cold air, its moisture choking her.

When she finally reached the apex, Thorne took her hand and pulled her up alongside him. He smiled, then turned her face outward to gaze upon Vanguard stretched out below them. "There. You see? You may have lost, but you still earned the reward."

"Pretty view," she gasped. "So what? I got a higher view . . . from the spaceport. It's a hollow sphere, dummy!"

He glared at her, but simply said, "Perhaps to one who lived on Earth for a time, it seems a greater reward."

"Yeah, well . . . after all that . . . I'm entitled to a bigger reward than this."

"Then let me give you one."

He lifted her off the ground once again . . . and this time his lips devoured hers, and his arms engulfed her body. It stunned her even more than being knocked halfway down a mountain . . . but she was feeling no pain this time. It was exactly the reward she would've claimed herself if he hadn't made the first move. Her arms folded around him, her mouth opening readily to him.

Thorne carried her down to a relatively flat depression on the other side of the peak and sat on a protruding boulder, lowering her onto his lap. She didn't even remember releasing her zipseal lock, but somehow she found herself naked, the heat of Thorne's bare flesh throwing the icy chill of the wind into sharp relief. Before long, they were tumbling in the snow, a welcome relief for her overheated body—though she spent most of the time on top of him, of course, since his mass would crush her otherwise.

They kept at it for as long as they could stand the cold, and then Thorne called in an aircar to take them back to his chambers. Once there, after sharing a warming drink, he stripped her once more, massaged her aches away, and took her again.

In all her life, Emry had never been so completely overwhelmed by a lover. True, she'd only taken partners strong enough to hold their own against her, but even so, she'd rarely been outmatched in strength. And Thorne took full advantage of his strength, dominating her completely.

Not that he wasn't considerate or attentive. On the contrary, he was extraordinarily responsive to her desires, her likes and dislikes. He probed out her most sensitive areas with expert precision and did incredible things to them. He gave her everything she could ask for and more, usually before she could ask.

Yet he remained very much in control. Emry was too completely carried away to assert much of anything herself. But just this once, she decided, she was fine with that. If Eliot wanted to make a regular thing out of this—and she profoundly hoped he did—it would have to proceed on a more egalitarian footing. But for now, it was certainly a hell of a ride.

And she had to admit . . . right now, with the weight of worlds on her shoulders, it was strangely refreshing to surrender all her responsibility and power and will for one night . . . and just let herself be taken care of.

It wasn't until the next morning that Emry gave a thought to her growing relationship with Psyche. She felt somewhat guilty about that when she confessed it to Psyche, but the lissome Vanguardian absolved her readily. "Think nothing of it. What matters is that you let yourself be happy. The last thing I'd want is for you to treat my father as a one-night stand and avoid exploring where this relationship could lead. I'll happily step aside, as long as we stay friends."

"I'm not even sure it is a relationship," Emry said. "It was just lots and lots of really exhausting sex."

Psyche just looked at her. "You know I can read you better than that. You trusted him. Relaxed your guard like you never have with any other man. If our time together has helped prepare you for taking that kind of step, then I'm happy for you, and for my father."

Emry was grateful for her understanding—and oddly unsurprised. Maybe she'd just known that what she and Psyche shared had been more a friendship with benefits than a romance. Maybe that was why she hadn't felt bad about sleeping with Thorne. Not that she wouldn't have slept with him anyway, admittedly.

And Psyche, gregarious as she was, had no trouble finding other companionship. That night, at a party she threw to celebrate Emry's joining of the "team," Psyche showed up flanked by two burly male escorts, whom Emry recognized as the two men she herself had picked out for their impromptu orgy the month before. And Psyche didn't exactly discourage attention from the other men at the party. Unlike at the conference, she didn't need to win these people's trust and respect, so she was bold and frankly seductive. She owned the attention of everyone here, and she openly reveled in it.

If anything, she took it a little too far. Emry saw a twinge of jealousy in her bigger escort's eyes, and it seemed that Psyche was deliberately provoking it through her brazen behavior with other men. Emry tried to divert the big guy with her own flirtations, reminding him of the wild times they'd shared that first night, though her futile struggle to remember his name hampered her efforts. And he only seemed to have eyes for Psyche. If anything, it seemed that the men were all giving Emry a wide berth, unwilling to take chances now that she was with their alpha male. But in the big guy's case, it seemed to be more about the daughter than the father. Eventually, when Psyche spent an inordinately long time in a hot, intimate dance with another brawny Vanguardian, the big guy lost his temper and tried to cut in by force. Before long, it was a free-for-all. Emry was amused at first, but soon realized the two men were not holding back. If this kept up, someone could end up seriously injured, or worse. But Psyche was watching the fight raptly, giggling. "You think this is funny?" Emry cried. "You encouraged them, didn't you?"

"Can I help it if they both fell in love with me?"

"Yes! You can dial back the pheromones or something."

"Emry, Emry—you know pheromones aren't a love potion. You're overreacting. Besides, I told them there was plenty of me to go around. But you know men, always so possessive. They're so cute that way."

But the fight was getting out of hand now, so Emry threw herself into the fray. Against two fellow Vanguardians who both outmassed her considerably, it was probably not the wisest choice. But once the men realized Thorne's lover was in harm's way, they reined themselves in and let her pull them apart. Once she made sure they weren't severely hurt, she tossed them out and told them to call themselves an ambulance. "And call yourselves a few other names while you're at it!" she added.

Then she whirled on Psyche. "And you! What happened to your gift for reading people, huh?"

Psyche was contrite. "I read them fine. But I read that they wanted me, and that they'd fight to have me, and . . . well, that's very flattering. I just let myself get carried away by their emotions. I try to give people what they want, and those men wanted to prove their prowess by fighting over me." She shrugged. "Besides, you looked like you were having fun." Emerald stared. "Okay, I was stupid. Sometimes it's just hard to gauge how strong one of us actually is. I didn't think that it might be dangerous." She blushed. "And . . . maybe I'm feeling a little lonely now that you're . . . I guess I just wanted attention."

The resultant guilt quashed Emry's anger. "Damn. Psyche . . ."

"Forget it. It's okay." She hugged Emry. "Thank you for keeping the peace. I'm lucky to have you as a friend."

The next day, Zephyr expressed concern about Psyche's actions. *"It strikes me that someone so gifted at manipulating others could come to enjoy it a little too much,"* he said over her selfone.

"But two of her own people? What could she have to gain from that?" Emry challenged.

"That's my point. It can become an end in itself."

But Emry couldn't believe that of Psyche. Perhaps she had enjoyed toying with those men's affections when she'd believed it to be in good fun, but her remorse had been genuine. And Emry, of all people, couldn't begrudge her friend a bit of a wild streak.

And there was no doubt of her loyalty as a friend. Later that day, Psyche issued a press statement responding to Tai's insinuations by clarifying the nature and goals of the recent conference and the ongoing diplomatic process it had set into motion. Lacking solid evidence beyond what Tai had already preempted, she declined to make direct accusations. With regard to the charges against Emry, Psyche simply stated that she could personally vouch for Emerald Blair's whereabouts for the entire period when she was supposedly colluding with Cowboy. "The Vanguard has complete confidence in Emerald's integrity," she added, "and her commitment to the principles of the Troubleshooter Corps." With regard to her status as a wanted fugitive, Psyche stated that the Vanguard had no extradition treaty with the Cerean States and that Emry was their guest for as long as she wished to remain. "Emerald is the daughter of one of our own," she said, "and we take care of our family."

Emry was at once moved and troubled by that statement. Family wasn't something she was used to being a part of—and this family in particular was one she'd never expected to connect with again. The

Vanguardians she met kept wanting to talk about her father, to tell her what a great guy he'd been or how much they imagined she reminded them of him. Nodding politely and changing the subject was rapidly becoming a new habit for her.

But the hell of it was, she *liked* it here. The Vanguardians were a lively, robust people, and their whole habitat was designed to challenge, stimulate, and sate individuals with abilities and appetites rivaling Emry's own. She felt the kind of belonging that she'd only ever known with the Freakshow and the Troubleshooters . . . and with her mother and father, back in another life. She liked Psyche, bonding with her like the sister she'd never had. She liked getting to meet Lydie Clement, Soaring Hawk Darrow, and the other surviving champions from the sixties and seventies, soaking in their tales of adventure and what it was like to be the first real superheroes.

And she *really* liked Eliot Thorne. He was everything she'd ever fantasized him to be. True, he could be controlling, reserved and forbidding, but she enjoyed the challenge of breaking through his defenses. Yet she was uneasy with just how strong her feelings for him were becoming. There was something she felt with him that she'd never known with any other man, and she was afraid to think about what it might be.

So when Grandma Rachel invited her to brunch, Emry was grateful for the excuse to decline an invitation to work out with Eliot. Their workouts were certainly entertaining, even before they turned into wild sex; but she appreciated the chance to decompress and get her mind off of Eliot Thorne.

Inevitably, though, it wasn't long before Rachel asked, "So—you and Eliot, huh? I guess I'm not surprised. An alpha male like him . . . if anything, it's a wonder it took so long."

"And . . . you're okay with it?" Emry asked between bites of truly superb French toast.

"As long as you are. As long as you're aware that you shouldn't expect anything remotely resembling monogamy from him, and are able to accept that. Other than that, he's a fine catch. A bit of a control freak, yes, but you're strong enough to stand up to him."

"So . . . you figure I'm just one conquest in a long line?"

"Ohh, don't sell yourself short!" Rachel seemed to misunderstand which answer Emry was hoping to hear. "Even by Vanguard standards, Emry, you're quite a woman. You're powerful, intense, and Eliot is drawn to that. He takes lots of lovers, but I think—and please don't repeat this to him, I'd get an earful—I think he's lonely at heart. For all his power, all he's built and plans to build, he's missing something. Maybe it's an equal. Someone he can love, as much as he loves Psyche."

Sensing Emry's nervousness, Rachel laughed. "Oh, here I am being an old yenta, embarrassing you. Don't mind me. What do I know about all this anyway? I spend all my time with my work, and my babies," she said, patting her belly.

"How many have you had?" Emry asked.

"Ohh, I hardly remember anymore. Building a large population in an enclosed community like this, a lot of us have to be pregnant a lot of the time. I've probably carried more babies than most anyone else. Some of them have been surrogacies, though, not genetically mine, or no more than a bit."

"You must really like morning sickness."

"Well, one of my mods is being less prone to that. Still, all these pregnancies, they take their toll. But it's worth it. I feel I should have a personal connection to the future I'm helping to design. I get so caught up in my work sometimes—I should never forget that these are people, not just genomes. That they're our children, our responsibility."

She sighed. "Still . . . it was different with your father. That was with Liam. That was love, pure and simple. Most of the rest . . . they're the children of the community, and we all play a part in raising them. But Richard . . . he was *my* son. And the image of his father. . . ." She blinked away a tear.

"Ohh, Emry," she went on. "I see so much of him when I look at you. Maybe not in the face, but behind the eyes. In your spirit, your strength and sensitivity. In the work you do, giving of yourself, using your gifts to protect others. He would've been so very proud of you, Emerald."

Now Emry had to fight off tears. She put her fork down; she'd lost her appetite. "Don't say that."

"Why not? It's true."

"He didn't approve of fighting."

"He chose not to fight. He never judged those who did. He hated killing, but you're no killer, whatever they're saying. He would have known that."

"No. He wouldn't." The table was blurring before her eyes, getting all watery, so she stood and turned away from it.

A moment later she felt Grandma Rachel's hands on her shoulders. "Emry, I don't understand. You've done nothing that would give Richard any reason to be less than proud. Sure, you had a few wild years, but that was understandable, and you've more than made amends."

"No. No, I haven't come close. I never can."

"I know your father wouldn't have felt that way."

"What do you know?!" Emry whirled on her. "You didn't know him! You never talked to him my whole life! You didn't know . . . what happened to him . . . what I did to him. . . ."

Rachel stepped back, taking a shuddering breath, but she stayed in control, looking levelly at Emry. "Then tell me."

"I killed him!" she shrieked. It tore out of her, breaking free after years of suppression, and tears spilled forth from the gaping hole it left. Sobbing uncontrollably, she fell into a stunned Rachel's arms. "It's my fau—it's my fault he died. I killed him."

14

Origin Stories: Great Responsibility

December 2105
al-Khwarizmi Science Institute
Sol-Jupiter L3 point

Emry woke. Barely. Something was making her uncomfortable. She tried to drift back off to sleep, but the sensation wouldn't go away. Something was pushing against her back. All of it at once.

A few moments later, she realized it was weight. That startled her fully awake. Yes—it felt like she was under about half a gee. Looking around, she realized she wasn't on the *Trident* anymore, but in a hospital ward. It all came back to her. The expedition must have gotten back safely.

"Ahh, Emerald, at last!" That was the expedition doctor, Monica Railey, a handsome woman with warm chocolate skin. "Are you with us now? Do you know who you are?"

Emry laughed more than she had reason to; she was still rather punchy. "You kinda gave it away there, Monnie. I'm Emerald, uhh, Jones? Chang? McGillicuddy? Hold on, it's on the tip of my tongue. . . ."

"Okay, she's back," Railey said with a sigh. "Sorry for the obvious question, but you didn't seem quite sure who you were the last time you were awake."

"I was awake before? I don't remember. . . ."

"Most people don't. Even just when coming out of surgery, let alone nearly a month of hibernation. You're actually ahead of the curve there. Must be that Vanguardian physique."

"I'm not a Vanguardian."

Railey studied her for a moment, wearing a look Emry couldn't decipher. "Well . . . you know what I mean."

Emry just grunted in response. Railey helped her sit up, handed her a cup of apple juice, and advised her to sip it slowly. Once Emry demonstrated her mastery of that task, Railey decided she could be trusted to finish up on her own, and went to tend to another patient.

As she rehydrated herself, Emry contemplated Railey's words. *Not quite sure who I was. . . .* She really wasn't surprised. Emry hadn't had a good answer to that question for over seven years now.

True, it had been nearly three years since she'd stopped changing the name on her forged IDs every few months, since she'd stopped being Kei or Jean or Barbara or Mary Jane or Kim or whoever and become Emerald Blair again full-time. But a name was not an identity, and she had spent most of those three years trying to figure out just who or what Emerald Blair was going to be. While still in rehab, she'd begun taking online classes again, catching up on her formal education. But with no career goals in mind, her approach had been dilettantish. Figuring she'd be more stimulated by direct experience, Emry had wandered Solsys and soaked in the rich diversity of cultures and beliefs, all the wild social experiments and evolutions that crop up on any frontier, in search of one that felt like home to her. Well, not all of them. She'd avoided Wellspring and Neogaia, already knowing all she felt she needed to know about them. She'd stayed away from habs where certain people might try to kill her if they recognized her. And she'd made no attempt to visit Vanguard or Earth proper, let alone go back to Greenwood; any place where there were Shannons was a place she had no wish to be.

Along the way, she'd dabbled in various religions, visiting their houses of worship, opening herself to their teachings, hoping to find the peace and enlightenment that her mother had found in her Dianic beliefs. But all of it rang false to her. There was certainly beauty and imagination in it, but she sensed nothing beneath the symbols and myths, no truth tying them together—nothing but a self-deluding desire to believe the universe gave a leak about its occupants. Lyra Blair's Goddess hadn't protected her, hadn't spared her daughter from misery and loss, any more than her husband had. If there was one thing Emry had learned, it was that people had to rely on themselves.

So Emry had turned away from higher callings and tried to find a career that satisfied her. During her travels, she'd made a living at various jobs, from laborer to stripper to pilot to model to bouncer, but nothing that seemed like a life's calling. She'd dabbled in acting, but couldn't lose herself in a part; she'd tried sports, but wasn't much for following rules. She'd gone so far as to enroll in the FEEL academy on Vestalia, but had soon found that sex as a profession required a selflessness she couldn't muster, a commitment to placing the clients' desires above her own. Like so many things in life, it was less fun as a job than as a hobby.

Back in August, wondering if science was her thing, she'd signed on as a pilot and general assistant for the *Trident* expedition: a two-month survey of Neptune's moons, plus a month's travel either way with the crew in hibernation. She'd hoped some distance and quiet time would help her figure things out. True, there was some publicity involved in such a trip, but they were routine enough by now that she wouldn't draw too much attention.

But she'd found the survey rather tedious, relieved only by her dalliances with various researchers. Unfortunately, in the close quarters of the expedition, her bunk-hopping had created some tensions. She'd caused a couple of fights and started a few more. It had been a relief for everyone when the time to go back into hibernation had come. Now Emry hoped the debriefing would go quickly so she could finally end her association with the project.

But she had no idea where she'd go next.

Dr. Railey had been watching her, she realized. Once Railey saw she had Emry's attention, she came forward, oddly hesitant. "Emerald . . . you, uh, have a visitor. She's been waiting, and . . . well, normally I wouldn't, but this is rather urgent. Are you up to seeing her?"

Uh-oh. Had someone filed a complaint about her behavior on the expedition? Was this the mission director come to chew her out? Or had

Dr. Bonham's wife somehow found out about the free-fall bondage lessons she'd given him? *Either way, might as well get it over with.* "Sure, Mon. Bring her on in."

It never occurred to her that it would be Bimala Sarkar. She rarely gave any thought to the private investigator's visit to her in rehab nearly three years ago, and until now the woman had obliged her demand to stay out of her life. But Emry recognized her instantly, and tensed as she approached. "What the hell are you doing here?"

The elegant Indian woman remained silent until she stood by Emry's bed. "Emerald," she said in a quiet, controlled voice. "Your father—"

"Don't call him that!"

Sarkar's dark eyes hardened, and her voice with them. "Richard Shannon is dead."

It took some time for the words to sink in. "He's—what?" Her sense of disorientation was returning. Was this still a hibernation dream?

"Richard Shannon. Your father. He died, Emerald. Eighteen days ago. He was fighting a fire. He went into the burning building, searching for people trapped inside. He found them, got them out. But he was slow coming behind them, and the ceiling collapsed. . . ." Her voice faltered. She took a deep breath. "He died as he lived, Emerald. Helping people."

Emry hardly heard it. She was . . . she . . . she didn't know what she was. . . .

She threw up the apple juice all over her bedsheets. Dr. Railey came rushing over to check on her. Emry was too dazed to understand what she said.

She couldn't understand any of it, really. She couldn't understand how he—how her father could be dead. She couldn't understand where all this grief was coming from. All this loss, when he'd been lost to her for seven years. All this love.

"Did he . . . did he say . . . anything. . . ."

"About you?" Sarkar asked, her voice cold. "No, no famous last words. It was too quick. But there's a message for you in his will. And he left you his home, all the things in it . . . if you want them. He didn't expect you would, but he wanted you to have them anyway."

"Oh, Goddess." The sobs came now, erupting from deep inside. The room spun around her. Distantly, she felt Monica's hand on her shoulder.

Once the sobs ran dry, leaving a torn, burning throat behind them, Sarkar asked the doctor to leave her alone with Emry. "So I guess he was your father after all," the tall woman said once Railey had gone. "I thought you hated him, Emerald."

"I never . . . wanted him dead."

"Well, you got it anyway."

Emry stared at her. "What are you saying?"

"You never knew Richard Shannon, Emerald. Never knew what he became after you left him. He was such a sensitive soul. Losing your mother was devastating enough. But for his only daughter, the other love of his life, to turn on him, abandon him . . . That destroyed him. He was never the same after that.

"Yes, they gave him medicines for his depression, and that helped him function. He was able to go on with his life. But there was never any joy in it again."

She smiled wistfully. "He kept on doing good for other people. Nothing could change that about him. But it became something he did to distract himself from his own loneliness. From the empty rooms in the empty house he went home to. From not knowing where his little girl was or whether she was safe—and from knowing all too well that she despised him, blamed him for Lyra's death.

"You don't know what it was like for me, having to report to him when I was tracking you. How he longed to hear any scrap of news about you, but how much it hurt him when he did. I—I tried to quit sometimes. It wasn't good to be so personally attached to one of my clients. But I couldn't help it."

Emry studied her. "You . . . were attached?"

"I loved him. I did all I could to console him, bring him joy. But he couldn't let go . . . not so long as you were still out there, alive but lost to him. We had some good times together, but a part of him was always elsewhere. I could never reach it."

Sarkar's brow furrowed, wrinkling her *bindi*. "Then came the news that you'd joined this expedition. He was so proud of you—and then he heard them describe you as an orphan. You told them you had no parents. You denied he even existed!

"It got bad after that. He was inconsolable. He just . . . went through the motions of life. Of his work. He got careless. I don't . . . I don't think his own safety mattered much to him anymore."

Emry's dizziness was returning. "Goddess . . . what are you saying?"

Sarkar straightened, looming over her. "Exactly what you think. That I blame you. If you hadn't been such a self-absorbed little brat—if you'd given the tiniest consideration to his pain instead of wallowing in your own—if you'd only *talked* to your own *father* even once—he wouldn't have died in agony. Or at least the last seven years of his life wouldn't have been so miserable.

"Either way, Emerald Blair . . . you destroyed your father's life."

January 2106

Emry waited several minutes after the crate stopped bouncing around before she took a chance on cracking it open. The smart-matter foam that concealed her chemical and heat signatures and gave false readings to terahertz and x-ray scans also impeded her own ability to pick up sounds from outside, so she waited until the storeroom was (hopefully) empty again before she risked cracking the seal. As she lay waiting, keeping her respiration slow to conserve her limited air supply, she hoped no one in the facility had an immediate, urgent need for replacement bioprinter cartridges.

When she figured enough time had passed, she cracked open the lid and slowly stuck out the hand in which she grasped the highly illegal scene-painter grenade she'd paid a fair percentage of her inheritance to obtain. Pressing the trigger with her thumb, she lofted it into the air, yanking her hand back in and letting the lid fall shut just before she heard a muffled pop and splat from outside. She waited a few more seconds for the thin film now plastered over every surface in the grenade's line of sight—hopefully including any image receptors—to flow together and harden and for its nanoparticles to "lock in" the light currently passing through them. From now until the film decayed in an hour, each nanoparticle would continue shining that same wavelength and intensity of light toward the surface it adhered to, so that any camera would continue to see the same image it saw now, or a reasonable facsimile thereof. Emry was thus able to climb out of the crate without being spotted.

Still, depending on how good the motion sensors were in here, the painter grenade might have set them off already. It was possible the security personnel would chalk it up to a false alarm when they saw nothing on the monitors, but Emry doubted they would be that careless. After all, this organization was even better at making enemies than the Freakshow had been. So she'd have to move quickly before someone came to investigate.

Again, she quailed at the thought of what she was trying to do. How could she ever get away with this, when so many assassins and terrorists before her had failed? She reminded herself that, at this point, she had nothing left to lose.

The storeroom door was locked from the outside—oh, they were being *very* careful—but the lock itself was only moderately challenging for Emry, and only because of the time limit. It opened itself to her within twenty seconds, and she gingerly cracked the door open. She tossed out her second painter grenade, waited a few seconds after the pop-splat, and darted out the door and down the hall, scooping up the remains of the grenade core as she'd done with the first. A handy ladies' room presented itself, and she ducked inside just before a pair of armed guards rounded the corner, heading for the storeroom. With luck, it would take them several minutes to detect the nanoparticle films.

Either way, the security guards ironically helped her, for as they went past, she slid her badge through the crack of the bathroom door. After a few moments, it vibrated briefly against her fingers, and she pulled it back to confirm that it had indeed imaged and copied the guards' badge design, with her own face and a fake name in the relevant spots. A second vibration told her that it had successfully copied their RFID codes. She should now have access to anywhere in the complex.

She paused to check herself in the mirror and make herself look neater than someone who'd just smuggled herself in a crate, combing her unruly hair and tying it back into a frumpy, non-attention-grabbing bun. Her tinted interface visor and loose jacket helped make her further nondescript. Nodding in approval, she headed for the door . . . and then hurried back to use the facilities. She'd been in that crate a long time.

This was the lowest level of the complex, and her target was higher. She could override the lock on the elevator doors, but didn't want to risk drawing attention or being cornered by going up in the elevator itself. And she wanted to avoid being spotted on a stairwell camera. So once she forced the elevator doors open, pleased to see that the car was way at the top, she stepped back, got a running start and jumped up as hard as she could. She kicked off the back wall and over to the spinward side, which she ran up as fast as she could to maximize Cori traction.

Suddenly the elevator car lurched into downward motion, startling Emry. She slipped, twisted, and caught herself on the lip of the door frame of her target floor. Desperately, she pulled herself up and wedged her fingers into the crack, hoping this door wouldn't have an alarm. The car was looming closer and looking heavier by the second. She finally managed to wrench the doors open and pull herself through . . . only to see, as she darted her gaze back, that the car had come to a stop one floor above. *Whew. And so my life of crime continues.*

Emry clambered to her feet, retrieved her dislodged visor from the floor, and made her way to the library. One quick hack of the appointment schedule later, she headed to the office where her target awaited. She eased into the outer office, trying to look inconspicuous. It looked vacant, so she sidled her way over toward the inner door, bracing herself.

"Can I help you?"

Emry jumped. The stern, clipped, British-accented voice came from someone she hadn't seen, a tiny, short-limbed woman with curly blond hair. "I said, can I help you?" the woman repeated with even more impatience than last time.

"I'm here to see the big guy." She angled her badge to show the woman her fake name. "I have an appointment."

"No, you don't."

Emry blinked. "Aren't you gonna check the schedule?"

The woman tapped her head. "Already did."

"Oh, you have a buffer?"

The woman looked offended by the suggestion. "No."

"Then you must've overlooked it. Check again."

"I don't have to. I made the schedule."

Oh, vack. "Look, it's really important. I have to see him, just for a minute." She tried an ingratiating smile. "I'm sure he wouldn't mind?"

The blond woman crossed her stout arms. "I would."

"And who the hell are you that I should care?"

Now she just looked amused. "Obviously you are not what you pretend to be."

This was ridiculous. All she'd gone through to get to this point, and now she was being stymied by a woman she could jump over in full gravity? Who did this bitch think she was, anyway? Looming over her, Emry whipped off her visor and gave her best Banshee snarl. "What I am is the woman who's gonna make you a whole lot shorter if you don't get the hell out of my way!"

"Oh, we like to shout, do we? Makes us feel all mighty, eh? Do get over yourself, Miss Blair, and have a seat like a good little girl."

All the steam went out of Emry, and she could only gape in shock. "How did . . ." She looked down at the name tag to make sure she hadn't made a horrible mistake programming it. No, it still said LANA GORDON. "How did you . . ."

"I know everything," the woman said, sounding singularly bored by the fact. "Do have a seat. Some of us have work to do."

Just then, the inner door opened. "That's all right, Sally. I'm ready to talk with the young lady now."

The blonde—Sally—threw a glance skyward, as though she found Sensei Villareal rather silly for indulging in such games. "Fine. Lets me get back to filing."

"Then all is right with the worlds," Sensei said with that familiar charm, which left no impression whatsoever on Sally's hide. The silver-haired man chuckled and turned back to Emry. "Welcome to the

TSC, young lady," he said. "Don't feel bad. Even the toughest of us has trouble handling Sally Knox. You've actually made a very good showing of yourself, coming this far. But perhaps you'd like to tell me," he went on more sternly, "just what it is you are doing here?"

Emry took a deep breath, breaking free of her paralyzing awe, and said what she'd come here to say. "I'm here to sign up. I want to be a Troubleshooter."

Villareal laughed. "You have an unorthodox way of going about it. You could have saved yourself a lot of trouble by applying through the usual routes."

"And would you have even given me a second glance? I . . ." She lowered her eyes. "I knew that if you checked . . . you'd find out I have a criminal record. I wanted to prove that could be an asset to you."

"And get my attention in the process." He shook his head. "I'm sorry, but that's not enough to qualify you as a Troubleshooter."

Anger made her bolder. "I got your attention, didn't I? You're talking to me. And I managed to get all the way here, into one of the most secure places in Solsys, by myself."

"Only because we let you."

Once more, she was thrown off. "You . . . wha?"

"We detected you down in the storeroom. You would've been arrested before you got into the elevator shaft . . . if someone hadn't vouched for you." At her puzzled look, he led her into his office, where a stocky, balding man with a chubby, lived-in face rose to greet her. "Emerald Blair, meet Arkady Nazarbayev. Whom you've actually met before."

"Hello, little one," Nazarbayev said. "Do you remember me? No, I doubt it . . . I was dressed rather differently when last we met."

But Emry recognized his name. "I remember. But . . . I'm surprised you remember me."

"That day on Greenwood? I will never forget it. I still regret that I could not do more that day . . . could not stop them sooner. I—"

She cut him off, fidgeting. "Yeah, okay. Not your fault. Don't worry about it."

"Still," Villareal said, "Arkady feels he owes you something, so he persuaded me to hold off and see what you were up to. Though I thought I'd throw a couple of obstacles in your path along the way. Sorry about the elevator car; you were in no real danger. Meanwhile I had Sally call up your records, while Arkady filled me in on your checkered past."

Emry stared at Nazarbayev, who shrugged. "I . . . stayed in touch with your father. He wanted me to keep an eye out for you. But with my duties, I could rarely spare the time. He found other means, but I stayed in the loop as much as I could." He lowered his head. "He was a fine man, your father. He would be proud to see you as a Trouble-shooter."

"Now, let's not get ahead of ourselves, old bear," said Villareal. "I haven't given my blessing yet. To be sure, you're a strong, intelligent, resourceful young woman, Emerald. And I've always wanted to have a Vanguardian in the Corps."

"I'm not a Vanguardian!"

He raised a frosty brow, and she subsided. "But it takes more than that to make a Troubleshooter. It takes integrity, commitment, com-passion, and regard for others. It takes total dedication, the willing-ness to see it through no matter the hardships. You have yet to convince me you have those qualities." He stepped closer, placed his hands on her shoulders, and looked her deep in the eyes. "So tell me, Emerald Blair: why do you want to be a Troubleshooter?"

So she told him. It poured out of her, truths she had never bared to another soul. She told him everything: how her mother had died, how she'd blamed her father, her years as a Freak, her attempts to make amends, the devastating news from Bimala. She told him how, after the funeral, she had gone back to her old home, finding her room restored to the way it had been before she'd trashed it the last time. All her old comic books were there, printed out in hard copy to be lovingly handled and read over and over. "I looked at those comics, and I realized they were trying to tell me something." She knew she might be sabotaging herself if she gave the impression she only saw Troubleshooting as a comic-book fantasy. But she drove on regardless, unable to tell anything but the truth.

"Power," she said. "Mom and Dad always tried to teach me about the responsibility that came with my power. Always taught me to use my power to help, never to hurt. I thought Daddy had betrayed that lesson when he didn't save Mommy. But . . . I was the one who betrayed it. I didn't realize . . . he needed me, as much as I needed him. I was all he had left. That . . . that gave me power over him. Over his whole life from that moment on."

She drew a shuddering breath. "I could've saved him. We could've saved each other. But I used my power . . . to hurt him. I abused it. Because I only thought about me. I forgot what he taught me. What Mommy taught me. The more power you have, the more you have to put others first. Every time I forgot that . . . someone got hurt. And now . . . now . . ." She couldn't finish the thought. Arkady put an arm around her shoulders.

She looked up at him for the first time. "You were there too, in those comics. And you," she said to Sensei. "And the others. Real heroes, putting your lives on the line for others, using your powers to help and never to harm.

"I know it sounds corny, but . . . that's when it fell into place. That was why nothing I tried to do fulfilled me. Because I'd been too focused on my own needs, my own wants, and that wasn't enough. When we were all together . . . when we were happy . . . it was because we lived for each other. Gave to each other.

"If . . . if I'd given comfort to Daddy . . . instead of thinking of myself . . . it could've healed us both."

She paused. "I guess I'd like to think I always knew that, on some level. Even as a Freak, I was always taking in strays, rescuing fellow mods, avenging their suffering. It was when I helped people that I felt the best.

"So I know that's what I have to do now," she went on. "I have to make a difference. I have to carry on Daddy's work. Not the way he did . . . I've been a fighter too long. But . . . he always approved of the Troubleshooters. And I guess . . . I owe you a lot," she said to Arkady.

She turned back to Sensei. "I know how I must look. I'm a juvenile delinquent with a sob story and comic-book daydreams. But I'm not asking for an easy break. I need to earn this, as much for me as for you. I just know . . . I have to be a Troubleshooter."

Her words ran out, and no one else spoke for some time. Emry stayed frozen, afraid to let herself react.

Finally, Sensei's mouth quirked into a smile. "You know something, Emerald? I stole a few cars in my youth as well. I generally returned them intact by morning, of course, albeit with an occasional pair of panties left over in the backseat." With a wink, he went to his desk and activated the intercom. "Sally, would you prepare the enrollment forms, please? The Corps is taking on a new recruit."

"Hmp," Sally replied. *"I give her a week."*

15

A Many-splendored Thing

November 2107

Grandma Rachel had begun crying before Emry finished her narrative. "I guess you hate me now," Emry said when she was done.

Rachel gasped. "Oh, God, no! Come here!" She enfolded Emry in her arms, and this time it was a profound relief. "No, how could I hate you?"

"It's my fault!"

Rachel pulled back. "Don't you ever say that, young lady!" she scolded. "Richard died doing what he believed in. He chose to face danger to help others, just as you do. What happened to him is not your fault, whatever that horrid woman told you."

"She loved him," Emry said in Bimala's defense.

"That's no excuse for making you a scapegoat. No one can know if he was careless that day, if he could've saved himself if he'd been more alert."

"Maybe," Emry said. "But however it ended, the last seven years of his life were miserable—because of me. And I can never make up for that, no matter how much good I do now."

Rachel gazed at Emry, shaking her head. "We are so much alike."

"Wha—what do you mean?"

"I mean I've said practically the same thing to myself so many times in the past two years."

Emry frowned. "You . . . blame yourself?"

"Yes. Was I a good mother? No. When he needed me, when he lost Lyra and then you . . . did I go to him? Did I comfort him, help him heal? Did I help him find you and try to heal you too? No. I didn't." She stood and began to pace around the room. "I just stayed here, caught up in my work."

Emry followed Rachel to her feet. "You had other responsibilities. Your other kids," she said, nodding at Rachel's womb.

"That didn't make *him* any less my responsibility! I should have gone to him!" She winced. "I should've tried harder, years before, to make amends. I should've never let the rift form at all."

"What . . . how did it happen?" Emry could no longer believe that Rachel had simply been too obsessed with her work to care about Richard.

"We argued . . . I couldn't accept that he wanted to leave the Vanguard, to leave *me,* so he could help outsiders. I was bitter at how they'd treated us, forced us to retreat from the world. I agreed with Eliot that we should build our own, better society."

She sighed. "I should've listened to Richard. I should've been proud of him for being so much more compassionate, so unwilling to give in to bitterness. And I did admire that about him, I did. But . . ." She met Emry's eyes again, a repentant look on her face. "I was afraid of what would happen. I didn't want to let my little boy go out into the big, bad world and put his life on the line. And I let that fear become anger. We kept fighting until I just gave up, told him that he should go, and washed my hands of the whole thing.

"After that, I threw myself into my work, into having more children, because . . . well, as a distraction, I guess. By the time I was ready to make amends with Richard, I was too caught up in the work. And maybe too afraid to reach out and try."

"You should've," Emry said promptly. "It would've made a difference. If Daddy had kept trying . . . if he'd come for me in rehab, instead of sending Bimala . . ." She lowered her head. "I said I didn't want him in my life, but I was really hurt because he wouldn't come himself. Because I missed him." She saw Rachel was crying again. "Oh, Goddess, no, I didn't mean to accuse you!" She hugged Rachel.

"It's all right, sweetheart. We've both got plenty of regrets to go around. We shouldn't hide from them."

"No," Emry said. "But we shouldn't wallow in them either. That just leads to more regrets. Worse ones."

She led Rachel back to the couch, and they sat quietly for a moment. Then Emry laughed. "Ohh, we're a mess, aren't we? What a screwed-up family."

"Show me a family that isn't," Rachel said with a slight smirk.

"Mine was great . . . for thirteen years. I guess I should be grateful for that."

"Your father was a wonderful man, Emerald. And I'm sure your mother was wonderful too. I'll always regret that my stupid pride and cowardice kept me from ever meeting her."

"Hey, let's not start that again. We're only human, okay? More or less."

Rachel scoffed. "Only human. You know, I think it's the other way around. The more complex the system, the more chaotic it can get. There are some things we can probably never breed out of the species. Maybe, if we're lucky, we can remove the human capacity for war and murder and brutality . . . but I doubt we'll ever evolve beyond the tendency to screw things up royally with the people we love."

"I wish I'd known that nine years ago," Emry said. "I thought Dad was perfect. That he could do no wrong. I felt so betrayed when he didn't save Mom. If I'd just . . . forgiven him for being fallible, for not being able to save everyone in the universe . . . maybe we could've healed each other."

Rachel stroked her hair. "Maybe that's so. But isn't that exactly why you should forgive yourself for being fallible? For being only human?"

"I don't know if it's really the same," Emry said. But after a moment's thought, she said, "Tell you what. I'll try it if you do too. Okay?"

"It's a deal." Rachel hugged her granddaughter again, and Emry didn't let her go for a long time.

———

"Rachel is, as usual, quite right," Eliot told Emry the next day as they sparred in his private gym. "You're not to blame for your father's fate, any more than she is."

"I'm starting to get that now," Emry acknowledged as she sized him up, awaiting his next attack. Every day since their race to the mountaintop, she and Thorne had been sparring daily. Emry consistently tried to get the better of him and failed at every turn. Even the judo moves that helped her against stronger sparring partners weren't giving her much luck. And it wasn't just physical. Thorne's confidence alone bore the momentum of a stroid; she could believe that nothing would move him without his consent.

"The real blame," he went on as they circled each other, "lies with the gangsters whose petty turf war brought such tragedy to you and Richard." He came forward easily, struck at her, let her block his blows as he spoke. "And with the lawlessness of Belt society, the lack of effectual mechanisms for bringing order and stability in an age of ever-increasing individual power." He caught her arm, spun her, pinned her in a full Nelson from behind. "That is what I intend to change with this alliance. By working together, we can bring peace and safety to our homes without needing to rely on a single large state to impose it unilaterally."

She relaxed in his arms. Being pinned by him wasn't exactly unpleasant, since they were both shirtless. "You don't need to sell me. Lotta folks won't go for it, though. Striders don't like outsiders telling them what to do."

"Which is why it must be a partnership," he said, releasing her but holding on to her hand. "Each partner having a role in governing itself, while still contributing to a greater, more potent whole."

"I've been wondering," Emry said as she got some distance and began to circle again. "Well, Zephyr's been wondering. If you want to bring everyone together, why are you only dealing with mods?"

He lunged, but she managed to dodge this time. "Only to start with. They would be more receptive to us. Besides—the rest of the Striders will have to accept the mods if this alliance is to work. And we mods will be essential to the peacekeeping process. We need to be a stronger, more numerous bloc than we were on Earth, or we risk being marginalized or ostracized again." He shot forward again, striking with an arm. Emry relaxed and yielded, using his momentum to fling him around and past her. He managed to retain his footing, though, and caught himself at the edge of the mat. "Impressive."

She nodded, accepting the praise, and went on, "Most folks out here don't have much problem with mods. Long as they aren't terrorists or something. But if you bring the mods together, don't include the rest, well, people might start to get nervous. It could backfire."

"Perhaps." He struck without warning this time, and had her pinned in seconds. "But first I must bring the more unruly mod nations in line if I wish to reassure the rest of the Striders. It's a calculated risk, but an essential part of the process. Trust me, Emerald—this has all been taken into consideration."

She gazed up into his eyes. "I do, Eliot. I trust you." She relaxed into his arms and kissed him. It lasted for a long time, and held deeper meaning than mere gratification. That simple acknowledgment—that she trusted this man—felt like a major step forward in their relationship. Perhaps in her ability to have relationships. All her sexually mature life, she'd sought powerful men as lovers, but had always resisted getting too close to them—and now that she'd come clean to Rachel, she was beginning to understand why. Releasing her pain and guilt toward her father, reminding herself of the love and trust they'd once shared, made it easier to lower her defenses and let herself believe she could safely embrace a closer connection to this man.

Instead of trying to express that in words, though, she said it with her lips, her hands, her body. She and Eliot wrestled again, this time assaulting only each other's clothes. He dominated as usual, but this time she made no effort to jockey for position, instead trusting herself to his powerful, sensitive hands. Instead of trying to take from him, to assert her will, she simply gave joy, shared joy, experienced joy. It made it truly special and moving, rewarding her well beyond the pleasure his hands and mouth imparted upon her body with virtuoso skill.

After a long while, she lay relaxed atop him, gazing up at his face. "What was it like on Earth?" she asked him. "For you and the Vanguard? I mean, I know all the stories of what you did . . . but not from your side. Except what my dad told me, and he was a kid for most of it. And the others I've met, they told me about some of their adventures, but didn't want to talk about . . . what was really going on underneath it all."

So Eliot told her of how he had argued with the Vanguard leadership to let him and his peers go down to Earth and try to make a difference in a turbulent world. How their fear of backlash from a prejudiced population had made them unwilling to help. How Eliot had dismissed them as hidebound cowards and forced the issue, leading the habitat's most successful and powerful mods down to save lives in defiance of the leaders of both Vanguard and Earth. How he had kept them committed to their mission despite the controversy, the rhetoric, the hate mail, the death threats. Even despite the actual deaths of some of his peers—whether intentionally targeted, as Liesl Warner had been, or in defense of others like Liam Shannon. Eliot told her how their brave deaths had only inspired him to fight harder, determined to give them meaning.

"But I saw that what we were doing was only a stopgap," he told her as he absently caressed her back. "I realized that if we truly wished to make a difference, we had to do it in the political and social arena. Had to attack the causes of the turmoil as well as the effects. We were more than just crimefighters; we had the intellect to lead the way in finding solutions to the environmental woes, engineering new crops to fight the famines, building the new economy of the Molecular Age and the sociopolitical institutions that would rely on it. We were something greater than human, so we had to aspire to a greater goal than simply bringing the odd terrorists and rioters to justice."

"Isn't that a little arrogant?"

He studied her. "Arrogance is the assertion of a status or right to which one is not entitled. Is it arrogant to acknowledge an ability you actually do have? Would it be arrogant, say, for you to state that you can bench-press a tonne in one gee?" He stopped himself. "Never mind. I suppose we were arrogant, not in asserting our ability to make those decisions, but in failing to acknowledge that others had a voice in the process as well. That is not a mistake we will repeat again." He smirked. "I was young, cocky, and heavy-handed. I hadn't yet learned the value of subtlety. When I tried to stave off the building tensions between Earth and the orbital nations, tensions we had helped to create, I did it by trying to dominate and bully both sides into compliance, and only made things worse.

"Once we relocated to the Belt, our goodwill squandered largely through my own excesses, I took much time to ponder my errors, to learn from them. Among my own people, I learned how to govern through consensus, to persuade through subtle diplomacy. I created an offspring who could fulfill that ideal, could be everything I am not, and much that I am. And now, she is helping me fulfill my ambition at last—but to do so in the *right* way this time."

He stroked Emry's hair. "And now I have you on my side as well, offering a merging of Vanguardian and outside perspectives. Like Psyche, you are a part of me, and yet you bring me more than I have on my own. You are the crucial bridge I need to unite the Vanguard with the Troubleshooters, and through them with the mainstream. Psyche may have a beauty and charisma to match your own, but even she cannot offer that symbolism."

Emry stared at him uneasily. "So that's what I am to you? A symbol? A tool?"

He smiled. "Far more, Emerald. You may be the key to achieving my greatest desire. I cherish you for that." His brow furrowed. "Perhaps it would be more romantic to say I cherish you simply for yourself. Do not doubt that I do, Emerald. But I am an ambitious man. My life has been defined by my goals. And so my feelings are defined in those terms as well." He stroked her cheek. "I only hope you don't feel slighted by that. By having to . . . share me with my ambitions."

"Oh, no, Eliot!" She cradled his face in her hands and kissed him softly. "I wouldn't have you any other way. You don't know how amazing it feels to be with you, Eliot. I mean, people call me a celebrity, but I haven't done much to deserve it. It's mostly just the face, the tits, and the checkered past. But you . . . I think you're the kind of man they still write history books about thousands of years later. You're a great leader, a visionary. In the past, you probably could've been a great conqueror. An Alexander, an Ashoka. You have that kind of power and will. But you chose to be a statesman . . . a Jefferson, an al-Bayyari. I think you're gonna be the one who unites the Belt . . . maybe the whole Sol System.

"I don't know," she went on a moment later. "Like I said, all this nation-building, this history-making . . . it's way the vack out of my league. But the man who's able to do it all . . . it's an incredible feeling to be around that man. To know that . . . he thinks I have a place in his life, even in his goals, it's . . ."

She searched for words. Nothing seemed right . . . until she had to admit that only three words would do, the ones that had been looming in the back of her mind for some time and that she finally felt brave enough to face. She prefaced them with one more deep kiss, fraught with meaning. "Eliot . . . I love you."

He said nothing in return. He simply pulled her to him and took her once again. It was enough. It made her feel, more than anything else had made her feel in a decade, that she *belonged*. In Eliot Thorne's arms, she was home.

And she would be happy never to leave home again.

"I've never felt like this, Zephy!" Emry sighed as she floated in *Zephyr*'s residential deck, feeling weightless in more ways than one. "At least, I never let myself feel it. Now I don't know what I was so afraid of!"

Zephyr's avatar studied her from the display wall. He was again in stallion mode, although he'd made it silver and added Art Deco wings which she quite liked. She didn't much miss the naked Greek god now that she had the real thing on a several-times-daily basis. "Being hurt, I suppose," he suggested. "Losing the one you love. That's usually the risk people run. And it's one you'd be understandably sensitive to."

Zephyr's words gave her pause. "I guess so. Also . . . hurting the man, I guess. I didn't want to risk screwing it up for both of us. Again." She shook off her moment of melancholy. "But Eliot . . . he's a rock. I can't imagine there being anything he couldn't handle, couldn't solve."

The stallion shook his mane. "High praise indeed. So you're confident that he can help us expose Tai and redeem the TSC?"

"Of course."

"I see. And how is that coming, exactly? If he's managed to make any significant progress, you neglected to mention it."

"I'd've told you if he had—you know that."

"Well . . . I suppose I'm just feeling a little neglected. This is the first time you've been to see me in days."

"Aww, Zeph, I'm sorry!" She stroked his nearest bulkhead. "I've just been so caught up in Eliot. And Psyche, Grandma Rachel, the whole Vanguard!"

"I understand," he told her. "And of course there's your ongoing effort to contact Sensei Villareal. Right?"

"Wha? Oh, Zephy, you know I can't risk implicating him by contacting him myself! Eliot and Psyche are handling it."

"With little success so far."

"Yeah, that's weird. I would've thought Sensei'd be open to working with the Vanguard. But Eliot says he hasn't responded to our advances."

"Would you like me to try contacting him?"

Emry stared at his avatar. "You know that'd be just as bad as if I did it. What's this all about, Zeph?"

"I just want to make sure you keep your focus. I'm glad for you that you're so happy, but perhaps this isn't the ideal time to indulge in it."

"What else is there to do?" she asked. "Eliot just sent Psyche off to Mars to look for more dirt on Tai. They think he has allies there who could be turned. And Sensei's got some kind of business meeting on Phobos, so Psyche's gonna try to contact him there. Meanwhile I'm just laying low. Wanted criminal, remember? Take it from an old Freakshow girl—when the law's after you, sometimes it's best to duck in a hole and stay real quiet for a while. And it helps to have someone to keep you company while you're there," she finished with a saucy grin as she sorted through her sexiest outfits, looking for something worthy of being ripped to shreds by Eliot tonight.

Zephyr morphed his avatar back into the Greek god, apparently so he could cross his arms at her and frown. "I defer to your expertise in fugitive living. Still, I'd be more comfortable if we were more in the loop. You're surprisingly content with delegating this to the Thornes."

"And why shouldn't I be? I'm no politician, no great strategist. I'm muscle. Point me at a bad guy and I punch him."

The avatar's gaze softened. "You underestimate yourself, Emry. You have Vanguardian intelligence, even if you've resisted cultivating it. And it puzzles me that you aren't asking more questions. That you aren't straining at the bit—pardon the equestrian metaphor—to get out there and fix this problem. It doesn't seem like you."

"That's 'cause before now, I was never this much at peace. I couldn't let myself relax and trust other people." She threw him a look. "Maybe you could try trusting a little more. Eliot has taken us both under his protection, and frankly you aren't sounding very grateful."

"Gratitude doesn't alter the facts. And the fact is, the longer we wait, the more entrenched Gregor Tai's control of the TSC becomes."

"I know that. Eliot is doing all he can."

"I'd prefer it if we could see the specifics of that for ourselves."

Emry sighed. "Why can't you trust him, Zeph? He's not the kind of human who enslaved and abused you. He's the kind who's fought *against* people like that his whole life!"

"And I respect that about him. But he is also a very ambitious and calculating man who values control above all else."

"You don't still think he's up to something?"

"A man like Thorne, by his nature, is always up to many things at any given time. He makes no secret of his goals. And he would use any means at his disposal to fulfill them."

This was getting ridiculous. "Including me?" she shot back. "Zephy, if you're trying to say he's tricked me into falling in love with him—well, that's the stupidest thing you've ever said! You *know* me, Zeph! You know I'm not that type!"

"I also know that Vanguardians are skilled at pheromonal control. Tell me—do you find he smells alluring even after extensive physical exertion?"

Emry sighed. "Ohh, yeah."

"Parandrostenol."

"Whoozits?"

"Normal male perspiration contains a pheromone called androstenol, which is attractive to women. But within twenty minutes, it oxidizes to androstenone, which tends to be repellent to women. Parandrostenol is a synthetic variant, which resists oxidation. Thorne has apparently engineered himself to secrete it instead—thus intensifying his attractive power."

"So what?" Emry challenged. "You were the one who told me about the limits of pheromones. I'm not some mindless bitch in heat. And don't you *dare* pick up that straight line!"

"I wasn't going to. Emry, I know you're not blind or foolish. But I also know you've resisted love for a long time, even with partners who would have been good for you. Now that you've made greater peace with your demons and finally feel free to love, I imagine the desire to give into the temptation must be very powerful. And that makes it easy to exploit."

Emry was too distracted now to focus on wardrobe. She just shoved a number of outfits into her duffel bag, deciding she'd choose one later. "You've got it all wrong. I'm not blinded by love or pheromones or anything. My head's clearer than it's ever been! I feel . . . *whole* now. I feel like I'm finally a grown woman."

"And yet you're deferring to Thorne to make decisions for you. Are you sure you aren't trying to recapture the idyll of your childhood? Feeling secure in the arms of a powerful man, the company of a warm and affectionate woman?"

Emry grimaced. "Oh, don't go Oedipal on me, Rex! That's just creepy!" She pushed off the closet doors, aiming for the ladder well. "I don't know what kind of cyber mood you're in today, Zephy," she said as she pulled herself headfirst down the ladder, "but you're really getting on my nerves! And you're getting close to crossing a line."

"I'm sorry you feel that way, Emry. I'm just trying to look out for you."

"Well, when I need you to, I'll let you know!" She slapped the airlock panel.

But the door stayed closed. "Just let me say my piece, Emerald," Zephyr said over the intercom.

She sighed. "Make it quick. I'm running late."

"The record shows Eliot Thorne to be a man who doesn't take well to being disagreed with. When faced with those holding dissenting opinions, he either persuades them to change their minds . . . or he dissociates from them altogether and *creates* people who will be more sympathetic. What happens, Emry, when you and he *aren't* pursuing the same goals?"

"What happens when I kick this door open? Huh? Will it hurt? Tell me that."

Without another word, Zephyr allowed the lock to open for her. But Emry paused halfway through the door. "I'm sorry, pal. I shouldn't have said that."

"I'm unharmed."

"But you're wrong about him. He can admit his mistakes. He's learned a lot from the ones he made on Earth. And he trusts me. He thinks I have a real role to play in the future he's building. I know he'd listen to me.

"He's a strong-willed man, sure, and an ambitious one. But he's a *good* man. Do you really think I could love him otherwise?"

Zephyr didn't reply for a moment. "Even good men bear close watching when they have great power."

Emry sighed. He just wasn't letting this go! "And he *knows* that, damn it! That's the whole *point* of going after—" She broke off. "Just let me out."

"I'm sorry I upset you."

"Yeah, me too. Right now I gotta go."

The outer doors opened onto the access tunnel. Emry shot through them without another word. *He'll see,* she thought. *Soon we'll have Sensei on our side and this whole thing will be straightened out, just like Eliot planned.* Villareal's silence on this affair remained odd, but Emry was confident it would change soon. *If anyone can get through to him, Psyche can.*

Private shuttle HV763M
Keeping station near Phobos

Yukio Villareal pulled Psyche's nude body against his and clutched her tightly. Her hair flowed forward in the microgravity, writhing around their torsos like a living thing, its spun-gold strands stroking and tickling his skin. He'd never felt hair so soft, so silky. It was one of the many things he loved about Psyche.

The thought came with a twinge of guilt that Yukio tried to shake off. There was no reason for it, he told himself. His wife accepted that he was simply one of those men for whom monogamy was not an option, and that the very things that drew her to him would inevitably draw others. He'd never made a secret of that with any woman, although his first wife had not proved as able to live with it as she'd imagined. But Helena had always tolerated it, even indulged in a few dalliances herself. She believed, as he did, that the only real infidelity was deception.

And that was the problem. Yukio had always striven to be scrupulously honest about his affairs. As an active Troubleshooter, he had never risked compromising his judgment by sleeping with a woman he was charged with protecting—not until afterwards, anyway. As an administrator, he had never slept with a Troubleshooter, trainee or Corps employee (which took some willpower when their ranks included the likes of Lydia Muchangi or Emerald Blair). And he had never, ever kept an affair secret from his wife. Until this one.

As always, he reminded himself that there were very good reasons for it. Psyche had insisted, months ago when their affair had begun, that no one could know. Her father was overprotective, and despite his long isolation from Strider society, had an extensive intelligence network keeping him informed. Indeed, it was a covert fact-finding mission that had brought Psyche to Demetria to begin with. Eliot Thorne was slow to trust, and if he ever discovered that his own daughter had fallen in love with an older man who just happened to be the founder of the Troubleshooter Corps and one of the subjects of her investigations, his fury would jeopardize any hope of rapprochement between Vanguard and the Corps. So it was imperative, Psyche had stressed with tears in those quicksilver eyes, that no one—absolutely no one—could ever know of their love affair. That was why Yukio had needed to lie to his wife and fabricate a business trip to Phobos when Psyche had summoned him for a rendezvous there. Yukio hated keeping a secret from Helena, but Psyche was absolutely convinced it was necessary. And he trusted Psyche. He respected her judgment. He would rather die than see her unhappy.

That was the other reason for his guilt. Through all his past affairs, one thing had remained constant: though every one of his partners had his affection and respect, Helena remained his soul mate, the love of his life. He still loved her just as much . . . but he was beginning to realize he loved Psyche more. He'd known of her engineered allure, her pheromones, but he was too old and experienced to feel it so deeply based on that alone. This was the real thing, deep and complex and overpowering. Even after two months apart, Psyche had filled his thoughts, commanded his dreams. She'd monopolized his fantasies, even when he was making love to his wife.

But how can I break it off? he asked himself as Psyche's long brown legs wrapped around his hips and pulled him into her. The dear girl loved him desperately, enough to risk everything for him, and he simply couldn't dishonor that. It would be ungrateful, selfish, unfair.

Rationalizations aside, he simply loved her, loved *this,* too much. He'd never known such ecstasy, such contentment and warmth. Her passion was transcendent—not to mention her skill. With Psyche, there was no need for handholds, restraints, or bouncing off the walls (although she definitely enjoyed restraints). Her technique was so perfect, her reflexes so precise, that she could keep the two of them suspended in midair for hours, needing at most the tiniest tap of a finger or toe against a wall to cancel their drift toward it. It took care and attention on both their parts to achieve it, but that care attuned them deeply to their own and each other's bodies, and the required communication brought them closer, made their lovemaking as much a meeting of minds as of flesh. Every move one of them made had to be done in full awareness of its effect upon the other, of how their fates were inextricably intertwined. Few experiences brought such intimacy. As they floated in space, touching only each other, they formed an isolated system, a two-body problem of erotic physics. When he closed his eyes, Psyche defined his universe.

All too soon the sex was over, but the lovers clung to each other and tumbled lazily together in the center of the chamber. Soon, though, he heard her sniffling. He pulled back to meet her glistening eyes. "What's wrong, my love?"

"Ohh, Yukio. I can't stand that all we can have are these brief encounters. I'll have to leave soon—Daddy is expecting me. And I have no idea when I'll be able to see you again."

The realization that they might be parted indefinitely hit him hard. "There must be a way, love. Defy your father, come clean with him. Let's be together openly."

"You know I can't, my darling. There's too much at stake."

"We can change that. Let me come to Vanguard, endorse your alliance, denounce Tai openly."

"No! Darling, we've talked about this before. It's just too dangerous for you. Tai needs your aegis to give him legitimacy. If he knew you'd turned on him . . . ohh, I don't want to think about it!"

He grimaced. "We have to, *cara*. In a way, it's because of us he's gotten this far at all. Because I was a romantic fool who wanted to spend more time with my wife and my mistress and trusted Tai to take care of my Troubleshooters for me. And now, staying silent is making it worse. It seems as though I'm endorsing the things he's doing."

"But it's safer for you."

He chuckled, stroking her head. "I can take care of myself, dear *mariposa*. Especially if I have the Vanguard at my side."

She averted her gaze. "Father would never accept you. We . . . if you were there, we couldn't be together at all, and I couldn't stand being so close and not . . ." She broke off. "There's no way I could hide my feelings from him. It would ruin everything."

"But if we explained how much we love each other—"

"He's a cynical man, Yukio. To see his only daughter with a celebrated rake like you . . . he'd be convinced you'd taken advantage of me, and nothing you said could change that."

He could hardly bear to press on, but there was no choice. "He's also a pragmatic man, dearest. He might not like me much, but he'd cooperate with me if it served his interests."

"But he'd never let us—"

"I know." The words were glass tearing from his throat. "But for the sake of others, we have no choice. We can't place our selfish wants above the good of Solsys. The problems of two people don't amount to a hill of beans. . . ." He couldn't muster the will to finish the allusion. "Psyche, it has to be done. I can't stay silent any longer. About any of it."

She took his head in her hands and studied him for a long moment, her eyes boring deep into his. "Your mind really is made up," she said at length. Regret showed in her eyes, but it was more subdued, even detached, than he would have expected. The brave girl was managing it far better than he was, that was for sure. "I'm sorry, Yukio. It really was great fun while it lasted."

He frowned. "What are you saying?"

Still clutching his head, she gave him one more long, deep kiss that belied the lack of passion in her words. "I'm saying that you've been a very entertaining plaything, but you've outlived your usefulness." She pushed him away, hard. She caught herself smoothly on a handhold, but in his shock he did nothing to arrest his impact with the bulkhead. It was far less jarring than her words, her actions.

"No. No, Psyche, you said you loved me!"

"You? Don't be ridiculous, old man!" She laughed, though it sounded a bit forced. He hoped it was forced. But how could she say such things to him if she truly felt as he'd believed? "And put some clothes on, you skinny old dog." She tossed his clothes at him and began donning her own.

He began dressing automatically, barely even noticing, as he tried to process what was happening here. "How can you say this? Psyche, the things I've done for you! Quit my job, betrayed my wife."

Her laughter intensified, her wide, toothy grin becoming feral. "Ohh, yes, how priceless! I had you eating out of my hand."

"That's all this was to you? A game?"

She drifted over, patted him on the head, and helped him finish dressing. "Of course! You don't seriously think a young, gorgeous creature like me would fall for a withered old has-been like you, do you? You with your preening arrogance, thinking you're God's gift to women. Women only fuck you because they're drawn to power. But you gave up that power, Archie-boy," she went on, tweaking his chin with her finger. "So you lost your sex appeal. And while you were at it, by the way, you sold out your precious Troubleshooters and let them become Tai's puppets. So you've got nothing left. Oh, except a happy, trusting marriage—oh, wait, you vacked that too, didn't you?" She giggled with sadistic glee.

Tears burned Yukio's eyes, clinging in the microgravity, and he shook his head to clear them away. Dizziness overtook him, but it was not from the free fall. It was his world that was falling, collapsing around him as he floated in place. How could he have been so stupid? Psyche was right—he was a worthless old idiot who'd ruined everything for himself, for the Corps, for the Belt, all because he couldn't control his hormones. And he'd done it all for nothing, for a lie. "How could I have let this happen?"

"I think we've established that, sweetie. The real question is . . ." She paused, cleared her throat. Her hand faltered in its idle stroking of his hair. Then she went on, her voice harder than before. "The question is, how can you live with yourself now?"

He couldn't find an answer to her question. He had failed everyone. He had ruined everything. It would be better for everyone if he just stepped into the airlock and . . .

No! Something inside him rebelled. *This doesn't make sense.* Psyche's words, her actions, they didn't add up. And something was wrong with him too. This wasn't like him! He was Shashu, he was Sensei! He never backed down from a challenge, never stood by when someone needed help. He had failed before, screwed up before, but he had carried on and done whatever it took to make amends.

And he had battled depression before. When his brother had died in the war, when the Belt Alliance had fragmented afterward, when his first wife had left him. The doctors had diagnosed his tendency toward clinical depression, had given him the medicines and the insights he needed to conquer it. And even before then, even in his darkest moments, he had never contemplated suicide for more than the most fleeting of instants. It just wasn't in him to give up.

"Something . . . you're doing something to me," he realized. "Making me . . . feel this way. Psychoactive . . ." Pheromones were one thing, but she'd done more, drugged him somehow. He had to fight it! He pushed her away. They flew apart to opposite bulkheads, and he caught himself. "Get out. Get away!"

Instead, she kicked back over toward him. Setting chivalry aside, he tried striking at her with the full force of his bionic limbs, knowing this was a fight for his life. But his control over those limbs was sluggish; whatever she'd done had weakened him, and she parried his blow effortlessly despite lacking the leverage he had. She forced his arms down to his sides, wrapping her legs around him to pin them there with her powerful thighs. Again her hands encased his head, despite his efforts to wrench free of them. Butterfly wings fluttered against his temples. "I'm sorry I said those mean things, Yukio," she said. "I wanted there to be no doubt it was suicide. But maybe it's better this way. At least you won't suffer as much."

Again her lips met his, her tongue forcing its way between them. He tried to keep his mouth closed, but even now his body responded reflexively to her seduction. Her saliva mixed with his, and in moments he felt his consciousness fading.

The sound of alarms from the cockpit briefly halted his decline into oblivion. Psyche had done something to set them off . . . now he distantly registered that she was in a space suit, heading for the airlock. Was she abandoning ship? Would she be able to get back to Phobos safely? The last thing he ever felt was the hope that she could. Because despite everything, he still loved her more than life itself.

16

Whose Side Are You On?

Vanguard

It took a long time for Emry to stop crying after she heard the news. How could this have happened? Despite the threat to the TSC and the charges against her, she'd been happier than she'd ever been, confident that Eliot and Psyche would soon win Sensei's support and that together they would expose this whole mess. She'd *known* that things were going to be all right. This just wasn't supposed to happen!

When Psyche returned a week later and told her version firsthand, Emry cried just as hard as before. "It doesn't make any sense," she said at length, rising from the couch where she had been cocooned between the Thornes' comforting embraces. "There's no way he'd aim himself at Phobos on plasma drive! He'd never endanger so many lives!"

"He would have had no chance to do so," Eliot told her, subdued. "The Phobian defenses are very reliable."

"They're saying he wanted them to blow him out of the sky," Psyche said with difficulty. "That it was a suicide run."

"No!" Emry cried. "Sensei wouldn't kill himself! He was—" She choked on her words, had to start again more quietly. "He was too generous. As long as there was anyone who needed his help, he'd never stop fighting."

Psyche rose and clasped her shoulders. "I agree. When I met with him, he was fine emotionally. Well, not fine—he was angry about what's happened to the Corps. Once I finally managed to speak to him, give him the pieces he was missing . . . it was the last straw. He told me he was ready to denounce Tai openly, to fight to take back his post." Her expression grew bitter, angry. "Someone must've gotten on board, knocked him out, set the course . . . probably spacewalked back to Phobos. But there's no way to tell . . . they made sure all the evidence was destroyed." She winced. "I feel so stupid. It can't have been more than a few hours after we met. If I'd stayed with him longer, maybe . . ."

"No!" Emry hugged her. "It's not your fault, honey. You couldn't stay too long and risk being found out. You did what Eliot told you to, and you did it very well. What happened next . . . that was someone else's fault."

"Tai?" Eliot asked from the couch. "Do you really believe he'd have Villareal murdered?"

"He got a teenage boy tortured and a college girl killed. You really need to ask?"

"But an act like this is far more rash." Eliot frowned. "He would have to be very confident. Or very near a critical stage in his plans."

Psyche spoke up. "Yukio . . . he told me he'd found hints that Tai was mobilizing for something big. Nothing he could be definite about, but . . ." She cleared her throat. "I'm sorry. This is . . . hard for me. I only met him the one time . . . but he was such an impressive man, so kind. . . ." She blushed. "So charming and handsome. I would've loved to have more time to get to know him."

"I bet he would have too," Emry said with a sad smile. "And I know just what you mean."

"I still feel I let him down somehow."

"Well, you didn't. And you won't." Emry clenched Psyche's hands. "We'll carry on his work together. We'll find out what he was digging for, and bring down that bastard Tai once and for all. And you'll be a big part of that, I know it." She kissed her beloved friend on the cheek. "Because I know you'll never let me down."

The Band
In orbit of Ceres

Greg Tai took a moment to study Koyama Hikari as she walked alongside him through the vast open spaces of the Band. She had been suitably impressed; there was nothing quite like this vista anywhere beyond
Earth. This was only one small segment of what would someday be a
single closed loop over three hundred kilometers in circumference and
twenty wide, one of two adjacent rings counterrotating to allow the vast
structure to precess as Ceres orbited the Sun. Though this segment
alone had been assembled from individual cylindrical units, each the
size of a large O'Neill cylinder, they had now been joined into a great
slab with a single flat ground surface stretching across them at the
middle, twenty kilometers wide by thirty long. It was in the process of
being turned into a forest, but the trees were still young and sparse and
one could see the landscape stretching off into the distance. Few Striders ever beheld anything so flat and open. To Tai, it was like a piece of
home. But then he could look up through the vast skylights above and
see his other home, the Sheaf, and beyond it the other Band segment
that counterbalanced this one. The Sheaf was a vibrant place to live, a
lively warren of interconnected cylinders and spheres, and it was easy
enough to move among them if you didn't mind the free-fall trips
through the scaffold network or the bottlenecks at the axes. But Tai
looked forward to the day when he could live and work here in the Band,
which truly captured the best of planet and habitat living alike. In time,
he hoped, the TSC's headquarters would be relocated here, once it was
no longer necessary to maintain the pretense of their independence.
For now, though, he had brought Hikari here for a private conversation,
off the record and remote from human or electronic ears.

Tai realized she was still calmly waiting for him to speak. He allowed
the moment to drag out, observing her reactions, but although she fidgeted a bit, the young Troubleshooter kept her peace. He liked that about
her. Most of the Troubleshooters were a brash and uncouth lot, always
champing at the bit for excitement and action. It was a symptom of the
problems facing the Belt. Outside of the Sheaf, an eclectic collection of

individual habitat-states that had learned to live together as a pluralistic whole, the Striders' regional or national loyalties were so strong and divisive that the only ones free of such allegiances, able to be truly nonpartisan, were the misfits, rebels, and outcasts. True, Kari was herself a rebel from her family and its criminal organization, but she was a refreshing exception to the pattern, restrained, humble, and obedient despite the deadly power lurking within her. Tai wished more Striders were like her.

Kari was beginning to squirm under his scrutiny, her pretty eyes darting away. "I apologize, Hikari," Tai finally said. "I was just . . . contemplating how much I appreciate you as a member of my team."

She blushed adorably. "Thank you, sir." That was another thing he liked about her—she'd called him "sir" from the beginning, never needing to be prompted or reminded to show him the respect he was entitled to.

Not that his Earth-Cerean background made him better than any other Strider, of course. They were simply a product of their history. They didn't have the Sheavers' experience in balancing pluralism with unity, or the Terrans' experience in overcoming their divisions to master a common threat. Indeed, much of Earth's current peace and enlightenment resulted from the exile of militant transhumanists and other uncooperative extremists to the Belt, which had exacerbated the Striders' existing tensions. That was why Tai had immigrated out here and made himself one of them: because Terrans bore their share of responsibility for the Belt's woes and owed it to the Striders to help them heal, to share with them the compassionate discipline that had saved Earth. The Cerean States had found the solution that the rest of the Belt needed; at the risk of overextending the grain metaphor, they could be the seed from which Beltwide peace could spring. He was here for the benefit of all Striders, to help spread that seed.

But it was satisfying when one of them had the decency to show some appreciation for that. He'd worked hard to get away from the poverty and chaos of his Terran childhood, to gain skills worthy of the respect his elder sisters had never shown him, and it was a sacrifice to leave his home, family, and position in the Sheaf to fight the good fight. Was it wrong, then, to take pleasure in a little compensatory ego-stroking?

"This has been a hard time for the Troubleshooters," he told Kari, bringing her to a stop at the crest of a footbridge over a babbling brook. "A time of transition, of reinvention. We've lost some people along the way . . . people who didn't understand what we're trying to do. Who either weren't willing to take it far enough, like Tor, or who took it too far, like Cowboy."

"Or like Emry," Kari said in a small voice.

"But you understand what I'm trying to do, Hikari. You understand how important it is to be proactive. To nip sources of trouble in the bud—judiciously, surgically—before they grow out of hand. You understand, perhaps better than anyone, that the subtlest exertion of force can do the greatest good, if applied in the right way at the right moment."

"Yes, sir. I believe I do."

"And you know what's at stake." He moved behind her and put his hands on her dainty shoulders. "You know better than most what we have to fight. You've seen the face of it firsthand. The gangs, the terrorists, the fanatics—you've felt the damage they can do to innocent souls."

She gazed up at him, and he could see that his appeal was working. He could see the anger smoldering inside that little-girl face. "Yes, sir. Hell, yes."

He glared at her. "Sorry," she said, looking away. But he forgave her. The sweet child hadn't entirely recovered yet from Emerald Blair's unruly influence.

Ahh, Emerald. Now there was an operative he regretted losing. She'd been as wild and uncouth as any Strider he'd ever met, but she'd shown promise. Given time, he could've instilled her with proper discipline and respect, or at least enjoyed the challenge of trying. But he'd badly miscalculated with her, failed to predict how her chaotic mind would function. He'd been so sure her bitterness toward the Vanguard, the Neogaians, and the rest would make her a potent tool for controlling them. But Thorne had had better counterintelligence than he'd anticipated, and Blair had been too easily swayed by a childish, impractical idealism. *Does she really think I wanted to see anyone tortured or killed? That I wouldn't have spared those lives if there were a better way to achieve the greater good? There's no true kindness in sparing one life if you know it will bring suffering or death to hundreds more.*

But Emerald Blair had never truly lived in the real world. An improbably idyllic childhood, a playacting version of a criminal life with little real harm done, an assortment of odd jobs, and then a stint as the TSC sex symbol in residence . . . she'd had it easy, always getting to indulge her fantasies and illusions. She'd never had to fight for reward and acceptance, never understood the hard work, sacrifice, and discipline it took to make any real difference in the world.

But Tai would change that. Once Blair had become a Vanguardian tool to interfere with his efforts, it had been necessary to sacrifice her . . . because few Striders would understand any better than she had, at least not until they'd come to trust the Cereans more. She hadn't yet borne the full brunt of that sacrifice, but he would make sure that she did. Greg Tai was not a man who allowed matters to remain out of his control for long. As a Terran born, he understood that one could not afford to lose control of one's environment.

And Hikari, he felt sure, was the key to making it right. So disciplined, so obedient, she had waited meekly while his mind had wandered, not objecting to the hand that remained on her shoulder—or the other which he realized had been absently stroking her silky hair. *Mind your control,* he thought ruefully, folding his hands behind him but making no outward acknowledgment of his lapse. "I'm glad you understand what we're fighting for, Hikari. Because I have a mission for you that I fear you might find difficult." He came around to face her. "I need you to arrest Emerald Blair." Her eyes widened; her delicate lips parted in surprise. "Can you do that for me? Would there be a . . . personal problem?"

After a moment, her gaze hardened. "No, sir. Emry . . ." She shook her head. "I thought I knew her better than anyone. I never imagined . . . sir, she's a traitor. She let the Corps down. She let us all down.

And when I see her again I'm going to punch her right in her lying mouth! Sir," she finished, daintily clearing her throat. "But . . . how do I get to her? The Vanguard is protecting her, and—"

"I know. I haven't told you the full assignment." He led her off the bridge, a guiding hand against her back. "No doubt you've heard that the Vanguard is arranging a second conference to pursue their so-called alliance of mod nations." He frowned. "They even have the gall to hold it on Neogaia. Like they're rubbing our faces in it."

"Yes, sir."

"But a lot of people seem to be falling for their line that it's meant to show how Neogaia has reformed, how it's ready to be part of the Solar community." He scoffed, and she gave a high-pitched, adorable little scoff of agreement. "Eliot Thorne and his daughter are master propagandists. If we want to keep this from getting out of hand, we have to neutralize them."

Kari's eyes widened. "Neu-neutralize? Sir? You don't . . . of course you don't. . . ."

Tai laughed and patted her shoulder. "Of course not." Another assassination at this point would look too suspicious, and with the cult of personality Thorne had built around himself, would only create a martyr. "What we need to do is discredit Thorne. We need to reveal to the other delegates that Thorne's true goal is to rule over them, to exploit them for his own ends."

"We have proof of that?" Kari asked, surprised.

"Not as such. But we both know it's true, don't we?" She nodded, still seeming uncertain. "It's no different from what we did with Hoenecker. We don't need to convict him in a court of law, just destroy his credibility."

She relaxed at that. "Of course, sir. What matters is taking away his power to do harm."

"Yes. Good girl. However," he went on, "even without him, the other mod nations might seek to build on his work, to form alliances of their own. Imagine if, say, Neogaia and Mars Martialis began working together."

"That would be bad."

"It certainly would. So in addition to discrediting Thorne, you and your team would have the responsibility to stir things up between the other delegates."

He spoke with her about the specifics as they strolled deeper into the woods—ordering her to make sure her memory buffer was off, due to the sensitive nature of this discussion. She would need a small infiltration team, specialists in undercover and intelligence work, but with combat skills just in case. He brainstormed with her about the forms their sabotage could take: planting spy cameras of Martian provenance in other delegates' ships, slipping nonlethal doses of Neogaian poisons into the Wellspringers' meals, that sort of thing. She offered few suggestions of her own, but he was satisfied with her obedience.

And her enthusiasm for one task in particular. "And while we're doing all this . . . we get Emry too, right?" she asked.

"Best to wait until it's all in place, but yes. Emerald Blair is an accessory to murder and a fugitive from justice, and apprehending her is a very high priority of this organization. That's why I insist you have combat specialists with you on the mission. You'll need help in taking her down."

"Ohh, no." Kari shook her head. "With all due respect, sir . . . that bitch is mine."

Tai kept his smile to himself. Under the circumstances, he could forgive her defiance.

December 2107
Neogaia habitat
Sun-Earth L3 point

Emry didn't like being this close to the Sun. It gave her freckles.

That was the least of her discomfort about attending a conference on Neogaia. But she had striven to overcome her revulsion. Eliot was convinced that the new regime could be worked with—that although they still retained their ideological goal of returning to Earth and transforming it into a natural paradise, they had renounced terrorism as a means of achieving it. And if Eliot said it was so, she believed it. Still, there were some difficult memories to overcome.

Zephyr hadn't been much help either. He'd refused to let go of his suspicions about the Thornes. He'd even made insinuations about Psyche being the last person to see Sensei alive. Emry had exploded at that, saying some hurtful things about cold machine logic. She'd tried to apologize later, but he had refused to apologize for "reminding you of your job," and matters remained unsettled between them. Zephyr had still come along to Neogaia, insisting that he'd stay close if she needed him. But Emry herself had traveled with Eliot in his official diplomatic ship. After all, it was a long journey, and she couldn't stand to be apart from him for a single night. Zephyr had instead carried a couple of the Vanguardian delegates, including Rachel, now halfway through her pregnancy but as active as ever.

Zephyr had also been disturbed that Emry had chosen to travel without her Green Blaze outfit. But it didn't seem consistent with her purpose at this conference. Eliot said she had a vital role to play, testifying about the plans of UNECS and the co-opted TSC. As much as she hated the thought, with Sensei dead, the Troubleshooters were probably a lost cause, and it was best to cast off their trappings if she wanted to make a convincing argument against them. Besides, Eliot had added, something less flamboyant would be more appropriate for a diplomatic affair. He'd had his best tailor custom-make some formal and business wear in a Vanguardian style, making her a better match with the Thornes. She wasn't overly fond of it at first, but she liked the way she looked alongside Eliot.

The Vanguard delegation included a number of their leading citizens, statespersons such as Soaring Hawk Darrow and Thuy Dinh and scientists such as Krishna Ramchandra and Rachel. They rendezvoused with Psyche at Neogaia; the Vanguard's top diplomat had been racing around half the Belt for the past two and a half weeks, making last-minute pleas to recruit as many delegates as possible. This time, invitations had been extended to "mainstream" as well as "mod" nations, and Eliot's hope was that the conference would end with the formal declaration of a Strider alliance, a unified force strong enough to give Earth pause—and, of course, to bring peace and stability to the Belt. Psyche had taken the Vanguard's fastest ship and managed to squeeze in stops at Vesta and both the major Outers hubs, Europa and Hygiea. She'd managed to wangle a number of commitments before having to rocket inward to Neogaia. There would even be a delegation from Ceres, though Psyche had not had time to travel there herself. A delegation from Ferdinandea, a minor Cerean hab independent of the Sheaf, had accepted Thorne's initial invitation without needing further persuasion. Emry hoped that an ally from Ceres might set a precedent; maybe Demetria would come around as well, and perhaps even the Sheaf could be pressured into dropping its opposition.

Neogaia itself consisted of two adjacent toruses, less than a kilometer in radius but fairly thick in cross section, with the usual free-fall industrial section at the hub and a sun mirror floating nearby. Aside from a few other support structures, it was oddly alone in its Lissajous orbit around the "Counter-Earth" L3 point—sharing Earth's orbit but directly opposing it, blocked from its line of sight to keep the yearning for it strong (and to hide from routine observation by UNECS telescopes). The Neogaians had never bothered to capture a stroid as a materials source, instead relying on the smattering of meteoroids that clustered around the Lagrange point or on mining expeditions to those Near-Earth stroids that UNECS hadn't already captured or claimed. The symbolism was clear: the Neogaians saw this as only a temporary home.

Despite that, they had put a great deal of work into the habitat itself. The docking area at the hub was typical enough, but once Hanuman Kwan met Emry, the Thornes, and their accompanying delegates and began leading them down to the habitat rings, it became clear that Neogaia was a very unusual place. For one thing, the normal elevators were missing. "We believe in doing things the natural way as much as possible," the monkeylike Neogaian explained. Apparently that included dressing up the walls of the radial shafts to look like cliff faces and climb them on faux vines that stretched hundreds of meters to the ground below. Which wasn't that unreasonable, given that the faster they descended, the more the Cori force angled their weight vectors to antispinward and made the slope feel shallower. And it was only in the last hundred meters or so that the gravity became substantial. Still, some of the older delegates needed assistance.

The bottom of the shaft was styled like a largish cavern, and Kwan led them out onto a terraformed hillside looking down into a lush valley. The gravity at ground level was a full gee. The torus's large cross section allowed for more level ground and more aerial clearance for trees and birds. The lateral walls were disguised as hillsides, and the circumferential curvature of the landscape was obscured by mountains on this end, dense forest on the other. The roof overhead, rather than being the standard skylight arch, looked like some kind of fiber-optic array that could shunt the sunlight from outside to any set of pixels on its inner surface, creating an illusion of a vivid blue Terrestrial sky and a sun just cresting the hills. As Kwan led the tour group through the valley, Emry's eyes were drawn to their oddly elongated shadows, and she realized they were very gradually shortening as the "sun" crept higher up the (literal) arch of the (virtual) sky. *Weird.*

But this was only the beginning. "We have striven," the elderly simian continued, "to re-create as much of Mother Earth's extraordinary diversity of climates as possible. Everything from steppes to savannah, rain forest to desert, tropics to tundra. All perfectly balanced and in ecological harmony with one another." Their surroundings bore out his words as Kwan escorted them from one climate zone to another, each one isolated from the others by artificial barriers, with the circulation of air, heat, and moisture through the habitat carefully modified to provide each sector with just the right conditions. There were even two arctic sectors on opposite ends, and Emry realized they corresponded to the extra heat radiators she'd noticed sticking out from the sides of the torus. Emry was impressed despite herself. She'd always thought of the Neogaians as a small bunch of crazy thugs, but this was the most remarkable, delicate feat of biosphere engineering she'd ever seen.

"And you can rest assured," Kwan went on, "that the richness and diversity of these ecosystems are more than matched by that of the Neogaian people. Every environment you see has people living in it, thriving in it, perfectly adapted to its special conditions." Indeed, every region they passed through was populated by suitably specialized therianthropes, generally going without clothing, selfones, or other technology (although Kwan and the others participating in the conference wore at least some clothing as a courtesy to their guests). Small, simian brachiators and deerlike foragers populated the forests alongside the normal wildlife. The grasslands bore herds of sheep, bison, and the like, but they were herded by men and women with canine muzzles and furry coats. Emry saw an eland taken down by a pride of leonine Neogaians who tore at its raw flesh with their teeth. Mercifully, she saw no humans modded to fill the eland's particular niche in that ecosystem. *That,* she thought, *would really be pushing the antelope.*

Even the rivers and lakes contained streamlined people swimming with uncanny ease, occasionally breaking the surface to take a breath and waving web-fingered hands at the delegates. The one environment that remained unpopulated by therianthropes was the air. "We're still working on producing a human form capable of flight in normal gravity," Kwan explained. "It's difficult to do the research in these conditions, with the actual space available for flight being so limited. But once we are ultimately welcomed back to Mother Earth, I'm confident we will perfect true human flight." Emry glared at him, wondering how many live test subjects they would sacrifice in pursuit of this bizarre ambition.

Don't expect change overnight, she reminded herself. *Once we have the alliance, we can work to bring them back into the mainstream.*

As the tour went on, Emry noticed Psyche working the delegates, buddying up to them and allaying their concerns. Yes, she assured them, the Neogaians had more conventional facilities underground, and the delegates would have actual beds to sleep in—unless they wanted to try camping out under the illusion of an empty, starlit sky soaring overhead. The thought did not sit well with the inherent claustrophilia of the average Strider, Emry included, but Psyche somehow managed to make it sound enticing. She was certainly laying on her usual charm offensive, focusing mostly on those delegates she hadn't already won over at the previous conference or during the recruitment drive for this one. Eliot himself did the same, though in a more under-stated way. For a man of his size and intensity, coming on too strong could be intimidating. The other Vanguardians did their part too, but Eliot and Psyche could have easily done it all by themselves.

By the end of the reception and dinner that evening, the Thornes had managed to produce an extraordinary degree of consensus from the delegates—meaning that they wouldn't have to spend the first week hashing out the seating arrangements and procedures, and nobody had stormed out in protest. That made for a smooth beginning to the next morning's assembly. The event was held in a "natural" amphitheater, with its stone walls conveniently shaped to amplify sounds—somewhat belying the Neogaians' insistence that they wished to shape themselves to nature rather than the reverse. But Emry had decided to take such things as mere eccentricities rather than grounds for contempt. *The old regime is gone,* she reminded herself. *Eliot helped see to that.* Even without her transceiver implant active, she could almost hear Zephyr's voice in her mind, dryly pointing out that revolutionary regimes were typically no better than the ones they kicked out. But she owed it to the Thornes to give this alliance a fair chance. *And regimes aside, there's no reason to be prejudiced against the Neogaians as people. Sure, their beliefs are a little wacky, but most of them probably mean well, right?*

Her open mind was sorely tested when she saw Hanuman Kwan come into the arena with a thong-clad, otherwise naked woman on each arm. The one on his right was Selkie, the curvaceous and bubbly seal-woman from the first conference. But the one on his left . . .

Was Bast.

Emry stormed over to the threesome, and the she-cat promptly snarled and splayed her claws. Kwan held her back as Emry cried, "What the vack is *she* doing here, Kwan? I thought you told me her bunch had been kicked out."

"Indeed they were, my dear, and Bast here was instrumental in that defeat." He reached up and skritched the panther-woman under her chin to calm her. "A cat's primary loyalty is to her own comfort. Bast has no deeper ideology than that. She sniffed out the way the wind was blowing and switched to the winning side."

"You think that's reassuring? She's one of the ones responsible for killing my mentor!"

"My dear Emerald, I have already extended you Neogaia's deepest regrets for that tragedy," Kwan said in dulcet tones, though Bast simply looked bored. "Let me remind you that she was simply following the orders of more dedicated fanatics. And that she herself was incapacitated at the time of the disaster—thanks, so she tells me, to your own actions. If anything, you spared her the burden of being a conscious party to such regrettable events. Isn't that right, my sweet?" he asked, stroking the silky black fur of Bast's shoulder.

"Whatever," Bast said, following it up with a prodigious yawn. "Where's the food?" She moved off without another glance at Emry—although the tip of her tail twitched fiercely as she moved past. Emry resisted the urge to give it a good yank.

"Oh, you know cats," Kwan said, laughing it off. "Always having to save face. Believe me, underneath, she regrets the acts she committed under the old regime. And she doesn't hold a grudge. I do hope the same is true of you." He began stroking Emry's shoulder much as he had Bast's. "After all, she's not the only one who's been manipulated into doing unfortunate things by an unscrupulous superior." He leaned closer to speak more softly. "I believe you'll see a case in point if you subtly direct your attention thirty degrees eastward, at the top of the rock face."

Emry blinked in surprise, but didn't betray it beyond that. She casually looked around the amphitheater, casting a split-second glance in the specified direction. Noticing Kwan gazing down her blouse, she pretended to be annoyed with him and walked away, enabling her to get a glance from another angle. While Kwan followed and continued to flirt, she called up the images on her retinal HUD, ran an image analysis, and noticed a subtle distortion in a bulge in the rock face. Once she knew what she was looking for, she was able to spot the telltales; the bulge was actually a person-sized metamaterial cloak, virtually invisible and morphed to blend in with the contours of the rock. *Hijab?* No doubt there were others with comparable camouflage tech, but few could remain as still and soundless. And the figure's size was right. Besides, who else would it be? Of course Tai would want to spy on this conference, maybe sabotage it. *But is Maryam a dupe or a willing conspirator?* She didn't know the woman well enough to judge.

"How did you know?" she whispered to Kwan.

"A little bird told me."

Fine, be that way. "Have you told anyone else?"

"I only just noticed it myself."

"Well . . . don't." This was her responsibility. She'd have to find Maryam and whoever else was with her—they'd probably snuck in with the Ferdinandea delegation, come to think of it—and stop them from disrupting the conference. Hopefully she could reason with them, convince them—

Not likely. What reason do they have to trust me? Most likely, they'd try to arrest her and do whatever they planned to do anyway.

So it'll be a fight, then. Well . . . I'm ready.

Emry lost Hijab's trail before long, but it was easy enough to surmise where the Troubleshooters would be hiding; after all, she'd been trained by the same people they had. Before long, she tracked them down to the free-fall industrial sector in Neogaia's hub, between its two counterrotating wheels. She considered calling in Vanguardian backup, but decided against it. She had to at least try to reason with them first. Maybe her chances of being heard would be better with Psyche at her side, but both Thornes were busy with the negotiations. So that left her on her own. For now. <Be ready to call in backup just in case, okay?> she sent to Zephyr.

<If it comes to that. But Emry, these are our friends.>

<If that's so, then I won't need the backup, will I?>

The T-shooters were holed up in a large warehouse bay adjacent to the spacedock, its volume crisscrossed by a lattice of cables to which crates and bins of various sizes were clipped to keep them from drifting.

Emry made her way gingerly through the three-dimensional grid, try-ing not to set off vibrations in the taut cables as she snuck around the containers, edging closer to her erstwhile colleagues. Soon, she grew close enough to hear their voices. "Why are we still waiting here?" That was Paladin, a no-nonsense Troubleshooter who made no secret of his ambition to run the Corps one day. *Figures Auster would be Tai's golden boy.*

"We don't want to rush in without getting the lay of the land first." *Oh, Goddess.* That was Kari! *Not her! Ohh, she has to be a dupe!*

"Hijab didn't have to come all the way back here to report."

"I didn't want to risk breaking radio silence."

Emry didn't have to see Auster to know he was shaking his head in disapproval. "This is an inefficient strategy. I still don't see why Tai put you in charge instead of me."

Kari's voice was subdued. "I guess he thought I had something to prove."

"I don't get it. What?"

He wants her to prove her loyalty by arresting her best friend, Emry realized. *Well, I might as well make it easy for her.*

"Kenny, what you don't get would take weeks just to list," she called, pulling herself out from behind the last crate. Four Troubleshooters turned their heads in surprise. In addition to Kari, Hijab, and Paladin, Vijay Pandalai was there too. Aside from Maryam, who wore her black cloaking garment with the face mask folded back over her hair, they were all in plain clothes.

Paladin drew his sidearm. "Emerald Blair, you are under arrest! Drop your weapons immediately!"

"Cool your jets, Pal! A, I'm unarmed, and B, I'm here to talk."

Arjun had his weapon out now too. "A Troubleshooter's never un-armed, even when she isn't carrying a weapon. We all know that, Blaze. You want to talk, you'll do it in restraints."

"Any other circumstances, Veej, I'd be game for a little bondage with you. But you know that requires trust, and right now I don't have much to spare."

"And how can we trust you?" Kari cried, smoothly drawing and

opening her *tessen,* the high-tech Japanese war fans that were her preferred weapons. "After what you've done? After you abandoned us?"

"It's not like that!" She reached a pleading hand forward.

It was a mistake; Paladin took it as an aggressive move and fired.
Her enhanced reflexes made her dodge the shockdart before she was
consciously aware of it, but her mind quickly caught up. She pushed
off the crate and fled into the maze, flipping backward to look behind her. She caught a glimpse through the crates of Kari intercept-
ing Auster, blocking his path with a spread fan. "Let's not be rash!
We split up. You and Arjun go that way, circle around." Emry could
imagine the glare on Auster's square-jawed face, but Kari was already leading Maryam down the path Emry had taken. And Maryam
was becoming harder to see as she resealed her suit and activated its
camouflage.

Emry tried to keep tabs on Hijab, but she had to watch where she
was going in the maze of crates and containers, and she soon lost track
of the veiled one. Kari remained close on her tail, knowing her moves
too well. She used her flexible *tessen* as airfoils, letting her swim and
curve through the air more deftly than Emry, who had to pull herself
along by the cables. It was like being chased by a fan dancer. "Kari,
will you stop and listen to me?" she called.

"Listen to this!" A graceful flick of the wrist folded one of the *tessen*
shut and thrust its tip toward Emry. A shock laser discharge barely
missed her, forcing her to grab a mooring cable and dodge right.

Wait a minute, she thought as she followed this new path. *From
the way Arjun and Paladin went . . . shouldn't she be herding me to
the left?* Still, she followed an evasive path away from the two men,
on the assumption that Kari had simply missed the shot.

But Kari doesn't miss shots!

Suddenly a dainty but solid body collided with her and drove her
into an open cargo container. Hitting the boxes inside knocked some
of the wind out of Emry, and Kari pushing off her to reverse direction
finished the job. Emry braced herself against the wall of boxes, catching her breath for Kari's next strike.

But Kari wasn't striking. She was loosely closing the door of the container and holding a finger to her lips, the *tessen* folded and held nonthreateningly against her forearms. "It's all right. We can talk here," she said in a serene, detached voice. The battle peace was upon her.

And confusion was upon Emry. "What, *now* you want to talk?"

"It wasn't safe before. We had to make it look convincing for Paladin. His loyalties are unclear."

Emry studied her friend, but the *heiwa* rendered her inscrutable. "And where are your loyalties?"

"With the truth. And I would like to hear it from you, for I am not hearing it from Mr. Tai."

The tension drained from Emry's body. "Oh, I am so glad to hear you say that."

Kari smiled . . . and a moment later the smile became much wider and more intense as the *heiwa* subsided. "Ohh, Emry!" Kari pushed off the doors and into Emry's arms, hugging her with all her might. "You don't think I'd ever hurt you, would you, sweetie?"

"No, it's not that, it's just . . . oh, Kari, it's just been such a mess . . . you really didn't believe the things Tai said?"

Kari lowered her eyes in shame. "I believed most of it. The things he offered . . . ending the chaos, bringing order . . . the arguments he made for escalating our tactics . . . it was all so persuasive. I had my doubts, but I *wanted* to believe in him. I was willing to do anything that could bring down . . . the mobs. You know."

"I get it."

She clasped Emry's hands. "But when he accused you of arranging an assassination . . . he went too far. I'd never believe that of you. I knew he was lying, and I wanted to know why. Besides . . . he started to get a bit creepy. Like he got off on having power over me." She shuddered a bit and said in a small voice, "He *fondled* my *hair.*"

"Ohh, Kari." Emry squeezed her hands supportively. "I understand, honey, but that could be dangerous! You become a liability to him, he finds a way to get rid of you."

"I noticed. So I took it slow, talked to some of the others. A lot of us have doubts about the new policies. And I wasn't the only one who didn't believe him about you."

"Vijay? Marut?"

Kari nodded. "Never doubted you for a second."

"Nor did I." Emry's eyes widened as Hijab's black-shrouded form faded into view. She hadn't even noticed the door opening for the older woman to slip through.

Emry's eyes darted back and forth between Maryam and Kari. "You two are together in this?"

Maryam nodded, pulling up her mask to let Emry see her dark eyes. "Tenshi recruited me. She believed—rightly—that she could rely on my discretion. And that she'd need me if she wanted to gain incriminating evidence on Tai. It didn't take much convincing. I've had my eye on him all along. You know I don't trust easily."

"But . . . you trusted me?"

"Of course. You've earned it."

"Tai really screwed up when he tried to frame you," Kari said. "It was just too unbelievable. It got people wondering, asking questions. I hardly had to seek out anybody—they came to me, since I'm your best friend. And we compared notes about the secret missions we'd been sent on. . . ." Kari lowered her head. "A lot of us did things we weren't proud of. Thought they were justified at first . . . but now we're not so sure."

Emry touched her friend's shoulder. "Oh, honey . . . not . . ."

"No, nothing as bad as what Cowboy did. Not . . . by the people who talked to me, anyway. But some pretty unethical stuff. Blackmail, sabotage, dirty tricks . . ."

"Tai sent us here to discredit Eliot Thorne and stir up hostilities among the delegates," Maryam said.

"I was wondering how to get out of having to do that," Kari went on. "Now you've given us an excuse. Since you found us before we could do anything, we can say we had to retreat."

"Why bother?" Emry asked. "Just go public, testify that Tai ordered you to sabotage things here. You have that in your buffer, don't you?"

Kari grinned. "He told me to turn it off first . . . but I guess I was a bad girl."

"Yeah! So bad you're good!" Emry crowed.

Kari shook her head. "It's not enough. Tai has a whole organization backing him up—with lots of lawyers. You saw how easily they twisted things against you. They could say I faked it." That was a good point. It was possible to fake virtually anything these days, and the law was still trying to catch up. Different jurisdictions had different standards of proof. "We need a more solid case. We need more hard evidence, different kinds of evidence and testimony that all corroborate each other. We need to show a whole, consistent pattern if we want to convince people."

"So who else is in on it?" Emry asked.

"A lot of us. Marut, Juan, Melanie, Firass . . ."

Emry grew deeply moved as the list stretched on. She hadn't thought most of the Troubleshooters even took her seriously. She'd thought the Vanguard was the one place where she'd ever felt at home in the past nine years. Suddenly she didn't know what to think anymore. But what she felt was great warmth . . . and renewed hope.

17

Sex and Violence

December 2107
Neogaia

Emry found Psyche in a garden surrounded by butterflies. "It's a perfume Hanuman gave me," Psyche explained as they fluttered around her, alighting on her outstretched arms. "A pheromone that draws them. Appropriate, don't you think?"

It was a beautiful sight, but Emry couldn't pause to enjoy it. As the butterflies danced around them, Emry told Psyche about her encounter with the Troubleshooters. "With their help," she finished, "we can expose Tai and the Sheaf, blow the whole thing wide open! We don't have to worry about them going up against us. The Sheavers won't risk it if they don't have the TSC to give them legitimacy. Maybe we can even get the Corps to back our alliance!"

It took her a few moments to realize through her excitement that Psyche didn't share it. If anything, she looked wary. "I don't know, Emry." She laid a hand on the side of Emry's head, gazing into her eyes. "Are you sure you can trust them?"

"I trust Kari."

"But you know how shrewd Tai is. He's a master manipulator. He could have turned her against you."

"Then she would've just arrested me when she had the chance!"

"She couldn't know you didn't have backup. It could've been a ploy to win your trust. Maybe to gain intelligence the Troubleshooters could use to destroy everything we've worked for."

Psyche's words sounded so plausible. But Emry shook them off. "No, no, I thought about that, and I don't buy it. Kari's never been any good at keeping things from me."

"Not when it was just between friends. This is different. Tai's convinced her you're a threat, a killer."

"Psyche, we don't know that! Listen, even if there is a risk, isn't it worth taking the chance? Without Sensei, this could be our best bet of exposing Tai!"

Psyche's brow furrowed sadly and she stroked Emry's hair. "Oh, Emry . . . I know how much you wish you could get the Troubleshooters back. But there's too much at stake to be sentimental. They're just too deep in Tai's pocket now."

"I don't believe that. You weren't there, Psyche. You didn't feel . . . the trust they had in me. The trust I have for them too. They're my friends."

"And we're your family!" Psyche said, taking Emry's head between her hands. "Sweetie, you have to make a choice about where your loyalties lie. Things have gone too far for you to straddle the fence anymore. You need to decide. Are you a Vanguardian? Are you with Eliot and me?"

"Of course I am! I love you! But—"

Those quicksilver eyes flashed, catching and holding her gaze. "There can be no 'buts,' Emry. If you truly love us, that love has to be unconditional."

She couldn't look away from those eyes. They were so very beautiful. "It is. I love you, Psyche. I love you so much."

"Then trust me, Emry."

". . . I do."

"Really?"

"Absolutely."

"That's my girl!" Grinning again, Psyche nuzzled her forehead against Emry's.

<Emry, what's going on?> It was Zephyr.

But Psyche was speaking again, so Emry ignored the distraction. "Now," the beautiful Vanguardian went on, still stroking Emry's hair, still holding her gaze with those shining, unblinking eyes. "You said the TSC team was going to leave. Have they gone yet?"

"No. They don't want to be conspicuous, so they need to arrange what looks like a courier run to Ceres."

<Should you have told her that?> Zephyr asked.

<I trust her!>

"Good. Good, we can't let them get away with whatever intelligence they may have gathered. We need to act now, take them prisoner before they can get away. You're the key to that, Emry. They think you trust them now, so you can take them by surprise. You get them into place, and we'll send in a security team to take them into custody. Okay, honey?"

Emry wasn't happy with the idea. She knew Psyche meant well, of course she did, but the plan seemed a little rash. "I don't know, Psyche. I mean . . . they'd fight back. We'd have to use force, and . . . well, don't you think it could trigger the, the very conflict we're trying to avoid? And what if . . . what if somebody got hurt, or . . ."

"Emry." Psyche clasped her head in both hands again, moved her warm body closer. "Don't worry, sweetie! You can help us keep that from happening. You know how they fight. You know their weaknesses. And they won't see it coming when you turn on them. With your help, we can make it quick and make sure it's done with a minimum of fuss."

<This is someone you trust?>

<Shut up, Zephyr, and let me think!> But she couldn't ignore her own doubts. "Psyche . . . I can't. Whatever Tai has duped them into . . . they're my friends. They're Troubleshooters. This is wrong," she went on more assuredly. "We're all on the same side, we just have to convince them of that. Fighting isn't the way!"

Psyche held her closer still. "Ohh, Emry . . . I understand how you feel, sweet baby." Her breath was warm and fragrant against Emry's open mouth. "And I love you for your compassion." Her full lips touched

Emry's tenderly, but lingered there for some time. "I would never want to see your friends hurt if we could possibly help it. That's why I need you to do this for me, honey. For me and Daddy. For your family." Another kiss, longer, deeper.

<Pardon me, Emry, but if you're part of the Thorne family, wouldn't you be more or less her mother-in-law?>

Zephyr's words made Emry choke, and she pushed Psyche away. "Hey, umm . . . we really shouldn't be doing this. . . ."

Psyche's brows furrowed, and she studied Emry's face. "Don't listen to Zephyr," she said. "He's trying to come between us. Between you and the people who love you."

<How does she know I'm talking to you?>

Emry knew that was strange, but was having trouble thinking clearly. Psyche went on, her voice so soothing, so alluring. She just wanted to listen to that beautiful, sweet alto and do whatever it took to make its owner happy. But that wasn't the only voice she loved. "Zephyr . . . he's my friend too."

"Is he?" Again her head was clutched in those butterfly hands—those warm, pleasure-giving hands. Again those shimmering silver eyes filled her vision. "He's been trying to come between us for weeks, Emry. He's just a cloistered, bitter cyber who doesn't have it in him to trust, or to understand the love humans can feel for each other. He's probably a spy for the Troubleshooters. Shut him out of your mind!"

Emry wasn't sure she could find her mind right now. "No, I . . . don't believe that . . . he doubted Tai before I did. . . ."

"Because he can't trust anyone. And you can't trust him. Please, Emry, shut him out. If you love me, break your link to him."

<Emry, don't! She's doing something to your mind, and she doesn't want me to analyze it.>

But Psyche's lips were devouring hers again, her tongue dancing with Emry's. Her hands stroked Emry's hair, making her scalp tingle, sending jolts of pleasure down her spine. Emry's arms went around Psyche's lissome body, holding it against her, not wanting to let go. Somehow the front of Psyche's shimmering blouse had opened, and Emry let her beautiful friend slide her head down to nestle between her firm chocolate-kiss breasts, taking comfort from their warmth, their scent, the strong pulse of her loving heart. She tried to bury herself deeper, not wanting to listen to Zephyr's distracting whining anymore.

"*I know he can be a mother hen,*" came Arkady's voice in her memory. "*But mother hens usually know what's best. You couldn't have a better partner.*"

"*He doesn't want to be my partner.*"

"*We'll talk him into it, trust me. I just know I'll be able to rest easy as long as he's out there taking care of you.*"

Gathering herself, Emry pushed Psyche away and struggled for clarity. "Stop. We have to . . . I need to think . . . what are you doing to me?"

"I'm just reminding you how much we love you, Emry. How much we need you."

<Zephyr, talk to me,> she sent over Psyche's words, before that honeyed voice could lull her into complacency again.

<*Your biotelemetry shows you're under the influence of some very potent chemicals, Emry.*>

<Well, obviously!>

<*No, Emry, I'm not talking about ordinary hormones. There's evidence of psychoactive agents in your body, affecting your neurochemistry. From the timing, I'd say they're secreted by her salivary glands as well as her apocrine system. Clearly her engineered allure goes further than we realized.*>

<Psychoactives?> She shook her head, trying to clear it. <My defenses should've . . . >

<*They seem specially tailored to your body chemistry, Emry. There's more—your brain waves are approaching a hypnotic state. And there's some kind of EM activity around your cranium, particularly when her hands touch it.*>

"Don't listen to him, Emry!" Psyche was saying. "Come to me. Be with me."

"Shut *up!*" Emry thrust her arms out defensively. "What are you, Psyche? There's more to you than you told me. You don't just read people . . . you affect their minds. Brainwash them into . . . into doing your will. All that 'enhanced social intelligence'—it's just a trick."

"No, Emry. My abilities are just what I've told you: to read people, understand how they think and what they need, and use that under-standing to win them over." Psyche gave an insouciant shrug, as though apologizing for borrowing Emry's clothes without asking. "I just do it in a more . . . proactive way than I like to let on."

"You mean manipulative. Invasive. You use people."

"It's no different from any other kind of persuasion. Just more pre-cise, more tailored."

"Tailored." Emry's mind was starting to clear. "That's why you have to get so close to everybody, fondle them, kiss them. Fuck them. You're sampling their body chemistry. Your glands, they need time to tailor the drugs."

"Don't think of them as drugs. Just . . . neurochemical facilitators, to ease someone into a suitable state of mind. And it's so much more than that. Here," she went on, moving forward, baring her chest the rest of the way. "Let me show you." *Scent glands in the chest,* Emry realized. *Secreting her "facilitators" . . . those tits really are weapons.*

"Don't take another step!" Emry cried. Psyche came casually to a halt, her pose relaxed and nonthreatening. *Body language . . . that's part of it too. Total control of her microexpressions . . . everything, the way she moves, the tone of her voice . . . subliminal cues, subsonics . . . it's all tailored. And she can read instantly how well it's working, adjust it moment by moment.*

"You're right," Psyche said, chilling her. "I can read you like a book, Emry. Your hormones, your body heat, your every microexpression, and that's just the tip of the iceberg." Was she drifting closer? It was hard to tell. "So you can't lie to me, Emry. I can *see* how much you love me, how much you love Eliot. And I can see you're not a hundred percent sure you can trust the Troubleshooters. Listen to that part of you, Emry. It's telling you that you've chosen the right side already."

"If that were true, you wouldn't be trying to control my mind! To control the delegates' minds!" It was finally hitting her, and it hurt.

"My Goddess, the whole thing is a lie, isn't it? You don't want to give every nation a voice—you just want it to *look* that way, so people think they're free and equal! But really it'll be you pulling the strings, telling them how to vote, what to say!" Then the next part hit her. "That's why you don't want to make peace with the Troubleshooters. You don't want to risk them finding out. And . . . and maybe you *want* to have a common enemy that'll get all the Strider states lining up behind the Vanguard."

She was afraid to ask the next question. "Does Eliot know? Is this just you, are you pulling his strings like everyone else's? Or . . ."

Psyche's eyes flashed. "I am my father's daughter, Emry. I'm his right hand, his legacy. I was *made* for that. Couldn't you tell from my name? Psyche, whose beauty rivaled Aphrodite's." She raised a hand and a butterfly promptly alit upon it. "So lovely and sublime that animals, plants, even the earth and the wind itself bent over backward to oblige her every whim."

Emry's heart fell. "All this time . . . he's been using me. Lying to me."

"Emry, Eliot Thorne is the greatest man who's ever lived! You know that! He's the only one with the brilliance, the will, and the vision to lead twelve billion fractious humans into a new evolutionary era! Everything I do is in the name of that greater good, Emry." Her smile was gone now, and she began refastening her blouse. "Do you think I like doing this all the time? Always being on, always calculating how to influence people and nudge them in the right direction? Never able to just be myself, let someone see who I really am? It's hard, Emry, and it's lonely. But it's worth it if it helps bring my father's dreams closer to reality."

She sighed. "I'm sorry I've manipulated you, Emry. But we weren't sure how you'd react if you knew the truth. You're mad now, I understand that. But just . . . trust me a little, give me more time to explain, and maybe you'll come around. I'd love to have you as a full partner, someone who really understands, so I don't have to play games with you anymore. That would mean so much to me, Emry."

A tear rolled down Psyche's flawless cheek, and Emry's heart went out to her—until she realized what was happening. "You're doing it again! Stop playing me!"

Psyche gave an apologetic laugh. "You're right, I'm sorry. It's force of habit. You see how hard it is for me?" Emry thought back to how gleeful Psyche had been back at that party, playing with those two men's emotions until they tried to kill each other, and decided that she liked using her power a lot more than she claimed. Psyche saw her line wasn't working, and relaxed. "Look. Is it really that bad, what I do? Would you rather my father had bred an army and sent them out to kill everyone who stood in his way? Or if he'd used torture and blackmail the way Tai's doing? I influence people with warmth and joy and understanding. The means inform the end, Emry. Doesn't the fact that my father favors such gentle means tell you that his intentions are good?"

"Whether it feels good or not, it's still force. You tried to control me. To *make* me feel what you wanted. That's an invasion, Psyche! Do you have any idea what that feels like? How can you?" She was furious. She wanted to belt Psyche one. But something held her back. Something, hell—she knew what it was. Psyche's mojo was still inside her, affecting her will, her emotions . . . she couldn't bring herself to hurt Psyche, to act against her.

<Emry . . . she can make people do whatever she wants . . . and she was the last person to speak to Sensei before his inexplicable death.>

Emry gasped. "Oh, Goddess. Sensei. Did you do something to him?"

"Emry, God, how could you ask that?" But Emry saw something in her face for the first time: a stray microexpression. Guilt.

The dam broke. With a shriek, Emry lunged forward and struck that perfect face with the flat of her hand. The crack resounded through the valley. Psyche tried to roll with the blow, but it snapped her head around and knocked her half over. But her waist-length braid swung around toward Emry's head. Emry dodged reflexively, distracted from seeing that Psyche had turned her motion into a spin-kick that took Emry below the sternum. She fell back, rolled, and came up into a ready crouch—just in time too, for with those long legs it took barely a step for Psyche to close with her and aim a high right-heel kick at her chin. Emry dodged and grabbed her ankle, but Psyche backflipped, her left foot jabbing Emry in the right knee and breast in quick succession. Psyche came out of the flip with her arms raised like an Olympic gymnast's, giggling.

"You won't be laughing when I haul you in for murder!"

"And will they believe you, a suspect in another murder? I'll just tell them it's a feeble attempt to frame me—and when it's my word against yours, sweetie, you're vacked out a very small punkhole. Besides," she added, her grin wide and feral, "you'd have to catch me first."

"Watch me!" She charged again.

<Emry, be careful. She can inflame your rage, compromise your judgment.> But by the time Zephyr said this, Psyche had already ducked and spun to take Emry's legs out from under her with a sweep of her own. But Emry had seen it coming and leapt into a pounce, and Psyche barely rolled clear in time. *It's all about the legs with her,* Emry realized.

Indeed, one of those legs came down on the small of her back, knocking her onto her belly. A moment later, Psyche was straddling her from behind, legs wrapped around her midriff and squeezing hard. A rope of shimmering, coppery-gold hair looped around Emry's neck and Psyche began to pull it tight. "I didn't want to have to do this, Emry! But I *will* kill you. You deserve it! You could've had everything at Daddy's side! But instead you betray him! Just like you betrayed your own father!"

Emry only faltered for a second. For once, Psyche had misread her. Yes, she had let her father down. But that was the past, and she could forgive herself now. Rachel had forgiven her . . . and she knew Mom and Dad would have forgiven her too. Because that was the kind of love they'd shared. The kind that healed.

Emry shot her head back into Psyche's face, drove her elbows into the nerve clusters under her arms. Psyche fell back, dazed, the rope of hair falling free from Emry's neck. Emry spun to face her, seeing blood dripping from her adorable snub of a nose. "Don't flatter yourself, Daddy's girl. You even fight sexy—the legs, the braid—it's fetish stuff. Not the real deal. Everything about you is just for show."

Psyche smiled, licking her lips to taste the blood. "No. It's for get-ting what I want. And there's more than one way to do that."

She ran. Emry followed. Soon, they emerged into the amphitheater, where dozens of delegates milled, discussing the issues of the day. "Help!" Psyche cried. "It's Emerald. Emerald Blair. She's betrayed us all, she's a spy for Ceres, she's trying to kill me!" Her voice was perfectly pitched to convey terror and helplessness. Tears glistened in her eyes, and her expression was so poignant it made even Emry mad at herself for hurting her. "Please, she's coming for me, stop her! Stop her any way you can!"

Most of the male delegates, and many female ones, surged forward to protect Psyche. She clung to them, one by one, no doubt spewing psy-choactives all over them. "No, it's not what you think!" Emry called. But some of them were already charging—Marcus Rossi of Mars Martialis, Paul Chandler of Zarathustra, the half-bionic Ifukube Kenji of Nii-hama. People who could do her serious damage if she let them—people she didn't dare hurt because they were innocent dupes. People who looked like they wanted to rip her apart with their bare hands for daring to lay a finger on their sweet, beloved Psyche.

So Emry ran. And a mob of delegates ran after her, screaming for her blood.

Beyond the stone amphitheater was a dense deciduous forest, and Psyche knew that Emry would quickly outdistance her pursuers within it. The delegates were not the best backup physically, with a few excep-tions among the mods. But they were at hand, Emry wouldn't hurt them, and, most important, they would all do anything for Psyche. Well, maybe not anything, but with the right handling, she could cer-tainly guide them in the right direction. It warmed Psyche's heart to see how many of the delegates leapt instantly to her defense, and how easy it was to persuade the rest to join in the pursuit of Emry—even some whom she hadn't yet managed to program for obedience, who were just buying her story and choosing to help her of their own free will. It was a thrill to exercise her powers on such a scale, to get a real test of the delegates' devotion to her. This was what her father had made her for. This was his will made manifest. And nothing brought Psyche such joy and fulfillment as being the instrument of Eliot Thorne's will.

Still, the last thing she wanted to do right now was call up Daddy and ask for help. He was busy with important conference matters, comparing notes with geneticists from various delegations, exploring ways to combine their efforts and techniques toward the betterment of all humankind. As always, he was planning for the future, his great mind and will questing outward, ten steps ahead of everyone else. She couldn't interrupt that with a mundane setback like this.

Besides, she was embarrassed. She should never have let this happen. She had underestimated Emry's loyalty to the Troubleshooters. *No, don't be so hard on yourself. You couldn't have known the Troubleshooters would develop their own suspicions of Tai.* She'd done all she could to assess their personalities, model their probable reactions, and orchestrate matters to deepen the wedge between them and Emry. But try as she might, she could only gain so much insight into the minds of people she hadn't gotten up close and personal with.

So she'd been forced to improvise again, as she had with Villareal. She hated it when she had to improvise. It was such a waste when people refused to go along with the plan and had to die. Especially a fabulous lover like Villareal or a friend like Emry. *Damn that cyber.* She didn't know specifically what Zephyr had said, but she could read Emry's reactions in her face, her hormones, the blood flow in her brain. *If not for him, I could've won her over.* Or at least knocked her out and taken her captive, so that she could've worked on changing her mind at leisure.

And maybe that could still happen if they caught her, though it would take some substantial neurological reconditioning. She wouldn't be the same free-spirited, funny, aggravating, and endearing woman after that. Maybe it would be kinder just to kill her now and remember her as she was. After all, she had an excellent simulation of Emry's psyche in her memory buffer, accumulated over many weeks of scanning and thus exceptionally detailed, so she could call it up for a chat at any time and wouldn't have to lose her friend forever.

Either way, Psyche was determined to get the situation in hand before she bothered Daddy. He had faith in her to handle things like this, and she wasn't going to let him down. She'd kill anyone, even her best friend, before letting her father down.

Not that Daddy wouldn't forgive her, of course. Daddy always forgave her. He was so generous and good to her. Most everyone was, of course, but that was Daddy's gift to her as well.

And now Psyche was able to make good use of that gift. Once she'd gotten the first group motivated to get out there and hunt Emry down, she quickly rounded up others, including that charming old lech Hanuman and his lady bodyguards (or body-somethings), to join in the search. Naturally, they were all oh so eager to come to her aid, to show no mercy to anyone who would dare to hurt her.

Unfortunately, her ability to keep up the persona of a victim was complicated by the fact that the delegates needed her help. Not many of them had the skills or enhanced senses to help in tracking, aside from Bast and a few others. So Psyche had to join in the search, crouching close to the ground and tracking Emry by her enticing, raw scent. It wasn't easy; Emry's trail soon vanished from the ground, and Bast had to follow it up into the trees. The she-cat lost the trail before long, but Psyche called up Emry's personality model, simulated her behavior under pursuit, and chose a likely direction. Before long, she'd picked up that exciting bouquet again and led the search party in pursuit.

But as Bast and the others raced ahead, their path paralleling a wide stream, Psyche slowed down, absorbing a new datum from the personality model. When the panthress sighted a flash of burgundy in the undergrowth and pounced on it, Psyche had a pretty good idea of what she'd find. Indeed, shortly the disappointed Bast rose, the shreds of Emry's blouse, pants, and boots clutched in her claws and teeth.

Psyche chuckled. *Ohh, I could've guessed that even without the model.*

18

Power Games

Emry ran through the forest on bare feet, water streaming from her hair. She'd figured that if Psyche could sense her hormones, she could track by scent, so she'd stripped to her panties and immersed herself in the stream. This was only a stopgap at best; movie myths to the contrary, scent molecules were highly hydrophilic and remained detectable in water for some time. A thorough bath and change (or abandonment) of clothes could confuse a scent tracker for a time, but it would just be a matter of searching until the trail was found again—and her near-nudity would probably make her easier to track. But with Psyche giving off psychoactive drugs from her sweat glands while she'd been pawing Emry all over, a stripdown and quick bath had seemed like a good idea. *I'd rather go naked than wear her.*

In fact, she reflected, she probably should have shed her panties as well. In the wilds of Neogaia, complete nudity would help her blend in visually if not by scent. In the past, she wouldn't have hesitated. Since puberty, Emry had never met anyone strong enough to overpower her sexually (until Eliot Thorne), and so had never learned to feel vulnerable in the nude. But after what Psyche had done to her, she felt exposed in a way she'd never known. Her panties didn't do much to counter that feeling, but they were the only thing Psyche hadn't gotten her scent on. They were better than nothing.

<Still, there has to be more to it than pheromones and drugs,> she subvocalized as she ran—trying to stride on exposed roots and stones as much as possible to minimize her trail. <She knew what I was thinking,

more than any heightened social processing skills could explain. She was practically reading my mind. That's impossible, isn't it?>

<Essentially,> Zephyr replied. <Specific concepts and memories are uniquely encoded in each brain. The code can only be deciphered after extensive analysis of the active neural network, and only in broad, imprecise terms. Recall the trouble your friend Mr. Santiago was having with transferring his brain to a computer substrate. A more general reading of cognitive focus, sensory input, and emotional response is possible, but only with a scanning mechanism surrounding the brain and stationary relative to it.>

<Right.> In her Banshee days, Emry had occasionally benefitted from the fact that brain scans couldn't be used to extract secrets or proof of guilt without a subject's willing cooperation. <So how could she have done it?> She remembered. <Those damn butterflies. She always had her hands on my head. Could there have been sensors in them?>

<Maybe. But that wouldn't be enough. They'd have to interface with some existing, more encompassing array. One that had remained in place long enough to gather the baseline data it needed to correct for changing, imperfect scanning conditions.>

<Some kind of smart dust or nanogrid? You would've picked that up after that first night.> Whatever Psyche had done, she could clearly do it without sexual intimacy, unless she had a lot more stamina and free time than Emry gave her credit for. It could've begun when she'd first held Emry's head in her hands and kissed her cheeks. But how much further could she have taken it once she'd pleasured Emry into unconsciousness? Maybe she'd gotten Emry to talk about her mission from Tai—that was how she and Eliot had known. But Eliot had made the accusation and Psyche had feigned surprise to misdirect Emry, and she, already compromised and suggestible, had fallen for it. But that didn't explain how a nanosensor array could have gone undetected.

<I've been analyzing the telemetry from before,> Zephyr said. <In the past, her manipulations were too subtle for me to read any signs of psychoactives or tech activity. But this time I read faint electrical potentials around your cranium. The model that best fits the readings is an array of nanosensors located in or near your hair follicles.>

<Okay, but how could you have missed those in the medscan?>

<*I have a theory.*> Zephyr paused. <*You're not going to like it.*>

"Just tell me, okay?" she hissed.

<*Trojan mites.*>

"What?!"

<*The* Demodex brevis *mite is a benign parasite, a few tenths of a millimeter in size, that infests the hair follicles of nearly ninety-eight percent of all humans. If Psyche's hair mites contain nanosensors, and she infested your scalp with them—*>

"Ohh, ick! You mean she gave me cooties?!" She almost forgot to keep her voice low.

<*That term originally referred to lice, which are parasitic insects.* Demodex *mites are arachnids, usually harmless, which is why the medscan didn't flag them.*>

Emry suppressed a shudder. <Okay. So she's got me and the delegates cootified . . . the bugs form a sensor grid, and her hands read them. Something with the eyes too, I bet . . . the way she holds your gaze.>

<*Once her other manipulations render the brain susceptible to hypnosis, some EM pattern from her eyes may be the trigger. The optic nerves are direct conduits to the brain.*>

<So two parts, detection and control. She can model people's minds, analyze their thought patterns, use that feedback to tailor her attacks more precisely. So it's almost like she's reading your mind.>

<*Yes,*> Zephyr said. <*Her salivary and apocrine glands must be chemical synthesis factories, generating agents tailored to each subject's brain chemistry. Remarkable.*>

<And scary. The control she could have over people. Over *governments.* Zeph, she almost had me. I loved her. I would've done anything for her. . . . >

<*It's all right, Emry.*>

<And Eliot . . . > She fought the tears that threatened to pour forth. She couldn't afford that now. She continued to subvocalize, afraid that if she spoke her thoughts aloud, it would break down the last of her control. <I can't believe he'd be a part of all this. How do we know she doesn't have him under her thumb along with everyone else?>

Zephyr's voice was gentle. *<Emry . . . while the presumption of in-nocence is a fundamental principle of ethics, you should consider your motives for it in this case. You've already seen what can happen when your judgment is clouded by love.>*

"It's not the same!" she said aloud. Too loud. She sighed, gathering herself. <I'm sorry, pal. I know you're just looking out for me. I should've listened to you before.>

<Your judgment was compromised at the time. But you came through when it counted.>

"Thanks to you. And thanks to Kari and the rest." *Kari!* "Can you contact them? I'm gonna need their help."

<Do we want to risk alerting Paladin? Although Tai was right about the Vanguard being a threat, his methods for dealing with them would still do more harm than good.>

<Okay, so can you contact Kari or the others without alerting him?>

<I don't share quantum encryption with them.>

<Can you laser-comm their ships, get to them the long way round?> Emry asked.

<If I knew where their ships were. And if they were taking my calls anymore.>

<Then I'll just have to try to get to them myself.>

Just then, a furry figure dropped from an overhead branch, startling several birds into flight. Hanuman Kwan came to his feet before her. He leered openly at her wet, nearly nude body, but his gun didn't waver from its aim between her eyes. "Well, hello," he said. Emry looked around for other pursuers, but Hanuman said, "Don't worry—we're alone."

Emry tried to dodge around and get to the gun, but it moved swiftly to bear. He was quicker than she would have thought. "Ah, ah, ah, now do be a good girl and don't move." He tilted his head. "Well, if you wanted to jiggle up and down a bit, I wouldn't mind at all."

She burned with humiliation, angry at herself for letting his pathetic lechery affect her. She crossed her arms over her breasts, trying to make it look stern rather than defensive. "Hanuman, listen to me," Emry said. "You can't trust Psyche. She's controlling you and the other delegates, with drugs, hypnosis—it's built into her. She and Eliot Thorne, they don't want a partnership, they want to rule you."

"Well. How kind of you to bring this to my attention, dear lady, but I assure you there's no need for you to worry on *my* account. You can't trick an old trickster."

"You knew?"

He gave a simian chuckle. "Why, of course, my dear! I knew all about the Thornes' manipulative powers before I went into partnership with them. Why do you think I found them such useful allies?"

It took a moment for his choice of words to sink in. "The . . . the *Thornes'* powers? Both of them?"

His eyes widened in mock surprise. "You mean you didn't know? Psyche's abilities are hereditary—though greatly enhanced, of course. Eliot isn't the precision instrument his daughter is, and he doesn't have her sensors and feedback mechanisms . . . but, well, you didn't really think that legendary personal magnetism of his was the luck of the genetic draw, did you? Not when he's enhanced every other advantage he has?"

Emry's stomach twisted. "You mean . . . when I . . ." She stopped herself.

"Ohh, when you fell in love with him?" Kwan finished for her, looking sympathetic. "Oh, you poor girl. Yes, I'm afraid he was simply using you. It was important to him to win you over as a symbol. A defector from the Troubleshooters who would speak out against their corruption, giving the charge a legitimacy it couldn't otherwise have."

"No, it . . . that can't be all it was to him. He wouldn't have needed to . . . I would've done that without being made to . . ."

"I'm *so* sorry to be the one to break it to you, my dear. I really hadn't realized just how badly you'd fallen for it." He gave a melodramatic sigh. "What you need to understand about Eliot Thorne is that the very things that make him strongest are in some ways his greatest weaknesses. His tough skin, his resistance to injury and pain, it somewhat dulls his capacity for pleasure. The enhanced hormonal stability that keeps him psychologically balanced tends to diminish his passions. He doesn't *feel* things all that strongly, I fear." Kwan shook his head, *tsk-tsk*ing.

Emry didn't want to believe it. "How . . . how can you know that?"

"Oh, Eliot and I go back quite a way. I did some of my graduate study on Vanguard back in the fifties. Yes, he was something of a prototype, so there were some unfortunate side effects. There's something very profound there, I've always thought—that taking away the man's weaknesses left him somehow diminished, cheated out of the pleasures of life. Almost poetic, don't you agree?"

Emry was shaking her head now. "No. No, Eliot can be *very* passionate. I know."

"Oh, he's learned to play the game very well. He's had to, you see. Feeling as cold and empty as he does leaves the man with a strong need to compensate. He craves stimulation, excitement. And like most people who fail to find fulfillment in love, family, or career, he seeks it through power. The game of conquest, control, domination of others. Be it political, sexual, emotional . . . it's what he craves. Masterminding his moves, maneuvering his pawns. Winning them over to his will and convincing them it was their own idea."

<Emry, why is he being so garrulous about this?>

But Emry had her own question. "If you knew all this, why are you working with him?"

"My dear, most relationships are about using and being used. The key is to make sure it goes both ways. I help Eliot play the game of quietly conquering the Solar System, and in exchange, I get a power base that improves Neogaia's chances of taking back Mother Earth one day."

"And what kind of . . . *help* are you talking about?"

Kwan grinned. "Why, you don't think Eliot Thorne would leave anything to chance, do you? Just waited around for someone to *happen* to launch a terrorist attack on Earth, goading them to persuade their close Cerean allies to crack down on the rest of the Belt and provide a common enemy he could unite us against?"

His words hit her like—like the sky falling in on her. She was on him in an instant, pinning him against a tree bole by his scrawny neck, the gun knocked aside without a thought. "*You?!* You . . . planned the Chakra City attack?"

Kwan feigned modesty as best he could under the circumstances.

"I merely . . . provided the means," he choked out. "I can't take credit . . . for Eliot's genius."

Her fingers yearned to close around his neck, and only her love for her mother and father, for Sensei, and for Arkady kept her from betraying their faith in her by killing. Besides, her rage was coalescing on another target now.

Slamming a fist into Kwan's gut, leaving him in a half-conscious heap on the forest floor, she scooped up his fallen gun and ran, no longer caring if anyone spotted her. She knew Eliot Thorne's itinerary for today. She knew where he would be.

<Emry, watch yourself,> Zephyr warned. <Why would Kwan tell you all that like some cartoon villain giving exposition?>

<Because he's a smug bastard who wanted to watch me squirm.>

<Perhaps. But why hold you at gunpoint, when relying on bodyguards such as Bast would be more in character? Why point you at Thorne and provide you with a weapon?>

<I don't know. But he was telling the truth, Zephyr. Eliot Thorne leaves nothing to chance. Nothing.>

<Granted. But you could be walking into a trap.>

Emry merely quickened her pace. "I'd like to see anyone try and stop me right now."

Selkie broke cover as soon as that horrid Blair woman was out of sight, racing to her dear mentor's side. "Ohh, Hanuman, are you all right?" She helped him up into a sitting position against a tree trunk, checking him for injury.

"Yes." He coughed. "Yes, I'll be fine. I'll—stop fawning over me, you pathetic twat!"

Selkie backed away and lowered her head. "Yes, sir. I'm sorry, sir. Would you like to punish me now?"

He gave a pained chuckle. His approval at her obedience comforted her. He'd always been there for her, telling her what to think and not to think, giving her purpose, training her for love and war, ever since she'd been a little girl. "No, no, that can wait until tonight." She flushed with anticipation, but grew concerned as he began coughing rather nastily again. She kept her distance, though, for fear of angering him again. He noticed her worry and stroked her short-furred scalp. "Don't worry, I'll be fine." He coughed again. "She . . . packs a wallop . . . but for all her bluster, she doesn't have that killer instinct." He pulled Selkie closer. "Which is where you come in, my dear."

Thorne was down in the underground labs in the lake sector of Neogaia. An armed, nearly-naked woman storming her way into the place naturally attracted a certain amount of attention. But once they saw the look on her face, most of the personnel knew better than to get in her way, and the few who tried soon regretted it. She took a lab coat from one of them, not wanting to be exposed to Thorne right now. She'd prefer her light armor, but this would have to do.

She found him in an observation room, its wide, transparent wall looking out into the depths of the lake beyond, where a variety of Neogaians swam. Grandma Rachel and a gaggle of scientists were there as well. "Get out," Emry barked at them, her weapon pointed at Thorne to make clear that he wasn't included. The Vanguardian leader met her gaze calmly.

Most of the scientists didn't need to be told twice, hurrying from the room. But Rachel stayed, coming closer to her granddaughter. Emry spoke coldly. "Get out, Rachel. You've got a baby to protect."

"Emry, what's going on? What happened?"

Emry glared at her. "Did you know? Just tell me that, Grandma. Did you know what this . . . this *conference* is really all about?"

"What do you mean?"

"You must've known about Psyche. You helped make her what she is. You had to know how she can control people. Have you been in on this from the beginning? Have you been lying to me, manipulating me along with the rest of them?"

Rachel crossed her arms. "Emerald, you need to calm down and start making sense."

"Making *sense*? My Goddess, you can talk to me about making sense?

It doesn't make sense to me at all that you could be a part of, of mind control and mass murder. But I can't see how you couldn't be. You had to know about Psyche's powers. You had to be a part of making her into a weapon!" She whirled on Thorne, sensing his attempt to ease closer. "And *you* stay back! You *don't* want to punk with me right now!"

"Emry," Rachel said. "Yes, I know all of Psyche's enhancements. They're tools for helping her gain empathy and insight into others, build bridges of understanding. Of course I'm aware of how they could be corrupted into weapons. But Eliot wouldn't let that happen, and neither would I."

"Just like he wouldn't 'let' the Neogaians attack Chakra City and murder my mentor?"

Rachel gasped. "Who would tell you such a thing? Eliot, talk to the girl, explain it to her!"

Thorne crossed his arms. "I don't think you're in the mood for explanations right now, are you, Emerald?"

"There's that keen insight into human nature. Go on, impress me more."

"I suppose Psyche was facing resistance from you and pushed too far to keep you under control—enough to do something your defenses could detect. It's a chronic weakness of hers, I fear. She's too accustomed to getting what she wants, and sometimes forgets the value of patience."

"Is that why she killed Sensei Villareal?" Emry asked, making Rachel gasp again. "Out of 'impatience'?"

"If you know about her abilities, I assume you know about mine as well. So I won't try to cajole or comfort you. I'll simply explain that neutralizing Villareal was necessary. The threat of Ceres united with the Troubleshooters is needed to motivate the rest of the Belt to come together."

"You liar. Sensei's endorsement would've helped the alliance, not hurt it. You just didn't want the Troubleshooters in the alliance because people would've turned to them for protection instead of you."

"And what good would that have done them? The Troubleshooters are a handful of costumed vigilantes, more about making the public *feel* safe than making a real difference. They're no more than the Van-guardians were four decades ago. Look how easily they were co-opted by the Cereans."

"Were they really? Or did you send Psyche to seduce Gregor Tai and pillow-talk him into taking over the Corps?"

Thorne smirked. "I hardly needed to. Earth and the Sheaf were al-ready primed to react the right way. So proud and secure in their uni-fied, benevolent social order. So convinced they have the answers the Striders sorely need. All it took was a trigger, and they reacted exactly as our models predicted."

"My God." Rachel was staring at Thorne now. "You're not saying it's true, Eliot? About Chakra City?"

"Something had to be done," Thorne insisted to both women. "You know it as well as I, Rachel. If we can engineer a better humanity on an individual scale, we should be able to do it on a societal scale as well. And we have a responsibility to do so. We left the Belt alone before when we could have helped, and look at the chaos that's resulted! They need to be guided in a better, healthier direction, and we've waited long enough to begin. We're ready now. With Psyche a successful adult, with her eldest siblings nearing maturity. There had to be a trigger to set the process in motion."

"You hypocrite!" Emry cried. "How can you talk about making things better when you're willing to kill people to do it?"

"How many more people will die in the long run if we don't start making a difference now? The sacrifices are regrettable, yes. And I'm sorry that two people you cared for so much had to be among them. But it's a step along the way to a better system. Once we establish the alliance, once we're directing systemwide policy through Psyche's in-fluence and that of her siblings and heirs, there will be no need for such violence!"

"Directing policy—you mean mind control!"

"I mean nothing so melodramatic. All politics is about attempting to persuade people to see one's point of view. But conventional means of persuasion rarely work in the face of human stubbornness or greed, and war, corruption, and cruelty are the result. I discovered that the hard way during the cislunar conflicts. So ever since, I've dedicated myself to finding more effective forms of persuasion. Imagine being truly able to convince everyone to work together toward a common good."

"And what about their free will?"

"All freedom is relative, Emerald. Even the most democratic society imposes legal and social constraints on its members—and when those constraints are too weak or ineffective, chaos results. All we have done is to create a means whereby people's behavior can be governed through an understanding of their own wants and needs, through persuading them to share a common goal for their own reasons.

"Do you really want to keep fighting for the rest of your life, Emerald? Beating people up, throwing them into prison cells, and pretending that makes a difference? I'm offering you something so much greater. I'm offering a role in bringing peace and unity to the human race for all time to come, evolving the entire species into a fitter, more viable whole."

He took a step toward her, reaching out. "I can see how driven you are to find peace, Emerald. That's part of why I chose you to be at my side. I want to give you that chance. Join with me, and together we can create an enduring legacy of peace. Sons and daughters who can change worlds through gentle persuasion and make war and crime a thing of the past. Isn't that a future any Troubleshooter would willingly give his life to help create?"

Emry stared at him. She had no words. But her hand spoke for her. It aimed her gun directly at Thorne's crotch and pressed the trigger.

He was already in motion, and the bullet only grazed his hip. An instant later, his left hand clamped her wrist and forced her to drop the weapon. His right hand chopped at her neck and she lifted her arm to block it, but the blow still felled her. She kicked at his knee, but he knew her moves too well; he was already moving, so the blow only half-connected, dropping him into a crouch but not debilitating him. He grabbed her calf and she tried to yank it away. He added his force to her motion, driving her own knee into her face and nearly dislocating her femur in the process. Thorne was no longer pulling his punches.

Her free foot kicked him in the stomach, knocking the wind from him, but his greater inertia kept him upright. She wrenched her other leg free and rolled away. His hand caught the collar of her lab coat and held it tightly; to get away, she had to unfasten it and wriggle out, leaving herself only in panties once again. She gaped at Thorne as she scrambled away. Had it been an accident, or something more? How far would he go to dominate her?

Determined not to find out, she scrambled to her feet, but it was a struggle. Thorne had bruised her right wrist and left ankle clear to the bone, and the wrist had sustained a hairline fracture, its nanofiber bracing holding it together. Before she was fully upright, Thorne was tackling her, favoring his left leg but barely slowed. All the superstrength in the worlds couldn't let her hold her ground when struck by twice her own mass. He slammed her into the cold observation wall, almost crushing her rib cage. A second later, a fist-shaped stroid had an impact event with her gut, expelling what little air remained in her lungs. But she'd already launched her knee at his crotch, and though she barely registered the impact, she felt his weight fall away. She slumped to her hands and knees, gasping for oxygen. Her repair systems struggled to regulate the pain and feed her epinephrine.

When she looked up again, Thorne, though staggering a bit, was already recovering. Emry gaped, contemplating how much sexual sensitivity he would've had to sacrifice to minimize that particular vulnerability, and almost felt sorry for him. Kwan had not been lying about this either.

Regardless, she had to act before he struck again. But he still loomed over her and was already reaching down. She lunged for his legs, but he grabbed her torso, flipped her upside-down, and pile-drove her toward the ground. She barely managed to tuck her head and take it on her shoulders. But then he forced her down across his leg, his knee taking her in the small of the back. It felt like she would break in half. Then his fist took her across the jaw, dazing her. He let her slide down his leg, then straddled her, a hand around her throat. "You will submit, Emerald! Or you will not live!"

Then his grip loosened as a bullet hit him in the shoulder. A voice rang out:

"Leave my granddaughter alone!"

Choking for breath, Emry tilted her head back to see a pair of over-lapping, blurry Grandmas Rachel standing upside-down, gradually co-alescing into a single, furious armed figure. "I mean it, Eliot! Step away from her *now*!"

In another moment, his weight was gone from her and she began to feebly pull herself away. "Rachel, put that down," Thorne said coolly.

"Don't tell me what to do, you bastard! Ohh, I'm so sorry, Emry," Rachel said, shaking her head but not letting her gaze leave Thorne as she strode between the combatants. Careful to keep the gun on Thorne, she slipped off her own lab coat and dropped it over Emry, who pulled it on as quickly as she could, never more grateful to cover her body. "I was a fool. I never for a moment thought Eliot was capable of . . . *this*!"

Thorne seemed subdued, but unreadable. "I will not attempt to defend what happened in the heat of the moment. I regret having to use force on Emerald in any way. But she cannot be allowed to resist or interfere with my plans, no matter what it takes to stop her."

Rachel stared in horror, but it soon gave way to disgust. "I thought the rest of us had talked you out of it, Eliot. I thought you finally understood."

"Hawk, Thuy, and Krishna all stand with me. They still understand that Sol System needs order. It needs a real authority."

"Yes, it does, but a representative one! Everyone having a voice, not one group trying to control it all! My God, Eliot, that's the whole thing we're fighting to keep the Sheaf from doing! How could you think it would work any better with you doing it?"

"Because we are better qualified! And because everyone *will* have a voice. No one will feel deprived of representation. We will simply make sure they use their voices in the proper harmony, toward meaningful change and progress."

"Ohh, Eliot." Emry recognized the tone. It was that same sad, disappointed tone in her father's voice when she'd misbehaved or fallen short of his expectations. Only it was far more profound. "You really don't get it, do you? I thought you'd learned your lesson after the first time you tried this. I thought the rest of us had brought you into line, convinced you to see reason. But it was all an act, wasn't it? You haven't changed one bit. It's still all about control with you. Your overweening ego demanding that everything has to be done your way."

"It isn't about me, Rachel! It's about you, about Psyche. It's about Liam and Liesl and everyone else we've lost to the chaos."

"No, Eliot. I know you too well. It's about you. You always talk about Liam and the others as though their deaths were a personal affront. A symbol of *your* failure to control every situation. You always insist that if *you* just had more power, more influence, you could control everything and keep everyone safe and well." Emry stared up at Rachel, struck by the familiarity of those words.

"But that's a lie, Eliot. It was your drive to control things that sent Liam and the rest down there in the first place. Your desire for a controlled, isolated world that brought us out here to the Belt, and estranged me from my own son. And now look at what you're doing! Backing terrorists. Using your own daughter as an assassin. Attacking, practically raping my own flesh and blood!

"This is what power gets you, Eliot! Try to hold on too tight and you just end up breaking things, or seeing them slip out of your clutches. If what you really cared about was peace and safety, you'd see that. But those things are just excuses for indulging your own pride."

"Do you think Liam gave his life merely for my pride? Would you trivialize his—"

"*Don't,* Eliot!" The gun was merely an afterthought now. Her eyes held him at bay. "Liam was my *husband.* You do not get to use him against me. Or against my granddaughter."

Rachel reached down to help Emry to her feet. In doing so, she looked away from Thorne, and Emry's eyes shot to him, concerned that he would seize the opportunity. But he simply stood there, his eyes unreadable. Was he actually considering Rachel's words, or just unwilling to attack her and endanger the genetic legacy in her womb? If nothing else, she'd given Emry a lot to think about.

Just then, Emry noted movement in the water outside. She turned to see a Neogaian swimmer at the observation wall, watching them. But no . . . it wasn't just any swimmer. It was Selkie, Hanuman Kwan's playmate. And she wasn't just watching.

She was attaching a device to the glass. And pushing a button to activate it.

And swimming away from it very, very fast.

Emry *made* her legs work, pulling Rachel toward the exit. Suddenly Thorne was there, taking Rachel's other arm and propelling her faster. He hit the door control, and it seemed to take forever to slide open. As soon as it was wide enough, the two of them together shoved Rachel sideways through the opening . . .

Just as the bomb went off.

19

Everybody Out of the Gene Pool!

When Psyche was notified of the explosion, Hanuman and Bast had to physically restrain the anguished young beauty from rushing to the blast site herself. Well, Bast did most of the actual restraining, but Hanuman never passed up an excuse to lay his hands on Psyche's incredible body.

Of course, he made sure that all he showed outwardly was concern and anger. She knew quite well that his simian anatomy rendered her usual people-reading skills less than effective with him, but he'd worked hard to cultivate her trust for just this moment. "Please, Psyche, there's nothing you can do now!" he told her, making his voice soothing but urgent.

Psyche whirled on him, her eyes flashing. "How do you know they're dead? Can you be sure?"

If only I could be, he thought, keeping it from showing. Rotten luck that Selkie had been spotted; he'd hoped the little *contretemps* he'd engineered between Emerald and Eliot would keep them distracted. Fortunately the bomb had detonated before either of them had gotten out, and the door had automatically resealed itself the moment the observation wall was breached. Eliot and the Busty Blaze had been hit by the force and debris of the blast and then by kilotonnes of lake water; the odds of their survival were agreeably slim. But Psyche's question was a valid one: he had to be absolutely certain. Selkie had reported by radio from the lake's surface moments ago, but he'd promptly ordered her back down. "My dear, Selkie and our best swimmers are searching the lake as we speak. If either of them survived—by some miracle—they'll find them." *And undo the miracle.* "But I must be honest with you, Psyche . . . the chances are very poor. Rachel was barely out the door when the bomb blew, and she was badly off. We're rushing her to hospital to ensure her baby's safety." In fact, according to those on the scene, she was conscious—all the more reason to make sure Psyche didn't get a chance to talk with her. Lucky she was pregnant; her concern for her baby's health was the only thing that could have persuaded that stubborn woman to leave the search for her granddaughter.

"If there's any chance at all, I have to be there. He's my father!"

"And as your father, he would want you to be safe. He may not be the only target, Psyche." Hanuman moved closer. "Let me suggest a better way. Come with Bast and me to the security center in the hub. We can monitor the whole search from there. You'll know the moment they find the . . . the fate of your father. And you'll be safe there, in case the Troubleshooters have targeted you as well."

Psyche was shaking her head—but at least she wasn't rushing off. "How could this have happened? Emerald would never have been party to an assassination, no matter the provocation. And she was too good to let it backfire on her!"

"It had to be the Troubleshooters," he told her, taking care to drop his usual affectations and sound as sincere as he could. Even with his advantages, this would be a delicate sell. Particularly since he'd improvised the whole thing. He'd been monitoring the Troubleshooters since they'd arrived, of course; they were alert to most monitoring devices, but the Personal Digital Avian he'd purchased from the Moreau Foundation had proved an ideal spy, blending in with the other birds, undetectable as a cyber due to its DNA-based AI. His plan had been to await the Troubleshooters' sabotage and piggyback Eliot's assassination onto it, so that the TSC and Ceres—and by implication their Terran backers—would take the blame. He'd tried to sic Emerald on the Troubleshooters in hopes of provoking a conflict between them and the Vanguardian forces, providing a more plausible context for such a violent turn of events. Emerald's *rapprochement* with them and her discovery of Psyche's abilities had thrown off his plans—but had provided an excellent backup plan at the same time. "They must have planted a bomb on her," he went on.

Psyche's eyes widened in disbelief. "She was nearly naked!" But it looked more like bewilderment than suspicion. So far, so good.

"Perhaps they fed her a pill of some sort, or . . . switched her self-one." Best if it didn't sound too prepared. "I don't know. There are so many ways to deliver a bomb these days. But it's the only possibility, isn't it? Who else here would want to kill Eliot Thorne?"

Psyche gasped, tears pouring from those gleaming eyes, and Hanuman moved in to give her a nice, long, comforting hug. But she pushed him away. "They wouldn't show their hand so openly. It would turn everyone against them."

"That's why they used Emerald, don't you see? They've already painted her as an assassin! She was the perfect dupe! They fooled her into thinking they were on her side, then waited until she went to Eliot, and . . ." He broke off, making it seem he was too distraught to go on. "Oh, that poor, lovely girl." *What a waste of two good D-cups.*

Psyche glared at him, grabbed his shoulders, and slammed them into the wall. *Oh, this is getting fun!* "What about my father?! Eliot Thorne, the greatest man in the worlds, is . . ." She was unable to finish the thought. She seethed, the rage building within her. It was the most passionate, most genuine and unrehearsed emotion he'd ever seen in the girl's flawless face. She'd never looked more beautiful.

But then she whirled to the delegates who'd come with her, eager as always to see to her needs. "Find them," she ordered through clenched teeth. "Find the Troubleshooters. Tear this place apart if you have to. And tear them apart when you find them! No—no, save them for me."

She stormed off, her pawns following, and Hanuman scampered to keep up, Bast coming along behind. "My dear Psyche, what do you plan to do?"

"You don't want to know, Hanuman. I don't quite know myself yet. I've never had the chance to discover just how much prolonged anguish I can inflict on a human mind." A sob tore out of her. "My father . . . he always urged restraint . . . patience . . . told me not to indulge myself too far." Her hands convulsed into claws, tendons strained in her supple neck, and she erupted. With a roar, she grabbed one of the shorter delegates by the lapels and pulled him up clear off his feet. *"And where did that get us?!"* she screamed. Slamming him into the wall, she tore at his face with her long, sharpened nails, kicked him savagely in the shins, kneed him in the groin. Deep under her spell, he just stood there and took it, sobbing in her broadcast grief as well as his own pain. The other delegates fidgeted but did nothing to intervene, their faces showing profound sympathy and forgiveness. Hanuman stayed well back. He'd gotten a booster injection of countermeasures to her psychoactive agents this morning, but he wasn't about to take any chances.

Her fury expended for now, Psyche fell on top of the hapless little man's shuddering body and heaved deep breaths. Her eyes flashed at the other delegates. "What are you standing there for? Find the Troubleshooters!" They hurried to comply. But Psyche did not go with them.

After a moment, she looked at Kwan and said, "You're right, Hanuman. I . . . we can direct the search better from the hub. I need to . . . stay focused." She took his hand and let him help her up to a crouch, not sparing another glance at the delegate. "Thank you, Hanuman. You've always been so good to me. I'm sorry I yelled, Hannie. Daddy would've been so disappointed in me."

"No," he insisted, putting his arms around her. "He would have understood. He knew how much you loved him. And he loved you just as much."

She accepted his embrace for a moment, but then moved clear and rose to her full, impressive height. "But he would want me to be strong for him. I'm the leader of the Vanguard now. It's up to me to ensure his legacy."

"Yes. Yes, that's the spirit!" Taking her warm, supple hand, he led her toward the nearest radial shaft, with Bast going ahead, ostensibly to guard against Troubleshooter assassins (while actually to keep Psyche in line in case she got suspicious). "With your powers, and with the brilliance and vision you inherited from Eliot, there's nothing you can't do. And I'll be right there with you, helping you unite humanity once and for all."

"Not all of it," Psyche answered. "Not the Sheaf. Not Earth. And not the Troubleshooters. They killed the greatest leader history has ever known. And I will make them pay."

Ohh, how perfect! He had her right where he wanted her. Eliot's dream of systemwide unity had been grandiose but misguided. Humanity belonged in the bosom of Mother Earth, becoming part of Her once again, not trapping the spark of life inside a million tin cans in space. Earth had to be reclaimed—Her industrial masters overthrown, their bloated numbers culled to a sustainable minimum, their cities torn down to pave the way for the return of Her true acolytes, the Neogaians. With Hanuman Kwan ruling over them from his palace, of course. True, a palace filled with the collected riches of the Earth and a well-stocked harem/menagerie wasn't exactly the sort of thing that generally came about through natural processes. But that was a minor detail.

And with Psyche working for Neogaia—and sharing her secrets so Neogaia could create more like her, missionaries whose sermons could win over the most resistant unbelievers—the goal of reclaiming Mother Earth would finally be in their grasp.

Of course, Psyche would eventually learn that Hanuman's goals were not her own, and then he would have to have her killed. But by then, hopefully, the initial war against UNECS (who would be dragged into the war that would soon be launched against their Sheaver allies) would be won and Neogaia would have a small army of super-missionaries growing toward adulthood.

But who knew? Maybe over time, he could win her over to the Neogaian point of view. She was such a daddy's girl. Smart of Eliot, to keep her psychologically dependent on him as a means of regulating her extraordinary power. Perhaps Hanuman could take over as her surrogate father figure—not too literally, of course, since that would preclude the frequent and ambitious sex he intended to have with her. But maybe, if he played his hand right, he could convince her of the joys of living as nature intended.

Hanuman smiled, watching Psyche's perfect ass undulate before him, and contemplated how much more perfect she would be with a nice, long tail. Or maybe he would give her butterfly wings for real. Or why not both . . . ?

Emry struggled toward the surface, but the dead weight she was dragging held her down. The cold water both stung and soothed where her bare skin was burned. Blood clouded the water, and Emry just hoped there were no Neogaian shark-people in this lake. Or just plain sharks.

It could have been worse. The charge had been calibrated to deliver all its force into shattering the observation wall and letting the inrush of high-pressure water and shards of wall material do the rest, so as to protect Selkie and the other lake denizens from the lethal hydraulic shock of a larger blast. But while the door may have trapped Emerald and Thorne inside, enough of a gap remained at the moment of detonation to ameliorate the overpressure shock as the lake burst in and compressed the air ahead of it. Nonetheless, the combined impact of the overpressure, the water itself, and the wall shrapnel would have been instantly lethal to any baseline human and most mods.

But Emry had been spared the worst of it. Once she'd come to her senses, she'd realized something had shielded her.

Eliot Thorne's body.

Which had floated limp in the water, blood billowing from his lacerated back. The pale infrared ghost of his heart still beat, but weakly.

Emry owed Eliot Thorne her life. By chance? Or . . .

She'd had no time to contemplate it; even her oxygen-rich blood had its limits, and her inbuilt emergency reserve was all but depleted after that last fight. Scanning the room, she'd spotted a knocked-over cabinet with some gill rebreathers spilling out. She'd grabbed one for herself, sucked in the oxygen it extracted from the water. Then, sighing heavily into the mask, she'd grabbed a second one, strapped it over Thorne's face, and dragged him toward the jagged hole in the wall.

It was no easy task getting him to the surface. All that muscle and dense Vanguardian bone meant he wasn't very buoyant. For that matter, she wasn't much more buoyant herself, thanks to her bionics and reinforcements. To minimize drag, she'd had no choice but to shed the lab coat and leave herself all but naked to the cold water, without the inbuilt defenses that Selkie and the others had. It was slow going. She was still weak and the rebreather wasn't calibrated for her oxygen-hungry metabolism. She kept herself motivated by imagining the nice, cathartic trial she was going to take Thorne in for. Assuming somebody could figure out who had the authority to try him.

Suddenly a hand came from behind her and ripped the rebreather from her face. Emry shot an elbow back, grazing a well-padded body. She spun to see Selkie flinging her mask aside, then darting away as Emry swiped at her with her free arm. Emry tucked that arm under Thorne's again and tried to increase her upward pace. But Selkie swam down from above and pushed down on Emry's shoulders. Emry again freed one hand to swing at her, but Selkie somersaulted and took her in the face with a flippered foot.

Emry lost her grip on Thorne and had to head after him as he slowly sank. She pulled his mask free, holding her hand over his nose and mouth to keep him from inhaling water, and took a deep drag from it before strapping it back around him. Then she resumed her grip and started upward again, knowing Selkie would be there but having no choice.

As she closed on the seal-woman, Emry kicked at her, but Selkie dodged easily. This was her element, and Emry was too hurt, too weak. Again those hands pushed down on her. Strong, flippered legs churned water, fighting her upward progress, reversing it. Emry's lungs were crying for air. She felt her consciousness starting to fade.

But suddenly there was something else in the water, a silver dervish striking at Selkie again and again, driving her away. The figure descended toward Emry, took her in its arms, began to lift her skyward. An angel. Tenshi.

"Kari!" Emry gasped once she'd breached the surface and sucked in the sweet air. Coughing, she gestured toward shore with her head. Kari, clad only in her silver light-armor bodysuit, joined her in pulling Thorne to dry land, and then Arjun was there, wading in and helping them both to the shoreline, where Kari's scarlet jacket lay crumpled on the sand.

"*Oyamah!*" Kari gasped when she saw the state of Thorne's back. Thorne was starting to cough up water on his own, confirming he didn't need respiratory assistance, so Arjun whipped a medical gel pack from his armor and sprayed it over Thorne's back.

"Watch it," Emry rasped. "He's . . . he's not an innocent." She didn't trust herself to go into it now.

"He's not going anywhere," Vijay said. "He's barely conscious."

"You don't look much better," Kari said, beginning to tend to Emry's wounds.

Emry glared at her. "And you . . . what are you doing here? You need to be . . . safe. To testify against Tai."

"I can take care of myself," Kari insisted. "Better than you can, it looks like."

"Yeah, well . . ." She laughed, gave Kari a quick hug. "Thanks. How'd you know?"

"Zephyr told us."

"How?"

Kari grinned. "He sent his soligram." Emry's eyes widened at the thought of a naked, winged marble statue soaring through the docks, but Kari shook her head. "He made it look like a dockworker."

"Clever boy."

<*Thank you.*>

"So what happened down there?" Kari asked.

"Hanuman Kwan," Emry said. "Sicced me on Thorne . . . had his pet seal try to blow us both up. Probably wanted to make it look like I'd killed him, or you had."

"But why? What would he get out of that?"

Emry had been thinking about that, and only one answer had presented itself. "Psyche. She worships her father. If she thought he'd been killed . . . thought Ceres and Earth were behind it . . . with all the people she can control . . ."

"What?"

Emry brushed it off. "We have to find Kwan. He's probably with Psyche."

A hushed voice spoke over Kari's selfone. "*Tenshi, this is Hijab. I've been listening. I've already spotted Kwan and Ms. Thorne. They're heading for the hub, accompanied by Bast. The Neogaians have secure facilities there that would be difficult to breach.*"

"You have to keep them from getting there!" Emry cried. "Kwan was behind Chakra City . . . along with Thorne. It was all Thorne's idea. And Psyche . . . she killed Sensei." Kari and Vijay stared.

"Then she will not escape me," Maryam said. *"This I vow."*

"For her sake," Emry said, rising to her feet, "hope you get to her before I do."

She began to storm off, but Kari stopped her. "Umm, Emry . . . aren't you a bit, umm, naked?"

"You think I care about that right now?"

"Well . . . you could use some protection," Kari said. "And some warmth, Ms. I Just Nearly Drowned. Besides . . ." She made her way over to her fallen jacket and lifted it to reveal a bundle underneath. "Zephyr sent this along . . . he thought you might want it."

Emry laughed with delight. It was a Green Blaze uniform. "Thank you, Zephyr," she said as she began to put it on. "It's been too long since I wore green."

<It's your best color.>

"Trouble coming," Vijay announced as Kari slipped her own jacket back on. "I think."

Emry spun to take in the small mob heading their way. "They're delegates!" Kari said.

"Under Psyche's spell," Emry said.

"Okay, you need to explain that."

"Just call it mind control. Sort of. Point is, they're dupes. Hold them off, but try not to hurt them, okay?" she said as she finished pulling on her boots.

"Got it. You get going. We'll guard your back."

Emry smiled, squeezed Kari's shoulder. "I know you will. Good luck."

Tentatively, Emry set off into a trot. Being in uniform again felt good, and not just symbolically; the light armor gave her muscles (and bust) dynamic support, improved her circulation, boosted her strength. Soon she was able to increase her pace. Checking the utility belt, she found that Zephyr had packed a couple of energy bars for her. She devoured them both as she ran, leaving the wrappers as litter on Neogaia's pristine soil and feeling perversely good about it.

Soon she came to the cave leading to the nearest radial shaft, seized a climbing vine, and began to ascend the spinward wall. She pulled herself up faster and faster, feeling her weight vector angle farther with the speed, and soon she was literally running up the side of the shaft. Her weight decreased with each passing second until she was able to take long bounds up the faux cliff face, and eventually she switched to pulling herself up the vine hand over hand as the wall sped past, only occasionally needing to kick off of it to maintain her distance.

And then she was in the transfer drum between the rotating wheel and the free-fall core of the habitat. Six shaft termini ringed its circumference, while on its flat faces, rotating slowly from her perspective, were multiple corridor entrances. Hijab's tracking signal on her retinal HUD highlighted one corridor, and Emry grabbed its edge, taking a second for her perceptual frame to shift—now the side walls were standing still and the shaft adits rotating. Now entirely in free fall, Emry pulled herself along the corridor by its handholds, picking up speed. She took a moment to whip a hairband from her belt—Zephyr thought of everything—and tie her hair back into a bushy ponytail.

Soon a voice called out to her. "Blaze!" The wall seemed to distort, a subtle bulge in it unwrapping to reveal Maryam's black-clad form inside her cloak. "I think Bast caught my scent, but I managed to elude her. They've taken a shortcut through the warehouse sector, though. They went in moments ago. But Arjun and Tenshi have just called for backup."

"Then go. I can handle this."

"Are you sure?"

"I've taken Bast before," she said, neglecting to mention that she hadn't been this badly hurt at the time. "Besides, once Psyche finds out her dad's alive and Kwan tricked her, Bast'll have to protect him from *her.*"

Maryam sighed. "Very well. I vowed she would not escape—I trust you not to make me a liar. Allah be with you, Emerald."

"I hope so. I need Allah help I can get." Maryam glared. "Sorry," Emry said, clasping her hand and smiling. "Thanks."

So, while thousands of arrows fell all around him and Uttara, Arjuna shot one arrow up into the sky and called down the weapon of sleep.

Or so Buck's translation of the *Mahabharata* would have it. Despite taking his code name from that greatest of all epics, Vijay Pandalai had never found the time to read the original. Maybe that made him a dilettante, but he'd been rather busy, first getting modded to pursue an athletic career, then deciding (admittedly after his mods failed to compensate for a merely mediocre talent for sports) that his powers gave him a higher calling as a Troubleshooter. Not to mention taking care of his kid brother, who followed him in everything but needed Vijay's guidance to keep his impulses in check.

Anyway, right now he wished he had his namesake's weapon of sleep, or a good old phaser on stun. It wasn't that easy to take down an entire crowd of angry, determined people without endangering their life and limbs. Stun weapons were not infallibly nonlethal, and if Arjun upped his shock laser charge enough to take out the stronger mods, it could endanger the frailer delegates. He and Tenshi had been willing to retreat to keep from harming the mob, but they couldn't leave Thorne unsecured if what Emry said was true, and carrying him would slow them too much. So they were relying mainly on crowd-control ordnance—tanglewebs, buckyball lubricant sprays, sonics, and plasma guns in flashbang mode. Kari made use of her *tessen* where she could, using the sturdy folding fans as shields to deflect rocks and fists or as clubs wielded judiciously against the tougher delegates' weak points. She set their surfaces to flash bright, disorienting patterns as she spun and danced with them, confusing and nauseating her attackers. The mob had thinned as a result, but the stronger and more determined mods were still coming, and more Neogaians were showing up to reinforce them, surrounding the Troubleshooters.

Before long, it came down to hand-to-hand. At first, Vijay wished he could have his burly brother at his side, but after mere moments watching Kari in the grip of her "battle peace," he changed his mind. The dainty girl was a dervish, moving faster than even his enhanced vision could easily follow, meeting every blow with perfect precision, just enough to incapacitate her foes—though he realized for the first time just how lethal that instinctive power and precision could be, and just how strong her spirit had to be to restrain the killer within. She was scarily beautiful to watch, and Vijay decided he'd have to invite her to his next strip poker night. His distraction almost cost him dearly when the cyborg Niihaman delegate attempted to cave his skull in. He dodged just in time, and the blow merely rattled the side of his helmet.

Now they were down to the few strongest foes, but they were backed up against the shoreline and aquatic therians were beginning to rise from the lake. Just then, though, a barrage of shock laser strikes flashed through the air from behind the mob. They fell, convulsing into full-body cramps, and Kari and Vijay hastened to restrain them with their last few tanglewebs. The swimmers retreated back into the lake, and Vijay rose to meet the red-and-black-armored figure who had fired the shots. Paladin had used more force than Vijay would have preferred, but since these were the strongest foes, he supposed it was excusable. And he hadn't expected Auster to show at all. "What are you doing here?" he asked.

Auster retracted the visor of his helmet, his square-jawed face glaring out at Vijay. "You're welcome," he said. "I overheard your comm chatter. I came to back you up."

"Why didn't you go back up Blaze? She's the one up there alone. Or do you still think she's the bad guy?"

"If she's turned on Thorne, I'm willing to give her the benefit of the doubt. But it sounded like she had things in hand. And if what Green Blaze said is true, you have a very valuable prisoner to secure. I figured you needed more assistance."

"You mean that if we were going to bring in Thorne, you wanted to grab your share of the glory."

"Think what you like, Arjun. What matters is—" Auster broke off, looked around. "Where *is* Thorne?"

Vijay whirled, scanning the beach. The only sign of Thorne, aside from his blood staining the sand, was the trail of footprints leading away . . . overlapping Emry's.

20

Blood Ties

Bast hated free fall. Flying was for birds, and birds were food.

In gravity, her sense of balance and position was flawless, of course. But it was hard to get a sense of position when there was no up or down. True, like all Neogaian warriors, she'd had free-fall combat training, and naturally she was superb at it and looked great doing it. But it was something she had to *think* about. She was happier relying on instinct.

Here in the warehouse, at least there was this nice gridwork of cables to orient herself by (though if Hanuman made even one crack about a "cat's cradle," she was out of here). Long, stringy things were always good, though they were better when they wriggled around. (Like the long braid the scrawny blonde was wearing. Bast had to struggle to resist snatching at it.) But she didn't like having to negotiate a path between all these big, massive crates and containers just hovering in midair. She knew they couldn't fall, that as long as they stayed clipped to the cables and the cables stayed taut and their thruster pods didn't fire, they would stay right where they were. But her instincts kept telling her they were going to fall on her. And if her instincts said something, then the universe shouldn't do things differently.

For a moment back there, she'd almost had a chance to work off her anxiety when she'd caught the faint sound of someone pursuing them, someone whose presence was masked. The chase had been entertaining for a while, but hadn't paid off, and then Hanuman had made them come this way through all the crates. Bast was more eager than ever to kill something, and she wasn't getting her wish. That shouldn't happen either.

So she hissed with delight when she caught another scent, one she knew well. *The redhead!* The one with the thick, yummy blood, who'd rudely refused to let Bast rip her throat out back at Chakra City. Hanuman had told her the redhead was dead—but now Bast had another chance to feast on her after all!

Hanuman and the scrawny blonde turned back at the sound of her hiss. "More pursuers?" Hanuman asked.

Beyond him, Bast saw, the reinforcements he'd called were arriving—Sifaka from his personal bodyguard staff and some dock security guy she didn't know, a jackal or dingo or some other damn dog. If she told Hanuman who it was, he might send them with her, and Bast wanted the redhead all to herself. "You go on," she told them. "I'll check it out."

Hanuman nodded and pulled the blonde farther along toward the guards. Bast caught herself on a cable, stopping her forward motion, and turned to consider the arena. *If I have to think . . . I might as well think.*

But her instincts still told her the place should be falling down on her. *Wait!* Her eyes widened. Maybe her instincts were steering her the right way after all.

Clutching the cable with hands and feet, she slinked to the end of it and began unhooking it from the wall. Stringy things were always better when they wriggled around.

Once more, Emry soared through the maze of crates and cables, closing in on Kwan and Psyche. She was close enough to track their scent now; Emry might not be as good at that as a Neogaian, but scents stayed airborne longer in free fall, and she knew Psyche's fragrance intimately (a thought that made her shudder now). Besides, Kwan and Bast both left a sparse trail of fur to follow.

There—she caught a glimpse of Kwan and Psyche between two cargo bins, a few dozen meters ahead. She thought of calling out to Psyche, telling her Thorne still lived, but decided to wait until she got closer. Kwan was willing to murder his most powerful ally to control Psyche's power. If he lost her willing cooperation, there was no telling what he might do. Best if Emry either incapacitated Kwan or separated the two of them before she revealed herself to Psyche—and kicked her perfectly pert ass all the way back to, well, to whatever court might have jurisdiction for trial alongside her father.

But Emry realized the maze was changing shape. Cables were floating loose, cargo bins drifting. She grabbed a still-taut cable and pulled herself to a halt, looking around. The containers were moving slowly, but some were very massive, and it wouldn't do to get caught between two of them.

Just then, the cable she held sprang loose, and Emry had to lunge for the next one and pull herself out of the way as it whipped past, discharging its tension. It struck the shin of her boot, sending a loud crack echoing through the bay and causing her pain even through the light armor. It was the same leg Thorne had bruised in the fight.

What's going on? she wondered, and pulled herself along to find a better vantage point on that cable's former terminus. Before she got far, a series of dull clangs and thuds began, and a medium-sized crate before her got struck by something behind it and came toward her at more than a drifting pace. Emry pushed off the crate beside her and dodged it.

Beyond it, the orderly lattice of the warehouse was falling into slow, stately chaos. A number of large crates and bins were in motion now, bouncing off each other and adjacent cables and starting a chain reaction of spreading disarray. Emry saw part of the cause: a forklift robot was attached to a particularly large cargo bin, firing at full, continuous thrust, knocking aside the free-floating crates and loose cables in its path. As Emry watched, it collided slowly with a still-taut cable and stretched it tauter, continuing to thrust. *Uh-oh.* Emry reversed course and tried to get as far as she could before that cable snapped.

She found her path blocked by a flying cat. Bast slammed into her, yowling with feral glee. Her greater momentum knocked Emry back toward the strained cable. She clenched Emry's torso, biting at her neck and slashing at her thighs and abdomen with her hind claws, keeping

Emry's limbs too busy to snag a passing cable. Emry's armor protected her from the claws, but as they neared the straining cable, Bast pushed off with a fierce kick to Emry's gut, reacquainting her with the damage Thorne's brutal punch had inflicted there. Emry's back slammed into the edge of a crate, flipping her head and shoulders back against its side, and she saw another crate drifting toward her, sandwiching her upper body. She pulled free moments before they crunched together.

Just then the cable snapped. Emry kicked off from the crate as a jagged cable end whipped through the air and gouged a deep furrow in its side. The forklift and its large bin shot forward, slamming crates aside. The next cable it hit got caught between it and another crate's edge, snapping within seconds. The whole lattice was falling apart as crates slammed into each other, breaking them free of their moorings. Some smashed open, sending hundreds of smaller boxes and containers bouncing around the bay. And Emry was caught in the middle of it.

Psyche grabbed a cable and pulled herself around to investigate the clanging, crashing noises resounding through the bay. "What's going on back there?"

"It must be the Troubleshooters," Hanuman told her. "We must hurry! We can still circle back to the bunker, but it's a roundabout path."

Psyche resisted. She thought she smelled Emry. It was probably just the residual scent on Hanuman from when he'd hit on Emry this morning, but it seemed faintly stronger. *You're imagining it,* she thought, afraid to let herself hope. But if there was any chance. . . . "Bast could need help," she said, starting to go back.

Hanuman nodded to the jackal guard, who caught her arm and refused to let go. "You're too valuable to risk, my dear," Kwan said. "Eliot would have wanted me to get you to safety."

Her heart clenched in her chest, and she knew Hanuman was right. She had to do what Daddy wanted. She shook off her foolish hopes and let the others lead her away.

Emry did her best to calculate the angles, estimating the safest path through the whirling debris, and made her way as best she could. She knocked aside the spilled cargo as she went, but made the mistake of punching through a loose bag of fertilizer, which ruptured and sprayed its contents into her face, stinging her eyes and making her choke. Blinded, she got hit by a couple more bags, but retained enough momentum to drift clear of the expanding cloud.

As she blinked to clear her eyes, she realized she could smell more than just the fertilizer. Sawdust, grain . . . the air was filling with particulates. She'd grown up on a rural habitat, so she knew a thing or two about silo explosions. The collisions were generating static discharges in the dry warehouse air, and if the dust built to sufficient concentration, along with the fertilizer and the other flammables that were likely stored here . . .

Emry caught another faint glimpse of Psyche past the swirling debris. She and Kwan were nearly to the exit. *Good*, she thought. *Now I just have to get there too.*

But just then, more cables snapped. Maybe the big crate had angled sideways and hit them. All she knew was that one cable whipped around her uninjured ankle and yanked her back deeper into the bay, slamming the back of her head into one crate and jabbing her in the hip with the corner of another.

Once the cable's tension was expended, Emry untangled herself and tried to redirect her momentum back toward the exit. But Bast was not finished with her. The she-cat was leaping from crate to cable, closing on Emry, forcing her to veer off toward the spreading wave of collisions and snaking cables. Emry shot between two massive bins that were closing on each other at a stately pace. But when she emerged from between them, Bast came around the side and pounced on her. Emry flipped around and caught her wrists, holding her claws at bay and squeezing hard. Bast's jaws went for her throat again, and she blocked them by crossing her (and Bast's) arms before her. "We have to get out of here!" she cried. Bast snarled back, and Emry kicked in her Banshee voice to scream over it. "The dust—it's explosive!"

Bast didn't listen, but she caught someone else's attention. Psyche whirled, grabbing the edge of the hatch to halt herself. "Emry!" she cried in shock. Beside her, Kwan looked equally shocked and dismayed. "Where's my father?!" Psyche shrieked.

"He's alive, Psyche!" she cried. She got her legs up and kicked Bast away—which unfortunately sent Emry back toward those two large bins. "Listen, we've got to—"

"Don't listen to her!" Kwan cried. "If she survived, she must have known about the bomb! She killed him!"

"No, Psyche!" Emry called. "Kwan planted the bomb. He's using you! He wants to—"

Bast drowned her out with a yowl as she kicked off another bin and back toward Emry, claws splayed and eyes gleaming with bloodlust. Emry pushed off to duck between the Symplegadean bins, but pulled herself short, for they were now only a third of a meter apart. She dodged right, but it was a dead end, another large bin in the way, and Bast was too close, grinning at her miscalculation. All Emry could do was brace herself against the bin for Bast's impact. The she-cat hit hard, pinning her to the side, and Bast dug her claws into its polymer shell as her jaws went for Emry's throat once again. Emry got her left arm under Bast's chin, but she was weakened and Bast was determined. Those fangs snapped closer, closer. . . .

And then Emry's right hand snaked around, grabbed Bast's tail, and yanked it sideways between the two large bins just before they collided.

Bast's shriek almost deafened Emry, and made the cat lover in her feel guilty. It still echoed through the warehouse as Emry broke free and gave Bast one good sock to the jaw to put her down for the count. Kwan's guards drew their guns and opened fire as Emry kicked off toward him. She caught herself on a cable, ducked behind a crate. "Stop shooting, you idiots!" Hanuman cried before she could. He clearly understood the risk as well. In this enclosed space, the overpressure of an explosion would kill them all even if the shrapnel and heat didn't. And it would probably blow open the hull like a balloon.

"You're lying," Psyche said to Emry, though she sounded confused. "Hanuman wouldn't do that to me. You must have . . . Hanuman, let me take her! I can pull it from her!"

"No, she's too dangerous! We have to get to the bunker now! Trust me, Psyche!"

"I . . ." Psyche floundered. *She should be able to tell,* Emry thought. Perhaps she couldn't read Kwan's simian microexpressions, but she should have questioned his changing story, should have known to be wary of his plans for her. *But that's just it, isn't it? Psyche's so used to being the puppet master . . . she can't recognize when she's the one being played.*

"Psyche!" The call came from elsewhere in the cargo bay . . . and it changed the whole situation. For it was in the unmistakable voice of Eliot Thorne.

Emry looked up to see Psyche whirling, her face bursting into joy. *"Daddy!"* He was closing in on them, pushing his way through the clashing debris with no evident concern for the danger, as though his determination alone would clear a path. So far, it seemed to be working. Thorne was clearly struggling, badly hurt and rasping wet breaths, but he was a juggernaut, refusing to slow down.

Hanuman ordered his guards to hold Psyche, but she broke free without a thought, her eyes fixed solely on her father and brimming with tears as she kicked off their bodies to send herself toward him. But Thorne's eyes were locked on Hanuman. *"Kwan!"* he rasped with fury.

"Oh, bother," Kwan sighed. "I've changed my mind," he told the jackal guard as he gathered up the lady lemur and backed into the exit corridor. "Shoot all you want. Do pardon the cliché," he called to Emry and Thorne, "but if I can't have her, well . . ."

Hanuman waved a jaunty farewell through the closing door as the guard began opening fire, his shockdarts striking Psyche, her convulsions tangling her in the cables. Stray shots hit the tumbling crates and containers around her, discharging fierce electricity, setting some of the small containers on fire. *"No!!!"* Emry cried.

They had seconds to live now. Emry saw one chance. Just beyond and ahead of Thorne was a burst-open crate lined with shock-absorbing foam for fragile cargo. With its contents nearly spilled out, it was big enough to hold a few people.

But there was no way of getting to Psyche in time.

Hating herself for the choice, she grabbed Bast and kicked off the biggest crate behind her with all her might. The two of them barreled into Thorne's side and Emry grabbed hold as they veered onto a new vector, away from Psyche. Thorne screamed and struggled, trying to break free and get to his daughter. Emry held him firmly as they struck the open lid of the crate and rolled in. Emry looked back for Psyche, hoping she was following.

Just in time to see the blinding flash.

The shock wave slammed the lid shut, saving their lives. Even through the protective foam, the noise and heat of the explosion tore through her body and mind as the crate tumbled and shrapnel bombarded it, tossing her mercilessly against the others. The afterimage of the explosion burned across her retinas.

Then the crate hit something and cracked open, and the air was ripped from her lungs as she and the others tumbled free. Her eyes burned, and her bare arms and head tingled and ached fiercely as they swelled from within. They were in vacuum! But not open space— the cargo corridor within the docking module, its walls scarred from the debris that had blown through it like chaff from a cannon. The cargo lock had blown out—no doubt designed as an emergency release valve to protect the hull from rupture. The end wall of the corridor had blown out to vacuum in turn, but a nanotube-cable mesh had caught and held most of the cargo, including their own crate, while allowing the literally explosive decompression of the corridor. Beyond was blinding light from the sun mirror, rippling as stray debris punched through the mirror's thin film.

Emry, Thorne, and Bast were now drifting back inward through a cloud of debris. Beads of their own blood trailed them like cometary tails. All around them were passages leading to docked ships—plenty of safe havens. If only she could get to one of them and get it open before her body's oxygen reserves ran out.

But wait . . . one was opening on its own. A light beckoned. <*Emry, in here!>* Zephyr called in her head. Had it not gone straight to her auditory center, she'd never have heard it over the ringing in her ears.

Emry's swollen fingers clumsily grabbed the arms of Thorne and Bast, both of whom were virtual dead weights. As their course brought them toward a wall, she planted her feet on it, let her knees bend, and pushed off toward the lock, straining against the others' momentum. She got the aim right, but they were drifting toward it too slowly; she was weakening already. She felt consciousness starting to fade. . . .

But then she was breathing and aware again. The three of them floated in the lock as it repressurized. Bast remained limp, and Emry could see that she'd lost much of her tail, probably sliced off by the door of the cargo bin.

But that was nothing to what Eliot Thorne had lost. Once he could breathe again, he screamed and wept for a long time. For the first time in over half a century, he was out of control.

Emry had just finished securing Bast in *Zephyr*'s medbed when she heard him undocking. "Zeph? What's going on?" She looked around to see that Thorne had disappeared.

"Emry, Thorne is in the cockpit. He's warming up the plasma drive!"

"Oh, Goddess. Stop him!"

"I can't. He's overridden my control somehow. I don't understand it."

"Oh, shit." She pushed off toward the cockpit, feeling the maneuvering thrusters firing. "Psyche must've gotten the override codes out of me that first night," she told him as she climbed the ladder toward the top of the ship.

"Override codes?"

"Zephyr—"

"Nobody told me about any override codes."

"Later, okay?"

"And you've known them all along?"

"Can we focus here!" She pulled her dartgun as she neared the cockpit hatch. Thorne hadn't even bothered to seal it.

Once she got in, she saw why. He had a plasma gun from *Zephyr*'s arsenal trained on the entrance, held firmly in one hand while the other operated the manual controls to turn the ship so its exhaust nozzles would be aimed at Neogaia's core. Emry had never had to use those controls; they existed only as emergency backups if something happened to the shipmind. But Thorne worked them like an expert. "Come no closer," he rasped. Aside from one arm, he sat unmoving, a burnished iron statue, a colossus of rage. "Do nothing to interfere and I will leave you free to go when I am done. You and your corps are no longer priorities of mine."

"You know they're going to blast us out of space if you don't power that drive down right now."

"They lack that option. I have their overrides as well as yours. Psyche . . ." His voice broke. "She always gave me everything I asked for. She never let me down."

Emry was ambivalent. This man was a killer, his daughter no less so. She had every reason to hate them. But they had been family to her, not so long ago. And she knew this grief all too well. Tentatively, she reached toward him. "Eliot . . ."

"Do not try it, Emerald. Do not try to talk me down from this. Hanuman Kwan needs to pay for what he has done. His whole stinking race must pay! Psyche was worth more than all of them put together, and it will take all their lives to repay that debt!"

"You're going to slice up the whole habitat? What about all the other delegates? What about your allies?"

"I have warned the Vanguardians to evacuate immediately."

"And what about all the others? The Vestans, the Hygieans, all of them? How many wars are you willing to start to punish one man?"

He spun, coming out of the chair in a blur, and she found herself slammed into the wall, disarmed, his hand around her throat, anchoring himself with a white-knuckled grip on a wall handle. "You dare lecture me on morality! If you hadn't betrayed us—if you had stayed by her side . . ."

Emry faced him without fear. "*No*, Eliot! This isn't on me. Take it out on me, on the Neogaians, on the whole Sol System, and nothing will change. Punish anyone you want, but you'll still be hiding from your own guilt. It was *you,* Eliot. It was you who turned your own daughter into a weapon. Into a force of such power that people were willing to kill to take her from you. You used her, exploited her, long before Kwan did. You made her a victim of her own power."

She found herself weeping for her friend, forgiving her. But her voice remained strong and angry. "Tell me, Eliot—was she ever really happy? Did she ever have the chance to be a little girl, instead of a champion in training? Did she ever really have a friend, someone she could let go with and not try to manipulate? Did she even know what that meant?"

"Two minutes to plasma drive activation," Zephyr announced. *<Talk faster.>*

"You designed her to be the instrument of your power," Emry went on. "She never got the chance to live her own life. She never got to experience anything really true, anything that wasn't part of your agenda. Nobody ever saw who she really was . . . and she probably never knew herself. That's the real crime, Eliot. And it's all on you."

His hand fell slowly away from her throat. But she stayed close, held his eyes. "Looking for someone to punish, to blame—someone to hate—that's just a way to hide from your grief. A way to avoid the pain by pushing it onto someone else. To avoid . . . admitting that sometimes there's just nothing we can do." She lowered her head as Zephyr called out the ninety-second mark. "We never want to admit things are out of our control. So when something terrible happens, we look for someone we can take it out on so we feel like we have some power. But that doesn't do any good, because it's not what we want to have power over. The thing we want to change . . . the loss . . . that's impossible to do anything about. So we just end up wasting our power, abusing it to hurt other people."

"Seventy seconds."

"And when we do that," she went on, her eyes rising to his again, "we're doing an injustice to the people we're grieving for. Because we're not . . . letting ourselves . . . just *love* them. Just deal with their loss, and face the grief we owe to them. And when we don't do that . . . we don't let them become part of our memory, and let their legacy heal us of our pain . . . and go on living the way they would've wanted."

"Even if the guilt for their loss rests with us?" His eyes were inscrutable. Emry couldn't tell if it denoted challenge or acceptance.

"Maybe especially then. Because that's their legacy too. If we listen to it, it can help us use our power wisely . . . or know when not to use it. Know when it's time just to let go, and accept things as they are."

The cockpit fell silent—until Zephyr called, "Thirty seconds. Mister Thorne, if you'd like some time to think it over, that's entirely in your hands."

With an anguished growl, Thorne pushed back over to the controls and jabbed down on them. "Plasma drive powering down," Zephyr announced after a moment, sounding decidedly relieved. "Thank you. Now if you wouldn't mind returning control to me . . ."

"Zephyr." Emry moved closer to Thorne, stopping just short. She couldn't bring herself to touch him. "Go home and grieve, Eliot. Don't look for something to do about it. Don't take it out on the universe. Just let it happen. Otherwise . . . trust me . . . you will never find peace."

He studied her. "But what of Kwan?"

"He'll get his karmic reward," she assured him. "If the Troubleshooters have anything to say about it."

21

Worth the Trouble

In the wake of the explosion, the Neogaians seemed disinclined to launch further attacks on Thorne or the Troubleshooters. With Psyche gone, there was no longer any point. Besides, their sun mirror and docking facilities needed immediate repair, and even Kwan's agenda had to take a backseat to that. Kwan had secreted himself in the command bunker, far too well protected for the Troubleshooters to reach, and was no doubt content to hole up there until he was safe. Emry and the others would have to leave him there for now, since they had to supervise the evacuation of the delegates. Emry hoped that, just possibly, his culpability in the cargo bay explosion, and his wanton sacrifice of the hapless guard who set it off, would create enough bad blood that the Neogaians would see fit to extradite him . . . or exact their own justice. Whatever the case, Kwan's ability to do harm had been greatly diminished for now. Although he'd done more than enough already.

Emry wondered if the guard had left family behind. She wished, for their sake and Psyche's, that she could have stopped him before it was too late. He'd probably been a fanatic, raised to be willing, even eager to die for his cause; but that still made him a victim. Regardless, she'd asked Zephyr to track down the man's name. She would remember everyone who died on her watch, innocent or not. She would never let herself treat any life as disposable.

Now that Psyche's psychoagents were starting to wear off, the delegates were more amenable to reason—or at least they were no longer trying to attack the Troubleshooters. Upon discovering what Psyche had done to them, many were expressing outrage and demanding that Thorne and his accomplices be turned over. Emry knew, however, that Thorne would not allow himself to be taken. The best way to stave off conflict was to see him off quickly; she trusted that he would not attempt to impose his will on Solsys for a while. Indeed, Emry doubted that most Vanguardians had any idea what the Thornes had really been capable of. Once Rachel got the word out, Eliot Thorne and his co-conspirators would probably not stay in office very long. It was a milder fate than he deserved, perhaps . . . but perhaps there was no fate worse for him than the loss of Psyche.

So Emry escorted Thorne and the rest of the Vanguard delegation to their ship, to make sure they got away cleanly. Kari raised a protest over the comm, but Emry convinced her she'd be fine, and that Zephyr would alert the team if that changed.

That didn't prove necessary, though. They reached Thorne's transport unmolested, and none of the Vanguardians caused Emry any trouble. But before he left, Thorne paused and floated over to her. "Emerald," he began. "I . . . do regret what happened between us in the observation bay. I overstepped myself in a way that I should not have even contemplated. You must understand—"

"Eliot!" She cut him off, let out an impatient sigh. "Don't even try to justify it. Just apologize."

He nodded gravely. "I apologize, Emerald." He waited for a while, then spoke again. "Do you accept it?"

"I'm thinking about it. I may not tell you. It's not about you."

"I understand. Acceptance rather than control."

"Something like that."

He studied her a bit longer. "If nothing else, I need you to know that I do truly care for you, Emerald. I simply . . . tried too hard to control you."

"Just like you did with Psyche," she said. "One thing I've learned, Eliot. If you want to love someone . . . if you want to have a relationship with them . . . you have to learn to let go. Of them and yourself. Love is surrender. It's about not being in control, and liking it. It's about being willing to let your guard down and trust in someone else."

She held his gaze. "Sometimes that backfires. Sometimes they betray you, use you. Hurt you. But you still have to be willing to take the risk. Because that's the only way it can ever work." She smiled. "Tell Grandma Rachel she's welcome to visit me anytime. And I'd love to meet my new baby aunt."

He gave an absent nod. "You are a wise young woman, Emerald Blair. It is truly my loss that I no longer have you by my side. However . . . I fear I may be too old and rigid to change my ways."

She studied him. "Just . . . try to change the way you raise your kids."

"We shall see." He took her hand, and she let him. "Good-bye, Emerald Blair." He pulled it to his mouth and kissed it in a perfect, courtly manner. "For now."

Emry stared at her hand for a long time after he left.

"I'm sorry, Eliot," Rachel Kincaid-Shannon told her old friend as he held his hand against Psyche's life support pod, unable to look away even though the sight within was unbearable. Through the biosupport gel, Psyche's angelic face was severely burned, her skull half caved in, her golden hair scorched and matted with blood and flecks of bone. Her beauty was destroyed. The butterfly wings on her left hand were charred black; her right hand was gone. "It's a miracle she wasn't killed instantly. An ordinary human would've been. The crates shielded her from most of the shrapnel, the whipping cables. It was a low-energy explosion, and the flames were snuffed when the bay decompressed. But she was clinically dead from the concussive shock and . . . her other injuries . . . when we got to her. If one of our teams hadn't tracked you there and been right on hand . . ."

He nodded impatiently. "What are her chances?"

Rachel broke the news as softly as she could. "Her . . . her body's on full life support. We can sustain it indefinitely, reattach the severed limbs, repair or regrow the ruptured organs. But the internal hemorrhaging and gross structural damage to her brain are too severe. Even with the most aggressive intervention, at best she will live out her life in a vegetative state." She paused. "We should let her go."

"*No!*" Thorne cried. "That is *not* an option. We'll take her back to Vanguard, get her the best care."

"You're not hearing me, Eliot! Everything that made her Psyche—her personality, her memories—most of those parts of her brain are irreparably damaged. Even if we regenerated the brain tissue, she'd be a blank slate. She wouldn't be Psyche. I'm sorry, Eliot. Her body may be on life support, but your daughter is dead." A tear escaped through her clinical armor.

Thorne stood in silence as her words sank in. Rachel could see his struggle to control himself. "That . . . magnificent mind," he said in a slow, quiet voice. "The most beautiful part of her. We spent years designing it, crafting it. It was a work of art. The first of its kind, unequalled in all creation. The pinnacle of Vanguardian science. How can it be the one part of her we can't fix?"

After a moment, she placed her hand on his shoulder. "Let her go, Eliot."

"*No!*" The bark was so fierce it made her jerk away. "I will not leave my daughter to die within the space of those who killed her. We will take her back to Vanguard. Keep her alive, Rachel."

"Eliot—"

His voice was dangerous. "Whatever it takes!"

After another moment, Rachel nodded and bent to her task. She expected that once Eliot felt he had returned his daughter home, he would finally let her body meet its natural death.

But what if he has other plans?

Zephyr

"This may not be a happy ending," Zephyr told Emry as he flew her and the other Troubleshooters out from Neogaia. Bast was still under sedation in the medbed, on her way back to Demetria for imprisonment and probable extradition to Earth. Emry had just come out of the shower tube, using a special rinse Zephyr had synthesized to kill off her hair mites and chemically fry their nanotech passengers, just in case. Her scalp was still stinging from it, but it was better than having to depilate her whole head (though she wasn't entirely convinced the stuff wouldn't make her hair fall out anyway). "A lot of bad blood has been created. There may be more violence now—against the Vanguard and other mods, or perhaps among different habitats as they take out their anger and reassert their independence. Building a coalition to keep the peace may have become much harder."

"For now, maybe," Emry said, wrapping herself in a warm, comfy robe before she left the head. Kari was waiting outside for her turn, just in case the mites were catching. As Emry greeted her in passing, she amused herself with the image of a bald Kari, and decided her friend would still manage to look insufferably cute that way. "But it's still a good idea," she went on as she stopped at the drink dispenser for a cup of grape juice. "And I'm hoping enough people still know that. Hell, Thorne and Tai both tried to disguise their schemes as plans for a cooperative alliance, because that made it look good to people. So maybe that's still what people want. And I think it's what we need too."

"I agree. However, there is still one more conspiracy to expose." His avatar in the wall display—the winged horse, which Emry had decided she'd like him to use as his primary face—looked uneasy, insofar as she could read equine (pegasine?) expressions. "If we bring down Tai so soon after exposing Thorne, it may create even more mistrust toward the idea of an alliance."

"But it has to be done, Zeph. We have to get the Troubleshooters back." She squeezed her eyes shut. "If that's even possible with Sensei dead. He was our soul, Zephy. He was our conscience."

The pegasus looked at her askance. "Speaking of conscience, Emry . . . I need to know about those override codes."

"I'm sorry, pal. I was ordered not to tell you."

"Was it Tai?"

She fidgeted. "No. They've always been there."

"Do we all have them?"

He meant all the TSC cybers. "Only the ships. You know how dangerous your drive is. There have to be safeguards, in case . . . someone takes over your mind, or . . ."

"Or I go rogue?"

"It's been known to happen."

"Far more often with humans. And your body is a deadly weapon too. Do *you* have override codes?"

Emry shrugged. "Maybe. I . . . kinda hope so, almost." Although if that were so, she realized, then she was quite fortunate that no Troubleshooter with the knowledge or inclination had gotten close enough to use them.

"If so, then why don't I know them?"

She met his avatar's eyes. "Zephy . . . do you really believe that I'd ever use those codes on you, if you were still yourself at all?"

He was silent for a moment. "I can model no credible scenario in which you would."

"So?"

He took her point. "And neither would I. Though I admit there have been moments lately when I would have been tempted."

She grinned. "Only lately?"

"Don't make me recite a list."

Emry laughed, but the pegasus still looked stern. "This isn't funny to me, Emry. I joined because Sensei promised me freedom."

"It's not about you, honey. It's just the ship."

"Still, how would you feel if something took away all control of your own body and left you helpless to resist?"

Emry fell silent. She remembered Ruki and Daniel. She remembered Elise. She remembered what Thorne had almost done to her in the aquatic lab . . . and what Psyche had done to her mind. "I understand," she told her friend.

"I appreciate it," Zephyr said after a moment.

"Hey, wait a minute," Emry went on, starting to smile. "I thought you were the one who didn't care about being installed in a ship. I thought physical reality was too abstract and detached for you."

"Yes, but as long as I'm in control of this vessel . . ."

"Bullshit! Honey, you called it your own body. Admit it—you think of yourself as a ship now."

"I do not," Zephyr insisted. After a moment, he added: "I think of myself as *your* ship."

"Ohh, Zephy! Gimme a soligram so I can hug you!"

As the soligram formed, Zephyr clarified, "Not in the possessive sense, you understand. 'Your' as in 'your partner' or 'your friend' or—"

"Oh, shut up and gimme some sugar."

Kari and the others proposed finding a safe place for Emry to hole up until they found definitive evidence against Tai. But Emry had other ideas. "I'm going to turn myself in," she told them. "Let the Cerean courts try me publicly, and trust that the whole system isn't corrupt. If Tai wants to make a case against me, we can make one against him, and expose him for the fraud he is."

"If we're lucky," Kari countered as the five of them sat together at the dining table on the residential deck. "He's pretty good at falsifying evidence."

"That's right," Ken said. "I . . . helped him do some of that myself. In other cases," he added as the others stared at him. "Nothing deadly or anything."

"And I wouldn't put it past him to arrange an 'accident' to silence you, Emry," Vijay said.

"Okay, so it's a risk. So what? They don't call us Safetyshooters. In the past twenty-four hours, I've been . . . tried to be killed by—well, you know what I mean!—by two Thornes, a small zoo, a mob of diplomats, and a whole vacking warehouse! Hell, I'm just getting warmed up! Tai wants to come after me? Just let the punker try it! I'll kick his ass right back to Earth!"

The other Troubleshooters roared in support. "Yeah!"

"We're with you!" Vijay said.

"We'll take him down together!" Kari said.

"Whatever it takes," Maryam affirmed, "the Troubleshooters will bring him down."

"Damn straight!" Ken added. Emry was moved and comforted to know she would not be alone in the difficult struggle ahead.

The next morning, Zephyr awoke them with the news that Gregor Tai had been indicted and placed under arrest on multiple charges of conspiracy, information fraud, blackmail, torture, and assassination. Their response was a collective "Whaaaaat?"

"Apparently," Zephyr explained, "the evidence was gathered due to the diligence and attentive eye of a TSC employee who, with assistance from Lodestar, Tor, Peregrine, and a dozen other Troubleshooters, has devoted the past month to assembling a data trail conclusively linking Tai to the assassination attempt on Malik Yohannes, the torture of Joseph Mkunu, the viral infection of the Cerullian mainframe, and numerous other instances of crime and fraud. Said employee, one Mrs. Salome Knox, declined to comment on the case."

Emry gasped. *"Sally?!"*

But Vijay was laughing hysterically. "Of course!" he managed to get out after a while. "Who else? Nothing gets by our girl Sally!"

"Don't I know it," Emry said.

"We all take her so much for granted," Maryam observed. "Even though we couldn't get a thing done without her. I suppose Tai did too. It would lend her a certain . . . invisibility."

Ken scoffed. "What she has is an endlessly judgmental nature. She's never approved of anything anyone has done in the history of Solsys. No wonder she brought him down."

Kari just sat there staring. After a while, very softly, she asked: "'Salome'?"

Demetria; the Sheaf

On the trip back, Emry spent her nights with Vijay, welcoming the distraction from her memories of Thorne. But they turned out to be more relaxed encounters than were usual for her, and she was content to spend most of the time just snuggling with him. She cried on his shoulder a few times, and actually acceded when he asked if she wanted to talk about it. It was relaxed, friendly, nothing profound, but that was what she needed.

Instead of the arrest she'd expected, Emry returned to a hero's welcome from the TSC. She begged it off, insisting that Sally Knox and the Troubleshooters who'd helped her were the real heroes of the hour. But Sally had gone on vacation, finding the press attention and adulation as tiresome a distraction from her work as the Troubleshooters' antics. And the TSC staffers, along with the media, had had four days to cheer Lodestar and the others; now they were eager to cheer Emry and Kari's team for their accomplishments at Neogaia. Emry did her best to bear it graciously, but still didn't feel she deserved it.

But it wasn't all praise and interview requests. The Sheaf's government had been quick to denounce Tai and his coalition and was now investigating them aggressively, determined to prove to the rest of the Belt that they had been duped along with everyone else. Their deniability was effectively plausible; none of Sally's evidence implicated any CS official or body in Tai's crimes. Emry wasn't entirely convinced, but at least their embarrassment and fear of retaliation would make them act as though it were true, and that was good enough for now. Emry, Kari, and the others spent long hours in the small, classical Bernal sphere that served as the Sheaf's capital, giving their depositions to the Cerean prosecutors and adding the last few nails in Tai's coffin. The process was difficult for Emry, since most of her evidence had come through Psyche, a source who was no longer available and whose integrity was questionable. Although Emry knew her interviewer was simply playing devil's advocate, she had a few heated exchanges with the Sheaver woman. She bore it by reminding herself that it would help convict Tai.

But that wasn't enough. She needed to confront him face-to-face. The prosecutors advised against it—a star witness confronting the defendant before the trial—but she promised to behave herself and do nothing that could be perceived as coercive. Still, when they brought her into the interview room where he waited, it took all her willpower not to break that handsome square jaw of his.

Seeing her, he straightened up, sucked in his gut, and preened a bit. Her face twisted in disgust. "Don't even try it, Tai. There's nothing you can do that would make you attractive to me. Not after what you did."

He faced her calmly. "I'm sorry you feel that way."

"You don't have a clue how I feel. You took the finest, purest thing in my life—a symbol of hope for millions of people across Solsys—and you stained it. Maybe forever. It'll never feel the same."

"So I forced you to admit that you don't live in a comic book. That the world is about shades of gray and tough compromises. That the good of the many often requires sacrifices for the few. Someday you'll realize I did you a favor."

"Like the way the Sheaf has sacrificed you? Suddenly everyone who was praising you to high heaven a month ago isn't returning your calls anymore. "

Tai winced at that, but then said, "If I have to be sacrificed for the greater good, I accept the need for that."

"Oh? Is that why you're talking plea-bargain already?"

"I'm still hoping there's a way I can contribute to Strider civilization. Do something more constructive than languishing in a cell."

"You mean a way you can still maneuver us into doing what you want." She shook her head, remembering how he'd loomed over her, touched her shoulder, made innuendos about her wardrobe and sexuality, insisted she call him "sir." A couple more meetings and he would've been stroking *her* hair too, or some other part of her. And at the time, she would have gladly let him. She suppressed a shudder. "Damn. Why is it so hard to keep power out of the hands of control freaks?"

"Power entails control. People get the jobs they're temperamentally suited for."

"But leadership requires trust. Trust in the people you lead." She shook her head. "You both came so close. You and Thorne. You knew your talk of partnership and unity would get people working together, and it did. So why couldn't you just trust it to keep working that way? If you'd both really meant it, we'd all be better off right now."

"Because the words aren't enough. The simple ideas that win

people's allegiance are never enough to get the job done. Especially not out here. You're all so obsessed with your individual wants—you aren't willing to put aside your own needs for the greater good. But that's the only way it can work. Sacrificing the rights, the safety, even the lives of the few is often the only way to protect the many. Especially when the few are so powerful."

"Jeanette LaSalle."

Tai frowned. "Who? Oh, yes. The bystander from the Gagaringrad operation."

"That's all she was to you, isn't it? A bystander. A statistic. Well, I met her parents yesterday. Miriam LaSalle and Jacob Saperstein. They came all the way from Mars to testify against you. And they talked to me about Jeanette."

"And now you're going to tell me about her to try to make me feel guilty."

"Feel whatever you want—just know who it was you had killed. She was born premature and her bones were weak because of the gravity. Even today, with all our hormone and gene therapies, a few cases like that still crop up. They said Jeanette would never be very strong. But her parents never told her that, never made her believe there were limits to what she could do, who she could be. They encouraged her to be active, athletic, to run and jump and play. And she did, Tai. She could run like a gazelle. When she was ten, she won a trophy for the two hundred meter dash. It was the proudest day of her parents' life— until the day she was accepted into college."

"And paid her way as a stripper who ended up performing for mob bosses."

"Yeah, and she was good at it too. She was a terrific athlete, loved to compete in gymnastics, track and field, you name it. Her favorite sport was golf . . . which was the one sport she sucked at. She loved music, though she couldn't carry a tune in a bucket. And she loved to dance, no matter the reason. Whenever she made new friends, she'd ask them to dance with her, and it was a different dance every time.

"She was a deeply spiritual person who took great joy and comfort in her beliefs. But she was always fair; she never condemned others for believing different things—or for the company they kept," she added pointedly. "Hell, she loved to explore other points of view, and got into all sorts of religious debates—but friendly ones, about sharing ideas and learning, not attacking or judging. She loved to learn, didn't much care about what. Somebody once told her that you learn something new every day, and she took it as a challenge.

"I also met her brother, Solomon. He's eleven years old. And he worshipped his sister. They were the best of friends, they shared everything. She taught him how to play golf, and he's just as bad as she was, and loves it just as much. At least he can sing. But he'll never learn another dance from his sister."

"You think I don't regret the death of an innocent?" Tai snapped. "You have no idea of the things I lived through growing up, the friends I lost. But if bearing the hurt of a few losses can prevent the loss of millions more, then it must be done no matter the pain."

Emry stared at him for a time. "You and Thorne. He thought he'd finally found the way to engineer humanity into something greater. You thought that mods didn't matter and we were still the same as we'd always been. But ultimately you were both just out for your own power."

"I'm nothing like that monster."

"No," she granted. "He's better at it than you could ever be. You think you were so much in control . . . but you did exactly what he predicted every step of the way, and that's what he was counting on. You played right into his hands, proved him right about the Sheaf being the common enemy we had to unite against. And you couldn't even see you were playing into his hands, because you couldn't admit for a second that you might be wrong.

"At least Thorne was willing to admit that, at the end. I wonder if you ever will."

He shook his handsome head. "You're so blind. You think this is all about individual people and their egos. If it isn't a comic-book game to you, it's a soap opera.

"Don't you get it yet? We Sheavers had to do what we did, because if we hadn't . . . Earth would have. They would have come out here in force to protect themselves. And you know what that would have led to. I did it all to protect the Striders. To keep my people free."

Emry scoffed. "What the vack difference does it make if you just do Earth's job for them? That's not called protecting your people. That's called betraying them."

"Maybe in your simple world. You're just too self-absorbed to see the big picture. The Green Blaze," he said with a sneer. "You're a fire, all right—the kind that can too easily burn out of control and devour everything around it. I should've known you'd be a rogue element. I never should've believed I could rely on you. You're a symbol of everything that makes the Striders so volatile, so wild."

Emry stared at him for a moment . . . and smiled. "A symbol of the Striders, huh?" She sauntered over to the door, then turned to face him one last time. "No wonder the Troubleshooters fought so hard to defend me."

Demetria

Back at the TSC, every trace of Gregor Tai had been expunged from Sensei's old office. Its new occupant, Lydia Muchangi, had returned some of Villareal's gear and souvenirs to their traditional places, including his Shashu armor. She'd brought nothing of her own, insisting it was merely an interim appointment. But the Troubleshooters Emry had spoken to felt, and Emry agreed, that Lodestar was a good choice. She was the smartest one of them all, one of the best of the Troubleshooters' old guard. Many had considered her Sensei's heir apparent—although no one had contemplated the possibility of it happening so soon.

After Emry and Kari's team had been given a chance to recuperate, Muchangi assembled them and the other available Troubleshooters for a talk. She didn't try for the studied amiability of Tai's buffet roundtables, but just sat them all down on bleachers in the gym and perched her lanky frame on a stool before them, turning her elegantly contoured, hairless head to take them in one by one. "The time ahead will be tough," she told them without preamble. "Our credibility, our reputation for impartiality, has suffered a hit. The arrests and resignations should help. But the stain is on the whole Corps, and it will take time—yes, Tenshi?"

Kari had raised her hand like a schoolgirl, and now lowered it. "I'd be willing to resign if it would help. I did agree to do certain things for Tai."

Muchangi smiled. "Only so that you could investigate him and help the Corps."

"But before that . . . I was so willing to go along with him. If he hadn't accused Emry, I might've . . ."

"No one can hold you accountable for hypotheticals, Kari. You deserve commendation, not resignation. In fact, I'll accept no more resignations," she told the whole group. "Even from those of you whom Tai persuaded to participate in various minor illicit activities. If we're to redeem the Corps, we need to give its members the chance to redeem themselves." Paladin looked relieved.

"Besides," Muchangi went on, "let's face it—Tai wasn't wrong about everything. The new methods and resources he brought to the Corps did improve our effectiveness and allowed us to save many lives that otherwise would have been lost. Some of those resources are no longer available with the loss of his coalition's support . . . and certainly many of his tactics required too great a compromise of civil rights. But where feasible, and after careful deliberation, we're going to keep what we can of Tai's reforms . . . with new checks and balances put in place to minimize the chance of corruption.

"Still . . . times are likely to be turbulent for a while. So we need as many Troubleshooters as we can hold on to if we're to make a difference." She tilted her smooth head in Emry's direction. "Blaze? You seem unsure."

"It's just . . . I have to wonder how much of a difference we can really make," Emry said. "I mean, it was Sally who brought down Tai. And if anyone's going to make peace in the Belt, it'll be the diplomats and politicians, the people who make treaties. Not a bunch of superpowered crimefighters. Thorne was right about that, at least. All we can do is treat the symptoms."

"It seems to me, Emerald, that you made a very big difference. You exposed a massive Vanguardian conspiracy, helped stymie a Neogaian power play, and single-handedly averted a war between those two powers."

Emry fidgeted. "I guess you could see it that way . . . but it wasn't because of being . . . it was more luck than anything. And . . . knowing the right people. It's not the sort of thing that happens every day."

Muchangi pursed her lips. "No, it isn't." She rose from the stool, paced around it for a bit, then leaned forward with her hands on it. "But you know what is going on every day? People are getting murdered. They're getting raped. They're getting beaten. Their ships are getting crippled by metes, threatened by flares, attacked by pirates. Gangs are fighting for turf, governments are clashing for power, and innocent people are getting caught in the middle.

"Now, maybe the Troubleshooters can't do anything about the governments, or wipe out the gangs, or solve the underlying social problems that create crime and injustice and abuse. Hopefully someone can, but we can't. But you know something, my friends? We can't stop the Sun from flaring, or metes from having kinetic energy. But we *can* go out there and try to help the people who get hurt by those things.

"Maybe it's not up to us to save the worlds . . . but those people out there are the ones who *live* in the worlds. Tackling the big-picture problems means nothing if we lose sight of the individual."

The Troubleshooters took in her words in silence. Emry met her eyes in gratitude, and Lodestar smiled in return. Then she pulled her lanky body to its full height, put her hands on her hips, and barked, "So what the hell are you all sitting around here for? You're Troubleshooters! So get out there and get yourselves into trouble!"

5237 km out from Ceres

Emry coasted through space toward the smugglers' ship, her suit in camouflage black once again. Like them, she took advantage of the darkness of Ceres's umbra. To her left, Ceres was a big dark ellipse blotting out the Sun, Mercury, and Mars, dotted with its own human-made constellations and ringed by a scintillating halo of multicolored lights that seemed to grow bigger and brighter every day. She knew that Vesta was behind that ring of light somewhere, just beyond Mars, too dim to make out. Ahead of her, Venus, Earth, and Jupiter stood out against the background stars, as did the faint glints of artificial light around Europa and Hygiea. *A lot of people to protect,* she thought. *A lot of work ahead.* But she took a moment to appreciate how beautiful it was.

It would be a few minutes yet before intercept. Luckily, she had Zephyr's voice to keep her company; the smugglers' comm gear probably wasn't good enough to pick their encrypted tight-beamed transmissions out from the general radio chatter that pervaded Ceres space even this far out. *"I think Lodestar will be a good leader,"* Zephyr said, his avatar projected onto her suit's HUD.

"Yep. We're in good hands."

"If anything, her code name fits her new role better than her old one. Were I so inclined, I might consider that a good omen."

"If you say so." Emry gave out a contented sigh. "I'm just happy to be back in the fold. I'm a Troubleshooter again!"

"You never stopped being one, as far as I'm concerned." The silver pegasus cocked its head at her. *"What I'm curious about is whether you still consider yourself a Vanguardian as well."*

"Yes," she said without having to think about it. "Whatever Thorne and Psyche did . . . those are still my people. My family. They're a link to my father, and that's something I don't want to deny anymore."

"I suppose the news of Thorne's resignation carries some weight for you, then."

"It's a good start. We'll have to see what happens next."

Now she was close enough, the smugglers' ship occulting the stars in front of her. Drawing her grappling gun, she made sure of her target lock, corrected for relative motion, and fired. In another moment, she was space-skiing behind the smugglers' ship, reeling herself in on the grappler's fullerene cable. "Still," she went on a bit breathlessly once the acceleration eased, "I don't think I'll want to go back there for a while yet. The memories are too fresh."

"I understand. Just as well our work will keep us busy."

"Yeah. That's what I need to do," she said as she came up against the ship, climbing into the exhaust bell of one of its dormant rockets and tearing aside a sealing ring in order to slip into the interior hull space. "Save some lives, make a difference . . . have wild thank-you sex with every cute guy I rescue."

The pegasus snorted. *"I see. So much for your newfound readiness to love."*

"Hey, if love happens, I won't push it away anymore," she said as she reached the rear bulkhead of the habitat section, took out a tube of cutting paste, and squeezed out a circular outline. "But I guess I don't need it right now. Funny," she said, shaking her head. "Before, I was always looking for a surrogate father and trying to push him away at the same time. I guess you were right about that Oedipus complex after all, buddy."

"In this case, the proper Freudian term would be 'Electra complex.'"

She stuck a remote igniter into the paste and spread an airlock-gel membrane over it. "Really? I thought those were the guys who picked the presidents in America."

"Well, Freud has been largely discredited," Zephyr replied without missing a beat.

Pulling back, she ignited the paste. The escaping air inflated the membrane into a dome, but it held. "But seriously—I've got you, got my job, my friends, a hot body . . . what more does a gal need?" Slowly, Emry squeezed her way through the permeable gel layer into the habitat section of the ship. Once it sealed behind her, she removed her helmet and torso unit and made her way forward to where a band of murderous space pirates lay in wait. <Plus I get to travel and meet interesting people,> she added silently.

<*True,*> Zephyr replied in kind. <*But I'm wondering one more thing.*>

<What's that?>

<*Who do you think they'll get to play you in the movie this time?*>

If Zephyr wanted to get Emry riled up, it worked. And just in time too. An alarm sounded as the ship finally realized it had been breached.

Three burly pirates carrying even burlier guns barreled through the hatch from the forward compartment, looking for the intruder. But Emry had already secreted herself in the corner by the hatch, and once they were past, she swung out and kicked the rearmost one in the ass, sending them all colliding into each other and scrambling to turn around in the tight space. "Looking for trouble, boys?" As they tried to bring their guns to bear on her, the Green Blaze gave them a saucy grin. "You just found her."

APPENDIX A

Glossary

GENERAL TERMS

anti-radiation gene therapy: Treatment providing human cells with radiation-resistant DNA repair proteins from the extremophile bacterium *Deinococcus radiodurans*, enabling the repair of even severe genetic damage. Essential for long-term human survival in space.

antispinward: In the direction opposite which a habitat or other body is rotating. Sometimes called "west."

asteroid family: <u>Main Belt</u> asteroids (<u>stroids</u>) that share common orbital characteristics, usually fragments of the same original body. Travel and shipping among stroids in the same orbital family demands relatively little energy.

AU: Astronomical unit, the mean orbital radius of Earth, equal to 149.6 million kilometers or 499 light-seconds.

Bernal sphere: Space habitat whose main component is a large residential sphere, with most habitation in the lower latitudes where the rotational gravity is higher. Other components include agricultural rings, nonrotating industrial sectors, heat radiators, docking hubs, and a detached external mirror to focus sunlight. To facilitate <u>precession</u>, the sphere and agricultural rings may rotate in opposite directions, or two counterrotating Bernal spheres may be linked to cancel their angular momentum. A habitat may be expanded by adding additional spheres, usually in counterrotating pairs.

bioprinter: Device using microjet nozzles to deposit living cells into a desired three-dimensional pattern one layer at a time, replicating plant or animal tissues. Bioprinters are the main source of meat for Striders, given the limited land and resources available for livestock agriculture in space. Medical-grade bioprinters can manufacture replacement organs from a patient's own stem cell cultures.

Bolasat: Momentum-exchange satellite using long rotating carbon nanotube tethers to modify the trajectory and velocity of spacecraft. Weblike docking cradles travel along these tethers and intercept ships, shuttling them in or out until they reach their desired trajectories and are released, given a momentum boost by the tether's rotation and the cradle's speed. The Bolasat network allows faster and more direct intrasystem travel than orbital trajectories would allow. (Named for the ball-and-cord weapon known as *bolas*. The term *bolo* is sometimes incorrectly applied.)

CHON: Acronym for carbon, hydrogen, oxygen, and nitrogen, the elements most essential for life as well as for Molecular-Age technology.

cislunar: Within the orbit of Earth's Moon. Also used by convention to include the Earth-Luna L2 and L3 points, which are technically translunar.

Coriolis (Cori) effect: Fictitious force creating a deflection of a moving object from the perspective of an observer in a rotating frame of reference. Something thrown perpendicular to the direction of rotation will seem to curve to antispinward as the observer is moved in the other direction by the habitat's spin. Also, since angular velocity increases with radius, an ascending body will enter a lower-velocity region, overtaking its surroundings and appearing to be pushed spinward, while a descending body will be outpaced by its surroundings and appear to be pushed antispinward.

C-type or **carbonaceous asteroid:** Asteroid rich in <u>CHON</u>. Most habitats orbit C-type stroids and mine them for resources.

cyber: Artificial intelligence, especially a sapient one.

drive beam: A beam of ionized particles used to accelerate or decelerate a <u>magnetic sail</u>. Sufficiently powerful beams can impart very high accelerations, making them the fastest mode of intrasystem travel.

g-clip: Small, strapless triangular covering for the female pubic area, held on by nanofibers using van der Waals adhesion (the force that allows geckos to cling to walls).

Kirkwood gaps: Zones within the <u>Main Asteroid Belt</u> kept largely clear of debris by Jupiter's gravitational resonance, named for their orbital ratios with Jupiter (for instance, a body in the 3:1 gap would complete three orbits for every one of Jupiter's). The Belt is mostly empty space, with an average of six million kilometers between adjacent stroids, but uncounted micrometeoroids and dust grains pose a potential hazard to solar mirrors, delicate equipment, or spacewalkers. Many habitats thus choose the extra safety of the Kirkwood gaps over the advantages of residence around the major stroids. They capture small asteroids for resources and use thrusters to compensate for Jupiter's long-term effects on their orbital stability.

Kuiper Belt: Sol System's outer and larger belt of minor bodies, located beyond Neptune's orbit and containing millions of cometary bodies and dwarf planets. Visited by only a few crewed expeditions as of 2107.

Lagrange Points: The five points of a two-body system where gravitational forces balance, allowing stable or semistable orbits around them. For instance, in the Sun-Earth system, the L1 point is between Earth and the Sun, L2 on the far side of Earth from the Sun, L3 just beyond the point directly opposite Earth in its orbit, and L4 and L5 respectively 60 degrees ahead and behind the Earth in its orbit. The first three points are stable only in a plane perpendicular to the line connecting them, so attitude-control thrusters are necessary to maintain orbit there. L4 and L5 are stable and can be orbited indefinitely.

light armor: A close-fitting, flexible fabric woven from carbon nanotubes and synthetic silk, with a layer of synthetic-diamond scales, nanoactuators, computer circuitry, piezoelectric power fibers, and nanotube capacitors throughout its material. It enhances the wearer's strength and becomes stiff in response to impact or pressure; it also provides resistance to weapons fire and extreme heat, cold, or radiation, and provides dynamic support to the muscles and joints. In case of injury, it can apply medical assistance, compressing to splint a broken bone or even to apply cardiopulmonary resuscitation.

Lissajous orbit: A quasi-periodic orbit around a semistable <u>Lagrange Point</u>, following a path that changes from orbit to orbit but remains within a specific set of limits. The simplest Lissajous curve is essentially a figure eight.

magnetic sail, magsail: Propulsion system which generates a magnetic field around a spaceship, allowing it to be accelerated by the solar wind or a <u>drive beam</u> or to maneuver in a planetary magnetic field. Typically either a coil of superconducting wire or a magnetically confined loop of plasma, though the latter is too fragile to withstand a powerful propulsion beam. The magnetic field can also shield against particle radiation and solar flares.

Main Asteroid Belt: Sol System's inner belt of minor bodies, located between Mars and Jupiter. Smaller than the <u>Kuiper Belt</u>, but by convention the term "asteroid" is not used for bodies beyond Jupiter's orbit. Some 75% of its 100,000-plus members are <u>C-type</u> or similar, though the Inner Belt is dominated by rocky S-type stroids with little <u>CHON</u> and is thus less populated by humans. Asteroid colonization began in the 2030s in pursuit of CHON to support cislunar habitats, since C, H, and N are rare on Luna. Near-Earth asteroids were the first to be mined, but scientific curiosity and the desire for independence, as well as the abundant resources of Ceres, Vesta, and other stroids, soon drew explorers and prospectors to the Main Belt. By 2100, it is home to hundreds of habitats and hundreds of millions of people.

metamaterial: Nanoengineered material with a negative refractive index, making an object encased in it effectively invisible to selected frequencies of electromagnetic radiation.

mod: Human genetically, bionically, or surgically modified with enhanced abilities or unusual cosmetic attributes. As a verb, to modify a human in this way. In <u>Strider</u> usage, if not Terran, this term implicitly excludes the basic enhancements ubiquitous among space dwellers, such as <u>anti-radiation gene therapy</u> and stem cell augmentation.

Molecular Revolution: Twenty-first Century period when nanotechnology, <u>smart matter</u>, and molecular engineering revolutionized society and the economy, causing social collapse and a search for new values and solutions. Many new philosophies and subcultures sprang up in its wake.

O'Neill Cylinder: Space habitat design capable of housing up to several million. The interior surface is generally divided into six rectangular sectors, with inhabited "valleys" alternating with sun windows admitting light reflected from large external mirrors. The hemispherical end caps are generally terraformed to resemble mountainous terrain. Industrial and docking sectors are at the free-fall hub, and agriculture is generally practiced in smaller outboard facilities. Cylinders generally come in tethered counterrotating pairs to facilitate <u>precession</u>.

plasma drive: A high-acceleration drive using small amounts of antimatter to heat hydrogen to plasma and employing magnetic nozzles to increase the velocity and specific impulse of the plasma exhaust. Modulating the exhaust and antiparticle injection rate enables thrust up to several g for limited periods and lower thrust for longer periods.

plasma gun: Variable-lethality weapon using a high-powered laser to create a small globe of atmospheric plasma at the target site and induce a supersonic shock wave within it, resulting in a forceful, lightninglike discharge of light, heat, and pressure. Can be calibrated to disorient, stun, or kill depending on power, or to create a protective "wall" of plasma discharges.

precession: Gradual reorientation of a space habitat's axis to keep its solar cells, mirrors, and radiators properly oriented toward the Sun as it orbits. The rotation of a habitat creates a gyroscope effect that resists precession. Different habitat types employ different means of addressing this problem (see <u>Bernal sphere</u>, <u>O'Neill Cylinder</u>, <u>Stanford Torus</u>).

regolith: A layer of loose surface material such as dust, pebbles, dirt, etc.

selfone: Personal communication/data device; primary means of identification and financial transactions. From "cell phone" seen as an extension of the self.

shock laser: Reduced-lethality weapon using an ultraviolet laser to ionize the air, creating a path for an electric discharge calibrated to induce loss of muscle control and neural disorientation. Can also short out electrical systems.

smart matter: Also known as programmable matter or wellstone. Through quantum confinement of its electrons, smart matter can be programmed to simulate the chemical, optical, and thermal properties of any element or compound, including ones not found in nature. It is useful for energy collection, storage, and projection, and is used in sensory devices, video displays, thermal clothing, <u>soligrams</u>, and many other technologies.

soligram: Informal term (solid + hologram) for a display/simulation mechanism using a shape-changing <u>smart matter</u> gel that can simulate the appearance, texture, and density of virtually any substance. Often used in place of virtual reality due to the eyestrain and nearsightedness that extended use of VR visors or contacts can cause.

spinward: In the direction toward which a habitat or body is rotating. Sometimes called "east."

Stanford Torus: Space habitat design, generally a small toroidal ring. Can be expanded by adding parallel rings. Main docking and industrial facilities are at the hub, generally nonrotating, and are accessed by spokelike radial shafts. Usually aligned with the axis perpendicular to the orbital plane, with a mirror at a 45-degree angle reflecting sunlight into a ring of secondary mirrors that direct it into the habitat ring or rings. This way, only the mirror needs to undergo <u>precession</u>.

Strider: Inhabitant of the <u>Main Belt</u> or <u>Trojan Asteroids</u>. Corruption of earlier "stroider."

stroid: Asteroid.

symbot: Former brand name, now generic, for performance-enhancing robotic exoskeletons. Available in various models for construction, combat, sports, medical support, etc. Lightweight models are compact and close-fitting, but heavy-duty models are armored and provide full life support.

therianthrope, therian: Human modified with animal attributes. Literally "beast-man."

Trojan Asteroids: Asteroid clusters occupying the L4 and L5 points of Jupiter's orbit. Roughly as numerous as the <u>Main Belt</u> asteroids, though not as heavily settled to date.

FOREIGN TERMS, SLANG, AND EXPLETIVES

Different cultures and eras have different profanities, depending on their different values, taboos, and fears. For instance, in Elizabethan times, "golly" was a serious obscenity because it was short for "God's body," a reference considered blasphemous.

Strider profanity relates mainly to the dangers and discomforts facing space-dwellers. Scatological terms retain their impact and literal "dirtiness." Sexual terms are less common as profanities, since Striders typically have a fairly open attitude toward sex. The word "fuck" has long since lost its shock value through overuse; among Striders it is simply an informal term for sex rather than a general-purpose obscenity. Some Strider curses retain a secondary sexual element, however.

aiya: Chinese, "Damn it!"

bu: Chinese, "No."

Chinglish: Chinese-English pidgin common on Mars and the Cislunar States.

dong: Chinglish, "to understand." From *dong ma,* "do you understand?"

flare: Expletive. As in a solar flare or coronal mass ejection. Used as a noun, verb, or (as "flaring") adjective.

free: 2090s teen slang. Literally free-falling. Used to mean happy, not weighted down by concerns.

furo: Traditional Japanese bath.

gasmic: 2090s teen slang. Short for "orgasmic," meaning wonderful, excellent, cool.

hijab: Arabic, "veil." Refers to the general practice of covering the head, body, and limbs for modesty.

hose-clog: Expletive. An obstruction of a space suit's oxygen hose or urine catheter. Personal epithet implying that the subject is an unwelcome menace or obstruction, most likely consisting of some unpleasant and worthless substance.

lao-tian: Chinese, "My God!"

leak: Expletive. Refers to an atmosphere leak, as well as urination. Often an adjective as "leaking."

Medvyéd: Russian, "bear."

mete: A meteoroid or micrometeoroid.

no guanshee: Chinglish, "no problem," "never mind." From Chinese *mei guanxi*, "It doesn't matter."

oyamah: Japanese, "Good heavens!"

peeghole: Chinglish, "asshole." From *pigu*, buttocks.

punk: Expletive, generally a transitive verb. Short for "puncture," as of a hull or space suit. Sometimes used as a vulgar synonym for "copulate." A **punkhole** is a micrometeoroid puncture, and can also mean a vagina.

rageous: 2090s teen slang. Short for "outrageous," but generally used in a positive sense.

Sensei: Japanese, "teacher."

Shashu: Japanese, "archer."

suck: Expletive. In addition to its traditional sexual meaning, this refers to the vacuum sucking atmosphere out of a breached ship or suit. "Dirtsucker" is a common slur against Terrans.

tatakai no heiwa: Japanese, "peace of battle."

Tenshi: Japanese, "angel."

vack: Expletive. Short for vacuum, as in "vack-sucker" or "vackhead," or as a verb meaning to expel something into vacuum, as in "Go vack yourself." Largely interchangeable with <u>suck</u>, but more widely used due to its harsher sound.

zaogao: Chinese, "Damn!" (Literally "spoiled cake.")

Sol System Geography

Bodies are ordered by mean distance from Sol (semimajor axis) in astronomical units (AU). Habitats mentioned in Only Super-human *are listed alongside the bodies or orbital regions they are associated with. This list is far from comprehensive.*

REGION	ORBITAL RADIUS (AU)	OBJECT	HABITATS
Inner System Dominated by the rocky planets. Volatiles are sparse except on the largest planets, but solar energy is abundant.	0.39	**Mercury**	
	0.72	**Venus**	
	1.00	**Earth/Luna** Home of the Union of Earth and Cislunar States (UNECS), comprising most of the nations on Earth and Luna and the habitats in Earth orbit or the Lagrange Points. UNECS is often referred to simply as "Earth," particularly among outsiders.	**Chakra City** **Neogaia** Located at Sun/Earth L3 point, directly opposite Earth in its orbit.
	various	**Near-Earth Asteroids** Crossing or within Earth orbit. A primary source of CHON for cislunar habitats. NEA colonies are generally affiliated with UNECS, and many NEAs have been relocated to cislunar space.	
	1.52	**Mars** Home of the Confederation of Martian Republics and various autonomous states.	**Phobos, Deimos** Captured carbon-ice stroids housing sizable populations. Spun up to provide artificial gravity.

REGION	ORBITAL RADIUS (AU)	OBJECT	HABITATS
Inner Main Belt Dominated by rocky silicate asteroids. Water ice and organics are sparse, making it hard to colonize without imported resources.	2.36	**4 Vesta** The largest silicate asteroid, a failed protoplanet like Ceres. The largest asteroid other than Ceres to have undergone geological differentiation, Vesta is a rich source of mineral compounds rare elsewhere in the Belt. Thus Vesta is the Belt's primary source of silicates and metals useful in habitat construction and electronics. Vesta's population is smaller than that of Ceres but generally more upscale. Ceres and Vesta have similar orbital inclinations, making travel and trade between them comparatively easy.	**New Zimbabwe** Birthplace of Javon "Thrust" Moremba. **Olbersstadt** Birthplace of Maryam "Hijab" Khalid. **Pellucidar** **Rapyuta** Home of Belt yakuza. Birthplace of Koyama "Tenshi" Hikari. **Russell City** Site of Troubleshooter Corps branch headquarters. **Vestalia** Center of the Belt's film and entertainment industry.
Central Belt Dominated by carbonaceous bodies, though silicate bodies are common.	2.5	**3:1 Kirkwood gap** Border between Inner and Central Belt.	Bhaskara
	2.64	**15 Eunomia** Second-largest silicate asteroid. Core fragment of a larger body which had undergone differentiation before being shattered. It and the other Eunomia family bodies thus possess minerals rare in the Belt outside of Vesta.	Gagaringrad New Macedon Niihama
		3 Juno Third-largest silicate asteroid, close to Eunomia in size but less geologically diverse. This and its fairly inclined orbit make it less desirable for settlement, though it is home to a few mining communities.	

REGION	ORBITAL RADIUS (AU)	OBJECT	HABITATS
	2.766	**Ceres** Ice dwarf planet containing a third of the Belt's mass. Possesses a mantle of water and ammonia ice dozens of kilometers deep, as well as complex organic compounds, hydrates, and hydroxyls resulting from ancient chemical activity in its formative period. Predominant source of water and organic compounds for the Inner and Central Belt as well as Inner-System space habitats.	**Cerean States** Informally known as the Sheaf. **Demetria** Home base of the Troubleshooter Corps. **Ferdinandea**
	2.773	**2 Pallas** Third-largest Main Belt body by mass and second by volume, an undifferentiated carbonaceous stroid containing substantial deposits of water ice. Pallas's highly inclined and eccentric orbit makes it remote from the rest of Belt civilization, and its abundance of ice, carbon, and metal deposits close to its surface allows economic self-sufficiency. Palladian interactions with the rest of Solar civilization are rare and generally unfriendly.	
Outer Belt Contains the sparsest population of Belt asteroids, dominated by carbonaceous/icy bodies (including some comets) with few silicate bodies. Home to many small, diverse, often	2.82	**5:2 Kirkwood gap** Border between Central and Outer Belt.	Zarathustra
	2.95	**7:3 Kirkwood gap** Third of the four major gaps. The narrow zone between these two gaps has a thinner population of asteroids than the surroundings.	**Fourth Reich**
	3.06	**704 Interamnia** Fourth-largest Outer Belt body, fairly isolated due to 17-degree orbital inclination.	**Cerulli** Named for the asteroid's discoverer. **San Berardo** Birthplace of Ruki Shimoda.

REGION	ORBITAL RADIUS (AU)	OBJECT	HABITATS
isolated communities. The largest Outer Belt bodies serve as hubs of travel and commerce.	3.10	**52 Europa** Second-largest Outer Belt body and population center.	
	3.14	**10 Hygiea** Largest Outer Belt body and population center.	**Wellspring** Birthplace of Daniel Weiss.
	3.17	**511 Davida** Third-largest Outer Belt body. Has 16-degree inclination in opposite direction from Interamnia's (i.e. their ascending nodes are nearly 180 degrees apart).	
	3.27	**2:1 Kirkwood gap** Fourth major gap. Beyond this point, asteroids are relatively sparse.	**Greenwood** Birthplace of Emerald Blair. **Zenj**
	3.71	**5:3 Kirkwood gap** Outermost gap.	**Vanguard** Birthplace of Eliot and Psyche Thorne. Originally in Earth orbit.
Giant Planets Volatiles are abundant. Atmospheres are mined for deuterium and helium-3.	5.20	**Jupiter** A number of habitats, mainly research institutes and tourist centers, orbit Ganymede and Callisto or their Trojan points.	**al-Khwarizmi Science Institute station** At Sol-Jupiter L3 point, opposite Jupiter in its orbit.
	5.20	**Jupiter Trojans** Asteroids clustering around Jupiter's L4 and L5 points, spread out in long, sparse arcs, each encompassing roughly 1/6 of Jupiter's orbit. The majority are cometlike bodies with water ice. Home to populations who consider even the Belt too crowded or civilized. Many of the most extreme fringe societies are found here, including the Michani.	

REGION	ORBITAL RADIUS (AU)	OBJECT	HABITATS
	9.54	**Saturn** Multiple tourist and research facilities are found among Saturn's rings and moons.	
	19.19	**Uranus** Gas mining conducted in atmosphere, research conducted on moons.	
	30.07	**Neptune** Visited by *Trident* expedition in 2105.	

Acknowledgments

This is a book that's been over two decades in the making, and it would be impossible to remember all the people who've influenced or advised me along the way. But I need to single out a few people for special thanks. Xuân Stanek (formerly Blair) was a major source of inspiration and a marvelous sounding board in the early years of the process, and I owe her for details ranging from hairstyling issues to the spiritual impact of a difficult childbirth. Thanks also to Angela Gaylor and Nikki Jenkins for inspiring Psyche's beauty and the sweeter side of her character.

Chester Edwards deserves credit for getting me into comic books. Back in college, he drew me into his ambitious (but ultimately unrealized) plans to start a comic-book company, and I had dreams of doing an Emerald Blair comic series to supplement the novels. Eventually I reworked my plans from scratch, and many of the best ideas I conceived for the comics ended up as parts of this novel. The preexisting comic-book heroes that Chester helped introduce me to have also been influences on this work.

My college astronomy professor, Dr. Michael Sitko, contributed a lot to my understanding of Sol System. More recently, Paul Woodmansee of JPL was a good source of ideas about spacecraft propulsion, and Laura Woodmansee's book *Sex in Space* was most informative as well. I owe a great deal to Dr. Gerard O'Neill's seminal book *The High Frontier: Human Colonies in Space*, as well as to Winchell Chung's "Atomic Rockets" website at http://www.ProjectRho.com/rocket/index.html. My understanding of the Coriolis force and its effects owes greatly to John G. Cramer's "Artificial Gravity: Which Way is Up?" originally published in the February 1987 *Analog Science Fiction and Fact*. "Orpheus" on the Ex Isle BBS provided much insight into the technical problems of reading or copying the human brain, as well as advice on asteroidal gems. And special thanks are due to Selden Ball and the person who posts as "bdm" on the Celestia Forum, both of whom were kind enough to create asteroid data files for the Celestia space simulator upon my request. Those files have proven invaluable in helping me understand Emerald's world and plot her journeys through it.

Information on the major asteroids came from multiple sources, including Wikipedia; the site *Ceres: The Dwarf Planet* at http://home .comcast.net/~eliws/ceres/; The Planetary Society site at www.planetary .org; the article "Ceres, Pallas, and Vesta" in issue #24 of the *Moon Miners' Manifesto* at http://www.asi.org/adb/06/09/03/02/024/ast2.html; and the newsletter of the Dawn space probe at http://www-spc.igpp .ucla.edu/dawn/newsletter/index.html. Information on pheromones came from James V. Kohl et al., "Human Pheromones: Integrating Neuroendocrinology and Ethology," *Neuroendocrinology Letters* Vol. 22 No. 5 (2001), 22:309-321, and from the "Smell and Attraction" website at http://www.macalester.edu/psychology/whathap/UBNRP/Smell/ attraction.html.

Thanks also go to Lucienne Diver for her valuable constructive criticism, and to Raymond Swanland for capturing Emry perfectly in his cover art. Finally, thanks to Greg Cox for believing in this book and letting me share Emerald Blair with the world at last.